Matriarch

An Australian Novel of Love and War

Geoffrey Hope Gibson

Modern History Press

Learn more at **www.GeoffreyGibson.com**

Modern History Press, an imprint of
Loving Healing Press
5145 Pontiac Trail
Ann Arbor, MI 48105

Tollfree USA/CAN: 888-761-6268
International: 734-417-4266
FAX: 734-663-6861

Distributed by Ingram Book Group (USA/CAN), Bertram's Books (UK).

Library of Congress Cataloging-in-Publication Data

Gibson, Geoffrey (Geoffrey Hope), 1937-
  Matriarch : an Australian novel of love and war / Geoffrey Hope
Gibson. -- First edition.
      pages ; cm. -- (World voices series)
  ISBN 978-1-61599-270-6 (softcover : acid-free paper) -- ISBN 978-1-
61599-271-3 (hardcover : acid-free paper) -- ISBN 978-1-61599-269-0
(ebook)
  1. Families--Australia--Fiction. 2. Immigrants--Australia--Fiction. 3.
Australia--Social conditions--20th century--Fiction. 4. Australia--Social
life and customs--20th century--Fiction. 5. Domestic fiction. I. Title.
  PR9619.3.G5247M38 2015
  823'.914--dc23

Dedication

Writing is a very singular occupation and I want to thank my daughters Alice and Sophie, who have stood beside me every step of the way and have done much to encourage me.

Author's Note

For some years, I have harboured a desire to write a story that would salute and encourage our young indigenous and part indigenous children. In my view, the original Australians have, for the most part, received a raw deal from those who have settled here since Captain Phillip sailed to these shores. Our forefathers came to an untouched treasure of immense beauty. For those of whom I write are descended from people who have lived upon this land since a time they know by story and tradition as "The Dreamtime." For thousands of years, they have kept this continent in pristine condition with not even a scar upon its magnificent landscape. We, who are privileged to also live here, owe a duty of care to all who will follow, to nurture this beautiful land we know as Australia.

About the Author

The seeds of this book were planted long ago when I was a school boy and they lay dormant until I retired and began to write earnestly in 1995. In 2010, I pulled it out and gave it a vigorous editing, and for a while I wondered if I had created two separate books. Then I decided that I had said what I wanted to say and that I was not going to toy with it any longer. If it had a genesis, it might have been a time when I was spending the school holidays with my father who lived on a sheep-grazing property he was carving out of the Australian bush. This was a few miles out from the village of Niangala, which in those days nestled in the heavily timbered hills of the New England district of New South Wales.

Out in one of our back paddocks there was a team of Aboriginal axe men ring-barking trees while their women and children were camped nearby. My father and I were driving to town, probably for some bread and to pick up a forty-four gallon drum of petrol, when we passed an aboriginal male lying beside the bush track. For what has stuck in my mind is a feeling of profound shame.

We may have slowed for a cursory glance, but we never stopped or got out of the truck to check if he needed assistance. The memory of our indifference has stayed with me ever since. On our way home, we again passed him, and I recall my father saying something offhand about their hitting the grog whenever he paid them.

I would say that that was the typical attitude of the time. They were not white and therefore they did not count; it was as simple as that. Some years later, I was working in central Queensland, where on a Saturday night at the local outdoor picture theatre, our indigenous Australians were corralled and made to sit down the front. They were second class citizens in their own home.

Much time has passed, and a great deal has changed, but still it is my hope that this book will do something more to tip the balance in favour of our young people of Aboriginal descent.

Geoffrey Gibson

1

My brother and I spent our childhood on an isolated and sprawling cattle station in northern Australia. Darain was very much his father's boy, while the greatest influence on my life was my great-grandmother, who in those years was a dignified and mentally alert old woman. She was the daughter of a white father and an Aboriginal mother and had married a young Englishman in 1909, and with much encouragement from him, had learned to read and write. But as I look back, what was remarkable was her ability to recall most of her life, especially those early years with her young husband. She had lived through the torment of the two World Wars, and wanted me to know the family story so I would tell my own children. My name is Alkina and I was named after her.

"The most famous of the Brancliff line," she told me, "was honoured for the part he had played in the battle to defeat Napoleon Bonaparte at Waterloo. We have talked of that, and mind you it was a very long time ago, even if you can imagine, before I was born," she said with a chuckle. "Your great-grandfather even told me it was before he was born. My dear child, I loved my husband's stories; they were so full of his Englishness, and I still recall them with a sense of wonder. His own father was a very distinguished soldier, one in an illustrious line, which stretched back to well before Napoleon. His name was Colonel Lord Handsmere Ponsonby Harry Brancliff, and father and son were very close, which was unusual, as in those days it was common practice to pack them off to boarding school at a very early age. Not so for Fritzhugh, who in his formative years had a tutor, and growing up in that family must have been extraordinary.

He told me an annex to the library held the insignia and decorations, dress uniforms, and battle trophies earned and gathered by his forebears, which gives you some idea. His father doted on him, and one of my husband's memories was of his father getting all the retainers out on the rolling grounds of the estate; there were cooks, butlers, housekeepers, and gardeners. The gardeners and the livery men might be asked to be the Royal Horse Artillery, the house staff to advance up the slope as the Grenadiers, all staged to show one little boy what had happened in a particular battle. It seems eccentric to you and me, but all the participants regarded it as great fun. He had a vivid memory of his father's manservant, a wonderfully wry Scotsman named Sholty, delivering the ultimate battlefield coup de grace. "Pardon, milord, but I have to report your right wing has just been overrun by the second gamekeeper's Brigade of Republican Guard."

We can try to imagine his early life, an idyllic one maybe, which certainly kindled his imagination. Had it not been for the loss of his father, I think he would have followed in his footsteps. Of course in a way he did, for they both had a wonderful way with people. Alkina, I want you to understand that your great-grandfather had no pretence, but in saying that, he was still the quintessential Englishman."

The old lady was very particular with her stories. She usually told them in the kitchen as she was teaching me to cook, or if it was a hot day, by our favourite waterhole where we could have a swim. "Alkina darling, if you have finished your swim, would you like to sit with me while I tell you some more about your great-grandfather and his side of the family?" And when she thought I was receptive, she would begin.

"He was a wonderful man, and when I met him, he had not long arrived in Australia. His name was Fritzhugh, a strange name to my ears; he told me the Brancliffs had been prominent in Somerset for over five centuries. Most of the males had attended the great public school of Eton, and they were farmers, politicians, explorers, philanthropists, and soldiers. They had been friends and loyal servants of each succeeding monarch for all that time. As he delighted in telling me, he, Fritzhugh Ponsonby Brancliff was brought screaming into the world on the second day of April 1891.

His mother, the Lady Sarah, was considered a great beauty who had married the dashing and very handsome Lord Handsmere Brancliff, Colonel in Chief of The Queen's Horse Guards and Captain of their polo team. Catching her was not easy, for she had refused several beaus. Now, your great-grandfather, our Fritzhugh, related the family story light-heartedly, so I cannot say that it is not overly exaggerated. However, he told it well, and I think it is more fun if we regard it as being true. He assured me that as a baby, he had the face of an angel; which may have been why his nurses, nannies, maids, and housekeepers, all vied to look after him, which gave them kudos in the eyes of the other family retainers. Perhaps all this attention during those tender and formative years may have nearly led to his undoing, as one day, when he was home from Eton, a neighbour's sulky was seen being driven up the drive. The squire had come to remonstrate with his father about Fritz's behaviour.

"I am scandalized," the irate neighbour said. "I deplore the behaviour of your boy Fritzhugh, and the next time I catch him behaving lecherously toward one of my daughters, particularly Emily, who is such a delicate thing, I shall have him horsewhipped. My dear Lord Brancliff,

I hope I have made my intentions patently clear?" The booming voice could be heard echoing through the front rooms. Lord Brancliff, according to the front of house staff, was exercising diplomatic restraint. They knew what was coming; he was merely being polite, and giving his neighbour a fair hearing. This was just a lull before the charge; after all, their Lord had fought in the Sudan campaign in an attempt to rescue General Gordon from the mad Mahdi, and he was getting ready to sail to South Africa to help suppress the Boers.

"He is a very likable lad," the squire continued, "and later on, when he becomes of age, he is welcome to pay court to any of my girls, after first paying the common niceties to their parents. Climbing up into their bedroom windows late at night is not behaviour that I will countenance." When the squire's voice had moderated, yet already the household bristled with the news of young Fritzhugh's transgressions. Indeed, some of the females among them felt distinctly peeved with the squire's three daughters, particularly with Emily, the youngest and prettiest one, whom they viewed as being a flirt, while it was said the male staff felt a surge of masculine pride. What is more, the household at the squire's had provided the rather scandalous news, which found its way to the hall, via the village, with the shocking, but nonetheless reliable information that their Fritzhugh had not been the first nocturnal visitor.

Hearing of this, they thought the young master hard done by, and there was much muttering of "poor, unfairly treated Fritzhugh; handsome, manly, hot-blooded Fritzhugh; our own dear Fritzhugh!" So incensed were they that later that very evening, the senior staff gathered in the kitchen, where they charged their glasses with their master's sherry and drank to the health of the future Lord Brancliff. However, the expected explosive confrontation over his son's misdemeanour did not take place, the Squire having joined the Lord in a few whiskies, which were offered with generous civility, the host later helping the visitor to board his conveyance. Quite the reverse, the incident acted as a catalyst upon his father, reminding him that the time had come when he must take his son and heir back with him to London, where, in the privacy of his club, he could talk with him about the fairer sex, tell the boy what was expected of a young gentleman in his position, which he viewed as a very delicate undertaking.

According to Fritz, this took place not long after "Fritzhugh old man, cigar, had a visit from Emily's father, disruptive business this, said you climbed up into her room, get a fellow into fearful trouble, that sort of thing, out of hand before you know what. Join me in a brandy, thought we should be together before I leave for South Africa? Delicate thing women, understand them do you boy? A chap has to get experience, very important how you handle yourself? Your grandfather fixed it up for me, like to do the same for you, very natural for a young fellow to want to bed a woman." "Pater, may I speak?" Lord Brancliff, ever conscious of the delicate nature of the subject under discussion, held back as his son explained. "She dared me to climb up, thought it was a great hoot, maid came in unexpectedly, screamed the place down. I scrambled out as quick as I could, most dreadfully sorry to have let you down."

Hearing this, Lord Brancliff tried his utmost to understand. "Lively girl that, gentle upbringing, bit flighty is she, a chap never can tell?" "Pater, my fault I am sure." "Deuced difficult this, steward, two more brandies, thing is boy, there are women for dalliances, chaps need that, love your mother; that is not the point; discretion, keeping it under the cush, follow? Happy to arrange it, just like my pater, give you a bit extra, to keep a chap out of trouble, respectable arrangement. Never mix the two, as your grandfather told me, 'a chap's private life should never be explained, and one should never try.' Your responsibility, tell your man, they understand, known about mine for years, works perfectly. There it is said."

"Sir, if you are not the best pater a chap could have, chums have pooled our resources to try it out, afraid I'm awfully keen." Lord Brancliff had rarely felt so content as he and Fritzhugh descended the steps of his London club for a leisurely stroll in an atmosphere of perfect accord. That dear old lady was a wonderful storyteller. "Nan, that was a lovely story, and it was so nice they had that time together before his father went to fight the Boers." She told her stories in easily digested segments in much the same way as she encouraged me to cook, for she well remembered her own shortcomings as a young bride.

"Alkina, you can stop me when you have had enough," she would say, usually from her favourite seat in her kitchen, while I was making a stew or whatever it was. "You have already done it very nicely and I think it is one of the easiest dishes you can prepare. When you are older, you will be a wonderful cook; just wipe down where you have been working before I begin."

"I'm finished Nan."

I have always had a fascination for my mother-in-law, whom you and I call 'the lovely Lady Sarah'. She must have been a very formidable person and I think it's sad we never met. Yet, perhaps in a way, we did, through her darling son, who delighted in telling me all about her. How she lived her life in the public gaze, she was like an actor, sparkling, expecting to be noticed, and needing the applause of her audience. I must say she kept Fritz and me alternatively very annoyed or highly amused, she certainly provided us with many lively hours of conversation.

Despite her disloyalty to her son, which I will come to later, and mind you he never saw it that way, for she was his mother whom he respected and loved with all his heart. However, when her husband was away fighting the Boers in South Africa, Lady Sarah's entertaining was restricted mostly to their immediate circle of friends and family; there were afternoon teas, whist drives, and her favourite pastime, following the hunt. I don't know that she would have taken all the fences, as women rode side saddle in those days, and she hoped the fox would get away, as often they did. Now the dashing Earl of Fairley was Master of The Hounds and liked to flirt with her, as I believe she did with him. That would have made the hunts all the more exciting, and it was said they kissed whenever the opportunity arose, which in those days would have been difficult to arrange, when circumspection was the rule, and the servants saw and heard much more than they were given credit for. Yet Fritz said they also knew when to turn a blind eye.

Mind you, I don't think that one could entirely blame her; after all, her husband kept a mistress, and I have to say that we thought she must have known. Fritzhugh and I often talked about it, and I am sure it would have hurt her a great deal, particularly as everyone, except her, apparently knew who she was, and that she was very vivacious and in the theatre. The news from South Africa was not good, Handsmere's men had got very sunburnt, and their bright uniforms stood out on the veldt, which made them easy targets for the Boers. Her husband wrote explaining they were going to try and use a new concept known as camouflage, which would help them to merge into the surrounding bush. She wrote, thoroughly endorsing the idea, although, as she told Fritz that as he was getting rather rotund, it was difficult to imagine his father disguised as a rock or a small tree.

While he was away, she made a point of travelling up to London to see Fritzhugh, and her letters said she found him much more settled and mature. There had been no more of his chasing around and setting the tongues of London society wagging. She also wrote that it was time she set about arranging a match for Fritz. Not that he had much trouble on his own, for they literally threw themselves at him.

"Nan, how would his mother know that?"

"Well darling, in fact she didn't, Fritz told me. I am quite sure he exaggerated a great deal, but that doesn't matter in the least, because he only ever did so to entertain me. While we are on the subject, his mother once observed that she was shocked at how the younger maids were easily flustered whenever he was home, and that she would not tolerate any funny business with them. Meanwhile, her husband's letters arrived a bundle at a time. They were full of action and thrilling to read, and she would have pictured her darling husband riding flat out after the enemy. They must be very stubborn to want to keep fighting, she often remarked, but she was pleased to think of him representing their glorious family name in the van of the Empire.

Sadly, the flow of letters stopped, and instinctively she knew. A polite letter from that wooden-headed Lord Kitchener followed, which informed her that Handsmere had been wounded. It went on to assure her that he was receiving the best possible attention, which gave her cause for confidence, or so she thought. For barely four weeks later, a fellow officer arrived to tell her that her husband had died of his wounds. "That was very sad," I remarked, and promptly made us a pot of tea while my young mind tried to digest this turn in the story. "Why not put out the biscuits we made yesterday? Shall I continue?" she would say when I was settled.

"Yes Nan, but I still think his father's death was very sad."

"Fritz was doing his best to bear up, but tried to conceal that he was drinking heavily, as I understand his mother was. It would have been a difficult time for them. And so it was that around eight months later, the executor of Lord Brancliff's Estate came up from London. There was a solicitor and a senior clerk. According to Fritz, they were serious-looking gentlemen in black frock-coats who gave the appearance of carrying the weight of the entire world upon their shoulders. Their manner made his mother uneasy. Fritz had travelled down from London and was doing his best to be the head of the household and to comfort her. After a desolate lunch, during which there was no cheer, and the air hung like a damp rug, the legal advice was dispensed by Bartholomew Craven, a solicitor, who presided over the proceedings.

'I must ask you to adjourn to the study where we have to apply ourselves to some very serious business,' he announced in a sombre voice, 'and indeed, may I assure you, my Lady, and you, my Lord, that you have the deepest and most sincere sympathy of all the partners of your solicitors, Messrs Craddock, Farnshure, and Branskin, who remain steadfastly at your service.' Fritz could recall all the minutia of this occasion, although he said he would disappear to fortify himself from a brandy decanter which was kept on the day-room sideboard. She could smell it on him, and was mortified to think that so could their visitors.

Mr. Craven began: 'we are gathered here today to read The Last Will and Testament of the Late Lord Handsmere, Ponsonby, Harry, Brancliff, Colonel in Chief of our most Sovereign Majesty's Horse Guards KC, MG, MC,' which he did in a solemn voice, stopping every now and again to clear his throat. The income from the estate went to Lady Sarah solely during her lifetime, or until she remarried. Upon her death, the estate passed to Fritzhugh. The will was a lengthy one with gifts and bequests to various worthy causes and to his retainers. Mr. Craven droned on and on about his responsibilities and about the great complexity of the estate. His monotonous voice made it difficult for Fritz, much fortified from the decanter, to stay awake.

There followed a long winded elucidation during which he revealed the alarming fact to the immediately startled audience, that in his considered opinion, the estate was well on the way to becoming insolvent. That edification out of the way, he distributed a list of assets and liabilities, the greater part of which appeared to be the latter. He went on to explain that Lord Handsmere had been a gambler, and that his estate had been rudely diminished. Mr. Craven recommended the sale of some of the less sound assets of the estate as soon as possible. Lady Sarah said her goodbyes to their visitors from London and requested a large brandy, as slowly she absorbed the ramifications of the day. She asked her son, the new Lord Brancliff, to join her.

When they were settled, in the east wing drawing room, she asked in a rather dismissive tone, which was how Fritz remembered it, 'Who was that woman, a Henrietta May, who takes three hundred pounds from your dear father's estate?' 'Oh, my dear, dear mater,' Fritz said, feeling not in the least bit remorseful for his pater's infidelities, and rather more like Wellington at Waterloo, quickly manoeuvring his forces to fill a gap. 'Nobody of any consequence, I would think just one of pater's many theatre friends in London.' Then in, he thought, a skilful stratagem, he feinted, to ward off her charge into the unmentionable, 'I did not know he owned a cattle station in the north of Australia, did you mama?' 'Dear Fritz, there appears to be quite a lot we did not know about my dear husband. He was a good man; I loved him with all my heart and will miss him dearly, but we should be comforted with the knowledge he died bravely for Queen and Empire.' 'We shall miss him, mama.'

The dreary days of that winter passed with uncommon delay, until one day a note arrived from the Earl of Fairley asking if he might call upon Lady Sarah. She accepted, and in no time, he had invited the fair lady to call him 'Bunty', a name he had acquired at school. She had made up her mind that a union with the Earl would be a very sensible match. He had in his favour, an excellent seat on a horse, a much smaller estate that was easier to manage but ideal for hunting, and an income that was said to be large. He was moderate in drink, and most agreeably, she enjoyed his kisses. Before long, they had taken to meeting at a friendly inn, an easy sulky ride from their estates, where they were made most comfortable. After a few dalliances, Bunty proposed, and the lovely Lady Sarah immediately accepted. They were married soon after."

"Nan, she didn't waste any time." The old lady smiled, "Dear one, in my opinion, Fritzhugh probably felt his father's death more keenly than his mother, as she soon resumed her busy, if restricted, social life. I think his loss would have hastened his coming to maturity. He was a self-confident young man when I met him, which would only have been a year or so later. Fritz never took to his mother's new husband at all. They encouraged him to follow in his father's martial footsteps. But

7

much to their surprise, Fritz announced he was going to Australia to gain experience on the estate's Australian cattle run. The vast selection was known as *Arrawatta*, which Lord Brancliff had purchased as a speculation, sight unseen, during a collapse of the Australian market. My husband told me that what really appealed to him was it being so large that much of it had not yet been seen by white men.

Those were difficult times, and he hoped the change might lessen his fondness for drink, which I must say he controlled; but it was always there during our life together. Fritz had also decided to separate himself from his mistress, whom his pater had so kindly arranged for him in London. Apparently, since his father's death, she had become very possessive; he said he could not move without her prying, and of course he was glad he had concealed these things from his mother.

So the more he found out about this faraway land on the very edge of the Empire, the more it appealed to him. There was also the advantage of being far removed from the odious influence of his stepfather. Also, as Fritz would freely admit, his behaviour at home was, in his own most benevolent view, erratic and his mother was becoming concerned. One evening she confronted him. 'Fritzhugh,' she said firmly, 'have you been drinking, and are you aware your tie and top stud are all askew? You know Bunty expects us to gather for drinks before dinner and I was sure I smelled brandy on your breath.'

'Mater, I may have had one or two.'

Of course it had been more; his relationship with Bunty had deteriorated, and as you would expect, his stepfather hid his own feelings from his new wife. So the Earl went out of his way to encourage Fritz's leaving. Hardest of all was the Earl's constant criticism of anything to do with his pater. The mere thought of that gauche man trying to follow in his father's footsteps was enough to drive young Fritz to the nearest bottle. He was still grieving, but he was determined to make his farewells with all the good grace that he could muster.

But the real shock of leaving England came with his arrival in the top end of Australia, where the conditions were very different from what he had contemplated. The sun shone down with a ferocity he could not have imagined, and a cloud of small black bush flies adopted him as their own. The harshness made the young Englishman blanch in genuine apprehension. Fritzhugh even began to entertain the thought that he may have acted in haste. The prospect of the long ride into Arrawatta with the mailman was no exception. Although they were to become very close friends for the rest of their too short lives, their first meeting proved to be a great clash of cultures.

He was fond of recalling those early days.

'No mate, you can't take all of those ports,' the mailman announced, pushing his old felt hat to the back of his head, so that he could scratch a habitual itch, while casting a disapproving eye over Fritzhugh's large collection of leather portmanteaus, all emblazoned with the family crest. 'Struth mate, I mean to say, out to where you're going is just a slab hut among the trees.' The caravan sat looking at them curiously as the mild altercation continued, and an aged Afghan began the loading. 'Well my good man,' Fritzhugh said, standing on his dignity, as if the well-being of the Empire depended upon it, 'we cannot very well leave my ports out in the middle of nowhere, can we?' 'Listen mate, if I had bloody well known you were going to bring this much baggage, I would have brought a dozen extra camels. I have never seen a cove with so much stuff. Tell you what, it is the dry now so we will stack them well away from the track and I will leave early to pick them up on me next run, no one comes through here except me, and one of the neighbours wants me to bring in an extra load.'

Fortunately Fritz gave way, and they quickly sorted through his ports, leaving those they could not carry under a tarpaulin. 'Flood or drought, the Royal Mail always gets delivered,' explained the mailman, 'though sometimes I might be a bit delayed. Right oh, mount up, tally ho you cranky old bastards,' the camel train rose and began to move. 'Now why,' he said earnestly, 'would a young gent like you want to come all the way from the mother country to the outback, and by the way, never mind this mister business, me names Percy?' This would have been his first major experience with the reality of Australia. 'I would say curiosity,' Fritz replied, 'and to remove myself out of the way of my mother's new husband.'

'Fritzhugh, now there is a beautiful name, very *la de da*, like your accent old chap, beats Percy hands down.' 'That is being ridiculous, it is certainly not, but for you Percy, we shall shorten it; I was known as Fritzy at school; how about using that?' 'Okay mate, Fritzy it is.' 'Percy, how long did you say to travel in?' 'Sixteen days in this weather; if we got caught in the wet, well, the truth is we can't get in. You could add a few days when it is hot. I have done it in thirteen with horses and a light load, and when there was plenty of feed about.'

'Percival, is a very illustrious English family name; were your pater and mater English, do you know?' 'You mean me mum and me dad?' Fritz began to realize how foreign he must seem. 'Me great granddad was a sent out in chains,' Percy continued, 'don't know what for, probably thieving I suspect, I think she was also. I didn't know I had a toff's name; perhaps I should tell the Royal Mail and they can pay me a bit more per round trip, ha, ha, ha... my dad was on the goldfields, met her there, six kids and lost four, lucky she lived, I reckon.' 'And what about your Afghan camel driver?' 'I reckon he probably came out with a load of camels.'

That evening Fritz found that any passing doubts he may have had about the wisdom of his journey were dispelled by the twinkling of a million stars, which stretched across the boundless sky and cast their pale light over the landscape, the sheer immensity of which he could only try to comprehend. The clang of camel bells woke him to the soft light of dawn to find that the mailman had already rekindled their camp fire and brewed tea. 'Here you are Fritzy,' Percy offered. 'Have a mug a tea, I like to put a gum leaf in mine.'

Anything further from the green of England he could not imagine; yet there was the delicious feeling of limitless space and that early morning mug of tea tasted very good. After much travel, they approached the boundary of the *station*, which, according to Percy, began at a stand of trees, and was marked by a faded Arrawatta painted on the side of an old kerosene drum, which had one end cut out and was fastened to a tree. That was the only evidence of white habitation. It was a poignant moment for Fritzhugh, who remembered it as a lonely sentinel, the only sign in all that vastness of the coming of the white man. This was the boundary of his new home in the middle of nowhere.

'Welcome home old chap,' Percy said expansively. 'I head east to see Craig and Jenny Miller on Springdale Station, which is another seven days on. Not long now mate, you can count the days and we will be there.' Fritzhugh thought it sad his father had never seen it, and he wondered what he might have thought. From that moment, it did not seem to matter how long the caravan took; he had immediately felt a sense of home.

'Percival, I see the country has changed; it is now just a flat plain stretching to the horizon.'

The mailman had the most good-natured patience. 'Mate, we are getting into the good country now. You can see how the roos like it; they are the best judges. There they are, camping under the scattered trees, like us, they like to lie doggo in the heat of the day.' Through the grass, curious emus came to gawk at them, like matrons window-shopping in the High Street. Fritz could not blame them as their own lumbering caravan must appear a very odd intruder. Time had lost its meaning; it was measured in wet or dry seasons, or the weeks or months it took for the swaying camels tethered one behind the other, to make their progress from one isolated station to another.

As their train swayed by, the mournful cry of the local black crows proclaimed the country as their own. Overhead was the bluest sky he had ever seen, where majestic wedge-tailed eagles soared in great circles. White and pink cockatoos, colourful finches, and a myriad of other birds shrieked and squawked and brought their sound and colour to the bush. They saw a party of Aborigines moving through the trees. 'Lubras and piccaninnies out after tucker,' Percy explained, 'they have a great time chasing about, the women teaching the young ones. There is good water in this country and plenty of tucker. Been here forever, they know the story of every tree and rock about the place and how the rivers and the ranges came about. They didn't like us coming, there is still a very occasional spearing, I never had any trouble meself, and they will come in for tobacco and a mug of tea. But them bloody missionaries want to chase them up, when I reckon they are happier being left just as they are.'

Fritzhugh found Percy to be something of a philosopher, yet it was strange that despite his solitary occupation, he was such a genial companion. He was a boundless source of knowledge about the bush, and went out of his way to teach him the practical things he would need. How to make a bed roll, set a fire, make tea, a damper, and turn the salted beef into a tasty stew using potatoes and onions. So much did Fritz feel in Percy's debt that he determined to reverse the flow.

'Percy, you might consider getting a lorry, dashed useful things for getting around; there are plenty in London, carry all manner of things, could take days off the round trip.'

'Go on, Fritzy. I seen pictures of them. I don't know, could I drive one, do you think?'

'Easiest thing in the world,' Fritzhugh explained. 'Pater had an automobile and a driver, but now and again he used to take over and trip all over the place.'

'Mate, you don't say?' 'Just put petrol and oil in and off you go, used to let me drive, absolutely splendid fun.'

That sojourn back to things English had been received very well. Percy wore a look of profound attention, which encouraged Fritz to give an enlightened dissertation on the telegraph and the telephone. To round out this journey into the developments of modern science, he explained about the sending of radio signals in Morse code. Although he had to confess that he had never seen or heard it being done himself, nonetheless he was delighted to find his companion was impressed.

Then, in the early afternoon, they rode out of the scattered timber and there on a gentle rise was a ramshackle slab hut, the Arrawatta homestead standing solitary among the trees. Further away was a set of cattle yards, a few other rough huts, an open iron shed with a blacksmith's forge, a large flat top wagon, two sulkies, and various pieces of harness and saddlery. This was his new home. If there had been anyone there, they would have heard the camel bells, but there was no one to greet them.

'Cheer up Fritzy, you will get used to it, and if the weather holds, you will soon have all your ports.' Percy left Fritz wide-eyed and not a little bewildered. A note had been left on the kitchen table: 'Boss, out shifting cattle to better feed. Good drinking water south of hut in *billabong*. Bert.'

Fritz was glad to have arrived, but sorry to say goodbye to Percy. He assured his new friend that the warmest of welcomes would always await him. Now he understood what Percy had meant about him having so much baggage, as in the hut there was not even enough room for those he had, and he laughed and laughed at just how ridiculous he must have seemed."

The old lady took her time, content to continue her story on another visit to one of our favourite spots. I would carry our tea things while she took my arm and used her digging stick as an aid. We would sit in the sand where the soft wind stirred the leaves above, and she would watch approvingly as I set a fire and when I was settled, she would begin. "Alkina dear, I want to tell you about my growing up and how I met Fritzhugh. I was born some forty miles from the Arrawatta homestead, and being with my lovely great granddaughter rekindles my memories of when I was a girl. My mother was a little rebellious and independent like me, and my father was a young white stockman named Charlie Dickens.

Mum said they loved one another and lived in one of the rough slab huts that serve as an outstation. My father attended my birth; his hands were sure, and he deftly delivered me on to a soft bed of grass, then severing the umbilical cord with his clasp-knife, and handed me to my delighted mother. Just like you, I was called Alkina, and when I was still a child, my father moved on when I was too young to remember him. I doubt my mother even knew his real name, but I have always accepted his going as a part of my life. My mother raised me in the traditional ways of her people, as we wandered across our land, just as our forebears have always done."

Nan paused, deep in thought, and when she was ready, continued the wonderful story of her life: "I delighted in learning the stories of the dreaming, and how all the animals and birds came to be, why the great rivers cut their way through the mountain gorges, where the geese came from, and how the rainbow snake made the wet. And now I think more than ever, it was very fortunate that I grew up among the women who kept our secrets, and could teach them to me. It was they who showed me how to set the sacred tokens in the ground, and what they meant, and how to paint and oil my body, and the meaning of our rituals.

My mother taught me how to stamp and sing our dreaming into the land, as could most of our people in those days; and when I was older, I became the keeper of the women's business. I knew who our ancestors were, except those on my father's side, who still remain a mystery. The old women told me that we had speared white men and had taken their cattle for tucker. The police took our men away in chains, but some of the squatters and their men would cruelly leave bags of poisoned flour lying about for our people to find.

But it was not until the missionaries came that they inflicted the greatest damage of all. They set out to destroy our beliefs, which they did by telling us our dreaming was nonsense. My mother said my father thought that when the missionaries came, it would be less disruptive for us if we just agreed with them. As it later turned out, his advice was a great help, and when I married Fritzhugh, I discovered he held much the same view.

I had seen Fritzhugh well before I met him, which happened early one morning as I watched the mist lifting over the billabong, and there he was, singing songs from Gilbert and Sullivan as he splashed about. He was a skinny young man engrossed in his song, and every now and then, he would keep time and bob down in the water. I had been standing motionless in the trees and thought it was one of the most unusual and prettiest scenes I had ever witnessed. I had heard talk of the new white boss who had come from a land far away.

The women had giggled at how he wore boots that went up to his knobbly knees, and how he had brought so many dilly bags they had to build another hut to put them in, and how he sometimes wore a red coat and galloped through the bush, blowing a small didgeridoo, jumping over anything in the way. I would look forward to the morning ritual, although there were often many mornings when he did not come. He would have gone after cattle, the women would know, because some of their men would have also gone out on the muster. They could be out for weeks, or maybe on a long drive to deliver a mob. However, one morning he was there again, and I was so pleased to see him that I stepped out of the trees and found his reaction very pleasant.

'Good morning young lady, I did not expect anyone to be here at this hour of the morning, and what is your name?' I told him.

'Damn me, if you do not understand what I am saying. I am Fritzhugh, but you may call me Fritzy, or Fritz, if you like.'

'Fritz, sound nice.'

'Good, I like Fritz, although everybody calls me Fritzy. I have enjoyed meeting you Alkina. Now be a good girl and run along while I get dressed.'

I was very amused by what my mother described as the great white modesty, and after that I would only emerge to say hello once he was dressed. About a month later, I heard that the station people were out searching for him. Mother said he was probably lost, having explained that my father had done the same thing. But once I understood that white men could not find water or tucker, I became very concerned for his safety, and on the second day, I set out with my dilly bag and digging stick, to look for him. I knew we had trackers, but knowing how our people think, I decided he would probably be in a place where they would be reluctant to go. This was dry, featureless, sandy country, and the home of many bad spirits.

The night had come and the bush rustled to the sound of animals, while the stars and moon seemed so low I could almost touch them. Our young people could read the signs, and I saw where dingo, goanna, emu, snake, and lizard had been; but I found no sign of Fritz. Toward the end of that long second day, I saw birds circling in the distance and I began to run. Closer, and I could see the crows, and my heart pounded.

I thought he might be dead; for me, this was a race for life, and I took in great gulps of air as I plunged down into a deep dry water course and clambered up the other side. I ran over the sandy waste, up the side of dunes falling down the other side until I saw him. The crows were waiting for the struggles to cease, before they rushed in for an eye. His horse was dead, with legs stiff in the air and Fritz was pinned under it. His pale skin had blistered and his lips were cracked and bleeding. I was elated that he was alive, and I clearly remember that this was my first brush with his English stoicism. I could have arrived for morning tea, yet he could barely whisper.

'Hello Alkina, how lovely to see you! We do meet in the most unexpected places and I must say it is always very nice when we do. I am afraid I cannot feel my legs; bloody horse must weigh a couple of tons. Would you oblige me by burrowing from the other side? It is probably lying on my water bottle, which was hanging from the saddle, and I dare say you could do with a drink yourself.'

I was so thrilled to have found him, and despite all this polite carry on, he was very weak, and using my digging stick, I tore away at the sand to retrieve his bottle. He was so ridiculously gallant: 'no, no... I insist... after you my dear girl...' I remember taking a quick sip so he would drink. Then I found he couldn't, until I let the water dribble down my fingers and on to his cracked lips. Fritz was in a terrible state as I did my best to comfort and shelter him from the last of the sun. He had already worked out what had to be done, and apart from anything else, there was terrible stench coming from his horse, which had blown up and attracted a large cloud of blow flies.

'Alkina, when you have had a rest, I want you to start digging under me, then hopefully, I will fall into the hollow you make.' It was clear that I could not leave, and with Fritz doing what he could to help, I dug like mad, which did much to ease his pain.

'Please try to pull the saddle out. I would dig under it from the other side, undo it first, then you may be able to wriggle it out. Then we should try to get my other leg free. I have had plenty of time to think about all this.'

Eventually I got the saddle out. The poor man was extraordinarily brave, and lay there gasping, but at least we were getting there.

'Thank you, please have a drink and a rest, and when you are ready,

I am going to push with my free leg and at the same time, I would like you to pull me straight back by the arms. Do you think you could do that?' Things had improved considerably. We got ready.

'Do let me know if I am gripping your wrists too tightly. I want you to pull on the count of three, one, two, three, pull! Nearly there, just one more, on the count of three, one, two, three, ahhh!' And poor Fritz had fainted. At least he was already a good way out from under the horse, and eventually I managed to drag him free of it. I was in a state myself. Fritz was unconscious, and could die before we were found. Should I run for help or stay with him? I bathed his face, and at last, the day had begun to cool. I can honestly say I was a very relieved girl when he came around.

'You did it Alkina; you are a first class girl! Now let's see, I am still in one piece and I think I am getting some feeling in my legs. We should try to make it over to that tree, and it would help if I had a decent stick to lean on?'

It must have been sheer willpower; we got him standing; he must have been in absolute agony, but with him leaning and me lifting, we shuffled a few steps at a time until we made it over to the tree.

'There we are, absolutely splendid! Now I am sure everything will be rosy. I am so glad the great dreaming spirit had the foresight to make trees.'

Working gingerly together, we managed to prop Fritz up so he was leaning back against the trunk with his legs splayed. 'Alkina, I cannot tell you how good it is not to be under that horse.'

Daylight was fading, but at least he knew what we should do. 'Alkina, I want you to go back to the homestead and tell Albert, the boss, where I am, and you can ride back with them?'

'I have never been on a horse.'

'Good Lord! Never mind, I will teach you when we get home.' Before I left, I did what I could to make him comfortable. 'My girl, you are wonderful, now I insist you take the bottle.' Obviously I could not, but I took a quick sip and left with him still making a fuss.

Albert was enormously relieved, and they were able to get the sulky in as far as that last deep dry water course. Poor Fritzhugh had to lie flat on his back for months while his pelvis knitted, and was most insistent that I visit him. He soon had me fossicking among his unopened ports so he could show me the family albums, which, with his vivid descriptions, opened up an entire new world for me, and I soon learned precisely who was who.

Fritz was a model patient, and as I found out, he was a wonderful storyteller with an inexhaustible repertoire of very funny tales from his former life. Being young and naïve, I discovered that my friend needed an audience, which was a new experience or as I had certainly never met anyone even remotely like him. However, I think we instinctively knew that we enjoyed our growing friendship. But, unknown to me, we did have a problem; Albert was nine years older than Fritzhugh, and, I imagine, felt duty-bound to protect the young English Lord. It was years later that Fritz described their awkward exchange to me.

Albert had been very apprehensive before he seriously confided his fears to Fritz. 'I wonder boss if we could talk about something which is really bothering me.'

'Fire away old man, talk about anything you like.' Fritz was completely open like that. At the time he was very uncomfortable and could not be moved from his bed, which, each morning, was trundled outside and placed under a tree. But he was fed up. Fritz needed people around him. Nonetheless, out it came that in Albert's opinion, I was smitten with him, which would have been perfectly true at the time, only I had no idea, and I honestly believe that in those early days, neither had Fritz. Yet Albert, who was very embarrassed with his task, must have felt it had to be said.

'I mean no disrespect,' he began, 'and I am sure Alkina is a very nice girl; it is just that I don't think you should feel obliged to befriend her.'

'Albert, but I don't. She has a wealth of interesting things to tell me about her people. Alkina has a lively mind, and I find her pleasant company.'

'I mean, begging your pardon Fritzy, but she is here every day; what I am trying to say is, of course, I admire what she did, but she was raised in the bush, and it would have been nothing to her.'

'Good Lord Albert, I have transgressed,' Fritz said, doing his best to tread water around the issue. Their exchange only made Fritz more determined than ever not to let Albert's sensibilities get in the way. 'Albert, I was thinking that perhaps her father was probably just like you and I, and I believe she is trying to understand us. I would be grateful if, when she visits me, you would accept that she is here as my guest?'

Fritz had the most wonderful sense of mischief. In time, he got Albert to bring in a quiet hack, so I and the horse could get to know each other, and Fritz would revert to playing the bumbling Englishman if he wished to put one over him. 'I am sorry if my being laid up is a bother, old chap, but I find being so out of touch with everything out here, is a difficulty, but never mind, I have taken her inside leg, waist, arm length, and across the shoulder measurements, and have written away for a few things for her, such as underwear, jodhpurs, and shirts. Oh, and a very strange thing, her feet are much smaller than I would have thought. I had no idea what size, so I measured toe to heel and traced an outline and enclosed that. I do hope it does the trick.' Fritz said Albert was speechless; yet, given time, he became my very dear friend. Several more rooms had been added to the hut, including a front veranda, a decent workable kitchen with a pantry, and best of all, a good fuel stove. The homestead roof was now big enough to collect rain water in large corrugated iron tanks for drinking.

Mail or not, Percy would make a detour and come all the way in to see him. The three of them were great mates and, after dinner, would sit on the veranda and talk for hours over a bottle of port. Eventually my new clothes arrived, and when Fritz was able to hobble about with the aid of sticks, my riding lessons began. He was a wonderful teacher and extraordinarily patient, it certainly gave him an interest, and he kept up a constant flow of encouragement. 'That's very good, an excellent seat, now forward in the saddle, nice hands, keep your mount collected.' One day he said to me, 'Alkina, you look very good on a horse, and when I saw you silhouetted against the lowering sun, I thought how pretty you are.'

During his long convalescence, he had taken on an excellent station cook. Dorothy Hobbs was a widow, and she took me under her wing and we became lifelong friends. I liked to help out in the kitchen, and after a while, Dorothy began to teach me. Each day we turned out an amazing variety of breads and pastries. There was no refrigeration in those days, and one of her biggest improvements was to have them acquire a small herd of dairy cattle, and under her guidance, they planted out a vegetable garden and build a decent *chook* run. Even those few improvements made an enormous difference to our diet.

Fritz enjoyed talking about his former life, and would encourage my questions. I suppose I did pander to him, by opening an avenue that he could explore, such as had he ever been presented to the King and Queen. Of course he had, and more stories would flow. Or we might talk about his mother, who was an endless source of fascination. After a while, I felt as though I knew her, as Fritz would tell of grand functions, perhaps a garden party at Windsor, who was there, what was said, and what they wore, and he would recreate the whole thing for me. Looking back, I think that he might have liked to have been an actor, or perhaps a writer, for Fritz enjoyed parodying his mother's polite society. He told me that she said that one could always tell a person's station by the way they drank their tea. Fritz would imitate their Vicar taking his tea, and act out the ridiculous stilted conversation, which, as he described it, was the art of talking at length about nothing of any consequence. He could be extremely funny.

As ridiculous as this may now seem, I began to take an interest in all this because for some time, I had wanted to give him a tea party. I suppose it was about trying to recreate something of what I imagined his life must have been. So, one Sunday afternoon, after my riding lesson, I asked if I could lay out all his tea things and serve a tea. I must confess that Dorothy and I had planned the whole thing, and I produced a magnificent sponge filled with jam and cream, together with scones still warm from the oven. Then with great ceremony, I poured from the magnificent silver teapot I had discovered among the salvers, servers, and cake stands, all of which were still in their original packing.

Of course Fritz rose to the occasion. 'If my dear mater could see this, she would be delighted.' And just to please me, as he was fond of recalling, he ate nearly all the cake and scones on his own. His obvious delight thrilled me, although he would never have dreamed of being any other way. Fritz was always the perfect gentleman, and so in between servings of tea and cake, he kept up a delightful flow of stories. That was an occasion we remembered with great fondness.

After his pelvis mended, he returned to disappearing for weeks at a time, mustering or working the cattle out on the camps. It was about a year or so later that I became aware of the effect the long spell of dry weather had been having on the station, and that Fritz was worried by it. This was also a period in my life when I realized how much I longed to be with him, although, strange to say now, but I don't know that I was even aware of why that might be.

In the following year the wet season failed to arrive, and the cattle market collapsed. There was day after day when the warm dry wind blew across the top-end, lifting clouds of dust to billow in the air, as fire, and vast mobs of starving kangaroos, took what little was left of the pastures. The gradual decline in the fortunes of Arrawatta was entirely beyond Fritz's control. They spent months shepherding the cattle from one meagre patch of feed to another, while Albert scouted about endeavouring to find a market, and when he would find a buyer, the cattle would sell very badly. The water holes dried up, and the land became a graveyard for the cattle; their bones and parched hides remained as the only sign of their existence.

Then a further blow fell, the Pastoral House, which had previously been so keen to have his business, informed Fritzhugh they had withdrawn his credit. It was a terrible thing to do, and a complete about-face. They said it was because the guarantee provided by his father's estate had not been honoured. Fritz was shattered; it seemed incomprehensible that his mother or the estate's solicitors had not forewarned him. That year was the first time Arrawatta had not been able to meet its debts.

My poor Fritz was weighed down with concern. We had discussed his bouts of drinking quite openly, and when I was around, he kept it well under control. He and Albert enjoyed a port or two after dinner, and if Percy arrived with a load, they would certainly celebrate the occasion. The effect of alcohol upon Fritz came to a head when Percy unexpectedly arrived. I think he sensed that he might carry bad news, for he would have witnessed the awful effect the drought was having on homesteads along his run. On this trip, he arrived with a large bundle of mail for his friend.

The greetings were no less enthusiastic: 'wonderful to see you Percival, we will have a lot to talk about over dinner.'

The mailman shrugged shyly. 'Same here mate, but the dry is worsening, and many have ceased ordering from town. And let's hope your mail has brought you some good news.'

I watched as, Fritz opened a letter from his mother; her salutation would have signalled that he was in trouble:

> 'My Dear Fritzhugh,
>
> I hope this letter finds my dear boy in good health. I worry about all the many things that I, as your loving mother, am unable to provide for you from such a distance. However, through a friend of Bunty's at the Colonial Office, I am recommended to furnish you with a felt spine pad, which you should wear against the damaging effect of the sun. They are very popular in India, and I have ordered that some be sent to you direct from London. They shall arrive under separate cover. Please do not neglect to wear yours.
>
> We are in the middle of a most exhilarating hunting season with masses of guests tripping up from London for the weekend. Your cousins Wallace and Constance are here. She is a ravishing beauty with red hair, so like her mother, and I feel sure she shall have plenty of beaus this season. Wallace cuts a very dashing figure and has taken to driving a motor. Tomorrow I ride Chancellor; he is wonderful at eleven years and gives me great confidence that I can stay the course.'

Fritz raced through the pages of her copperplate hand in a search of the nub of her letter. He was not disappointed, for her words stung him deeply. Fritz felt more put down than he could hide and shook his head in disgust. He put her letter down and opened those to which she had referred; there was one from his stepfather and another about the estate from Messrs Craddock, Farnshure, and Branskin, which he read.

> 'My dear Lord Brancliff,
>
> I write as the Executor named in your late father's will, and it is now my duty to report to you upon the winding up of his estate.
>
> Probate was granted, as you are aware, on the sixth of March 1904, and it was only of recent date that we were confident that we had received the last of the claims, and that every asset of the estate had been identified and recovered. This, you will recall

was reported to you on the fifteenth of February 1906. I must explain that the claims amounted to almost double the amount that we had earlier assessed. I assure you that all were verified to ensure they were authorized by your father. He was a man of honour, and would have expected me to meet them. Unfortunately, after the disposal of the main assets, the estate was left with a debit balance of a little over three thousand pounds. However, I am able to report that this sum has been generously lent to the estate by your stepfather, thus saving your mother the embarrassment of having to juggle her affairs.

I now come to the Australian assets, namely the cattle-raising venture known as Arrawatta Station. This was to be a long-term investment, and was part of the assets of the British and Australian Pastoral Company, which failed in 1895. The holding was purchased from the mortgagee using favourable terms of finance, and secured by your father's personal guarantee. The estate was not able to honour the personal guarantee, and again, your stepfather has come forward and done so. Accordingly, the mortgagee has transferred the property to his name. I am therefore instructed to advise that you may carry on at Arrawatta and that he has appointed The Commercial and Australian Pastoral Company to oversee its operation as a viable investment.

It has been an honour to serve your father over so many years, and to be his legal adviser and friend. I would be singularly honoured, if you would be good enough to communicate with me when you are next in London and be my guest at luncheon.

I remain your obedient servant.

Bartholomew Craven.'

Percy had obviously seen similar distress and was very concerned for his friend. Fritz never commented, but his mother's unveiled comments had hurt. They were completely out of place, considering the Herculean efforts that he, Albert, and their stockman had put in. That she should attribute their financial difficulty to her son's poor stewardship was unfair and quite ridiculous. She never stopped there, for what she had really wanted to convey was toward the end of her letter, and it seemed to Fritz that she wished to destroy him.

'I raise a matter that concerns me greatly; I have received word that you are cohabiting with a native woman. Your dear father would be as deeply shocked and as disapproving as I am. Fritzhugh, I beg you to put an end to this relationship forthwith.' I could feel his distress, although the contents of her letter were never revealed to me until much later. The bush telegraph had done its work, who knows how; perhaps it was the orders for clothes and other things for me, or someone's innocent remark to a neighbour.

But at that moment the drinking began in earnest.

'Percy, I have been done, and I still have to read a letter from my stepfather, but not without a drink, would you join me? He is the most abominable man you could ever meet.'

The letter was embossed with the seal of the Earl of Fairley. The expected derogatory comments about his dear pater followed, and with an undisguised oath, he suddenly tore it to pieces, and topped up their glasses. I had rarely seen our people drink; they were too isolated, and unless they got it from passing itinerant workers, liquor was never a problem. But never could I have imagined Fritz drinking himself into a stupor. But he did, and by mid-morning of the following day, Percy had been loaded on to the camel train, still so drunk he was in grave danger of falling off. He had left his great friend in a worse state, and Albert, who had come in late, was not much better. Fortunately, Dorothy and I thought to hide the bottles, and when I could bear it no longer, I saddled our horses, and with Fritz swaying precariously in the saddle, led him out into the bush. He slept most of that day in the sand, spluttering and mumbling incoherently to himself, until he eventually woke up.

'Good God, how on earth did we get here? Oh my head! Do we have any water?' I helped him to his feet and led him through the paperbarks to the pool. He was putrid and very embarrassed.

'I am so sorry my dear girl, I have honestly never felt worse, that damned drink, serve me right. I don't remember riding in, what a pretty place this is.' With that, he plunged in fully clothed and for the remainder of his life, that rock pool became our favourite place. There was plenty of bush tucker about, and I watched over him until he was calm. However, he and his clothes desperately needed a wash.

'Fritz, take them off, they are putrid.' He dithered coyly about, for I had forgotten about the great white modesty, and so I washed his clothes as best I could and draped them in the sun to dry. Then I took off my clothes and swam out to join him. This was such a pretty place, being just below where the water gently tumbled down from above the rocks. Fritz's pale skin looked strangely out of place as we frolicked about. When we kissed, it was the happiest experience of my young life.

There were so many feelings, and we were overwhelmed by their intensity. That was the moment that we became aware of how much we meant to each other. It was so beautiful to realize our feelings as we clung in an embrace that had no beginning and no end. I can still remember the exquisite joy at being able to run my fingers through his hair, and to kiss the face I so adored. We mated with overwhelming joy on the grassy bank. When our passions were exhausted, we lay by the warmth of a fire in wonderment. It was beautiful to have him call me his darling, and to know that he loved me as I did him. Late into the night, he told me a little of why those letters had so upset him.

'I am so sorry for putting on such an awful bender my dearest, but apart from everything else, she does not approve of us. I do not expect you to understand. I am embarrassed by it. My mother is on the other side of the world where they have all those tea parties we have been talking about. There is nothing worse than bad news from one's own family.'

'Shush,' I said, stroking his brow, 'my darling, her letter seems to have had the opposite effect to what was intended.'

'My darling,' he declared, 'I do believe that you are right.'

I am sure we both felt that in that moment, it was our laughter that broke his mother's hold over him. Fritz adored his mother, but how that lady, and her awful husband, could cause him so much hurt, when he was so far away, was unforgivable.

'Darling,' he said, 'I am sorry, but I cannot help being angry, and at the same time so disappointed at the unfairness of my mother's letter. Neither she nor my stepfather has any idea of just how isolated Arrawatta is, much less me trying to explain to them that I have no control over the weather, or the cattle market.'

'Fritz, one day, perhaps not even soon, what has been done will be shown to be wrong. You and I understand, and you must accept that it may not be possible to please them. Darling, I want to show you my land; there are so many things for us to share.'

We lay in each other's arms until the dawn.

Although this was a joyous time for us, it was a difficult time for Fritzhugh. The station was by then under the control of the Pastoral House, which, although they had no physical presence, began to exercise their authority all the way from Melbourne. This they did by way of a succession of long-winded letters and returns, which had to be filled in, and which took months to arrive. And it was a good job the writers were not there when Fritz opened them; they would be from someone with the exalted title of Pastoral Inspector, who had no idea of the extent of that drought, and what conditions were like. They went into such piddling detail that he and Albert would have a good laugh, apart from being very irritated; they answered what had to be answered, and just got on with it.

Looking back to that time, my attitude now seems ridiculous, but that is what love can do, and I set out to create a home life for Fritz with only a very rudimentary idea of what to do. Fortunately, I was unwittingly assisted by whoever had packed his things, for they had included a book with the pretentious title of 'A Guide to Housekeeping', by Lady Portia Hamilton-Reed. As I found out, Lady Portia knew a thing or two, and recommended keeping a strict eye on the consumption of the household's alcoholic beverages, a proposition with which I wholeheartedly agreed. Lady Portia also said there should be little fraternization between the kitchen and the other household staff, lest there be a breakdown in discipline, thus leading to an increase in the consumption of food and beverages, and of course household expenditure. We all thought that was hysterical; Lady Portia had never lived on an isolated cattle run in the top end of Australia.

We had many laughs while reading it; however, it had many traditional recipes we adapted to suit the climate. Much amused by all this, Fritz said he did not think that jugged hare, or the hearty barley and mutton broth, both of which came highly recommended, ought to be on the menu. However, much to my delight, there were two whole chapters devoted entirely to the serving of teas.

I was unstoppable, and wrote away for cookery books and scanned all the old newspapers and magazines for anything remotely English. I unpacked all his ports, which had sat unopened for years, and had him explain the uses of all his paraphernalia. There was a copper bed warmer, a hat block, a shooting stick, and so on. Port after port of it, I unpacked a full sterling silver table setting, of cruet sets, mustard pots, sundry containers for butter, cream, and sugar, complete with silver food holders to serve from. There were cheese boards, butter curlers, salvers, two carving sets, crystal decanters, cigar cutters and a beautiful pair of his father's matching guns. He had not seen any of this for years, I enjoyed it hugely, the two of us falling about, as we contemplated how they might be used. However, he never once said to me that he missed the trappings of his former life.

When at last the drought had broken and the cattle numbers were recovering, I wanted to show him my land. When we eventually set out, we carried little more than a water bag, my digging stick, tea, sugar, flour, and a billy can. I gathered and hunted tucker as we walked. I sang the ancient songs for him, and told the stories that been passed down from generation to generation. He had shared his life with me, and I wanted to show him something of mine. We went to places where it was unlikely any white man had been before. That time was one of the happiest of our life together, and Fritzhugh came to understand how my people lived so lightly upon the land. I think he came to see it through my eyes, and he came to love the country just as I did. Many months of this idyllic time passed, and one morning I tweaked his beard and kissed his face and told him, 'My darling man, I have learnt over the past few days that I am carrying our child.'

When my time came, the neighbouring wives delivered the baby. We named her Sarah, after his mother, which says a lot about our continued fascination. Then quite suddenly, and just as if we had been caught in a cyclone, our young lives were changed forever. This was at a time when our love was in its full bloom. For far away in a distant place I hardly knew existed, which was somewhere across the narrow sea from England, the thunder rumbled on battlefields where Fritz's forebears had fought before. The flimsy borders of Europe, where the trees and the grass were the same on either side, crumbled under the fire from a thousand guns, as the Kaiser's infantry hurled themselves across the border.

Fritz, Albert, Percival, they all volunteered, and that ghastly war bled us dry. All the boys from the neighbouring stations rallied to the flag when they heard the clarion call of 'Duty and Empire'. They and thousands upon thousands of wonderful young Australian boys rushed to join up. 'I must go,' he told me, 'it is what my pater would have expected; it is my duty to my country and my King. My love, do try and understand, I must, as the males of my family have always done so. For you and I, there can never be a parting, as I shall think of you in every moment of every day. We have the greatest joy there is, a love that will last forever.'

Fritz left his hereditary title in England, where he felt it belonged. His enlistment papers into the Australian Imperial Force were simply signed as Fritzhugh Brancliff, stockman of Arrawatta station. Those men were so innocent, so young, and so brave. The stinking mud, shrapnel, and machine guns devoured them with an unquenchable thirst. The Generals behaved like petulant boys, losing whole units, as if they were toy soldiers on an English lawn."

'Nan, you are crying?'

'Yes, but it is not so sad now; yet they are always in my thoughts. The English Generals considered the Australian troops had a larrikin strain and lacked unquestioning discipline. They misread that for their natural independence, for they made wonderful soldiers who looked after each other, and they were tough. One morning, after a fearful allied barrage was unleashed in the grey of dawn, the boys from all around here were ordered over the top, which meant those fine young men had to stand up and advance across the torn-up ground in front of the enemy machine guns and to an almost certain death.

'Come on, boys; let's show what we can do!' they yelled to each other. The Sergeant blew his whistle and they clambered up the ladders to walk in their extended lines across the deeply pitted ground and slush. My Fritz would have seen men going down all around him, the Sergeant and the young Lieutenant, like most of them, made no sound when they died. The line thinned, as somewhere ahead a German machine gunner fired to halt the advancing enemy, he slowly traversed his gun so his bullets thudded into my husband's chest and he died in the mud.

They had sensed they were to die; the losses had been simply horrendous; little did their loved ones know. Somewhere in the rear before his death, he wrote his last letter home. I brought it with me today; I would like to read it to you as I know your great-grandfather would have loved you, as you would have him." As she began to read, her voice was tremulous.

> "My darling one,
>
> What a joy it is, in the quiet warmth of a summer day, to write to the great love of my life, to tell you how I long to hold you in my arms once more. I am sitting under a tree in a green field, just as green as I have described to you. I can hear the buzz of bees and watch the wild flowers bending in the wind. I can only say that this place is so peaceful, without the fearful racket of war, which goes on night and day. After the casualties we have endured as we slam away at each other, day after day, I have to tell you that you may have to adjust to my not returning home. This would be a fearful prospect were I not so confident of our love for each other, and your ability to cope with all the difficulties that life may hold, and to bring up our child in the ways of your people.
>
> The battlefield teaches one that life is as fleeting as the blooming of a flower. I believe wholeheartedly in the great cause for which we are fighting, and I am prepared to give my all for it. Darling, if I should fall, I would like to think that I will return as a dreaming spirit to watch over you and our lovely child, and to see my loves from the stars, and to watch the flickering flames of your campfire. Should the Great Spirit spare me from the battle, then I shall be sailing home, and my darling, you and I will know that every day brings us closer to being united once more. You and Sarah are always in my thoughts; would you tell her that her father loves her and longs for that day when we three shall again be together?
>
> Until then, with all my love.
>
> Fritz

≈ 2 ≈

In the cooler winter months, Nan and I would go to our favourite place in the river bed, where the sand was warm and when we were comfortable, she would begin her story.

"As you know, I outlived our lovely daughter Sarah, who would have been your grandmother had she not succumbed to cancer not long after having her second child. But this story began when she was a little girl and the missionaries arrived. It seemed they came like the monsoon, although unlike it, they stayed. Our people were unprepared for the emotional onslaught, and assumed it was just another short stay to conduct a 'mission' as the missionaries called them. They had been coming through on and off for years, and if they came with a nurse or a doctor, it was a very good thing.

My people assumed they had a right to be there, just like all the other white people who had settled on our land. We can appreciate it now, but the strange thing was, my father, and much later Fritz, had foreseen this might happen, and had serious misgivings about the missionaries coming. Nonetheless, one day they just arrived. They made several trips in with an enormous truck. They brought with them building materials, a piano, stoves, showers, folding furniture, blackboards, and so on. We watched it happen; they set up a mission school and then began to teach the children to sing and clap their hands in time with the music, as young ones love to do. I felt overwhelmed, not only by the preaching, but by the subtle bribes of toys and games aimed at the children.

I have to admit that our Sarah had a wonderful time at the mission school, until one day she came home in tears, very upset by a frightful story about how God, the father of Jesus, had allowed his son to be nailed up on a wooden cross because she and all other children were wicked sinners. Fritz and I had discussed all this long ago, but I let this go on for too long; how absurd it seemed to fill their fragile minds with such guilt? That was the last straw, and so the next day, I sat quietly at the rear of the hall while the evangelist told the white man's version of the creation stories.

'Children, God made the earth, the trees, the clouds up above, the sun, the moon, the stars, the sunshine, and the rain. Our Almighty God,' at this, his eyes looked up to the sky, 'created everything, children, everything, the birds, wombats and kangaroos; did you know that?' With his arms outstretched, he proclaimed, 'God made everything on the earth and in the sky?' I was furious. The evangelist had the most

26

frightening glassy-eyed stare as he made a mockery out of everything I had taught. I listened as the little ones clapped their hands in time to the music.

> 'Since the Lord saved me,
> I am as happy as can be.
> My cups full of running over.
> Running over.
> Running over.
> My cups full of running over.'

An accompanist slammed away at the piano, the children sang gustily and followed the evangelist's actions. When the music stopped, I collected Sarah, loudly announcing, 'Come along, darling; we have our own spirits and we don't need theirs.' The missionaries were taken aback, and the other children giggled as we walked out. But this spiritual independence had its consequences, as they simply saw me as another soul to be saved. Not immediately, mind you, the visit came quite unexpectedly some months later; it was around mid-morning when I was sewing. The missionary seemed pleasant enough, but as they are, he was very single-minded.

He had caught me by surprise, as apart from my extended family and Sarah's friends running in and out, I lived quietly. As you can imagine, Fritzhugh's wonderful stories of their Vicar's visits, in all their exquisite idiosyncratic detail, came to me at once. I confess the thought amused me, and I found myself doing what the lovely Lady Sarah might have done under the same circumstances; I was charm itself as I ushered him to a seat in the living room.

'Would you care to take tea?' I offered brightly. 'It is so nice that you have called, although I rather think the weather has been unseasonably hot for this time of the year.'

My visitor could hardly do more but agree. 'My very word Mrs. Brancliff, it has been.'

'I find tea,' I commented, 'at this time of the day most welcoming; it settles one down and prepares one's digestive system for the delights of lunch. I am quite sure the work of the church must be very taxing, particularly so far away from the comfort and convenience of the big city.' And so began a flow of inconsequential small talk. My brow was furrowed with interest. It even occurred to me, that indeed, there may even have been spiritual intervention, for that morning I had just taken a teacake out of the oven. He seemed nonplussed by my warmth and interest, and ran his finger around his clerical collar, which did look uncomfortable, crossed his knees and fiddled with his straw hat, before placing it on the floor beside him. I set out the tea things.

'How nice, what beautiful silverware. Mrs. Brancliff, you do me proud.'

'Thank you, my husband brought it out with him from England.'

'He was from the old country? I had no idea.'

'Yes, he came out as a young man, and we lost him on the Western Front.' I regretted it as soon as it was said; I had no wish to dramatize it or have my visitor see me as being in need of comfort. Worse, I did not wish to give him an opening he could use toward the saving of my soul.

'My dear, dear lady, I am extremely sorry,' his head had inclined piously, and his voice had lowered in solemnity.

'Never mind,' I said brightly, 'my daughter and I have to carry on; do you take milk Reverend?'

'Yes, thank you so much Mrs. Brancliff, and would you mind if I inquire if your husband was a Christian gentleman?' I could imagine Fritzhugh's satisfaction.

'Yes, my very word he was, and a very fine Christian gentleman too, although you must forgive me for being biased over the matter.' I served the tea and sat eagerly waiting to see how he acquitted himself.

'This is very nice tea and the cake is delicious.' Lady Sarah would not have approved, for a wayward finger was protruding straight up in the air, and he was making the same frightful slurping noises as her Vicar. Ah, and there was the steady avalanche of lost cake. Oh dear, the Reverend had become over-anxious about the spillage, and held his plate directly under his chin. I served him another wedge and renewed his tea.

'Mrs. Brancliff, this is really most enjoyable. May I inquire how you and your late husband reconciled your spiritual beliefs?' The question rather shocked me, but I could imagine how Fritz might react, and I had it in one.

'Oh, very simply, we respected the culture and beliefs of each other.' I had not wanted to sound sharp, yet the Reverend's brow puckered with the immensity of it.

'Did he not try to bring you to Christ?'

'Not at all, I think we handled it very well, and it certainly never came between us. But since you ask, my husband was keen to understand our beliefs, as I was his. He was a wonderful teacher and raconteur, and it was lovely to learn all about his former life and his family. The dear man seemed pleased with that, and said, 'I think it is reassuring to know that he found rest in the arms of our Savoir, Jesus Christ.' What was I to say? Neither of us had given it a moment's thought. But these people tended to pursue these things.

Then he said, 'It would have given your husband great strength to face the terrible perils of war.' Damn! The conversation was slipping out of my control and heading where it shouldn't. Lady Sarah would have deftly steered around the heavy going, and I could see Fritz looking down and shaking his head.

'Perhaps it did, but I don't think my husband or his mates were overly concerned with dying. They were more worried about doing their duty, and looking out for each other.' I was wading into deeper water. 'My husband took a broad view of it; he was attracted to our beliefs, and mind you, it was never a matter of one influencing the other, but the subject of much lively discussion.'

"Ah yes, but Mrs. Brancliff, a Christian would not fear death because they have the promise of everlasting life.' At this point, the Lady Sarah would have pleaded another engagement, whereas I was becoming agitated.

'My husband liked to think that his spirit would return to watch over us as a star in the night sky. He was also very fond of rock formations, and spoke of being part of the landscape. I am sure he is a star; I can see him up there looking down at us. I said I would sing to him, and I still do.' I felt my civility had been extended far enough. The churchman wiped the perspiration from his thinning dome with his handkerchief. I felt he may be marshalling his forces, so I parried first. 'My husband said you might come and it worried him as he thought it would be confusing for our people. Having witnessed it myself, I am sure he was right.'

I may have felt better, but my visitor had barely reacted. 'Mrs. Brancliff, I was hoping you might come to chapel and learn about the word of God.' I had to hang on.

'That is very kind of you,' I said. "Why don't you and I agree that you may pray to your God, and I can sing to my spirits? My husband used to reckon they were probably great mates anyway.' My visitor was not deterred in the slightest.

'Would you allow me to read some passages from the Bible? There is great comfort in his word.' I wished someone would magically appear to defuse the situation for me. 'Particularly,' he went on, 'for someone who has been left so alone.'

'I would rather you didn't,' I announced firmly.

'Then I should like to pray for your salvation.'

'No, please don't; thank you Reverend.' What else was there to say? But there was no stopping him.

'Then before I go, allow me to ask our dear God for his blessing,' and the man of God began to pray. 'Dear Heavenly Father, who watches over us, be with your humble servant Alkina, and fill her heart with your love, so that she may come to know your loving son, Jesus Christ, as her Savoir and Lord. Be with her in her bereavement; give her and her daughter the strength to carry on in the footsteps and knowledge of the Lord. For I ask it in his name. Amen.'

His head came up and his eyes opened brightly, as if the hopes of all mankind had just been much uplifted. 'I do hope Reverend,' I said, 'that your prayer made you feel better. My husband was killed some time ago and I no longer feel the terrible emptiness, and nor do I consider myself as still being in a state of bereavement. However, I do miss him very much; he was such a lovely man, and we adored each other.' I could see Fritz shaking his head in dismay, but having wound myself up, I could no longer leave it there.

'Furthermore,' I went on, 'I think what you white people did to this Jesus person was grossly inhuman, and I object to you trying to make my daughter feel guilty about it. She had nothing to do with it; in fact none of our people did, and the very idea of you saying we did, is quite ridiculous.' Much to my satisfaction, he blushed, and we chatted amicably until he left. But the Reverend's visit had an effect, though it was the opposite of what would have been intended. That visit motivated me to teach the young ones everything I knew about our lore."

Nan's stories also sparked my own imagination.

"Nan, what happened to the lovely Lady Sarah after she married that awful Earl?" "That's a story for another day," she explained, "but I would say that before Fritz's death, contact with his mother had been strained. After he was killed, she and I had a brief correspondence until it ceased altogether."

"Nan," I said, unable to stifle my imagination, "and I imagine the Earl made an enormous fortune and left her for a much younger woman and went to live in Kenya. Or maybe, and luckily for her, he was killed in a duel over a dishonoured gambling debt, or she married an Argentinean cattle rancher and lived happily ever after."

"Ha, ha dear, that's a funny one, but if we start down that path, the family history will be out of sequence. My darling girl, I want you to marry someone you love, so each day will be a delight."

"Nan, perhaps I will be the one who meets an Argentinean cattle rancher. I was hoping you would tell me how mum and dad met, and that time before Darain and I were born."

"Okay, just a short story and one that I remember well, which began when a small party of *Myalls** unexpectedly walked out of the bush. They were in a terrible state, many of them were elderly and they had walked all the way from the coast. Among them was a young hunter known as Ganan. He and Tilly, your mother, just seemed to click, and each morning he would arrive on her doorstep, and walk with her to the mission school. But there was no way he would venture into the classroom. At first he would not wear clothes, nor would he let anyone trim his hair. However, I persevered, and nicely trimmed and dressed in

---

* Italicized words and phrases in this book are explained in the *Glossary* at the end.

some of Fritz's old work clothes, he looked very presentable. We fed him up and in time his people recovered. One morning they slipped away in much the same manner as they had arrived, and naturally enough your mother was upset. But Ganan was needed to hunt for them, for the elders were homesick and wanted to return to their land.

For Tilly, the intervening years must have passed very slowly, and my granddaughter grew into a lovely young woman, but it was to that tall young hunter that her heart belonged. Until one morning there he was, beaming his shy smile at her, as if he had never left. Understanding why he had returned, I got him a job in the blacksmith's shop. He became very good with horses, and later he got work out on a camp. After the initial excitement, your mother's life went on much as before. But I was mindful that Ganan had made that long journey on his own and had obviously come for her, and I decided I should move things along.

One day your mother and I were out on one of our walks, when I laid it out for her. 'My dear Tilly,' I said, 'I believe that when you find your mate, you must understand that the opportunity is not given to everyone, and you must seize it. Just like my husband, Ganan is a long way from home, and he has come all the way back just for you.' I had wanted her to understand where she was in the cycle of her life, and told her that a lifetime passes very quickly. We talked about my life with Fritz, and I told her I would give her some of her grandfather's things to keep for her children. Some of this gentle persuasion must have worked, as not long after, Tilly confided to me that they were very much in love and wanted to get married."

I could listen to Nan for hours, for ours was a very loving relationship. We used to wander out into the bush after honey. I would shinny up a tree to milk a familiar hive, and we would gorge ourselves. Then finding a suitable spot, she would carry on narrating the family story. "Tilly was a very good housewife, although in my view, she could be a little too impatient with your father. I have always loved children, and when she became pregnant, it was the thought of holding the baby in my arms that kept me young, and what a great joy to me you are. And as the lovely Lady Sarah is one of our favourites, why don't I tell you how a visit by the English owners put us back in touch with that side of the family?

One day there was quite a commotion up at the homestead. Dick Lacey was the manager in those days, and he and his wife Hope were well liked, although she could get a little over-anxious, as we shall see. When Tilly arrived that morning to work in the homestead, Hope was in a state of panic, the Boothroyds, the new English owners had written to say they were coming out for the running of the Melbourne Cup, and were going to pay us a visit on their way South. What an upheaval! Hope and Tilly turned the place upside down. Hope was fastidious at the best of times, but she and Tilly polished the homestead from top to bottom, which, having been altered so many times over the years, it has always been difficult to keep clean.

The Laceys were terrified that their visitors had no idea what they were coming to. There had never been much of a proper homestead garden, although the fruit trees and the vegetable garden had been kept up. In those days, other than rainwater for drinking, all the water had to be taken up to the house in forty-four gallon drums mounted on a dray. The pressure mounted, and the decision was made to install a windmill down on the lagoon so there would be water laid on at the homestead. The original tanks are still in use today. A huge amount of material had to be brought in, and the work went on in a race against the clock. The only outside help was an itinerant tank maker, who could turn his hand to anything.

I found it quite amusing as Tilly told me that with all the building work going on, as fast as they cleaned the homestead, it got dirty again, and she doubted Hope was going to last the distance. But when it was finished, it all looked pretty good, and the Laceys could not get over having water on tap. As the big day drew near, news of the steamer's arrival came over the peddle radio. Meanwhile, the housework never stopped, and the mounting tension in the homestead was terrific.

The mailman made a special trip to drive the Boothroyds in. It could have been a state visit, for we had seen nothing like it. They arrived in a large green Chrysler sedan, the square-looking model, which must have been current in those days. I recall that it was a particularly hot day and I believe they stopped a little way out, to remove the worst of the dust, and to make themselves presentable.

Tilly said she and Hope could not believe their eyes. Caroline Boothroyd had arrived wearing a Harris Tweed suit, with a long skirt and with a fox fur stole draped around her shoulders, with a fashionable felt hat firmly pinned to her hair. She reckoned they looked a bit like the King and Queen arriving at Balmoral. Hector, the husband, was very regal indeed, with winged collar, a heavy three-piece suit and a Homburg hat, while the temperature on the homestead veranda was one hundred and three degrees in the shade.

The welcome was very formal, after which Tilly served the tea on the shady side of the veranda. It must have been an incredible occasion. 'How does madam take her tea?' your mother inquired, and after serving their guests, then stood back to observe the proceedings. He made sucking noises as he drank, whereas his wife was exemplary. The calamity happened just as Tilly was getting her a second cup; with a sigh, their tweeded visitor quietly fainted and slid to the floor; they took off the heavy jacket which prompted her husband to remove his own jacket, collar, and tie.

When she came to, they got her to their bedroom and removed her long skirt, which wrapped around her lean frame. She was wearing a full set of cotton undergarments, which would have been more than sufficient on their own. Hope was just beside herself; they bathed the patient with cold towels and fanned her, and Hope was very relieved, when she managed a self-conscious smile. Hope went to check on the state of the husband, and to keep an eye on the kitchen, while Tilly kept applying wet towels and fed the visitor sips of water. From then on, things began to look up, she turned out to be a very charming lady who insisted they call her Caroline.

She and Tilly got on immediately; your mother always did have a nice way with people. She offered to unpack Caroline's summer frocks and to iron them, which was when it all came out. 'Thank you so much,' Caroline said, 'and before I jump under the cold shower, I will let you into a little secret. On the ship, we had two trunks with all our clothes very methodically packed in each, one with all our winter wear, and the other with our summer clothes for the tropics. The steamship company has sent the wrong trunk on to Melbourne, and left us with only our winter wear for our stay here.' With that she began to laugh, 'and we are, ha, ha, very annoyed and very embarrassed.' It must have been very funny, as when Hope rushed in to see what the trouble was, she found them in hysterics.

That incident began a lifelong friendship, and as it turned out, the visitors loved their stay, and all the trouble everyone had gone to had been very worthwhile. Having new kerosene refrigerators, and water on tap at the homestead had really saved the day. But to return to the problem, Tilly soon ran her up a few simple frocks to get by with, while Dick was able to outfit Hector, so they could enjoy their stay. Dinner the following evening was an unnecessarily formal affair, but that was Hope, being overly nervous and trying too hard. The conversation began with the awe the visitors had of the immensity of Australia and of Arrawatta.

'There are parts of the run where we never go,' Dick explained. 'It is either desert or so rugged and steep we can't get in, and we leave that to the goannas. We work the cattle around the good country, muster around the feed and the water, we lose a few, but as much of the boundary is unfenced, there is not much we can do about it, and every now and again, we come across a mob that have never been branded. We shoot the rough bulls and bring the rest into a camp. This is a climate of extremes; in good years, the numbers go up and we start walking a mob to market. We take the stores over to the Queensland channel country or we walk them down to Adelaide.'

Hope had planned the meal for weeks. Tilly was to do the serving; it was a rib roast, followed by rhubarb pie with clotted cream, which was quite ridiculous in that weather. Over the dessert, they had been talking about the history of Arrawatta, which of course Tilly was very familiar with. Perhaps she wasn't thinking, but for whatever reason, Hope spoke disparagingly of Fritzhugh. 'I imagine he would have been the black sheep of the family,' she said, 'who was sent out to get him out of the way. Mind you, he would have been one of many, too much money, trouble with gambling and drink, and I understand he was something of a London fop.'

Tilly would have none of this, while telling herself the Laceys had only been on Arrawatta a few years, but even so they should have known better. 'That is Fritzhugh Brancliff's portrait in the hall,' Hope continued unwisely. 'There would have been plenty of his sort packed off to the colonies in those days,' Dick, put in; he simply would not have known, which was all too much for our Tilly.

'I beg your pardon,' she said, 'he was nothing of a sort. My grand-father died a hero's death on the Western Front, so that you could sit here and criticize him when he was no longer alive to defend himself. That portrait is not of Lord Fritzhugh Brancliff; that is his father, Lord Handsmere Ponsonby Harry Brancliff KC.MG.MC Colonel in Chief of her Majesty's Horse Guards, who also gave his life for Queen and Empire fighting the Boers in South Africa. The only reason that portrait is hanging in the hall is because it is the only wall strong enough and with sufficient space to hang it on.' Having well and truly blown off steam, she fought to calm herself.

'The smaller painting beside it is a formal study of Fritzhugh's mother and father. She never visited her son's family in Australia, but as she was a great beauty in her day, she is fondly known to us as the lovely Lady Sarah.'

'My goodness, she married my great-grandfather,' Caroline exclaimed. 'But she was married to the Earl of Fairly,' Tilly added. 'Then that is definitely her,' replied Caroline, 'and Matilda, I am dying to hear your family history. You see, my grandfather was her third husband. I believe the Earl died sometime after the 1919 flu epidemic. By all accounts, she was considered a great prize. My grandfather was a widower with two sons, and I am the second daughter of Errol, who was the eldest. So you and I are just a blanket or two away from being related?'

That evening the dinner-table talk went on into the early hours, and I think it would have been fun to have been a fly on the wall. Caroline and Tilly often referred to it in their correspondence. The program called for Dick to take Hector out to see something of his holding and to experience life out on a cattle camp. Caroline had wanted to have a walk through the bush and to try to gain some understanding of it. Having toured the mission and the school, and met the staff and most of the local elders, and hosted several afternoon teas, she was looking forward to it. She and Tilly set off one afternoon, your mother carrying her dilly bag, the tea things, and her digging stick.

Her visitor was dressed in one of Tilly's creations, matched with a wide-brimmed straw hat and a pair of boots with her husband's socks spilling over the top. Tilly explained how to note the position of the sun and the relationship of the shadows with the hour of the day. The warm breeze rustled the grass and the leaves and she showed her how the moss formed in places where the sun never reached, she described the birds and where and how they nested; she collected bush tucker for her to try, and told her something of the surrounding trees and grasses. Caroline seemed enchanted by it all.

'How pretty it is, and how at home in it you are! I do hope you do not mind me dawdling along. I am drinking in the strangeness of it. These are sights and sounds I could never have imagined.'

No doubt your mother enjoyed it as well. 'Caroline, you should notice the trees, the rocks, the larger tussocks and patches of baked earth, the changes and the different signs that tell you where you have been.'

Tilly told her of the trees that she had climbed as a child. Every now and then they stopped to smell the leaves and wild flowers, and Caroline collected what she fancied. As luck would have it, Tilly came across the recent track of a snake, which they followed until they found the only one Caroline had ever seen. She watched in frozen fascination as her guide dispatched it and added it to the bag. 'I thought we should try some later,' she suggested.

Through the timber, they came to a sheltered place where in a clump of creamy paperbarks a mob of kangaroos waited until the cool of evening. As they watched in silence there came the muffled thumps as two bucks stood chest to chest in an ageless battle for dominance. They slashed at each other with their powerful hind legs, with a terrible thump across their chests. Later they watched as emus moved down a fence line on the edge of the open plain, their heads working to and fro with their inquisitive look and delicate gait, as they came right up to them; curiosity satisfied, they sauntered away.

They saw where the goannas lived, dug around the roots of an acacia bush for witchetty grubs, which Tilly added to the bag. Then she went straight up a tree, much to Caroline's alarm, coming down with a piece of comb, the honey oozing out of it, and gave it to the visitor to try.

'I have been robbing that hive since I was a little girl. Now we will make a fire by the billabong, and listen while the birds settle in the trees around it and tell us the night is coming?' The cockatoos fought and screeched, the sky turned pink, and the kookaburras began their evening chorus and they saw the sky's reflection on the water as evening came.

'Now I will light our camp fire in the old way, and we can talk women's business.'

She sat in the sand and blew gently until the handful of dry grass caught. 'That was extraordinary,' the visitor said. 'I would not have missed this for the world; they will never believe me when I tell them at home.' Tilly made tea and threw the grubs on the coals.

'Caroline, try one, they are delicious.' She made a face.

'I am only doing this for England; yum, so they are.'

The snake went on next, at which she balked. 'No thanks, not even if I was starving to death. If I am ever lost in the bush, I will have to survive on witchetty grubs.' But her guide was not to be put off.

'Go on Caroline, try a little bit; it is a favourite.'

'I hate snakes; maybe I could if I don't think about it,' which she did. 'Imagine you and I sitting by a camp fire under that beautiful sky and me eating snake. I can't unravel the primness of my upbringing, but I am really enjoying this wonderful experience. I feel profoundly moved. It has to be the work of one creator, I think we have been talking about the same Great Spirit all along.'

Nan told me Fritzhugh said the same thing.

"They had walked in a wide circle, and along the way, the conversation had turned to Lady Sarah and her marriages.

'When I return home, I shall find out everything I can about the great lady, and send it to you. What a shame, those two never met,' Tilly said.

Nan was fascinated by her and would have wanted her approval.

'Your grandmother is lovely; they had none of our communications and he was a long way from home. All they had was each other, which I think is a very romantic thought. That was a terrible war; we lost the flower of a generation; that young men came from such a faraway place to fight for King and Empire astonishes me. What have you and Ganan got planned?'

'He wants to show me his country and to walk the places of his dreaming. I hesitate because he may be the last of them. I think it needs time. One day we shall. I have never seen the sea, so I am looking forward to that. Nan and I did what we could, but he was very sad for a long time.'"

"Nan, that was a nice story. I like Caroline, she and mum still write. Could you tell me what happened then?"

"The long walk to your father's land had to be put off when she became pregnant with their first child. Later they delivered the baby at the very spot where Tilly's grandmother, after whom the baby was named, had first mated with Fritzhugh so many years before. It was her favourite place, and where she would go when it was time for her to join her mate."

"Nan, why did you say that?" I was too young to realize why Nan expressed life and death in such a practical way to me. "I loved their story, and now you have gone and ruined everything by giving it a sad ending."

Nan started, "I do not believe it is sad at all; births and deaths belong together. Darling one, I will not mind, because I will be joining my Fritzhugh, and I want you to sing to me every day and tell me what you are doing. I will be listening for you, and I certainly would not want you to be sad. My only regret is that it would have been a delight to have known your mate, although I am sure he will be lovely. I am sorry if I made you sad, and as you have been a very good girl, I thought we could spend the afternoon baking, and then have a nice afternoon tea, and I will tell you how a packing case arrived one day from England. Would you like that?"

"Yes Nan, very much."

"You can make a batch of date scones and a sponge. They used to serve those and dainty sandwiches at Windsor Castle. Fritzhugh told me all about them; your great-grandfather used to adore date scones, and he quite liked my fluffy sponges as well. At our tea party, you can play at being the lovely Lady Sarah and I will be Her Most Gracious Majesty."

With that the old lady sat in her favourite chair across the table from the iron stove from where she could watch, and see if any more wood was needed for the firebox. As I got organized, she opened an album, removed a letter, and continued her story:

"Now that Tilly and Kirra had a new baby, the missionaries were very keen to have it baptized, and so that harmony would prevail, and heeding Fritzhugh's advice, they went along with it. However, before the christening, a small packing case arrived for Tilly from Caroline. She and Hope opened it on the veranda. On top lay an envelope and a family photo album tied with pretty red ribbon. While Hope nursed the baby, Tilly read her letter. I have it here.

> My dear Matilda,
>
> I cannot tell you what delight your relationship through Fritzhugh to his mother, *the lovely Lady Sarah*, has given me. So much time has passed since her death, and over here, it was believed she had left no descendants. The children of her nieces and nephews know little of Lady Sarah or her son. This is very understandable, with Fritzhugh being an only child and living in Australia. However, my inquiries have had some rewarding results. The staff at Eton could not have been more helpful; there were his school days beautifully documented; you will find copies of his school reports, in which his work and behaviour are described on most occasions as *pleasing*. When you read the extracts from the school magazine, you will find he is mentioned

several times, and I am sure you will love his poetry, which was published in his last year.

Now to the most interesting part, through the school I tracked down his closest known school friend. I have enclosed what I am sure will be a most delightful letter to you. Our meeting is another story on its own. The writer is one Dicky Althorne, a retired Bishop no less, who remembered him well. From his endearing remarks to me, I can only guess at what a character your grandfather must have been. Then a descendant of Wallace Brancliff, one of Fritzhugh's cousins, sent me a photograph of Fritzhugh taken with his father, which takes pride of place on the first page of the album. Dicky thought it would have been taken in London just before the father left for the South African campaign. The Bishop is a dear old man, and has enclosed the last letter he received from his old school friend. But Fritzhugh left England so early in his life, I am afraid that is about all I could discover.

However, researching the Lady Sarah was no difficulty as she was such a prominent social figure. I found her obituary in *The Times*, and you will see how they gushed over her. She was always *the beautiful*, *the very lovely*, or *the vivacious Lady Sarah*, and was widely reported in the social pages of the best magazines. I must tell you, we are indebted to a charming lady named Gwendolyn, who's a second daughter of Constance Vincent, one of Lady Sarah's nieces on her side, who had an understanding of who was who, and to whom I shall return. For after her second husband's death Lady Sarah married another military man (my connection) who kept a string of race horses and served two terms as the member for South Durham. He was The Hon. General Marjoribanks Sparswick-Soames, *Winky* for short. I thought you would like that. Anyway they travelled extensively, and you will find photos from across the race courses of Europe.

Believe me, I could have sent you boxes of clippings about her, her husbands and their notable friends, but they tend to be repetitive. However, there is the moving account of the memorial service for Fritzhugh's father. The personal things, including the letter of condolence from H.R.H. Queen Victoria have come from Gwendolyn, who proved to be a delight. I am sure she will explain herself in her enclosed letter. She told me how the few things she had were passed down through her parents, they being unaware there were any of Lady Sarah's descendants still living.

I think it is lovely that such a lively lady did leave a family behind. Gwendolyn expressed the same view, and she is very pleased to have found a proper home for the remaining mementos. I wrote a separate letter to Hope, but please give her my love. I can picture you both on the veranda of Arrawatta having a great giggle and chin wag as you rummage through this.

I have the good fortune to be your friend.
With much love.

Caroline

Tilly was very touched by this marvellous gesture, and of course they had a great time going through everything. Hope was incredulous, 'oh do look at this; here she is arriving at Windsor Castle, looking quite superb; I bet the other ladies had to hang on to their men with her around. She was extraordinary, just look at her hats, her outfits; she must have kept a team of milliners and dressmakers working flat out. There she is on Lord Brancliff's arm; he was such a handsome man; you can see where Fritzhugh got his looks, you, and baby have them as well.'

They spent the remainder of the afternoon utterly enthralled.

The next major event was when Tilly and Ganan produced a son, who was born some forty-seven months after you. Darain's name came from his father's people, and it is to do with their totem. Incidentally, the missionaries must have prevailed, because like just like you, he was christened in the mission chapel. Ganan was keen to bring his son up in the ways of his people, and prepare him for his initiation."

I was so lucky to have Nan. She was a marvellous lady who made my time with her such fun. "That's enough story for today. The oven has a nice even temperature and they should be ready, you can let the sponge stand before you lay on the jam and cream. Do not forget you are taking tea with the Sovereign, so don't forget to address me as 'Mum.'"

⚡ 3 ⚡

Nan told me that in her day so much of what happened in Australia was still decided in London. One can imagine the ecclesiastical tones of men of religion who gathered by the Thames to consider the future of our people. Although much of this is anecdotal, the evidence suggests that their knowledge of indigenous Australians was at best, superficial. Their views having been fermented by traditional church morality, perhaps tempered in the teeming cities of pre-partition India, and much vindicated by a belief in white superiority that had been further encouraged by their experience in Africa.

For in the traditional way of missionary societies, it was decided to send the Reverend Michael Whiteside and his family to Australia, where he was to report on the state of the church's work amongst the unfortunate Aboriginal people, and to assume responsibility for their pastoral care. A canon of senior years was the first to offer his congratulations as the young missionary's mind swam in the glory of it.

"A wonderful appointment Michael, well done, taking the gospel right around the globe to a primitive people, who have never known the love of Almighty God, or the beauty of his word; it makes me wish that I was a young man again."

"Here, here," his colleagues echoed.

"Thank you canon," the young missionary responded, his face glowing with pride. "I shall pray for his divine guidance, as I prepare to spread his word, just as my father and grandfather did during their missions to Africa."

"And very appropriately spoken," commented a Bishop who knew the family well. "They were truly remarkable men, who dedicated their lives to spreading his glory, and now you are to follow. How proud they would be; your grandfather died upholding the faith in Matabeleland, and of course your own dear father, who was my close friend, joined our heavenly father in Bechuanaland, when you were still a boy in short trousers. A word of warning here, as I think the colonials are inclined to be over-familiar, the trick is to maintain standards. Do drop me a line and tell me of anything you need; sometimes the simplest things are just not available. But whatever it is, I am sure we can always raise the funds."

"Thank you, your Grace. I take your point. I am a firm believer in setting the right standards and sticking to them."

"Quite so," said the Bishop. It was said the young missionary was dizzy with it. And so it began. Although the financial circumstances of the society were not in a necessitous state, it afforded the young missionary, his wife, and their four children only a lower-deck steamer passage to Adelaide, where they arrived on a baking summer's day.

"My goodness!" Nora, his wife, exclaimed, almost swooning as the dry heat of Adelaide closed over her. "It is almost as hot here as it was in the Red Sea. I think I am going to melt."

"There, there my dear, do remember our position," said Reverend Whiteside.

"Never mind Mrs. Whiteside," said the President of the Adelaide Auxiliary, who was there to greet them. She was a woman of considerable influence, the second daughter of Sir Walter Packworth-Lloyd, who owned enormous sheep and cattle stations across the continent. Nora, being of a retiring nature, felt she might succumb to the heat and disgrace herself, whereas the demeanour of her hostess implied that she gave way to nothing.

"We will have you out of the heat shortly, and I think you will find that your new home is delightfully cool. We have filled your ice box with the staples, so there is no need for you to go out to shop." With that, the Whitesides were loaded aboard a small bus, their trunks being strapped to the roof. When they arrived, the children giggled when they were met by an Aboriginal girl in a white frock.

"This is Rose," Mrs. Packworth-Lloyd announced. "She is learning to be a housekeeper. Aren't you Rose?" The girl maintained her silence, her eyes diverted to the floor, causing the children to giggle and nudge each other.

"That will do," their father ordered. "You must all have a cool drink," said Mrs. Packworth-Lloyd. Rose appeared with a tray of glasses and a jug of orange cordial.

"You will find Rose a very helpful lass. Each week they send a different girl across to gain experience. They are thoroughly trained in personal hygiene, so you should have no worry on that score. They can wash and iron, do the floors, and dust and polish. Tonight she will bring dinner across from the kitchen."

"They do go to school?"

"Oh yes, and Rose lives in the home." Nora felt relieved. Mrs. Packworth-Lloyd continued to reassure. "The girls are learning to read and write, so they will not be under your feet."

The Reverend's ministry began with a visit to a home for Aboriginal boys. "Good morning Reverend Whiteside," they sung in unison, in time with their teacher's hand. Their discipline seemed satisfactory, although he was surprised that some were indistinguishable from white. The morning was becoming uncomfortably warm; the annoying little black flies worried him, yet the boys ignored them, and kept their eyes diverted to the ground.

"Boys, I have come to Australia," he explained, "from a small island on the other side of the world known as England. It is where most newcomers to Australia have come from, and with them they have brought a glorious Christian civilization. I want to bring you the word of Almighty God, so you may take your place as fine young Christian men in the Australian community. The training and education you receive here will give you an opportunity to make something of your lives." While he spoke, he felt the heat of the sun beneath his jacket, and it was not yet nine o'clock. He would not show weakness and ignored the rivulets of sweat dripping down his face and neck. "March them to class," he told the Superintendent.

Whiteside found their artwork strange. "Did I offend them? I could not catch their eyes."

"Not at all," the Superintendent explained, "it is nothing personal; they divert their eyes to ward off evil spirits, and so they won't jump from you to them." He was after all an educated Englishman, and the Superintendent's offensive explanation cut him to the core, although he maintained his silence. The Reverend left on a tour of their missions in the early autumn. He was in awe of this vast country, where the vehicle tracks were sometimes non-existent, or wound through the timber, across dunes, or there were three or more versions of the same track, or it petered out to nothing. The merciless sun bore down on the carcasses of long-dead cattle, and he battled to keep the truck's front wheels from getting stuck in the ruts. As he drove the bull, dust rose up through the floor boards, and under the doors so that it caked his lips and made his mouth and throat as dry as the landscape. There were long stretches with no shade, and every now and then, he took a drink from one of the canvas water bags suspended outside.

This strange land made him feel insignificant. "Merciful God," he prayed, as he hunched over the steering wheel, "deliver me from this place, and grant me the strength to take your blessed word to these heathen people. Guide your faithful servant, and I earnestly beseech you that your humble servant's truck does not break down in the middle of nowhere." Slowly the country changed, to where there was an endless sea of grass, and here and there stands of trees. With profound relief, he got his bearings and recognized the landmarks mentioned in his directions. He was to follow the left track at the stand of majestic gums, and continue due west for thirty miles, until he came to a cairn of stones.

"Oh blessed Lord, I have been delivered."

It said six hours to the Arrawatta homestead and he had sufficient fuel and water. He had been appalled by the state of the Aborigines, but one just had to get on with it. The brave outback women were always so welcoming. Hope Lacey could have been a matron from Adelaide, while her companion was obviously of mixed blood.

"I cannot tell you ladies what a welcome sight you are; for a while I thought I was lost. But one must never lose faith. For once I was lost and now I am found," he said brightly.

Hope and Tilly had looked forward to it; he had written in plenty of time, and a new face was always welcome. They wondered what sort of man he was. Hope's husband Richard commented bluntly, "Only mad dogs and Englishmen would have bothered." Once there, he found the mission staff had adapted to the ways of the local people. After meeting him, Hope said she thought it was absurd for a young Englishman to be alone on the track, and her husband said he must be very naïve. As soon as he had showered, they served a welcoming afternoon tea. The next day Tilly fixed bright green bows in Alkina's hair, in honour of their visitor, before sending her to school. "What did you do today?" she asked her daughter, when she came home.

"We had a visitor from Adelaide, and we had a lovely time singing. And mum, he talked about the little baby Jesus and all that. We had practiced, well you know, I have sung them for you." Alkina clapped her hands to the time.

"It is not do right because I must
but right because it's right," she sang with great
concentration.
"And mum, another one was:
'There is a green hill far away,
outside a city wall,
where the dear Lord was crucified,
who died to save us all.'

Mum, we had a tambourine and a piano, and we did that one we always sing.

'Since the Lord saved me,
I am as happy as can be,
My cups full of running over.'"

"That was very nice dear."

"Mum, those silly river kids did not wear any tops to school, and I don't think our visitor was very happy about that," Alkina said gravely, and her mother laughed. There were farewell prayer meetings for the staff, and when it was time to leave, the Reverend Whiteside thanked Hope and Tilly warmly, and set off in a cloud of dust. Before he had even driven through the horse paddock, the thrust of his report was already taking shape.

"Your Grace,

I have the honour to report to you upon the completion of my five-month tour of our missions in Australia.

Their pastoral work proceeds with great enthusiasm in bringing the word of Almighty God to the Aboriginal people. The Society has good reason to be proud of all they have achieved. This is carried out in an environment that affords little comfort. Your Grace, will note that I have taken leave to enclose a separate report that deals particularly with the state of the children. That is because I believe their condition is so appalling it needs your Grace's urgent attention.

My recommendation is that they be taken into care as soon as possible. This is a task far beyond our limited resources. My prayer and thoughts are that you may take the matter up with the Home Government, in the hope that they may confer with the appropriate authorities in Australian.

My family has settled down nicely in Adelaide, and were it not for the hot climate, it could almost pass as a warmer clime of England."

⚡ 4 ⚡

Many years had passed since the old lady had gone to join her Fritzhugh in the night sky. I had become one of the country's leading chefs, owned my own business, and was the author of several books, and also produced a popular syndicated column on food and wine. My mother had sent me Nan's journals through which I hoped to fill in the missing years of my life. Reading them was a very emotional experience, as she and I could have been sitting together in the sand on a winter's day. Her telling of our great walk brought it all back.

"When the summer began to cool, and there was plenty of feed for the stock, Ganan left with his family on the great walk to see his country on the coast and to visit his dreaming places. There he would instruct and groom his son in preparation for his initiation. Tilly was thrilled and she and the children had taken to calling him "The Mighty Hunter". Tilly would teach Alkina the women's lore. They left before dawn, the boy trotting along with his father, who carried his spears, thrower, and hunting bag. The women chatted happily as they gathered bush tucker.

Boy and father strode ahead, and in a while, they came to a place where the father carved a cutdown spear and thrower for his son. "We travel to the land of our ancestors," he told him, "where I hunted with my father, and where the spirits of my people dwell." Darain did his best to keep up with the great striding legs, and if he was tired toward the end of the day, his father would wait for him to catch up, and lift him up so he could ride on his shoulders. They found the water, chose the camp, made a fire, and put what they had hunted on the coals. After they had walked for many days, they came to a place of high cliffs riven with gorges. In the shadow of the towering cliffs, the Mighty Hunter showed him the sacred ochre deposit, which had been mined since time began.

By the light of their camp fire, he told his son the story of how the ochre deposit had come to be.

"Many, many moons ago, a giant red kangaroo lived on the cliffs above. He could see far away to where his land met the sky. He bounded about from one high place to another, from where he could keep watch over his country. But one day a great wind blew the evil spirit Modong to where he had camped, and when the giant roo came bounding along, Modong leapt up and speared him. After a terrible struggle, the giant kangaroo toppled over the cliff, and was dashed to pieces on the rocks below, which is why the rocks turned the colour of his blood; or where his other juices fell, they turned yellow and white. And so the evil spirit of

Modong cannot leap up and take us by surprise, we must not turn our backs to this sacred place, and must always leave walking backwards."

They took enough ochre for their ceremonies and mother and daughter decorated themselves; and then they sat down and wove dilly bags in readiness for the arduous journey across the range. On their last night, they feasted on wallaby.

Their father explained, "Tomorrow we leave in the cool of early evening and must travel all night, because we must not stop until we reach water on the other side."

They filled their bellies so as to keep Marmoo and other evil spirits away during the crossing, and when they reached the top of the escarpment in the moonlight, they briefly looked back over a silvery land, before they hurried on. As the sun climbed, the temperature on top of the great stone plateau rose. Tilly and the children wondered if the teeming geese would really be so thick they would block out the sun, and the fish so easy to spear they could eat them whenever they wished. Hurry, for they must not stop. They were heading for the land of Pikuwa, the great crocodile, the stealer of wives; but with the Mighty Hunter, there was nothing to fear.

They scrambled over deep gullies, willed their great mother Yhi, the sun, to give way to Bahloo, the moon, and let them through. When the sun was at its fiercest, they daydreamed of cool billabongs and when at night it cooled, Tilly and Alkina sang to Fritzhugh's star. They saw where Yarandoo, the Southern Cross, was marked by Monyi, the Pointers and were relieved their ancestors were watching over them.

As the dawn approached, Ganan smiled broadly, as for the first time he could see his land, which stretched beyond where scattered clouds dumped dark grey cascades in the half light and rivers snaked, like silver rope, into the distance. They were enchanted by it; far away lightning flashed, sending claps of thunder rolling over them. Ganan swept an arm before him. "This is all our country," he threatened his enemies with his spear and danced and whooped with joy while his family shared his delight. He was once more in the land of his spirits, and they replenished his whole being. As the dawn broke, they clambered down to the plain below, and lay down to fill their bellies with water.

This was where every river, bluff, and waterfall had a story, where their ancestral spirits were in the night sky, or leapt in mighty bounds across the plains, or were creatures of the rivers and the sea. They soared motionless above, or waited through all time in the scheming eyes of a crocodile. Banks of black and grey cloud unloaded their moisture, then gently floated away to allow the shafts of sunlight through. They were enthralled by it, and spent their days splashing across the plain and feasting and swimming in fresh water lagoons.

"We are getting fat," their mother remarked a few weeks later, "and you have not yet shown us the sea. It is a beautiful land and already we adore it." The soft grass held their tracks, which quickly filled with water, while in the distance, great arched rainbows formed between the showers. Ganan would spear a lazy water bird or fish, and when it was cooked, they would eat it on water lily leaves, then splash onward toward the sea. They played in the shallow water, dived among the swans and black and white magpie geese that had gathered in their thousands. The Mighty Hunter taught his children to call the water birds, and they felt great joy as they lay in the reeds among them. As they neared the coast, for the first time, they stared into the half-submerged watchful eyes of the wily crocodile, while the Mighty Hunter protected them.

The air became heavier, and soon they saw the coast for first time. They stood in wonder at the exquisite expanse of shimmering water before them, and in a while, they played along the shore. Tilly touched her husband's face and pulled gently at his beard, and shook her head.

"Ganan, this is the most beautiful sight the children and I have ever seen." He rubbed his face against her cheek.

"Follow me along the shore and when we near the place of my father's totem, I must leave you, so I can reveal our secrets to our boy. He and I will talk, and then we will dance and sing to our ancestors, I will tell them of our family, and that I have brought my son to the *bora* of our people, and I will make a ceremony for him." The children squealed in delight as they chased stingrays, octopus, and crabs through the shallows.

Father and son left a few days later, He led his son to an inlet, where, at low tide, he cut out a section of tree root, before they walked inland for a few days. All the time, he explained the significance of their journey, and why they were returning to their bora, and how it rekindled his memories of his own boyhood. He swept his spear around.

"The spirits of our ancestors are all around this place." Then he took the boy to a low mound of rocks, from where, with great care, he removed their ancestral totem.

"This is our sacred *kurduru*, and when you are initiated, you may set our totem up just as I do, and sing to the spirits of our people and stamp your dreaming into the land. But you will become a man in your mother's country, with all your aunts and uncles on your mother's side around you, and you can show this place to your sons, and teach them all that I have taught you. Now my son, as our ancestors watch, I will carve a *nulla nulla* for you, just as my father did for me, and then we will hunt and make a *Jarrajarra* ceremony."

The hunter sang softly as he carved, and in two days, it was done and he gave it to his boy, who had watched his every cut, and the way he smoothed it with sand and rock, and thought his club was the most perfect object he had ever known, and he pressed his face to his father's. Ganan continued with instructing his son. "Our people have hunted here since the dreamtime, and now we must talk of things that are the concern of men. Then we will dance and sing to our ancestors, telling them we are at our bora; I will tell them what a fine boy you are, and how you will grow into a great warrior."

Ganan daubed the signs of his people on his son and himself with great swirls of ochre. Darain felt like a warrior as he followed his father carrying his own spear, thrower, and new club. His father lengthened his stride and increased his pace as there were many privations for his son to endure, and much to learn before he became a warrior. The memories of his own preparation and initiation were of the grizzled elders, spirit-figures, his many uncles, his father, his grandfather, the anguished cries of the women, and a boy's fear of the unknown.

"Look, the bees have built their hive level with the apple blossom," he had stopped to ensure his boy had seen them. Another source of food, and in the great cycle of the seasons, that meant life. "Smell the coming rain," and he pointed to a bank of dark scudding clouds leaving a sun shower behind, wanting his son to be aware of everything around them. The Mighty Hunter led them to a place long in his memory, where the shy animals would shelter before they went out on the great watery plain to feed. He had his boy track quickly, although the moist earth had made it easier than was good for him. "Hurry now," he must learn to move fast; how pleased his own father would have been, and he would also have talked of the great hunters.

Darain missed nothing as they walked through the bush leaving hardly a trace of their passing, and when his father propped, so did he. At times they trotted along in silence, the father pointing to the things he wished him to notice, until they were where the roos had camped. The hunter spoke to him with signs and disappeared into the trees. Darain crept forward, every muscle in his small body ready to strike. Soft noses searched for the sweet new shoots; they had not caught his scent and some of the mothers lay in the grass preening themselves with their paws, their eyes half-closed, as their joeys played in the grass beside them. Others grazed nearby and every now and again the ruling buck perched, ears pricked, nose sniffing the breeze, checking the safety of his harem.

Darain chose a young male that grazed a little too far away from the rest. Each step was as light as a fallen leaf; his breathing had slowed; he struck and his spear thudded home deep in the animal's side. The great buck led the mob crashing through the bush. The legs of the stricken roo would not obey; it turned a somersault in torment, made sideways hops, then lay panting in the grass, where he made his first kill with his club. Then his father showed him how to bleed the animal and to smear its blood and kidney fat all over their bodies until they shone.

They hollowed out a pit and built a fire from where they could see the totem, and Ganan buried their kill among the coals. They talked of the things that young men need to know, and when their feast was ready, he gave his son the choicest pieces so that he would gain the speed, strength, and courage of the Great Spirit Kangaroo.

"Gurundaroo, Daranga, Baranbaran, Amajilli—may my son gain the strength and power of the Great Jarrajarra."

When they had eaten, they began to dance, the boy following his father, crouching, suddenly perching motionless, peering one way then another, sometimes jumping high in the air, taunting their enemies to come in out of the night. When that was done, they began to sing and stamp their dreaming into their land. Then they talked in the soft glow until the young hunter was asleep. Ganan was jubilant, and when the ashes had cooled, he threw them over himself, and sang and danced to his ancestors until the dawn.

They rejoined the women and the family began to walk the dreaming trail while the Mighty Hunter told them the stories of his land. When the season turned, and the weather warmed again, they set out on the long walk home. They returned without incident—the adults back into the routine of the station, the children back to the mission school. Each morning, during the singing of the national anthem, the children faced a picture of Her Most Gracious Majesty, who looked down at them from the wall above the piano. They imagined her to be another powerful white spirit, like God, and little baby Jesus. They sang enthusiastically.

> "God save our gracious Queen.
> Long live our noble Queen.
> God save the Queen.
> Send her victorious,
> Happy and glorious,
> Long to reign over us.
> God save the Queen."

They closed their eyes as the missionary intoned a prayer.

"Dear, and most merciful God, who looks after us, and who sent his only son to die on the cross for our sins. Bless us this day, as we learn about all the wonders you have created, and about thy holy word. Through Jesus Christ our Lord. Amen."

"Today boys and girls," said the teacher, "we are going to learn about trains and the long journeys they make. Has anyone seen a train?" No hands were raised, so Miss Phipps held up a large picture book with a photo of a bright green locomotive which spanned two pages. She had her eye on Darain, who with his sister, had gone walkabout with their parents for around eight months—a disgrace, and about which she had written to Adelaide, saying that in her view, the parents had been very neglectful. "These poor children," she wrote, "were taken out of school to go on a walkabout, during which they lived a primitive existence. Apart from missed schooling, this was far away from any assistance that this mission might have offered for their well-being." The boy's attention was likely to wander.

"Darain," she called, "I want you to stand out the front and help me point out how the locomotive pulls the carriages." He had been far away, remembering a whale shark gliding by only a few arm lengths away. It took a prod from the child behind to bring him back. Out in the front, she had him recite with her, "this is the engine that pulls the train." When Darain was distracted, he stared through the domed window above the cross. He could see the sky and the branches of a gum tree, on which a kookaburra, he called Kra-Kra, would perch; and if his feathers ruffled and the leaves moved, he knew the wind was blowing. Or he might think of how his father and he had chosen the timber for a larger thrower and spear.

The pattern in the domed window was very different from the cross they nailed Jesus on, and the outline of the panes cast strange shadows on the floor. Alkina said it was just a pretty shape. She was taller and faster than he was, and quicker up a tree. When the teacher told them they were all sinners, he was much comforted that he and his sister were not. Their mother said they were talking about the white people who had nailed him up. She was the best storyteller, and when she giggled, it was infectious. His mother said it would not be long before he was taller and faster than Alkina; it was nice to fall asleep to the sound of her voice. The teacher played the piano, and they sang the words without thinking much about them. His sister smiled at him as the hall shook with their singing.

> "Since the Lord saved me,
> I'm as happy as can be,
> my cups full of running over.
> Running over, running over,
> My cups full of running over."

"That was lovely children. Now this time we will sing using hand actions." Their teacher's face glowed with evangelical fervour. That winter was the second since Alkina had become a woman, and the men were aware of her, for she moved gracefully. When the children were taken, Ganan was away driving a mob of cattle to where there had been good rain, and that morning, Tilly had been working up at the homestead. The mission teacher simply shepherded the children on to a grey bus, then stood in front of the hall to wave as they sped away.

Alkina stared at Nan's words; what courage it would have taken to write them down; her tears streamed down her cheeks, as she imagined the dear old lady's anguish.

≈ 5 ≈

That awful day is engraved in my memory. Darain had joined the other children at the rear of the bus to watch the swirling cloud of dust we left behind. We had never been in a bus before, and I enjoyed the novelty of it. We were supervised by a thin-faced lady. "Here dear," she said to me, "we will pin your name tag on, that's the girl; then we will know who we are, won't we? Is that your younger brother playing up the back?"

"Yes it is."

"Lively little fellow isn't he?"

The bus grew hot and dusty and several children said they felt sick, and the thin lady handed out paper bags.

"Where are we going?" Darain asked.

"On an outing; it might be a picnic; wait and see, go and ask the lady."

"No, you ask her; going fast aren't we? Sis, I feel sick."

"Use the paper bag like she said. Dar, do be still. Look out the window. We have never been here before. Open the bag up and hold it close to your mouth, and bend over; don't be silly, I don't want it; throw it out the window."

It was about then that I began to have doubts—why wasn't Miss Phipps with us; why hadn't they been told the day before, as they usually were before an outing? I was upset at not knowing what to do, and Dar said he needed to go to the toilet, as I did myself. In a little while, we pulled up beside the track. And the thin lady clapped her hands to gain our attention. "Now children, it won't be long before we have our lunch, but before we do, girls may go to the toilet over there," she was pointing to some tussocks, "and boys may go on the other side of the road and face away from the bus."

"Everyone on board," she called, "another half an hour and it will be time for our lunch." Lunch was a bottle of soft drink and a brown paper bag containing a jam sandwich and an apple. "Off we go, girls and boys; we are on our way to see a train and to have a ride on it, won't that be exciting?" The lady had made it sound like the best school excursion there had ever been. I knew the rail was nowhere near Arrawatta, and by then, we were speeding along a two-lane road. The bus stopped at a general store, which had diesel and petrol pumps out the front, and filled up. There was nothing but hour after hour of the roar of the motor, and the sound of rushing air. Alkina was comforted with the thought that Fritzhugh was watching from above while Darain was asleep beside her.

"Wake up children," the thin lady called from the middle of the isle, "we are at the train." The night was bathed in yellow light. "Girls use that toilet, boys use this one, then we will see the engine." The huge machine spewed steam; the driver and stoker were busy taking on coal and water. We were offered milk or tea and buttered toast in the station cafeteria, and we drank from thick white mugs. The remark never registered with me at the time, or that she was referring to us. "Bloody boongs! They shouldn't let the little bastards in here," a waitress yelled across the room. The thin lady checked her roll as we boarded the train. The compartments were on one side of the corridor. The train began to move, and we ran up and down the passageway in excitement, and looked at the toilet, the brass baskets, and the water jugs.

"Where are mum and dad?" Darain asked when we had settled.

"Dad is out on a camp and mum is at home." He seemed content with that, and in my exhausted state, I assumed Miss Phipps must have told our parents. Those events of so long ago have remained locked away in my memory. But what had been the effect of our taking on our mother? Nan's journal described the utter chaos of our taking. "The barking dogs woke Hope after midnight, when she heard Tilly in the hall calling for her.

"Hope, they have taken my children," which came out in deep sobs. "Tilly, no one has taken your children; don't be ridiculous," Hope replied. They sat in the kitchen and made a pot of tea. But they soon discovered that they had taken them. Tilly was traumatized, and Hope gave her a brandy. Their husbands were not due back for weeks. Later Hope was to recall that Dick had said something about reading of a scheme to take black children into supervised care, which he had laughed off as so much city politician's hot air. There had seemed no connection with that and their isolated station life.

Hope did her best to comfort her. "When the children did not come home at their usual time, I assumed they were with their friends," their mother explained, "and when it got dark, I went down to the mission school and found most of the other parents were already there. We assumed they may have gone out for an afternoon by a lagoon where it would have been cooler. It was only when I confronted that dreadful Sister Phipps that she told me that they had been taken into care, where they would be brought up in a loving Christian atmosphere."

Tilly's anger in fact helped her to compose herself. "I demanded them back; it had not sunk in, and I still cannot believe it. Hope, I told that woman that she was mad."

Nan's journal continued:

"Those people broke our hearts; neither woman could drive a truck, and in the morning, the pedal radio confirmed what had happened."

All these years on and my mother still had difficulty speaking of it, and my own recollections are clouded with emotion. The train had stopped and it was morning. We were given cereal to eat, which we had never had before. I got us some toast and bacon. My younger brother was beyond crying, and trying to comfort him worsened my own distress. I was disoriented, and felt dirty and exhausted.

Of course I now understand that we would have been in shock; there had been another long bus ride, and I remembered waking up in a dormitory. Darain had been numbed by it. In the morning, we sung the national anthem and were marched into school. One day was followed by another. The home was almost hidden behind a bank of trees. There was a Scottish Superintendent. He was an older man and married to the Matron. She gave the sewing lessons and seemed the most approachable person there, and after a while, I went to see her.

"Matron, I don't think my mother and father know where we are."

"I understand Alkina that you write quite well. Why not sit down and write them a letter? I will help you. There is no point in upsetting them; you could tell them about having hot and cold water, about our refrigeration, having light at the flick of a switch, and then there is the radio and the telephone. It is fun to listen to the radio Alkina, isn't it? You could tell them you have been to the Zoo and for a ride on a tram. They would not know about those things. Tell them you are learning all the things that white boys and girls do. Make it a happy letter, and tell them how well you are doing at sewing. And you do well at English and arithmetic, and please tell them how you like to help in the kitchen."

After that, Matron and I spoke quite often, so unlike the others, at least I knew what was happening.

"Alkina," she told me, "you are nearly old enough for the training home for girls; that is where you will learn to be a housekeeper. It is a very respectable occupation for a young woman. And while we are on the subject, tell your younger brother he must improve his behaviour." She appeared to like me. "You obviously enjoy cooking," she said, "I think I would have liked to learn more of that at your age. The Superintendent says your brother is a natural athlete, and he recommends that he learn shearing; there is plenty of work and they make good money doing that." The Reverend Whiteside appeared to get great satisfaction in teaching us about God's love and the promise of eternal life.

"Boys and girls," he would proclaim, "it is important to remember that Almighty God created all children of every race and colour." But his instruction may have had the reverse effect than he intended. I would smile at my brother as the preacher began on his favourite theme. I was never surprised to see that Dar and our cousin Ernie were miles away.

"On the third day, he rose again from the dead!" And there was the unconscious expulsion of spray as the flushed face looked heavenward. "So we may be saved," he would exclaim, with arms open wide as if to embrace the whole class. But we had switched off, and all the emotion was wasted. I would think of one of Nan's stories, perhaps of Imberomberra arriving with her womb full of children, and her dilly bag stuffed with the bulbs and plants that would feed them forever, and I would wonder what she would have made of this.

But slowly the months passed until the day I gave Dar a final hug and asked him to promise that he would remember to sing his dreaming before I was driven away to the Training Home for Girls. I did my best so he would not see me cry. That move was a shock as all the girls talked about were boys and sex; the language was foul, and I felt alienated. At least I had been forewarned. "I have confidence in you Alkina," Matron had said, "you have a very pleasant disposition, and I think you will do well. And as embarrassing as it might seem, let me give you a gentle warning. You are going to be a very attractive young woman, and there will be demands made of you, and in my view, it would be a great shame if you got pregnant before you had made something of your life, and were happily married." The Matron would have done this before, but she was still embarrassed; but I was grateful that she cared.

"There is one more thing before you leave. Do you understand about homosexuality?" I had not, and Matron must have sensed it. "I am referring to an unnatural sexual relationship between two females, or it might be a male with a male; these are called homosexual relationships. The women are known as lesbians, and are attracted to other women and girls. It is something for you to watch; there has been trouble at the home before, and you would not want to fall into one of those relationships." Her description made the home sound like a pool full of vicious crocodiles. I found the girls treated it with good-humoured annoyance, and as something they could do little about. "Watch out Alkina, or Miss Page will take a fancy to you; she is as butch as they come, and will offer to dry you down after your shower." The extraordinary thing about all this was that I found that I knew more than I was aware. For Nan had told me in most loving detail all there was to know about her courtship and mating with Fritzhugh. At that time, I had not been aware that Nan had died, as knowing how upset I would be, my mother had kept it from me.

These were the thirteen or so years after The Second World War and thousands of Europe's displaced persons had or were settling in Australia. Unknown to me, my life was about to be transformed, which came about when a wonderful continental chef took over the kitchen. Until then our diet had been a monotony of overcooked cabbage, potatoes, and meat, the meat often so tough it was inedible. This was a miracle, as I had never tasted such beautifully prepared food, and I decided I would scrape dishes, wash pots and pans, and to do anything as long as I could remain in the kitchen and learn. I had simply entered the kitchen and introduced myself to the cook.

"Hanna Franks is name. How is yours?" she asked?

"Alkina."

"Please to meeting you. Say name, you tell me good?"

"Alkina."

"Hal-keen-a," she mimicked; then we fell about laughing. "You learn kitchen, I speak English, how you say, you talk me, we have café and gateau, I make good." I had met an extraordinary lady. Hanna may have been learning English, but she had no trouble in recognizing that she had a dedicated fan in me. When she disapproved, she would shake her head and take the whisk, or whatever it was, and demonstrate how it was done. Hanna recognized my potential and set about training me. As she told me later, I had been taught an old-fashioned English style, but there was much to build upon. She is the bravest woman I have ever met, and after the final cleanup for the day, we would have coffee and talk.

"I lose husband, our boy, everything. I starting all over again here in Australia; we are same, you and I. Jewish, wrong religion, you, wrong colour; we start new life. You learn good, my cooking much rich for here; I make plain, is all budget will afford. Is good, but boring, you and I will make beautiful chocolates and gateau, you will like?" Most evenings Hanna would demonstrate a new dish, telling of its origin, where she had cooked it, and we would eat together. When there was a birthday, under Hanna's watchful eye, I would venture into an untried cake or new confection. Despite her suffering, Hanna had retained a zest for life and was very good to me.

"One day Alkina," she foretold, "Australians will demand good food, new arrivals from Europe; they will not want potatoes and lamb, you see. We get ready, your day will come, they will demand lovely food, believe me, I am right. I teach, you learn good, then will be ready. I am very strict, is best for you, you will end up best chef in country, they come knocking at your door."

Hanna hurried against the day when she would lose her pupil, as she was determined not to let me enter a life of drudgery, and strove to lift me to the exacting standards that would help me prosper. But my last day came unexpectedly. A prospective employer had arrived and I was summoned from the kitchen to be inspected in the main hall as if I was a horse for sale. This was my never-to-be-forgotten first meeting with the very assertive and extremely neurotic Mrs. Thompson.

"Are you a clean girl?" The tone suggested she expected the answer was likely to be negative. However, before I could decide how to reply to such an awful question, the Matron answered for me. "Yes she is; they are all trained in personal hygiene and I am sure you will find Alkina is very good in that regard."

"What else can the girl do?"

"She is a competent housekeeper, a very friendly girl, who is also a very good cook. I think you will find her a great help."

Then followed the awful comment that was meant to establish her authority over me. "As long as she understands that if there is anything missing, I will not hesitate to call in the police. Have her get her things; she can come with me." With that, Mrs. Thompson sat down on one of the entrance hall seats as if she had just paid a deposit. I scrambled to get ready, pinned on my regulation hat, and ducked back to say goodbye to Hanna.

"Oh, my dear Alkina," and tearfully she hugged me to her. "Please, how you say, keeping up chin, remember, getting out of housekeeping as quick as you can? Future is professional kitchen. You are ready, I know truth, and you keeping this for emergency." She had thrust a twenty pound note into my hand.

My first day with my new employer was so traumatic, that in later years, I had difficulty in recalling much of it; however, there was one moment I will never forget. After washing up the dinner things for the third time, so as to meet with Mrs. Thompson's unattainable standard, then drying each item under her scrutiny, I had been dismissed for the evening. Mine was a small and sparsely furnished room at the back of the house. Utterly physically and emotionally exhausted, I sat on the bed and wondered how many other housemaids had been overwhelmed by the same feeling of hopelessness. It was then that I noticed that my one prize possession lay open; it was a pretty black leather handbag Hanna had given me, and its matching purse held the sum total of all my worldly wealth.

Then I noticed that my unpacked clothes had also been disturbed. The shock of these discoveries prevented me from sleeping, and if it had not been for Hanna's caring words, I would have fled: "We work for reputation, you must have excellent references, is more important than money." On the upside, I was out of the home and one step nearer my goal. Nothing could dampen that, but much to my dismay, things under the iron rule of Mrs. Thompson only got worse. There was just so much angst packed into one small lady whose very presence was enough to make me shiver.

"You must keep your room spotless, including the drawers. I will inspect it from time to time, including under the bed. So my girl, don't think you can get away with anything." All this over an old timber-framed bed sitting on a linoleum floor, a worn mat, an old wardrobe, and an equally decrepit-looking dressing table. My days passed in a haze; they were about brass and silverware polish, the excessive cleaning of everything, and that awful lady's mad search for elusive dust. At night I would fall asleep with sore elbows and knees. That obsessed lady could not drag herself away; she was engaged in a life and death struggle against, mostly imagined, dust and dirt.

But as I settled down, I began to absorb some of the idiosyncrasies of life at 27 Bayview Crescent. Alfred Thompson, the timid husband, appeared to suffer from chronic constipation, or that is what I had assumed, as he occupied the downstairs toilet from 6:30 to 7:30 each morning, not that his wife gave him any privacy.

"Alfred! Are you still in there?" she would call out, knowing perfectly well that he was, while her penetrating voice reverberated throughout the house. The poor man obviously went in there for refuge, and to read the morning paper. He never said much, and I was at a loss as to why he put up with his wife's constant nagging.

Sometimes he would shyly smile at me as if to say, "Don't worry, you are not the only one; just look at what I put up with." But it was the son who was the mystery. James disappeared for days at a time, or if he was in, was very wary around his mother and would scoot straight out again. I don't remember ever hearing him utter a word. The shrill of Mrs. Thompson's voice haunted me, and probably the rest of the household, until the bliss of exhausted sleep. That lady never stopped. "Alkina, that will not do at all; I can see the ingrained dirt from here; just look at it; it is an absolute disgrace. I want it spotless. Do I make myself clear?" Despair was never far away. I had promised Hanna to stick it out so I could get a decent reference.

The weeks went by until one Sunday afternoon I was sitting in my room, reading an out of date women's magazine, and wondering if I had enough energy to visit my brother, when there was a tap on the door and much to my surprise it was the elusive James.

"Hello, may I come in?"

"Yes, of course."

"They have gone for a Sunday drive and I wanted to say hello," he explained.

"That is nice, so thank you. I was just wondering what I should do for the rest of the afternoon."

"My mother works you to death, doesn't she?"

"I have Sunday afternoons off," I offered in her defence.

"Please, don't feel you have to be polite with me." I was really surprised to hear the son talk like this. "She is a tyrant. I know what is going on, and I am embarrassed by it. I want you to know that I don't approve of it. But I am damned if I know what we can do about it. It is just so unfair. I refuse to watch. I cannot stand the bloody woman myself. God only knows why my father puts up with her; she makes his life a living hell!"

I invited him to sit on the bed but was still rather startled by his frankness. "Perhaps, it is because he still loves her," I offered, "he must have at one time; after all he did ask your mother to marry him."

"What a nice comment," James said, "but no, let me tell you what my theory is; she would have nagged him into submission; and she has kept a tight lead around my father's neck ever since."

"James, we never see you."

"I am in love, darling, and it is heaven to get away from this place." I was enjoying what was becoming a revealing exchange.

"That sounds nice; have your parents met her?"

"Hell no," he answered, "it's a *he*; that's the way I am; it is a hell of a thing; and it does present a few problems." I was taken aback, but very flattered to have been told.

"It would kill them if they knew; her, I would not mind, but not my father. Perhaps one day. I think I became one just to spite her. So you see I am almost as much of an outcast as you are. Believe me, I feel for you. Do you have a boyfriend?"

"James, I hope one day, but I have to establish myself first and look after my little brother."

"And where is your little brother?" I told him, and all my pent-up unhappiness came out in a flood of tears. "Alkina, I am sorry, I did not mean to upset you."

"James, I have not been able to talk about it; I think it must be the relief."

"No, the other way around, you are the only one I have told outside our circle; I can't believe I have. But then again, I don't feel so bad when I see what you put up with. We should be friends; let's form a support group for the downtrodden."

"I would like that," and I really meant it.

"Alkina, what are you going to do with your life? You cannot spend the rest of it scrubbing floors for my mother. The thought of that scares the hell out of me." I told him all about Hanna, and our plans.

"Yet, with all she has lost, she still has a big enough heart to help someone like me."

"She must think you are worth helping."

"Thank you, James. I have tried, and now I must stay with your mother until I can get a good reference. Hanna says without one, I will not be able to get a job anywhere." The beginning of my new friendship with James was a wonderful experience for me.

"Holy shit!" he exclaimed, shaking his head. "Now I know you are in the wrong place. What can we do? As a matter of fact, my dear young lady, I think this thing is bloody urgent. Let me throw it around; there has to be an answer because you cannot possibly stay here. Tell you what, meet me in the little park around the corner next Sunday and I will organize a lift so you can see your brother; make it 12:30. Wait in the shade near the swings. You know a few minor adjustments and you could be a model."

I was not used to this sort of praise. "Don't be silly," I said sharply, "and if your mother sees we are friends, that will be the end of it." This had not the slightest effect on my new friend.

"Surely we can handle her." I was very much encouraged by this declaration. "Let's do it together," James continued, sounding as if he meant it, "we have to get you that reference. I had better go. I will see you next Sunday."

He blew me a kiss through the door and was gone. That week flew by and when Sunday came around, I had been up before dawn to brush my hair, try on each of my two dresses, and decide which one I should wear. Even Mrs. Thompson's viperous criticism could not dampen my excitement. Other than becoming a friend of James, I had lived on the memory of my last outing with Hanna, who had taken me to a little Italian restaurant she had heard about. There had been an immediate rapport with the chef-owner, who had conducted us through his spotless kitchen. We talked of his favourite regional dishes, and how he prepared them. It was a marvellous night, my first meal in such a restaurant; Hanna had opened my eyes to the world of fine food and wine.

"Authentic cuisine like this will catch on; all it needs is time," she explained. "Luigi and his wife bring the traditions of Tuscany with them. Other people from Europe will also bring their cultures and soon we will see their new restaurants opening up." When Sunday came around, I almost forgot to wear my regulation hat, and with one final inspection, I flew out the back door to meet James. It felt so foreign to be sitting in a neat suburban park, with trees planted in a precise straight line, and where the air carried the smell of hot Sunday roasts, a meal Hanna said was quite unsuited to the Australian climate, and a ridiculous hand-me-down from England; but best of all, I was out of the house and free of that woman. Away from that place, James blossomed and exuded a delightfully free and easy manner, and greeted me with a peck on the cheek, and introduced me to Patrick, his partner, who seemed equally at ease with the world. I was greeted with a hug and a big "Hello, so you are the poor, downtrodden, but adorable Alkina?" We had hardly driven around the block before James turned around. "Bloody hell, Alkina! Where did you get that bloody awful hat?"

"It is regulation," I said in its defence. "I am supposed to wear it when travelling to and from work."

"Well, please take it off and give it to me. Show Pat your gorgeous hair. There you are. Now isn't she the prettiest thing you ever saw?"

With that he threw my unloved hat out the window.

"What if they want it back again?" I asked in panic.

"You just tell them you were accosted in the street by a poor hatless woman, and if you need a witness, I am a volunteer. Now, I am being quite serious, because I never want to see your lovely hair covered again." Patrick was nodding his head. "And James tells me you like to cook."

"I do, very much."

"Well, it may be a long shot," Patrick said, "but I think that I may be able to help. One of mum's friends has tearooms in the city; they do Devonshire teas, cakes, light meals, nothing startling. As a sideline, she makes marzipan, fudge, chocolates, sugar-coated almonds, you know, and that sorta thing. Anyway, I heard she is looking for someone to do the waitressing and help in the kitchen. How does something like that sound?"

"Oh, Patrick, I would love it, and please tell her I adore making pastry and confectionary."

"Okay, we will come home via her place, and you can meet her."

"What about James's mother? Won't she report me and then I won't have my reference?"

"Leave her to me," James said over his shoulder. "I am quietly hatching a plan to free you from the tyranny of my mother. Here you are. Enjoy your visit. We will be back for you at around four."

Very encouraged, I went to meet my brother. Darain had grown between visits. We went for a walk and I told him my news, and judging from the state of his knees and scars on his arms and legs, he had obviously been in the wars. I tried not to scold him as he would have had enough of that. But I did have to say something. "Dar, please don't get into fights because it worries me. I don't like to see my little brother covered in bruises and scratches, and you did promise me you wouldn't."

"Awe sis, it was nothing; just some big kid reckoned he could take me on; he started it, but I bloody finished it."

"Dar, please listen to me. If you behave like that when you are grown up, the police will put you in jail. That sort of thing is bad white business, and I expect better from you."

"Sis, we was playing these kids footy and they got stuck into us when the ref wasn't looking, and when I took the ball, this big bastard yelled at me, 'Why don't you coons learn to play?' So I waited until the ref wasn't looking and smacked him right on the nose; ya should have seen the blood and him crying; jeez it felt good. But sis, it worked, 'cos we beat them easy, a real big bastard he was."

"Dar, you heard what I said. Now how is your school work; are you paying attention in class?"

"Yeah, the teacher reckons I am doing okay. But I can't wait to get out of this place and learn shearing."

"Dar, you must remember all the things mum, dad, and dear old Nan taught you. It is important to always try as hard as you can."

"Yeah, I do, but they go on and on about Jesus until the little kids are bawling their eyes out. Poor mum and dad, they don't understand all this stuff, do they?"

"No Dar, they don't."

"One day sis, I am going to buy a truck and go and see them."

"Good, that's why we have to do well, to be proud of ourselves and so will they. I am so excited; Nan made cooking such fun. If I get this job, it will because of her."

"Yeah sis, but if they are a couple of poofters, you have to be careful, because they act all friendly like, then perv on ya. Sis, they are pathetic, and worse thing is the bloody super won't believe it." I could understand my brother's dilemma.

"James and Patrick are quite open about it," I explained. "With them there is no pretence. The ones you are talking about are secretive, because they don't want people to know how they get their kicks. I know, I've seen it myself, and it is often the married ones. But can we leave all that? And Dar, I want you to be proud of what you do, of who you are and to believe in yourself."

I felt very different upon my return to Mrs. Thompson's; I had hope, and washed and starched Mr. Thompson's collars, and did them again and again on his wife's whim. Her complaints about imagined grime no longer mattered, as every day brought me closer to leaving. I daydreamed of working in the café, of greeting the customers and inviting them to return, and watching their reactions as they ate. Hanna said she had taught me some unique techniques, and had explained that if the customers asked for my recipe, I should see it as the compliment it was.

The Golden Café, with its marbled counter tops, large silver soda siphons with their pretty handles, and the high backed cubicles, where our customers would dine, had a lovely warm feel to it. I was determined to do everything so well, there could be no better place to eat. But there were things to do, what a contrast, and I treasured the owner's welcoming smile. I had to shop for pinafores with matching white collars. Hanna would be thrilled when I told her my news.

Of course I saw James on his rare visits home, where I dared not show the warmth I felt for him. Perhaps, this was not going to be easy for him to pull off. But he did, and the first signs that something was happening occurred while I was vacuuming with the new machine that Mrs. Thompson had acquired at considerable expense, as she never tired of telling me. I had been working in the gloomy lounge room, vacuuming the carpet surrounding the large centre rug with its ugly design, with Mrs. Thompson coming out of the kitchen every few moments to check on me. My thoughts had been miles away; yet part of me was intent on finding every speck of dust, every wayward human hair with my searching nozzle, when I became aware I was being watched. I had never seen Mrs. Thompson smile before, nor was there the usual admonishment.

"Alkina, that will do for now. You may switch the machine off." And what followed was the most extraordinary thing. "That is very satisfactory. I am making a cup of tea. Do wash your hands, and we can have it together in the kitchen." If I was surprised to hear this expression of satisfaction, I was astonished at her invitation. In total confusion and fear that I was about to be dismissed, I joined Mrs. Thompson, who had set out the tea things on the kitchen table. "With milk isn't it? And do help yourself to sugar and the biscuits? They are the shortbreads I bought home from town the other day." I was so nervous I could hardly pick up my cup, and that thinly spread smile was still there. "You and I may talk freely. I do understand boys, and of course, it will come as no surprise that I certainly understand my son. We are a very close family, and James has always been a very affectionate boy, and of course he has the same primitive urges that men have had since the time of Adam and Eve."

The shock of hearing those words from her bored right through me, and a flurry of conflicting thoughts milled around my head: had he told his mother of Patrick? No, of course he wouldn't have. I was incredulous and fearful for him?

"You are a very pretty girl, so I can understand how our son has become infatuated. He has told his father, and naturally we understand his pain and his carnal desires. But of course we would not dream of letting him make such an unthinkable match. Mr. Thompson holds a very responsible position in the city, so it would never do. But I should tell you that James takes full responsibility, as we would expect him to do." I had not touched my tea.

"I am being dismissed?" My comment had come out of its own accord.

"Certainly not; this is not your fault, but under the circumstances, we could hardly expect you to stay. James has told me he has been able to find a suitable position for you in the city. It will only be helping in a café, not everyone's idea of progress, mind you, but it may have to do for the time being." I had great difficulty containing myself. "My husband and I would like you to accept a month's pay on top of what we already owe you. There will also be an extra fifty pounds, which, under the circumstances, we should like you to accept on the understanding that none of this is discussed outside our home. I have written you a glowing reference, which states that you have been entirely satisfactory, and have been with us for a full six months, as we would like to help in your advancement. We are not throwing you out; you may stay until we find you somewhere to live. Alkina, you haven't had your tea. Let me get you a fresh cup."

Suddenly I was free, and it was an unbelievable feeling. Patrick and James moved me into a pleasant room in an old-fashioned rooming house, and I was immediately swept up in my new life at the Golden Café. Hanna was ecstatic, and my first six months disappeared in a frantic whirl. Joanna Shaw, the owner, was a war widow, who could not believe her luck when she discovered that she had an artist in the kitchen. The reputation of the Golden Café was spreading. Eight months later, the restaurant, as it had now become, was booming.

Looking after the front was Mario, an exuberant former Italian prisoner of war, who hung up the row of orders in front of my station and recited them as if they were a papal proclamation. "Two osso buco, one saltimboca, one goulash, and three tureens as entrees." This was his first decent job since his release, other than several years on the end of a jack hammer for the Tramways Department. He had delivered a pile of dirty cutlery and plates to the kitchen, picked up an arm full of meals, backed out through the swinging doors, and collected three bottles of wine with his free hand.

I worried over every presentation, as always in the back of my mind was Hanna's plea never to drop my standards. My mentor occasionally ate there with her friend. She could tell at a glance how the restaurant was going, and she and I would often discuss the menu and my presentation. I was beginning to understand just how well I had been trained, when we were given a glowing review in the local paper. I can still vividly remember Hanna and Henri's first visit as I had greeted them with some formality, just as Hanna had taught me. It had been a slow winter's night when Mario told me a Mrs. Franks wished to be remembered to the chef.

"Thanks, I will go out and greet them."

"Ah, your mentor," said Joanna. "Ask them to stay for drinks; there is only Patrick and James; the other tables are just leaving."

A quick check that my uniform was spotless, Mario knew his job; everything was as it should be as I approached their table.

"Good evening chef."

"Lovely to see you Mrs. Franks, Monsieur Raymond," the slightest of inclined heads to show deference, then imagine you are greeting guests into your own home.

"Charmed," he said, "she has been telling me so many nice things." They were always so thoughtful.

"Perhaps chef, you can produce something I might like," Hanna suggested. She was looking at me, having read the menu, and knew perfectly well. "Henri?" Her eyebrow was raised.

"Yes chef, we leave it to you." It was late, and I had an open-ended invitation to do as I wished. They would not want anything heavy. Hanna was not a big eater as the war had left her with a profound dislike of waste. Mario delivered the verdict, "compliments to the chef from table five."

Hanna was most insistent that a chef return the compliment, which I immediately did, and invited them to inspect the kitchen. James and Patrick wandered in to join us. Those two were always over the top anyway, and they made a great fuss of Hanna. "A small menu of quality," Hanna commented, "is good to see. Henri and I are thrilled."

We stood around with drinks and listening to Hanna and Joanna talk menus. My mentor was in her element. "How nice is meeting Patrick and James. I am the stern Hanna she would have told you about."

"No," James said. "Alkina told me you are the kindest person she has ever met."

"No, no, my dear friend is worth helping; believe me, I know." Whatever James had done, he had certainly grown in confidence.

"James, how on earth did you do it?" Henri asked.

James scratched his chin, obviously thinking what he was going to say. "There was never really an option," he said with some deliberation, "as my mother was intent on grinding our poor girl into the concrete."

Patrick laughed. "We are all dying to know," he offered while James drained his glass, "as long as it doesn't go any further."

Then he began: "Pat and I have been together for some years, and if anything, we are closer; I can see him nodding. Our friends accept us, and of those who would not, there is nothing more that needs to be said. But it does have its problems. I love my father; he is a very nice man, and I know he would not accept our relationship. But his real problem is being married to my mother, as eventually she will nag him to death. For me, it is not as if she is unaware of what she is doing; I think she knows exactly. So that is the background to it.

When I met Alkina, she had become my mother's latest hobby. For me the outcome was clear; either Alkina would succumb to exhaustion, or the house would collapse from over-cleaning. Think about it; they were alone all day and she had Alkina working like a slave. When I spoke to this gorgeous thing, I found she possessed great charm, was fun to be with, and had absolutely no idea what was going on, except that there was no end to it. She was being exploited by my mother and I hated it. Then I learned of Hanna, who has trained her to be the marvellous chef we know. We took Alkina to see her younger brother who was still in a home. And the more we learned about what had happened to them, and believe me, it was horrendous, the more deeply it touched us. I could see Alkina's problem; and in my view, she had no chance. The idea of anyone getting a reference, let alone a decent one, out of my mother seemed remote.

The question had become how I could help Alkina and square things with my father at the same time. My father and I talked about Alkina, and of course he was aware of her, and we agreed she was a very pleasant and, indeed, a beautiful young lady. But it was the talk, and I could see how chuffed he was. When he and I met for a drink, we would end up talking about her, and the more I did, the better he liked it. I had planted the seed, the thought that his son was a regular bloke with a growing attachment to her, and suddenly his world was looking rosier. We were mates, yet when he went home, my mother would smash him down again; it was awful to see.

But I still had not thought it through, and one day, over a drink, the idea just fell into place, and I asked dad how he would feel about having Alkina as a daughter-in-law. There was no hesitation: 'Son, I would love her as much as you,' and I could see it, and that night we got joyously plastered, which was how it nearly came unstuck, as I had yet to plant the seeds of this idea with my mother. I planned to let her catch me hanging around Alkina. But dad was so carried away he let it out of the bag, and I never had the chance to do the groundwork.

My mother immediately had a fit that her maid, whom she so badly mistreated, was going to become her daughter-in-law. Meanwhile, Alkina had no idea what was going on, but it was soon very clear to me what would happen. My mother, maybe half believed it, but she wasted no time in trying to pull my father into line. Fortunately, he and I had already discussed what a hopeless situation Alkina was in, and he immediately went to bat for her. My mother's life had been turned upside down, and the next thing, she was calling me at the office to tell me how well Alkina was doing, and that she is taking good care of her. But the wonderful thing for me was seeing my dad stand his ground; he simply refused to let my mother say a word against her."

I remember James's story as the most poignant moment of my life, and with tears streaming down my cheeks, I just folded him into my arms. Week by week, the restaurant grew busier, until there would be a queue waiting to get in. Fortunately the opportunity came to expand next door. By then my food was being written about. Hanna had seen it coming, and we were being asked to do weddings and corporate functions; the new enlarged restaurant had just opened, and the direction we should go was looming as an issue. The first wedding reception virtually walked in the door, and it grew from there.

"The groom and bride were here on Thursday night," Joanna explained. "Naturally I am delighted, but I'm not quite sure if we should take it on."

"Mama Mia! I know, she was flower, and he made big tip," Mario beamed proudly.

"Yes, but it means closing the restaurant to the public," Jo continued, "and they will feel let down, and if we are not careful, we could end up doing nothing but wedding receptions." We took it on, but instantly producing a hundred-and-sixty meals is some undertaking. This presented an opening for Hanna, who was by then running a traditional, old-style Adelaide hotel kitchen, catering for visitors from the country, and where she found the hotelier's idea of running a kitchen very much in conflict with her own. That first reception was a great success, Hanna's wedding cake, confections, and desserts were a dream, and as it had been a society wedding, it was widely reported in the press. Hanna was the closest thing to family I had; she and Henri were always there for me.

"Being asked to do these functions was a personal compliment to you," she said. "Henri and I see a wonderful opening, and when you are ready, we think Sydney is the logical place to be." Patrick and James had already announced they were taking their business over there, where they also thought the opportunities would be greater. But I had Dar to think about; Hanna understood as she and Henri had given it much thought. "While your brother finishes his schooling and training, we would like to see you get into the catering business for yourself," she explained, "you and I can start it up in a small way over here in Adelaide. I have enough to set it up and to carry it for a while; Henri is a great fan of yours, and will back us should we need it. I would like us to do it; there is only you to think about, and we would like to see you established. We know there is a big market for our continental cakes and confections; they sell themselves. Henri says what appeals to him is that very little capital is required. When I wish to get out, I will sell you my share on terms that are easy terms for you to handle, and by that time you should have a trained staff and a good cash flow." I was overwhelmed that they should have cared so much.

☞ **6** ☜

My brother will tell his story...

I recall being a small boy and reporting in sick to the Superintendent's office with a pain in my tummy.

"Son, do you mean to tell me that you have not had a bowel movement for over a week?" the man was offended by it.

"Yes sir."

"Trousers off, up on the table on your tummy; you must not leave it so long; this will not hurt."

I can laugh at it now, but the poor man had to wear rubber gloves to rub soap and warm water into my rectum. Then he used a rubber syringe to squirt in a soapy solution and delved around to remove several hard lumps of my rock hard excrement which I saw lying in a shallow white dish.

"That should soften it up for you son; lie there a few minutes, then wipe yourself with this towel. Disgrace, you know, not going to the toilet." He peeled off the gloves and washed his hands. "That is about all I can do. Now put your pants back on and drink your castor oil."

It was bad enough losing my sister to the girls' home, and not being able to shit; and what if that Williams kid wanted to pick a fight? Alkina said I should behave like the Mighty Hunter, and that Fritzhugh was watching over me from the stars. I had stopped waking up in the middle of the night and by then I had a gang; but how was I supposed to handle what Ernie had told me? "Dar, that Mr. Peters, the housemaster, is a poofter; he tried to feel me up after class. I had to stay behind so he could explain the lesson. Dar, what are we going to do?"

"Awe shit Ern, we gotta tell the boys; another married bloke; why do those bastards pick on us?" A gang had a chance, and I would get them together and we would fix this poofter like we had fixed the others. Even the big kids would stop their bullying for a while, and once the target realized the boys had closed ranks, that generally screwed them.

Ernie and I liked to kick a football, and we practiced day after day. I would leap to take a high one-hander. "Go on you mug lair," Ern would yell, "two hands for beginners." I usually took the return kick on my chest.

"Jeeze Dar, won't it be a ripper when we can play them white bastards? I reckon we could beat them hollow." Ern sent a soaring stab kick back to me.

"Watch this torpedo Ern. I will make her curl right around; geeze it's

a beauty. Kick one over me head and watch me mark like Cazaly."
Thereby, he incensed me by invoking the name of my favourite
Australian player casually.

"No, ya can't!" I yelled, "because I am Cazaly; I bagged him first,
when we first come here. Let's ask those kids for a game; you and me
would beat them easy."

"Heh, yous kids want a game?"

"Dunno, suppose so."

"Dar and I versus yous; that's fair."

"Short kicks Ern, we hang on to the ball and let them do the
chasing."

"You watch me take the marks Dar; them blokes won't know what
hit them."

When trouble struck, it felt like the end of the world, because the
Superintendent did not muck around.

"Darain stand still, and do not fidget. Before I administer six of the
best, I like my boys to know why. Do you understand why?"

"Yes sir."

"Well, tell me."

"For getting the boys to teach that poofter housemaster a lesson, so
he doesn't try to feel us up no more."

"Do not use that sort of talk with me lad. I will not stand for it; is
that clear? Answer me! Do I make myself clear?"

"Yes sir."

"Your teacher comes to us with an impeccable record. He is a young
man with a degree in Divinity. Hear me Darain? He has a wife and two
children. He completely denies any such conduct. He is a young man
trying to make a future in education. If you were older, I could have the
police charge you with assault; this sort of thing has to stop. Son, let me
give it to you straight; you are being given the opportunity to be
educated and trained the same as white children." I could only look at
the floor in despair. "Pay attention, and grow up to be an honest citizen
just like all the other boys and girls. Here we have a fine young man
trying to teach and prepare you for the world, and he is subjected to this
cowardly attack. We are lucky he was not injured. Now bend over with
your hands on the desk."

Ernie was waiting for me. "Jeeze Dar, you okay, how many?"

"Six."

"Awe shit! Dar, thanks for what ya done." One day, a week, a
month, a year, and I was king of the kids. "Listen you blokes, we play
Wingram Boys High on Saturday arvo, when they played us last year,
they played dirty. They slag off at ya real bad; they called us 'black
bastards'. Now boys, this time we are going to call them 'white
poofters'; now that should fix the bastards."

"It's great you're our captain Dar; now we got a chance; we got a meeting and a smoke after school tomorrow to plan the game."

We met out of direct sight of the home.

"Who's got a smoke?"

"Here Dar, it's an Ardeth I pinched from the cook."

"Yous blokes listen to me," I had no idea of how to give a pep talk, and mine probably would have gone something like this, "this game's important, cause this mob beat us last year; so this is revenge. We play dirty, but ya gotta make sure the referee does not see us; then ya gotta smack em across the kisser, and put the bastards off their game."

"Jeeze Dar, ya should see the bloke I got to mark; he is a real big bastard. What will I do?"

"Look Eddy, ya let him get the ball and when ya got the chance, knee him real hard in the goolies. That ought to stop the bastard. We gotta let them know real early who's boss; then we hang on to the ball like it is bloody gold."

"Dar, some of them blokes will have sheilas watching; what are we gonna do?"

"When I start shearin', I'm goin to have all the sheilas I want. I saw down the cook's blouse the other day; shit, does she have a good pair of norks, didn't mind me looking neither?"

But all too quickly there came a day when my days at the home were about to end forever, and the Superintendent had those of us who were leaving report to his office.

"Boys, some of you will learn plumbing, carpentry, bricklaying, and so on. They are all good trades, but whatever you learn, you must work hard at it, because your future will depend on it. You have been given a fair bit of leeway here, but at the training home they will expect mature behaviour. If you don't do as you are told, and pay attention, the only person you will hurt is yourself.

Those of you who have played sport, I recommend you keep it up; it will keep you fit and help you make new friends. Ernie and Darain, keep up your football, but no foul play; good players don't need that. Eddy, Jack, and Mick, keep up your cricket, and we have a couple of budding athletes in Ben and Archie. It will not be long before you are earning a wage, and with that comes responsibility. I want you to open a savings account, and get into the habit of putting your wages into it, so it accumulates, and then you have to be careful to spend it wisely. Out there you will see others who ruin their lives with alcohol. It is a terrible waste; it destroys their health, leads them into trouble with the police, and they neglect their wives and children. However, I am confident that you will make a success of it.

And so it is time to say goodbye, and for me to wish you every success, which, as I have said many times, will largely depend on you."

We all shook his hand. "Darain, please stay behind." What had I done? I was completely taken back as he began; "it has been some time since I have had to call you in here, and I hope you maintain this improvement in your behaviour. However, in general, I must say that I have had to see more of you than I would have liked. But son, I have tried to be fair with my punishments. A while back I called you in here for a serious breach of discipline, and I wanted to clear the air over it before you leave. Whatever you do in life Darain, you are bound to make mistakes, and I wanted to tell you that on that day, I made a bad one. About the best I can say to you by way of an apology, is this—I did listen to your comments, and although his references were excellent, the world is sometimes a smaller place than we think. I wrote to a friend of mine in Brisbane and asked him to do a little checking up. He found there had been other incidents. Son, I let you down, and I offer you my sincerest apology. I would like you to accept it. Will you?"

"Yes sir, thank you sir."

"Good, now let us shake hands. If anything like that ever happens again, see your supervisor straight away, until something is done about it. Never take it upon yourself to act outside the law, because that is when we revert to the law of the jungle. Anyway, I can tell you I have done my best to see he never works with children again. But, on a lighter note, Matron has saved some articles about your sister. She has followed her progress, and it has been wonderful to see how she has made a name for herself in the food industry. We would like you to have them. Alkina has set a fine example for you to follow. And just one last thing before you go, please drop me a line when you first shear two hundred sheep in a day. Thank you lad; now off you go." I was a lucky boy, for those well-meant comments have stayed with me ever since.

≈ 7 ≈

"Join The Australian Workers Union," our shearing instructor exhorted. The man was a wizened battler from the bush, a doubled-up former shearer, who kept the remains of a rolled cigarette stuck to his bottom lip, and urged us to get behind the industrial muscle of the union.

"Do that boys, and you won't go far wrong, cause you will be covered if any of them flaming cockies try to take you for a ride. Lovely life, I wish I was young enough to have another go meself, and that's the truth. You gotta support your union; they was what won you all the conditions you will enjoy when you are out working your run. I tell the boys to always pay their union dues with a smile. I can recall the days when we worked Saturdays and had lousy quarters. Yous young blokes are going to cop it sweet, because of all the tough industrial action of old codgers like me.

As I was saying, a shearer must keep his handpiece lubricated and running sweet. That's what we gotta learn today, how to get them sharp and keep them that way. There is a lot of work on smaller places where they only want a couple of shearers for a week or so, and you can bet your life the cocky won't know how to properly sharpen your combs and cutters." After our training, they set us free.

My cousin and I were elated, but it did seem funny to be heading for the bush, because that is where we came from in the first place. But we believed we were on the threshold of earning a lot of money, and had already decided to save so we could buy our own truck, and be able to make our own way from station to station (large landholdings).

"Mate, at last some dough in our pockets and don't forget all them sheilas," my cousin Ernie remarked. "Jeez, the old bloke says it gets bit hard on your back, and he does look bloody crook himself. We will get out before we get old, but it was bloody nice of him to recommend us to his mate."

And so we set off to sign on with a shearing contractor in central Queensland. The long unhurried train crawled through the monotonous plains of northern New South Wales, and where the gauge changed, we had to swap trains at the border. We reckoned we could walk faster. I remember being elated to see a mob of roos, and thinking that it would be good to have a shower, not that the contractor was likely to notice. Or an excited Ernie with his head out the window yelling, "This must be it; there's the river; waa-hoo, Goondiwindi, here we come!"

The train disappeared down the track as we trudged into town. The meeting place turned out to be the public bar of an old two- story pub with a veranda running around the top floor. It stood on a corner of the main street. They all have that smoky, beery smell and even at that early hour, the drinkers looked half-*shickered* to us.

"Hey Greeny, we gota couple of visitors for ya," the barmen said back over his shoulder into the gloom.

"G'day boys," and we met our new boss. Greenie was a small man with a big voice, not much hair, and a friendly manner. "Throw your *ports* in the back of the yellow truck; it's the Ford out the back under the pepper tree. I won't be long, like a jug of beer; you can take it outside and drink it behind the shed?"

I looked at Ern and shrugged. "I dunno; we're *skint*." He should know we were broke.

"That's okay," Greeny offered, "she's on the house." We took our jug and sat in the shade of a big old pepper tree.

"This has to be the life," I said. We were free and it seemed remarkable. We were on the threshold of manhood, and this was our first jug of beer, and nothing else in the world mattered, and in a while, the contractor came out with another jug of beer.

"Won't be long boys," he remarked with a wry smile. We were asleep under the tree when he finally came out.

"Throw your ports in the back of the truck and hop in, meet Mick and Chassa," which still looms large in our memories as our introduction to the shearing life. The two shearers in the front shared a bottle of beer with Greeny while we sat on our ports with our backs to the cabin and were soon immersed in a cloud of red dust. Our doss at our first shearing shed had corrugated iron walls and two iron cots on either side of the bare boards. On one wall, the sheets of corrugated iron had been cut out and hinged at the top, and propped open so they served as a window. A smelly, carbide lamp stood on an upturned box.

"Gee Dar, terrific, our very own doss. I bags this one!" Ernie had thrown his cardboard case onto the mattress of an iron framed cot. We could not wait to get down to the shed; there were milling sheep, yelping dogs, and a lot of dust. The first person we met was a young aborigine station hand who was darker than either of us. We patted his friendly black kelpie that came sniffing around our boots.

"G'day, I am Billy," he said.

"G'day, he's Darain and I'm Ernie. You from around here?"

"Yeah mate, this all our country."

"That your dog?"

"Yeah, a black dog for a black man." We laughed.

"We got twenty thousand ewes in this mob; you blokes can push them up to me." Shafts of late afternoon sun shone through the split timber walls and on to the greasy floor of the sprawling woolshed. Behind the wool bins, which would later fill with white, pearl, and cream wool, were four huge timber wool-presses. High above from the rough sawn rafters, wool staples hung like dirty snow.

The shed sprung to life in the early morning to the thump of a diesel. Steel combs and cutters screamed as they were sharpened, and great leather belts slapped and creaked as they sent each handpiece slicing through the warm fleece. Above the line of bent over shearers, the overhead shaft whined and stuttered, like cicadas on a summer's day, as the men cut in and out. The old shed shuddered to straining cogs, as bulging bales of wool were pressed, and shed hands whistled and whooped, as they forced woolly sheep into the catching pens. We could not get over the selection of cakes at the morning smoko, and I remember eating three chocolate éclairs and a lamington. One shed followed another and we settled into the itinerant life and began learning to shear by finishing a sheep at the end of each run.

"Dar, how many did you knock the wool off?"

"Eight, but I had a real bad one, and one of the boys had to tidy it up for me."

"Ern," I yelled, "you stick at it, because we are on our way."

We were eventually given a start in a team that shore from the top of Central Queensland down to the Monaro. But out west the sheep could be rough. Our comments described it exactly.

"I heard the wethers on this next place are so big you can throw a saddle on them," Ernie said.

"As long as the bastards aren't carrying two years' wool and are covered in sand and galvanized burr," I replied.

"Dar, a hundred and forty-five for you, and one forty-three for me; fancy you and me with pens on the great 'Brigalow Plains'. This is it. I can feel it; the first day we crack a hundred and sixty each." That day we went at it side by side.

"Dar, they cut like butter." I dragged my last sheep out seconds before the morning smoko. "Ern, our best run yet mate; this could be the day; just take it nice and steady."

We topped up from our water bags and waited for the bell. My fleece came away easily as I moved up the neck and opened up the shoulder, and in no time I was cleaning up and pushing the animal down the chute. Four strides and I had another, my handpiece glided in and I covered the back with smooth unbroken blows, and the wool fell away like a wave. My call of "wool away" sent a boy scrambling to pick up the fleece. We were travelling well, but we were not in the same league as the guns who shore upwards of two hundred and forty a day. The sweat dribbled down my nose as the animal kicked and struggled, and when it was done, I guided it down the chute. In a moment, I was stripping off a belly before the lunch bell. I picked at my food, at one hundred and sixty, we were on the way to big money.

We waited for the bell and were off again. At the last break, I towelled off and fitted a new comb and cutter. Ernie wasn't saying much, and then it was on. I shore one after another until I had four to go; then it was three; the minute hand crept around and when it was done, I dared not look. I grabbed another and tore the wool away from the face and raced up the throat to open the fleece up; the wool hung ragged. I swung around and began the long blow, and the fleece peeled away. I pushed mine down the chute as Ernie was cleaning up.

"One sixty one for me," I reported triumphantly.

"One sixty for me," Ernie added, "mate, we made it." The contractor gave us our cheques and offered us the run for the following year. One of the guns—the fast shearer—gave us a lift to town.

"We'll join the boys for a couple of celebratory beers," he said. "You know from now on, you blokes will just get better and better." The bar was crowded with shearers, and the background noise, the babble of drinkers.

"Three beers, struth, does that tastes bloody good, or what?" said the gun, nodding to the barman to go round again. But Ernie and I were wary of pubs and the cops, so I asked the barman, "Do you think we are all right in here?" Not only were we not supposed to be there, because we were collared, but it was well after closing time, and going on their usual form, the local cops would get stuck into us before anyone else?

"She'll be right mate; the cops never come in here," the barmen advised.

There was the pleasant flow of good-humoured talk, the occasional raucous laugh and Ernie and I were enjoying being a part of it. He reckoned I was wearing a fixed grin as if I had just won the lottery. One of the guns was telling a long-winded story about a horse he had a share in, while the barman pulled beers and played benevolent host.

"Right oh, right oh, home you go," said a booming voice, and there in the doorway stood a copper with three stripes on each arm.

"Now, where do you think you two are going?" he said, and bundled me and Ernie into the back of a paddy wagon—a police van. I tried to explain, "We have been shearing with Alf Morton's team and were just having a drink with the boys."

"Mate, I hate coons," by which he meant full or part Aboriginal. I could see we were in big trouble when he herded me into a cell on my own. I did my best to ride the blows. When he was through with me, he started on my cousin. We were thrown out next morning.

"Ern, how much did he pinch from you?"

"I'm down about a neat hundred," he said. I was missing about the same. Ernie shook his head, "Dar, forget about it; let's get the hell out of here."

But as I banked my check, I inquired from the teller. "The local police Sergeant gave us a lift into town, a nice bloke; would you happen to know his name?"

"That would have been Owen Nash; I understand he's a very nice bloke." We had never had a holiday, and a day and a half later, we were on the Gold Coast. "The best place for a young bloke to meet some sheilas," or so the team had told us. Our motel overlooked the beach.

"Dar, we can lie in bed; listen to the radio, or jump in the pool; and we can make a cup of tea whenever we like. And it says here, they got television in the lounge." Then he opened all the cupboards. "And mate, we can hang our gear up," and Ern spread the brochures on the table. "This has to be the best place."

We stood on the shore with the waves washing around our feet.

"Bloody fantastic," Ern said, "and no one seems to give a stuff about sharks." Some distance out, board riders were floating around, or paddling on to a wave and riding it in, only to turn around and do it all over again. We watched in awe. "Those blokes have got more colour than us, but, I reckon we'll have to work on our swimming." Ern laughed. "And now for the sheilas, we need some decent gear if we are going to do any good."

Kitted out, we returned to the beach.

"Over there," I said, leading the way, toward a group of sun-baking girls, their tanned skin glistening with oil as their heads and feet kept time with a tune blaring from a portable radio.

"Hello girls," I said, "are you here on holiday; lovely day for a swim don't ya reckon?"

"Which bloody question do you want answered first?" replied a fantastic blonde in a red bikini, a cigarette dangling from her lovely lips.

"We was just trying to be sociable," I explained.

"If you two blokes want to join us," said a plump girl, displaying a fair amount of nicely rounded breast, "you can sit down and get on with it. My name's Maureen, this is Adele, Ade for short," she giggled, referring to the lovely blonde with the cigarette. "And this is Joyce, and that's Mandy. You blokes look as though you have just blown in from way out west." I laughed.

"We just finished our shearing run. My name is Darain and this is me cousin Ernie; we started up the top of Queensland and worked our way down. It is bloody hard work so we came across for a break, and to meet some beautiful sheilas like you, and let me tell you that we are bloody sick of looking at sheep." Ern had made a beeline for Maureen and had spread his towel so he faced her.

"Well that's a nice thing to say," Maureen protested, "I would have thought that we are a lot better looking than sheep."

We all laughed, and I had spread my towel opposite Adele, whose lipstick had smudged her cigarette, and whose eyes were gorgeous pools of blue, and returned my gaze.

"We are comptometer operators from Sydney," Adele explained, "we're with Australian Global Risk and Funding; this is our second time up here; we love it, and we got a lovely flat overlooking the beach." Ernie was beside himself with expectation, and was already deeply engrossed in explaining to Maureen how to shear a sheep, while his eyes bored into her cleavage. I was impressed, but I had no idea what a comptometer operator did, but it sounded impressive. I had immediately formed a picture of Adele in a white uniform, a clipboard in one hand, her lovely blue eyes framed by spectacles that emphasized her great intelligence and her complete mastery over her machine. In my mind, they were part of the technical elite.

"What's a comptometer?" I asked, trying not to display my ignorance. I was already thinking that where they worked would be like a scene out of a movie I had seen in Goondiwindi, in which the leading lady was extremely important, and had worn a tight jumper that displayed her delicious contours as she hurried in and out of meetings. There was the feeling that anything as beautiful was unobtainable until Mr. Right came along. She exuded a sexual power, and would sit with her long legs crossed on the edge of her boss's desk as she gave him the eye, and there was a view of the canyons of New York in the background. The cigarette smoke from her pouting lips lingered in the air like an unanswered question. She made things happen, and her boss yearned to take her in his arms, but for some reason never did. I remember it clearly, because as blacks, we were made to sit down the front and had to look up at the screen.

"Oh, I thought," Adele said, "everybody knew what a comptometer operator did; it is like an adding machine and typewriter combined; we use it to post the book entries." I had no idea what she was talking about, but was very impressed nonetheless.

"Girls, after the beach, Ern and I were wondering if we can take you all out for a drink." We had already sussed it out, and our taxi driver had assured us that things were very different on the coast, and there would be no trouble going to the pub.

Mandy hopped right in. "That would be lovely, the pub has a terrific beer garden and a barbecue." The invitation had gone down a real treat, and we were on the way to having a great holiday. I gazed contentedly at the surf. Mandy and Joyce were nice, not beautiful like Adele, but they both had faces that appealed to me. I was eager for a swim. Adele wanted to sunbake, so I found myself walking across the sand with Joyce.

"Darain, you can swim, I mean you would say?"

"Yes, but it was a long time ago."

"Good, we can swim together." We trod water between the waves.

"Joyce, you swim like fish." A wave sent me flying toward the shore.

"Dar, dive under them like this," she instructed.

"This beats shearing hands down," I said.

"And Dar, bashing out account cards all day." Then my cousin swept past facing the wrong way.

"Joyce, we gotta keep an eye on Ernie before he ends up in New Zealand."

"Don't fuss, Maureen is a strong swimmer, so I wouldn't worry," she explained. I must have looked a bit self-conscious. "Do not forget we live near the beach, and none of us can shear a sheep."

The day, the surf, and the girls were just fantastic. Joyce and I lay on the sand and watched the others, and I could not imagine how life could get any better. Maureen emerged with Ern, with an enthusiastic "There you are, one cousin, delivered safe and sound. And now we are going back to the flat to make ourselves even more beautiful than we already are. We will meet you in the beer garden in about an hour and a half."

It was not hard to see what Ernie was thinking, "that Maureen is a real peach and she is giving me more surfing lessons in the morning. It's harder out there than you think."

"I would not get too carried away," I said, "because Joyce reckons they fly out tomorrow afternoon."

"Not to worry Dar, a couple of smart operators like you and me will have to find some more *crumpet*. Let's concentrate on tonight; I reckon it will be great."

"Ern, how are we going to work it if one of us gets lucky?"

"I dunno, crikey. I suppose the first one home gets the room; the other takes his girl down the beach. Dar, you got any French letters?"

"Nah, but we better get some." The sea had calmed and a cooling sea breeze ruffled the feathers of the seagulls on the shore.

The hotel was one of those mock Spanish places with Moorish roof tiles, and white plaster walls with purple bougainvillea spilling down. I lifted my glass to Ern. "This has to be the go, not a bad looking pub; we got music and everything." We were keeping the beat in time with a combo playing at one end of the bar when the girls arrived. We were awestruck.

"S'truth," Ern said, "they're bloody beautiful." Ernie greeted them with a, "Hi ya, girls; what will it be?"

"A schooner for me," said Maureen, who was spectacular in a Hawaiian skirt with white flowers through it.

"I was wondering," said Adele, who was a breathtaking vision in yellow, "if I could have a Porphyry Pearl."

"The same for me," said Mandy.

"And for me," said Joyce. "Boys, we want to put in for this because there's four of us and we think it's only fair," she said, and tucked a fold of notes into my shirt pocket.

The pianist tried to sing like Louis Armstrong, but didn't have enough gravel in his voice. Mandy told of the married bloke from Accounts Receivable who was always putting the hard word on her. We all offered advice, ranging from ringing the wife to sending a heavily scented love letter so she would read it. While we considered that, Ern went for another tray of drinks. The sun went down, the tables filled up, and the air was alive with music and the babble of people with the glow of the first of the evening's drinks.

"I am really sorry we have to go," Joyce said confidentially into my ear, "it has been such a nice day," and she gave my arm an affectionate squeeze. Her lovely hair hung down to her shoulders, she had taken a shine to me as I had to her; and she spoke sadly about the end of her holidays. We volunteered to cook the barbecue, and with a glass in one hand, she accepted my arm around her waist and slid hers around mine, as we manoeuvred around the barbecue. We chatted about nothing in particular, gazed at each other, and sipped our drinks.

"Try some of my wine dear," she suggested. It did not do it for me; then she spooned some of her potato salad on to my plate. Perhaps it was the Porphyry Pearl, because she gave me a moist peck on my cheek.

"Having a nice time?" I asked.

"Really nice dear," she said, fluttering her eyes as we snuggled closer. Another band had taken over, and Joyce said she had most of the latest hits on high-fidelity at home. She was by then sitting on my knee, and strands of her hair dangled in my beer. We kept the beat to the music and the whole place vibrated.

"Dar, can we dance?" Which was all very well for her, but I had no idea what I was supposed to do, other than to hold her hand and try to be nonchalant as she twirled this way and that with her petticoat billowing out. Maureen and Ernie were twirling around nearby, and he was wriggling his bum and shaking his head to the music. I hoped I did not look as silly. Mandy and Adele were out on the floor flying around in all directions, their partners knew what they were doing. Joyce twirled in and planted an affectionate kiss on my cheek and complimented me, "Dar, you're pretty good." With her twirling about, I decided there was not much to it.

As I headed for the bar during a break, I had to pass four drunks who were obviously looking to put on a blue. "Jesus Christ, they have let in the fucking boongs!" Loaded with a tray of drinks, I chose to ignore the comment. With Joyce once more on my knee, I promptly forgot about it, as we kept time to the music. "Hey lady, ya wanna dance, ya doan wanna drink with them fucking boongs?" One of the drunks was swaying about just a few feet away. I got to my feet. "Listen mate, get lost; we were having a nice time until you arrived; now go back to your mates and leave us alone." It wasn't going to happen, and the haymaker was that long in coming; it was like a fully laden trailer accelerating from a standing start. I hoisted him up as if he was a sack of wheat, took him well away from the girls, and heaved him into a garden pond, to much cheering from the crowd, as if it was part of the nightly entertainment.

However, the girls sensed danger. "Come on," Maureen said, "down your drinks and let's get out of here before there is trouble." I was walking arm in arm with Joyce with the road on one side and a hedge of oleander on the other. The other four were walking in front. I remember that Maureen was carrying a bottle of wine when I was knocked out. I came to in hospital, wearing a blue smock.

"Son, that was nasty," the doctor said, "you were hit with a bottle from behind. We will keep you under observation overnight just to be on the safe side." Ernie turned up with sticking plaster across his swollen nose.

"There were four of the bastards and they got to you first, then they put the boot in. I got a few decent ones in so it was not all loss, and Maureen laid one of them out with her bottle of wine. When the girls made statements, the cops knew who they were. Joyce said to say goodbye and hopes you will be alright. I think you had something going there; they left a couple of hours ago."

"Are we in trouble with the cops?"

"No, everything's sweet, and apart from the blue, it was a terrific night out."

We were soon back on the beach, but it was pretty obvious that we had been in a scrap and so we were not given any encouragement. A day or so later, we were walking along the shore and in the distance I saw a banner announcing "The Beach Mission to Children", and we wandered over to have a look. A great-looking blond was singing and playing an accordion to a group of kids; they were the mission songs of our childhood and she could sing. She was even more beautiful than Adele, and she gave us a dazzling smile, before launching into her biblical story. She worked with an auburn-haired girl who was also very pretty and deftly illustrated each scene. At the end of each story, she ripped the sheet off and gave it to the children. As quick as a flash, she drew three wise men and their donkeys, before dashing on to the next scene to keep up with the storyteller.

I leant across to whisper, "Mate, these two are a sensation?" Ern whispered back, "Hang on; they are not going to come to the pub, or want to jump in the sack with us."

"Who says?" I must have been brash in those days. They had begun to sing.

> "It is not do right because I must,
> but right because it's right."

I sang along and made a great play of the hand actions.

> "Since the Lord saved me
> I am as happy as can be.
> My cups full of running over."

"Christ, this turns the clock back,"

"Ern, they are bloody gorgeous," I said, but the mood changed as they laid on the guilt.

"Dar, bugger me; here we go again." She was my idea of an angel and 1 was hooked. Her companion sketched with deft strokes as they launched into the grand finale. They went for the children's commitment and the blond was playing her accordion softly.

"Hello boys," she said, after they had said their goodbyes to the children. "It is nice you came along." Her companion had joined us and I made the introductions. My angel was Jill, and her companion Coreen.

"Girls," I said, "we are just going up the road for a sandwich; it would be great if you would join us."

We sat on the grass, eating our lunch. "Dar, tell me about yourself," Jill said. I gave them the abridged version, and then changed the subject. They were school teachers and this was their second beach mission. Ernie was going great guns with Coreen.

"And where did you learn to be such a great artist?" he asked.

"I have always loved drawing and I just developed this side of it as an aid to our missionary work," Coreen said as if her talent was nothing special.

"You must be a great teacher," Ernie said seriously.

"I don't know about that, but thank you. My subjects are geography and history, and as a matter of fact I do find it quite handy. How about a caricature Ernie? You have an interesting face." Coreen reduced Ernie to his essentials, which we thought was terrific. Jill reminded us that they were on again soon, and I said we would come back to help them pack up. I was walking on air. "Mate, they are so nice, I wonder if they would have tea with us?"

"Who knows? Let's have a swim; it looks great out there." We re-joined them after our swim, and invited the girls back to the motel for a barbecue.

"We will bring the salad," Jill offered.

It was that simple. We went back to our shearing run, and they to their teaching, and we kept in touch so we could meet during the school vacations. By this time, we were shearing over two hundred a day, and had as much work as we wanted.

"Do you realize," Ernie remarked, as we were driving along between sheds, "we each have nearly forty thousand in the bank, all our own gear, and a brand new truck? That's not bad for a couple of layabouts who could not afford the train fare to get to our first shed."

My cousin could see his future crystal-clear, whereas my relationship with Jill was destined never be quite so simple. Sure, I wanted to marry her, but I could not imagine continuing with my itinerant life while we were trying to settle down. As I told Ernie, my idea was to give shearing away and for us to buy a little business with potential to grow, and as we both enjoyed the beach, we thought in a coastal town somewhere.

"Coreen and I are pretty keen, but we decided I should keep at it for a while because it is such good money, as a bloke like me would never make it doing anything else."

"Ern, let's stop at the Post Office in the next town, so I can ring my sister and see how she's going."

Ernie went to buy the drinks and sandwiches for our lunch, while I made my phone call. He said he found me sitting on the Post Office steps with a stunned expression on my face.

"You are not going to believe this," I told him.

"Why? Is she sick?"

"No, there's a letter from the Commonwealth Government; I have been called up for National Service. Me in the Army, you wouldn't read about it, and just when we are in the big money."

My number had come out of the barrel. There was the certainty of my regular shearing run and my plans for a life with Jill. The idea of it was overwhelming, but at that age, you ride with the punches.

"Where is Vietnam anyway?" I asked. "I have to go to Brisbane for my medical. Fancy me having to defend you and all the other *bludgers* around the place. Wonders never cease."

"The boys were talking about it the other night," Ern said. "The North and the South hate each other's guts; we reckoned it was a bit like Queensland having a go at New South Wales."

⚡ 8 ⚡

I reported to the depot, wearing old jeans and a tee shirt and a sharp-faced soldier began ordering us about. "When your names are called, fall in over there and we will get you kitted out." The Army moved slowly while we got to know each other. "I hate the Army already, and I only just got here," was the shared sentiment as we were waiting around to discover what the Army was going to do next. That loss of control over our own lives, and the feeling of apprehension, seemed to be the common bond.

"Form up, three ranks," ordered a well-fed Corporal who probably reckoned he had the makings of a General, "by the left quick march, no talking, left right, left right, halt, stand still, in twos, queue here to be measured, draw your gear, if it is the wrong size bring it back later and change it." We were slowly discovering that we would have to get used to the army bossing us around and that it could go on twenty-four hours a day.

"You will keep your kit, your bed, locker, and this hut clean at all times. Recruits will now change into the following: singlet white, underpants white cotton, socks khaki, trousers khaki, work jacket khaki, boots black, gaiters webbing, belt webbing, work beret, cotton, khaki. Hurry up Private, we do not have all day. Form up, three lines, stand still, face the front, on the order 'move', fall out and wait over there in an orderly line to get your hair cut."

"No! I really can't." At least that produced a few laughs.

"There's nothing personal about it Private; it's for Queen and country; just explain to the barber what style you would like and they will look after you. Soldier, your gaiters are on the wrong feet and upside down; fix them now; I said NOW!"

"Darain, do you play five hundred?"

"Yeah."

"Mate, we'll get a school together." The hut smelled of unwashed men. Suddenly in the dark of early morning, the door was flung open, the light came on, and we met our Sergeant for the first time.

"Wakey wakey, rise and shine! On your feet! Everyone outside NOW! NOW! NOW! Right NOW! I said right Now! MOVE IT!

"Christ, it's bloody freezing."

"No talking in the ranks; answer when your name is called. On the command 'fall out!' you will shave and shower and go to breakfast."

Later that week, "Platoon, by the left quick march, left right, left right. Platoon, halt! Private, what's your name?"

"Popodopolous."

"Private Popodopolous, you don't appear to know your left foot from your right, and you are out of step."

"GET FUCKED! I am not a going to march."

"You're letting yourself and your Platoon down soldier."

"Don't come near me or I KILL YOU."

"The Platoon, with the exception of Private Popodopolous, by the left, quick march, left right, left right." The army had obviously struck this before and we were intrigued by how they handled it. Month after grinding month and slowly they turned us into soldiers. Had we been onlookers, we would not have recognized ourselves, and suddenly there we were, saying our goodbyes. Jill and I were looking forward tremendously to my homecoming and our marriage. She could not make it down because it was midway through school term.

Alkina and I chatted while we waited for the final call to echo over the PA system. Every now and again, one of the boys would bring their wives or girlfriends across; they all seemed to know her from her column. Our last Will and Testaments had been made, and there was something about deciding how to dispose of your possession that brought home the reality of it. I made sure Alkina met all my mates, and we made light of it.

"It's been a lot of fun; we were a pretty wild lot when we came in, and look at us now. We are proud to be part of a well-trained unit." I had told her about Popodopolous, but not the outcome.

"Remember that Greek bloke I told you about, who we left standing in the middle of the parade ground. Much later we were having a beer and I asked the Sergeant what had happened to him. 'The MPs picked him up and put him in the slammer; he is the second one I've had,' he told me."

"Dar, do shush, James and Patrick send their best wishes, so do Hanna and Henri, and I think you look very smart in your uniform, and everyone is very proud of you. It is so lovely Hanna and Henri are getting married, and Dar you are invited to the wedding, but never mind, I will send you some photos, and please drop them a line, care of me. Do be careful over there; promise me that you will try not to be heroic. I would like my little brother back in one piece. Mum and dad send their love, and I will send them plenty of photos."

She made my going to war easier, and had brought so much food; it was as if she feared we might go hungry.

"This has all been too much for mum and dad. You can go and see them when you get back. Poor dad thinks he will never get us back together again; he still talks of our walk to see his country as if it was yesterday. One day maybe you and I could take them in by boat or helicopter, and wouldn't he just love that? And I wanted to say that I am very fond of Jill. I think she will make a lovely sister-in-law. But I do hope that what you two feel for each other is the real thing."

Alkina obviously had doubts then, but the subtlety of her comment really never really registered with me. "Sis, of course it is, but what is the point of a marriage when suddenly I am gone? Jill thought so too. We will do it when I get back. Here is the plan. Can you keep a secret?"

"Don't be silly."

"We are having a double wedding with Ernie and Coreen."

"How lovely, I am absolutely thrilled for you both, I really am." The PA system made the final call.

"There it is, thanks for everything, don't worry about me; we will look after each other."

There was an unreality about standing on the flight deck of HMAS Sydney with my cardboard identification stuck in the front of my slouch hat. Down on the wharf a military band had struck up; the hawsers had been let go and the old carrier drew away to the sound of 'The Maori Farewell'. It was one of those moments you never forget. I waved until she was lost in the crowd.

"The Army will not leave us alone for a second," I wrote to Jill. "If we are not doing push-ups on the flight deck, we are blazing away at balloons from the back of it. We train from dawn until we hit the sack." No matter how hard we went at it, there were always the occasional cock-ups. Like the time I was asked to be a casualty to give the medics some practice, I came away convinced that if it been the real thing, I would never have made it. But somehow the army had managed to weld us together. But had they? Men like the "Log" who reckoned he had never had a proper job, except the odd casual one here and there, and said he lived on his mother's war widows pension. Had they really managed to make a soldier out of him?

What of "Dolly", our Lieutenant, who was always so immaculate? How would he go for days looking and smelling like a dead dingo, and lead us into battle? There could be no doubt about our Sergeant, whose patience and bark had melded us into whatever fighting Platoon we had become. He was a soldier's soldier, a professional, but only one of thirty men. My friend "Toots", who carried an M60 machine gun, would never flinch when it mattered. It seemed right that "Brasso" should be a soldier; he was our Corporal, and had come up through the CMF (Citizens Military Reserve) and was the only one I knew who had actually volunteered. I think he saw his service as a bit of a lark, and an opportunity to practice his soldiering. There was "Books", our very own SP bookie who would run a book on most events, including the big race meetings back home. He was a cellar man, that is, when he was not out at the race track, or studying the form.

It worried us that "Stroller", who must have been approaching seven feet tall, would stick out in the jungle like a giraffe. As it was, he spent most of his life ducking under things, and found life on board a constant misery. He worked on the wharves, and kept greyhounds. And what about "Barrel," who was everyone's friend? In civilian life, he was a bricklayer, who now lugged a mortar around. A tailor of gentlemen's fine clothing who went by the name of "Rabbits" now made his living as a dedicated infantryman, who besides other things, toted a grenade launcher for us.

The Platoon had a collective sense of humour, and whatever we were going to come up against, we were going to face it together. At night we practiced stripping our rifles and putting them together again. "Harbouring" was making camp for the night, a drill we practiced until our stealth had become routine. It was after one in the morning and the air was damp.

"I would rather be up here stuffing around playing war games, than being stuck down below any day," I whispered to Toots.

"Ships stink; this one smells like a camel driver's arm pit," my friend replied. "Okay Dar, they're off again." We rose and went another few yards before going down again.

"Quiet you blokes, Dar to relieve the picket." I hugged the deck as I crawled out to the dark shape; then I lay on the deck, listening to the ship and looking at the sky until Brasso called us in.

"That was a bloody good exercise, but we must learn to keep still and maintain our silence in the bush. Now a few heads and arses stuck up more than they should have tonight. I know it is uncomfortable crawling around the deck, but over there I want you to hug the fucking ground like you are an earthworm. The weapon drill was okay, without being anything to write home about. Practice, practice until it's instinctive, and again, nobody beat Dar, which should give you something to aim for."

We lounged about, listening to Dolly running his HQ exercises. "Stroller, keep your messages as tight as possible and the noise level down, it carries like buggery at night, otherwise that was pretty good. Boys, I can't say it often enough, keep it brief." Brasso wandered over, muttering under his breath, "Christ, it's too bloody sticky to sleep."

"Brasso, what's it like being married? Do you two have many arguments?" I asked.

"Dar, all the bloody time, mostly it's about who spends what. I think the money side of it is very important. It would be the same for any couple, because by the time you set up home, and start having kids, the bloody stuff just runs out the door. Not that our differences ever get nasty, but I would advise a bloke like you to tie a knot in it for the first few years." That was said loud enough to get a laugh.

"No, seriously," he continued, "you got to talk it through, and the best thing is making up."

"Thanks, Brasso, now tell us about your boy."

"Well," he began, "Tim's going on three; here he is, a happy little bloke; spread it around, he is going to be open bat for Queensland, but we got a few years to get ready for that. Dar, did you ever play cricket? They say you blokes have a good eye for a ball."

"Yeah, but they were probably referring to football. I never had a proper game of cricket; as little kids, we used to muck around with pickup sides. None of us could bowl for shit, and when I got in, I would have a slog. I am talking about being a station kid at a mission school. Later, when we played at the home, we made up the rules as we went along. Footy was our thing; we would have kicked a football all day long if they had let us. We used to like playing other teams, and would do anything to put them off; and I would have been the worst offender. I mean knuckles, knees, the lot, and of course, they did the same."

"I heard shearers make a lot of money. Is that true?"

"Brasso, you got to get in, earn enough dough to set yourself up, and get out again. Most of them don't; they either drink it or they end up with crook backs, and besides, you would not want to live with a gang of shearers; it's a pretty rough life. I want to buy a business and settle down."

"Jill sounds like a real nice lady."

"She is. Jill's a teacher; she taught me a few things I can tell you; there is no rough-house around her, and I don't mind admitting she has smartened me up no end. I am going to look around when I get home. Any suggestions?"

"Have a look at lock smithing, a mate of mine got into it and has done well anyway; they got a nice home out of it."

"Yeah, and Brasso, how do you make a quid?"

"I got my start as a carpenter, I did okay out of selling my share of a business some mates and I started up in the Valley. We fabricated aluminium doors and windows, until I got sick of all the hassles. Mate, once you got a lot of people on the payroll, you got trouble."

HMAS Sydney anchored off Vung Tau, and we waited while the Army got itself organized.

"Vung Tau is not my sort of place," Barrel commented. "As a matter of fact, I don't think South Vietnam is my sort of place. What are we doing sitting here?"

"Do not whinge," Brasso mocked, "we are waiting for our limousines, but they have been unavoidably delayed; but don't worry, there is to be a ceremony with the keys to the city and a welcoming lunch." Chris knew exactly, "a party will take our gear into Nui Dat by truck. The Yanks are laying on Chinooks for the rest of us."

"Thank you Sergeant, and what will be on the menu when we get there?"

"Nothing for you Barrel; we forgot to tell them you were coming."

"Sarge, here they come; stuff me; will you look at that? I don't think we have that many Hueys. Struth, you can't help but be impressed. My old man was a digger, and he always said the Yanks knew how to turn it on." They kept on arriving until we were airlifted out.

On the ground our Warrant Officer, a very sweaty fellow named Mick Story, was directing the traffic. "You men get moving, take your men to the lines, come on, move it along and get your stuff out of here. This is no drill." We did not hang about.

"The Company will move out at 1600 hours to sweep this grid," the Company Commander explained. "In the morning, you will swing norwest through here and into the next grid, which is a defunct rubber plantation." Our time had come. Major Barry Holt was one of those eager-eyed officers on his second tour. This was his first as a Company Commander. Those guys could not wait to go to war.

"I want a radio check before we move out," he said. "The New Zealanders will cover us from their positions here. This should show the enemy, who no doubt are aware of our arrival, that we are not just a mob of home bodies." Those guys made it sound like a stroll in the park. The Nui Dat base housed us four to a tent, not that there was any time to try the accommodation out.

"Brasso, Dolly has a meeting; he wants you there right now." He was back in a few minutes. "Boys, we got twenty minutes, fill your canteens and strip your packs of excess gear."

We were anxious to get out; we had heard too many disaster stories about men sitting around minding their own business, and copping a rocket in their lap, and anyway we were trained to be out in the bush. Brasso gave me the thumbs up when I was about the right distance out. I was soon soaked, and now and again through the foliage, I caught a glimpse of the man carrying the M60. We patrolled over damp earth and rotting vegetation, I came across a spoor and decided it may have been from a native deer. What would the Mighty Hunter do? There was no hiding my footprints, which were the unmistakable sign of my passing. I ran my thumbs up under my pack straps, in an effort to make it more comfortable. We were all weighed down with grenades, claymore mines, ammunition, rifles, and the rest of it.

The night was closing in, and Brasso signalled we were going into harbor. I went out and set my claymores. There was no good-natured kidding about; our lives depended on not being heard or seen. They were all just as tired and disoriented as I was. After our exhaustive training, we were in the land of our enemy. That night we had a fitful sleep among unfamiliar sounds; mine was softened by thoughts of Jill.

Enemy elements of D445 were said to be active in the area, their trademarks were RPGs launched in the early hours, which would be during my picket.

I listened to the birds squabbling and resettling on their perches. The morning air was thick under a bank of low cloud, and from a distance came the crump of artillery. I went out to collect my mines, exchanged a "thumbs up" with Brasso, then humped my gear and began walking. The rain came in mid-afternoon, and I cupped my hands and washed my face. Now and again a thundering jet passed unseen above, while with every step, my boots sucked and squelched. Brasso signalled a halt and we went to ground; he called me in, "The boys on the right have a problem. Dolly says stay sharp while they sort it out."

I sheltered in the low scrub as the visibility worsened, we were among rubber trees with low scrub underneath. Would I be able to detect our enemy in the rain? And I wondered what was happening. My eyes played tricks on me by making imaginary faces in the foliage; I was desperate to see them first. Brasso whispered, "No contact, but Talbot has gone down, and they think it might be appendicitis; as he is lifted out, it will pinpoint us, so we move out straight away, good on you champ." I lay in the rain, the Huey came in, hovered and was quickly gone. On Brasso's signal, I walked on.

We had fallen into a routine of patrolling, and some months later, we were not long back from an extended patrol, when we were paraded before the Company CO, while he launched into an explanation of an operation to be known as "Dingo Drive". There was no doubting his enthusiasm.

"Gentlemen, we are going to patrol the Long Hai Mountains in Battalion strength and Charlie Company, reinforced by elements from Bravo Company, will act as a blocking force here," he used his swagger stick as a pointer. Toots had only a day or so previously joked that Holt may mistakenly believe he was a reincarnation of General Douglas MacArthur, and that even Dolly was beginning to sound gung-ho.

"The situation will be that when the other companies have completed their sweeps, they will have driven the enemy down out of the hills and on to our position. This will have been well prepared with interlocking fields of fire. The aim is to put our force across the tracks, which Special Air Service tells us are the only way in and out. Our responsibility therefore is to have thoroughly prepared our position before the attacking forces commence their drive." Major Holt appeared quite chuffed with his scenario, his bush hat and swagger stick sat on the trestle table in front of him; his maps were displayed to one side, pinned to several whiteboards; at least he had everyone's attention.

"There is nothing required of us that we have not been thoroughly trained for. Success will depend on each of us performing our individual tasks to the best of our ability. US Forces will be in support with two Batteries of heavy artillery, positioned here and here, while our own and the New Zealander batteries will be in close support from positions here and here, and of course their spotters will be forward with us. Gentlemen, the entire operation will have a Battalion of Air Mobile US Infantry standing by as a reserve, should we run into unexpected strength. However, we should have more than adequate fire-power. As I have said, artillery will be able to blanket the whole area, and of course, weather permitting, we shall have close air support, so all up, it is a very significant force."

As Holt spoke, he gave the impression that it had all been well planned. "The hills are tough going on the slopes and are broken with gullies, rocky outcrops, and cave formations. The topography begins to level out further down the slope. The most significant feature is a thick mat of thorny scrub and bamboo through which there are concealed tracks, which lead to the villages below. That mat forms a skirt which has been hatched in on the maps, and I want you to study them. This is a natural barrier over which the attacking force will be airlifted. But it also means that to get off that mountain, the enemy have to use these tracks.

Intelligence has identified the area as a safe haven where the enemy goes to regroup and recover. We believe they have a hospital up there, as well as weapon, ammunition, and food stores. Our job is to engage these forces as they are driven down those tracks and to destroy them. The key to our success will be accurate situation reports that keep us fully informed at all times. I have every confidence you will acquit yourselves well. Good luck to you all. I will now hand over to Captain Hickey, who will give you the latest intelligence assessment."

The Captain wore no insignia, and had a rumpled look, as if he might have been just come in from doing the gardening. Perhaps he was trying to tell us that he took a more intellectual view of the war than the rest of the Army.

He began, "This comes from Special Air Service, who have swept the area, and from interrogations as recent as a few days ago. So we have a pretty good picture of what to expect. You may encounter assorted elements of regular North Vietnamese forces, who have made their way to this base after being wounded or separated from their units. Small elements of Unit 274 have been encountered, and they are a battle-hardened North Vietnamese outfit. The object, as your CO has told you, is to destroy and deny them the use of this sanctuary. But for the longer term, it should do much to remove their influence over the province.

It is of great value to us to interrogate prisoners, and assess any documents that are found. Precise estimates of their strength are always difficult to assess, but we think there may be a ceiling of four hundred, with a more likely figure of something like two hundred. Their weaponry is the usual array of AK-47s and RPGs and any other heavier stuff, including M60s, they may have captured." The Captain's comment may have been made with some levity, but if they felt like me, it had the opposite effect. "There will be sappers with the dislodgment force to deal with mines and booby traps. Extreme caution should be exercised around any of their caves, tunnels and bunkers. The cover for your insertion will be increased helicopter activity, with simulated insertions over four days before you are flown in, and they will continue afterward, so as to add confusion. The SAS will maintain a presence, and everything will be done to sow maximum confusion and doubt among the enemy. Are there any questions?"

We were endeavouring to take it in, and privately wondering what screw-up the army may have dreamed up this time. After a few patrols, any barriers between Dolly, Chris and the boys had evaporated. A lot would have been Dolly, who, at first, may have been seen as a bit soft, but we had soon learned that Russell Tanner was a competent and likable bloke we could follow. He knew when to be one of the boys, and how to keep our respect. Some of that would have rubbed off on Christopher Palmer, our Sergeant, who came across as a knockabout bloke who had found his niche as a soldier. He looked and sounded like one; he had once driven a truck for a living; and had a daily produce run into the Brisbane markets. He could be tough and get what he wanted out of the Platoon, but he also knew when to switch off.

We got ready to leave. "Boys," Brasso said, "it would be better to lump the extra ammo there and back, rather than risk being short. Pete, you can lump in our spare M60; some of you bigger blokes can carry the ammo for that; okay, let's get set. I want plenty of water, so load yourselves with extra canteens; it gets bloody hot out in the bush, as we have all discovered." We were put down in a thinly timbered area about two miles from the nearest hamlet and what was supposed to be an easy two-hour march to our objective. Scrambling away, we found ourselves at the edge of that very same skirt of thicket where everything grew in tight confusion. Our route was meant to be through moderate to lightly wooded country. The reality was that twenty minutes later, we were hemmed in by a thick blanket of thorns and interwoven bamboo.

I was the scout, and the rest of the Company was strung out behind. Progress was slow; someone had stuffed up; the difference was being there on the ground. My instinct took over and I waited until Brasso had clambered forward.

"Mate," Brasso whispered, "we got the whole fucking Company behind us; have you gone on strike?"

"No, but we are not going to make it; the bloke who mapped this route has us too far up the slope. I doubt he ever walked it. Tell Dolly it's hopeless. I reckon we should go back and head down the slope and out of this shit, then circle around toward our objective."

"No sweat, stay here until Dolly can get the word back to the CO; good work champ." The air was still and hot, and the sound of Chinooks and Hueys in the distance were the only signs of war. A few minutes later, we began to retrace our steps.

"Okay," Brasso said. "Dolly says good work, and the CO wants us to mine back along this track, just hang in here until I call you through." Further down was much easier, and we spread out through the timber where there was a good cover of low scrub. There was still plenty of daylight when we got there. We set up a perimeter and began to dig in. We were just below that belt of thicket. The tracks through it passed right through our position. Down the slope was an old tunnel complex that had been destroyed. The broken ground around it provided good cover; I thought the SAS had done it well.

Chris organized his mining parties. "Get these fuckers up those tracks," he ordered, "before it gets dark, a couple of you guys mount a picket further up while we get set." The man was laden down with them himself. Dolly and a party from Company HQ, including the CO, were supervising the layout of the position. I was forward on the left and moved some of the debris from the old bunker out of my field of fire. Toots was beavering away in his pit, which was on a slight rise and further back and over on my right. We would cover each other. The soil was damp and musty as it came out, the spewy earth sticking to my boots and clothes. I made my pit deep and wide, scooped a shallow channel in front for my rifle, then inspected my handiwork from the outside. I added moss-covered timber from the old bunker, and endeavoured to make it merge with the surrounding ground.

I felt much safer as the silvery light faded into night. The Company Sergeant Major did his rounds with his party, and squatted beside my pit.

"Good job today soldier; this place could get very busy in the morning; spend your time making your position as strong as you can," he gave me an encouraging slap on the shoulder and went over to check on Toots. It had just occurred to me that Story and his men had to know exactly where everyone was, so he could organize the resupply of rations, water, and ammunition. His party was followed by Holt and gaggle of others from Company HQ. Our ambush was set like a spider's trap and we quietly waited for our unsuspecting prey. I had dismissed the possibility of my own death as there was just too much to look forward to. There was no telling what I was eating, and it occurred to me that perhaps the Army could get Hanna and my sister to work on their menu, and the thought amused me. Right then, a decent mug of tea and a cold lamb sandwich with tomato and pickles would have been a feast. The stars paraded through the canopy, and the myriad sounds of the forest kept me company until the pale of the new day stole gently through the trees, just as stealthily as the previous one had crept away.

The battle began with the continuous crump of artillery, and the pulsating thumps of Chinooks and Hueys as they darted in and out and hovered about like angry bees. The contact on the ground began slowly as the sporadic small arms fire rose and fell in intensity. My eyes were glued to that thicket. Occasionally a gunship lumbered in and let fly with a spray of metal into the jungle below. High above, Phantoms circled to scream in and dump a load of napalm wherever they were directed; the canisters landed with a fearful WHOOMPH and left the smoke to drift across the trees. It seemed inconceivable that somewhere on that mountain, men hid and waited. Scrub fires had started high on the slopes. The day wore on, and I wondered if the whole thing might turn out to be another military stuff up.

Up there, the boys would be clambering about trying desperately not to get wounded or killed. I was safer in my pit; they could never be sure; one wrong step could mean sudden death, or the loss of one or both legs. It had been a stifling day, and you did not need to be a staff officer to work out what the options were. Our enemy either stood and fought where they were or they must make an organized withdrawal down those tracks, unless of course they had a way down the SAS had not discovered. What would I do? I thought they would be holed up waiting for the right moment to attempt their break-out. To hell with them; what about us? I knew our own situation would deteriorate if we had to spend another day living in the ground like a wombat. HQ had to be worried; because our water would be getting low and everyone in our force would be hot, tired and very much on edge. What the fuck would we do when we began to smell? Our CO could not have a resupply without giving away our position.

Our second night and still no contact; I massaged my left leg to stop it from cramping, which might have something to do with letting myself be talked into shearing a mob of still damp sheep so we could finish a shed. What if I did not see them first? I calmed myself by thinking of our last picnic together. How come I was living in a pit like a bloody animal? I crawled out to stretch and to get my circulation going. Cradling my rifle, and with one eye on the thicket, I crawled very gingerly over to say g'day to Toots who was very pissed off. "Thanks for coming; if they don't kill us, the fucking stress will; Jesus, am I fed up with this!" This whispered conversation helped a lot, and I had figured a way to establish some communication between us. I gave him one end of reel of black darning cotton to tie around a finger. "Two quick tugs if they come, one to say g'day'." It was better than nothing.

At night the forest sounds seemed amplified; the crickets and the previous night's squadron of mosquitoes had returned and in the canopy above, bats defecated on the litter below with a splat. The birds squabbled, and every now and then, an owl swooped up a small animal from the forest floor. My eyes never strayed from the thicket. What would I say if somehow she could hear me? How melodramatic, but if I was ever going to see her again, I had to stay focused. I pummelled and pinched my face, I had to stay alert, for nothing else mattered.

Through the canopy the moon sent its gentle light, and the musty air was thick with the smell of rotting vegetation. I gave my troublesome knee another good rub, and in that moment, I caught the faintest whiff of dried fish, and probably spice and tobacco. I pulled my weapon into my shoulder, eased into my firing stance, and gave two quick tugs on the line and was relieved when Toots acknowledged. They would be trying to figure out who was there. Could they have found and disarmed the booby traps? They may not have come down the main tracks. Not a shadow moved.

They were running toward me in the soft light and I squeezed off three shots, which thudded home. One momentarily made a few spasms on the ground, and suddenly we were in a battle. The dark figures emerged from the thicket and Toots fired short bursts and they went down, but others came out in a spread and were missed. Parachute flares floated lazily overhead, lighting everything up like a weird stage, where the players fell or ran off into the dark. Some made zigzagging runs to one side, but most trotted steadily straight ahead. The string of oaths had come from Toots as the flares had destroyed his night vision. The shadows ran past; muzzle flashes came from the thicket; and there was the fearsome crump of detonating mines. I talked to her as I fired, "Darling, I am doing my best to keep out of danger, crack, crack, crack, hang on, and I will come home in one piece, crack, as I promised in your arms."

Our mortars marched down the hill until they fell in a deadly hail. The 105 howitzers had found the range and pounded across the thicket to fill the air with blast and steel. They were coming en masse, and I reserved my fire for those running directly at me. The bombardment marched from side to side; how could anyone survive? I had my own battle, but as it died down, I wondered what might be happening elsewhere.

At Company HQ, Major Holt listened to the reports, made his assessment, and reported to Battalion HQ. "They are breaking out from the tracks to the left and middle of our front. Positions holding, enemy passing through, artillery called down, request ammunition and water at first light, strengthening forward positions, no organized counter attack, estimate two to three hundred. Position holding, repeat Charlie Company holding." There was a lot happening.

"Sar-major, your resupply as quick as you can."

"Sit rep, First Platoon: Under attack, enemy passing through."

"Make: resupply on the way."

"Second Platoon HQ hit by RPGs, two dead, three injured, one critical, need medics, position holding."

"Make: 'help on way.'"

"Sergeant, take five men to Second Platoon, and report."

"Weapons ready, we may have visitors." Holt reported he was moving his people forward in support. Over on the left, someone from the sar-major's party arrived at my pit with water and ammo, almost as casually as if he was delivering a pizza. They were hesitant now, one or two at a time, or a small group in a sudden mad rush. Behind me, Toots was ripping short bursts into the track. "Darling one, I am still alive and now I have ammunition and water." Nothing moved, and I took a drink. WO Story's mob were angels. There was firing coming from behind. What now, one last great charge to get off the mountain? My heart was pounding.

Well behind us the senior Medical Officer had the first aid post functioning as well as he could; at first light, they would blow the trees and get the wounded out. In the meantime, men were dying. The doctor put a suture around a throbbing artery and tied it off. "Hang on Sunshine, won't be long now", he was not sure if his words were doing any good, as his patient's chances were fading with every passing second. What the fuck, no one was listening anyway! While he comforted and worked flat out, he pleaded silently: "Where are you bastards? I have men dying here; please come and take them out. Christ, I am losing him!" The instructions were imprinted on his mind. "Make comfortable those you can't save and concentrate on those you can. Calm and clear thinking saves lives; the evacuations will not take long; and your casualties will be airlifted to Vung Tau as soon as we can get the choppers in."

"Is that right?"

"Fuck no, another boy with no pulse." Nearby others were fighting to stem the bleeding, and still they came in. "Here, give this bloke another shot and put him to sleep." They worked feverishly. This was nothing like a city trauma ward; this was condoned mayhem and slaughter. At last there was an almighty crack as they blew the trees and in they came. "Thank bloody Christ!" The grenades had exploded among the HQ of Second Platoon. Stroller, the lanky radioman, was only just with them, with much of his skull cap missing. One had terrible blast damage and was just a bloodied muddle of perforated flesh.

Although I remained hunched over my weapon, at least I had survived. Somewhere to the rear, a dust-off was taking place, and now they had all day to fly in and out. The flares signalling the link-up shot skyward over the battlefield.

"You okay Toots?"

"Yes mate." They were our troops emerging from the thicket. I was looking over the remains of those whose lives had been snatched away, and found it overwhelming. Toots must have been thinking the same thing.

"Hey Dar, it was either them or us." I was glad it had been said. Then Toots yelled, what we all must have been thinking, "Mick Story and his boys deserve a fucking medal; I was desperate for a resupply when they came."

At that point, the extent of our casualties was not known. Holt was collecting his troops and moving up through his company. Just behind our position, he met up with the sar-major's party and the WO took him over to where the ground was littered with dead.

"Mr. Holt, these men have done very well." They conferred, and I overheard the WO say we would be unaware that our Lieutenant and Sergeant were dead, and that "Stroller" was critical and had been lifted out. I was too shocked and stressed out and I do not remember how I reacted. But Major Holt had not been aware and had gasped in shock. "That's terrible, they were such fine men." Toots was staring over his machine gun when Holt knelt down, "Well done soldier; the fighting is over now."

As for myself, I think that I was so relieved to have survived that I found it hard to react even as Major Holt's party stood over me. "Private, you can stand down now; the firing has stopped and we have had a great victory," and they helped me out. "Make sure these men brew up and have something to eat, and I would like you to inform them of their losses. Thank you, for showing me." At that point, I did not know my good mate Brasso had just died of his wounds, which I later wrote to Jill about.

> My Darling Jill,
>
> How I miss you. I spend hours dreaming of our future life together, and how we are going to make a home and kids, and how happy we will be. I am very well, and am now a corporal in charge of our Section, and I worry that I can lead them through all our future actions.
>
> My good mate John Braithwaite has been killed in action. Brasso was such a nice bloke that it is difficult to accept that he is no longer with us, and it hurts to write about him. But I want you to understand why I am acting in his place. Our sergeant, lieutenant, and radio operator were all killed in the same action; we were all such great mates that we feel a terrible loss, which is

how close this war has made us. I am so sorry that this is such a sad and short letter, but they don't give us much time to sit around, and now I have to go to a meeting for new NCOs.

No more sad talk. I must think of our future. Please keep your eye out for anything that might suit us. Please give my best to Coreen and Ern, and I know we are all counting the days. I am sorry that your mum has not been well; please give her a big hug from me. Like you have said, every passing day will brings us closer and I cannot wait to hold you in my arms.

With all my love, Your Dar

We had long realized that it was the Warrant Officers who ran the Army. Sticklers for detail, the training was largely left to them. Mick Story was typical, and having been a beneficiary of the selfless bravery he had inspired, he had our respect and at my first parade of NCOs, I listened carefully to what he had to say.

"We realize that your promotion has happened through very sad circumstances. However, after the grieving, we all must get on with it, and as it is not practical to put on a course over here, Mr. Holt has asked me to have a few informal chats, so you are aware of how the Army stands on things. We also wanted to open a door, so that if you have a problem, you know where to come. Sad as it is, we now realize how good leadership inspires others and saves lives.

You have also seen and have a feeling for what sort of standard you should expect from your men, and you must realize that it is your job to maintain it. There should be no wavering on that; you have been chosen for command because you are the cream of this company and the very stuff upon which our army depends. I want to discuss what we are doing over here. Our Government and that of The United States have drawn a line in the sand and said Communism shall not advance any further South. That is really what it is all about, and that is exactly what we are doing, we are holding that line right here in Vietnam. NATO does the same thing in Europe. Are there any questions on that? Yes son." I had to stifle a smile as the question was from a soldier who, the other day, I had watched sink a large bottle of beer straight down without drawing breath.

"Sar-major, do you believe Australia is at risk from what my old man calls, 'the yellow peril'?"

"That is a very good question, and yes, I do. You men are going to have to defend Australia from them in your lifetime; think about it; it is going to happen. They will want our food, our land, our energy, that is the oil and coal and so on. They will want our iron, wool, and our clean air and water." There were a few exaggerated coughs of protest among the boys, but he never wavered. "No, I am being fair dinkum about this;

after stuffing up their own country, they will want ours. That is the point, because you are the men who will have to stop them, just like your fathers did in New Guinea."

We discussed that for a few minutes. "Okay," he said, "now does anyone know what makes a good leader?" The sar-major was trying very hard to be seen as a good bloke, and to break down the barriers. That was the way the military worked, as nice as pie one moment, and all blood and guts the next. "Someone who leads by example."

"Correct!"

"Men, we don't have to look very far for that. I mean you blokes led by example when you showed great courage under fire, and stood your ground." He had ventured into sensitive territory, but to our shared relief, he left it there. "Okay, that's about it. Go and have a beer with your mates, and I will see you here at the same time tomorrow."

But no one could replace Brasso, and I was not about to try, and as for my stripes, they did nothing to save me from their good-natured ribbing. As soon as I returned, it was on.

"Hi Dar, how's your career as a top military commander going?" Toots asked, a beer in one hand, and a tits and bums magazine in the other.

"Dunno, load of crap if you ask me. Mick likes to talk, but it is going to add another hour to the day; but what can you do? Mate, the army is a worry, and he does goes on about all those yellow hordes invading Australia. Toots, I wonder how he feels about having to instruct me, I mean he has an Abo in his Company, and he's worried about all them collared hordes. I reckon it's a wank, no risk. And anyway, how in the hell did you get out of it?"

Toots grinned, "Mate, easy, I was not chosen, and I have a chit to have the MO treat my tinea."

"That's bullshit; yours is no worse than mine; you don't have any ambition. You will stay just a bloody grunt, and the poor bloody country will be invaded by all those hordes. And mate, when they come and screw the place up, and drink all our beer, it is going to be all your bloody fault, and all because you did not dry between your toes!" Toots was not put off.

"Corporal, this is what I will do, if they get down there and it looks critical. I will start to dry between my toes. I think that's fair enough, Corporal, mate, me old buddy?" Then he began to sing:

> "Only a hundred and sixty eight days to go,
> Only a hundred and sixty eight days to go.
> "We're having a cxxx of a time,
> with only a hundred and sixty eight days to go."

"Dar," he continued in a serious tone, "Mate, we are nearly there;

each day that passes brings us closer to going home. Please don't get all conscientious on me and get us selected for any silly business out in the bush. The way you're going, you will end up a bloody General, and the next thing we know, you will be mounting a bayonet charge, and we will end up being heroes and covered with medals. The only problem with that is we will be dead. Remember what we decided, we never ever volunteer. It's true, out of sight, out of mind. Put it this way, I would rather be a private in your section for the rest of our tour, as that way I reckon we are both going to make it home."

There had been a deadly seriousness to Toot's sending me up. Although I made light of it, I was interested to hear what the sar-major had to say. Most of our days were crammed with exercises, or we were out on patrol. Our new Lieutenant, Myles Dunphy, appeared comfortable in his roll, and so was Eric Sanders, our new Sergeant. They were on their second tour and seemed nice enough. However, there was never that closeness again. As Toots said over a beer, "You can't replace great blokes like them," and I remember thinking he was right.

≈ 9 ≈

Having just come in from patrol, it was strange to have to report to the Company CO. Major Holt looked up from his paperwork and smiled. "At ease Corporal, take a seat. As you know the battalion's service over here is slowly coming to an end, and we will be going home. You have a very fine service record, one of which we are all very proud, your peers hold you in high esteem, something even the most junior NCO or commissioned officer should aspire to. You have done very credibly, and the army likes what it sees. The General Officer Task Force Command has asked me to outline to you what your future might be if you were to sign up for a career in the permanent force."

I remember gripping the chair in shock, but there was no mistaking Holt's enthusiasm. "Immediately you would be promoted to Sergeant, and within your first year, you would be given every opportunity to rise to Warrant Officer. Normally it would take an outstanding recruit years to reach that level, however in your case the army will fast track it." It seemed unbelievable, and my heart was pounding furiously.

"Corporal, what the army is saying is this: we have an outstanding indigenous soldier we wish to hold up as an example to all young Australians, particularly our indigenous young men. The Chief of the Army is obviously keen to give you every inducement to stay. Should you transfer to the regular army you, would have to work hard, but your progress will be closely monitored and would be assured. I have your record right here; the Battalion Commander has kindly given me permission to quote from it. Let me do so now.

> 'This National Serviceman has shown great bravery, and composure under fire. He is, in the view of his immediate commanding officer, a natural leader of men, and has shown outstanding ability as a rifleman in a frontline platoon during his service in Vietnam. I have no hesitation of approving his posting in the field as Corporal and Section Commander. This National Servicemen exemplifies the highest traditions and ideals of the Australian soldier.
>
> Signed Colonel E V James
> Officer Commanding,
> Twelfth Battalion RAR Vietnam.'"

Christ, what had I done? Was this some sort of payoff for our losses? Was the Army trying to make something sweet-smelling out of a tragedy? If they were, they were wasting their time, as nothing could; but Holt was doing his best to make it easy for me.

"Corporal, this comes from the highest level. Most young regular army NCOs and officers would never achieve a report like yours during the whole of their service. If you were to stay on, you would have a flying start. We do not expect an immediate answer, but do write home and kick it around with your family. I understand you are engaged; we could patch a line through if you two need to talk. In the seven years since leaving our staff college at Duntroon, I have never heard of such an offer. Having observed you at first hand, I think you are very suited to service life."

"Thank you sir."

"Corporal, do you have any questions?"

"This is about me being an Aboriginal?"

"I think the army would like to hold you up as an example of how well your people can do, and there is nothing untoward about that."

"Thank you, sir."

"Corporal, I suppose it says to the Australian people, we called these young men up to serve their country, and look at what they have achieved. And one more thing, in the morning, I would like you up here at 0800 hours to meet Captain Gregory Bolton from Army Public Relations. He will run some media interviews, and I suppose that if it were to come up, you could say the army has asked you to stay on; but I would not go into the details. Captain Bolton is a very experienced hand and a nice chap; he will look after you."

Nui Dat was hotter than it was out in the bush, and everything was covered in a fine layer of dust. I had come out of Holt's office with the feeling the army was about to consume me.

"Mate, where have you been?"

"Toots, the Company CO wanted to see me, and I have to go back in the morning." "Yeah, you are not in any shit are you?"

"No mate, they want me to join up." Toots was shaking his head. "Didn't I say you would end up being a fucking General?"

"No, it's a lot of crap; it's because I'm an Abo."

"Dar, tell them to piss off."

"Thanks Barrel, and end up in the brig."

"Bugger it then; if the army has any payola they want to put your way, you may as well go for it."

"Dar, we should ask Chunky?" Chunky was regular army, and one of those knockabout guys who fitted in anywhere, and had been sent up from Townsville to bring us up to strength.

"Well, I am not so sure," Chunky said. "If you sign up, you are in for the long term; you can't just wander in and out of the army. But guys, this war is not all that popular back home; the public are starting to say we bloody well should not even be here." I had detected the same sentiment in Jill's letters.

"What do you think Barrel?"

"Dar, you know my view; we do our time, stay in one piece, and go home and get on with our lives."

"Barrel is right on the money," Toots added, "let's go up and grab a cold beer." The next morning I found myself waiting for a Hercules to set down.

Captain Bolton hardly seemed a typical officer. "Thanks for doing this," he said, and I was surprised by his politeness. "Corporal, I am sorry but we need to get on with it. You have a mother and father, and brothers and sisters?"

"Yes sir, parents and a sister."

"That's nice, and where do they live?"

"My parents still live on a cattle station up in the top end, and my sister lives in Sydney."

"You were born up there?"

"Yes sir."

"Look, it is very nice of you to be so courteous, but could we drop the 'sir' business while I am here? The Army is glad to have you along for this, so when we are talking to the members of the media, 'Captain' or 'Mr. Bolton' would be fine. When there's only you and I, just call me Greg. And what do your parents do on the cattle station?"

"Dad's a stockman, and mum helps in the homestead."

"What happened to you after your life there?"

"My sister and I were removed to a home for Aboriginal kids in Adelaide."

"What is this 'removed' business? You make yourself sound like a load of second-hand furniture. I would prefer to say you were 'sent to'; and what did you do there?"

"We had schooling; my sister is the eldest; she was sent to a training home for girls, and I went to one for boys."

"What training did you do there?"

"I learned to become a shearer."

"That must just about bring us to when you were called up, your occupation is listed here as shearer."

"Yes Greg, I was a gun, before I came in."

"So Darain, this has meant a huge drop in income for you."

"Yes, it certainly has."

"Darain, thank you. At 0900 hours, we have scheduled a session with the media, who are due from Saigon. Would you please talk to them, just as you have to me? But let's say that they throw in a few curly ones, as they sometimes do, I will be there, and you can refer them to me. That will slow them down while you and I consider how we deal with the question. They know perfectly well they are not allowed to ask anything that might put the security of our forces at risk. If they do, just decline to answer; they know the form. You are a smart-looking soldier; just be yourself while they film and snap away. Same drill with an interviewer, ignore the camera. The army will put on morning tea. I want you to mix and chat with them, so they get a feeling for the Australian contribution."

The journos stood around as if they had seen it all before. "Good morning, my name is Greg Bolton and as many of you know, I am the Media Officer for the Australian Task Force Vietnam. Thank you for flying in this morning, and you should have your media kit about an Australian mounted operation known as 'Dingo Drive'. The aim of which was to clear an enemy staging and resupply base out of the Long Hai Mountains, and to reduce the enemy presence and influence in the province of Phuoc Tuy. This morning I would like you to meet a young National serviceman, who is an indigenous Australian from northern Australia. He was part of a blocking force comprising Charlie Company, who, with other supporting elements, was positioned across the expected breakout point.

An estimated three hundred enemy attempted their breakout, and emerged from a system of tracks, one of which came out opposite the Corporal's position, and a fierce engagement raged until daylight. Although considerably outnumbered, the Australian soldiers, most of whom were National Servicemen, held their positions. This soldier fought on until the successful link up with the pursuing Australian forces had been made. The Commander Charlie Company tells of finding the ground in front of this man's position strewn with enemy dead. He will be happy to answer your questions." I wished he had not put it that way.

"Nigel Holmes, Consolidated News. How far away was your position in relation to where the enemy emerged?"

"Around thirty to forty meters and to one side, so I was not in the direct line of fire from our other positions."

"Tim Holland, ABC-TV. What were you armed with?"

"Our standard FN 7.62 SLR."

"Jan Tennyson, Channel Eight, 'The News Hour'. How did you feel when they burst out of the jungle?"

"Very tense and scared." My answer raised a few laughs; they had obviously heard that comment before.

"Could you tell us what it was like?"

"That was our second night of waiting, so it was a very stressful time."

"Delores Foster, NCB. What did you think about killing so many?"

"There were other positions in support, and when they came straight at me, it was either me or them."

I was glad to have Toot's comment. "Mike Crab, MVS TV, and what do you do in civilian life?"

"I have a shearing run that starts in Central Queensland and often extends as far south as Tasmania."

"I guess you would earn big money?"

"Well, more than I do now." They chuckled at that.

"Married?"

"When I get back." Some were scribbling away; others used tape recorders and filmed in such a nonchalant manner, I'm never sure if they were recording or not.

"Richard Small, *Canadian News*. The US Command reports on the war effort in very positive terms. How do you see it?"

"We are winning it around here." My interviewer gave me the impression that whatever I said would not matter either way. The Captain announced a coffee break.

"Hi," she was a good-looking brunette in a bush hat and a military shirt from which the sleeves had been removed. "Have you experienced any discrimination in the Army?"

"No, I am just one of the boys."

"That's nice; would you mind doing a little segment with me in front of a camera, same sort of stuff? It won't take long." She told me where to stand for the right light and background.

"Hello, this is Ruth Dagnovich for *Australia Today*, reporting from the Australian Army base, Nui Dat, Vietnam. It is another hot sultry morning in Vietnam and I am talking to a young soldier doing his National Service over here, just like all the other boys from right across Australia. Good morning Darain, could you tell the viewers the circumstances of how you became a Corporal?" The question was unexpected, and I did not like answering it.

"I replaced a mate of mine who was killed."

"And could you tell the viewers who else in your Platoon were lost?"

"Our command bunker was hit by RPGs and we lost our Lieutenant, Sergeant, and Signalman."

"You are telling me you lost three dead out of a platoon of thirty odd men?"

"No, sadly it was four, as we also lost a mate of mine who was our Corporal and manned our M60."

"Would you talk us through that?" Bolton was looking on unperturbed, but she was aware that I was struggling.

"Viewers, this action was code named 'Dingo Drive' and was mounted by the Australian forces." I felt as though she had ambushed me and did my best to complete the segment. "We were airlifted in, and took up a blocking position across the tracks they used to get in and out of their mountain sanctuary. Other units were inserted to drive them down and on to our position."

"Tell the viewers what the enemy casualties were."

"Ruth, there were many, and other than that, I prefer not to comment." I wished she would get off it.

"Viewers, we are told there were many in front of this young soldier's position."

"They ran straight at me."

"Viewers, we were told, that he held his position while under continual attack. I think you will agree, he is a very modest young man. What are you going to do when you get home?"

"Get married."

"Sounds good."

"Thanks."

"Thank you for talking with us. This has been Ruth Dagnovich for Australia Today, with the Australian forces, Nui Dat, Vietnam."

The calls started coming in several days after the interview was shown on Australian TV, and was followed by an avalanche of mail.

"Corporal, your sister will be calling you at 1800 hours, please go up and take it?" Much to my surprise, they had sent a Signaller down to tell me.

"Hello, little brother, you were on the television last night, and I was so thrilled to see you. Everyone sends their love. I am so proud of you. I just had to phone and the Army kindly patched me through. Not long to go now and you will be home; you and Jill can come and stay here while you get organized. I must not stay, all my love, and we are all counting the days until you are home. Please write soon."

"Another call, the name is Green and he says he is a friend of yours from Goondiwindi. I can only spare you thirty seconds." The booming voice came through like we were standing in a shed. "G'day mate, Greeny here; we were watching the box last night and bugger me dead, there you were. We had to call and tell you how proud we are. We are all looking forward to buying you a beer. A gun soldier, we should have known; the bloke on the line says I have to get off, so good luck sunshine from all your mates."

A week later and the mail began. Normally I only got letters from Jill, Ern, mum and my sister. "You're a popular boy," said the CSM. "Probably all bills." Story laughed, "Any problems, come and see me." I found her longed for letter and put the others to one side. The much cherished 'My darling one' was missing and I knew immediately.

Dear Dar,

I am afraid I am going to hurt you enormously, but I can see no other way but to tell you that I do not wish to become your wife. I have prayed and sought God's divine guidance, and have begged for his forgiveness for the hurt this will cause, and now I beg for yours.

I have been deeply shocked to hear how you have killed. I abhor it, absolutely abhor it. 'Thou shall not kill,' is one of the fundamental of God's commandments, which separates us from the animals. You are no longer the gentle boy whose love and respect I sought and returned, and whom I thought loved our dear Lord as I do. I think I was so caught up in my own selfish plans that I never saw you as you are. I want you to know that I pray that God will forgive and comfort you. Over recent months, I have become involved in the anti-war movement and am implacably opposed to that wicked, vicious, and unfair war in which you are engaged. All over the world, people are protesting against it, and telling the Americans to stop their bombing and to get out of Vietnam.

Whatever the faults of the Vietnamese, they do not need our soldiers or those of the Americans to tell them how they should conduct their affairs. Their peasant existence in their peaceful villages has been going on for hundreds, perhaps thousands, of years, doing no harm to anyone. That the Americans could go in and spray their fields and forests with toxic chemicals is an abomination, to shoot and bomb them as well is an insult to the glory of God. I shall write a separate letter to Alkina to tell her of my decision. Darain, many people will applaud your soldiering and I hope you find happiness. Please respect my wishes as I must tell you that this decision has not been taken lightly. I do not wish you to write or phone me, as I would like our parting to be respectful.

Yours in our loving Savoir Jesus Christ,
Jill

I simply could not absorb it and her words hit me with the deathly sigh of a bullet.

"Jill has just given me the big heave ho." Mine was not the first, they understood, and the radio had been turned down while we read our mail.

"Shit, I am sorry," and other than that Toots was lost for words.

"Would you like to get pissed," offered Barrel? And Chunks commented, "My old lady writes those all the time; it's probably premenstrual tension; I never know from one day to the next whether

I'm Arthur or Martha."

"Would you like us to get lost?" Toots asked.

She had floored me. Brasso and Toots had already put it to me that religion did strange things to people, as they were never really convinced we were a good match. Toots later said he was half expecting it. It was said that being in Vietnam made us cling to people back home. Jill and I had written page after page, full of our love for each other. "Jesus Dar, I'm sorry; here mate, give me that pile of shit and I will weed out any crappy letters." There was one fantastic note in a copperplate hand and we pinned it up.

> "Dear Corporal,
>
> I write as a returned man of the Second AIF who fought in the Middle East, Greece, and in New Guinea, and I never got so much as a scratch, and looking back, I realize how wonderfully lucky I was. My father and his brother were on the Western Front where dad was gassed and his brother badly wounded.
>
> Corporal, your interview made me very proud to be an old soldier and an Australian; to me, your story brought it all back—the many mates who were killed, wounded, captured, and endured incarceration. Mostly, I remembered the friendships, some of which are still strong today.
>
> Keep going, doing your best, remembering always that there are thousands and thousands of us who have been there and understand. We salute you, and wish you every success, and that you come back to these dear shores safe and well.
>
> Yours very sincerely,
> Burt Russell

"Let's go up to the boozer," Toots suggested, giving the nod to the others. I had not cried since the service to farewell the boys. But living in one another's pocket, as we did, there are few secrets, and in time I got the message. Toots and the boys reckoned I was better off without her.

⚡ 10 ⚡

That morning it seemed the whole hamlet, old people, mothers, babies, and little kids had turned out to stare at the patrol amid the squeal of piglets and the cluck of chickens scratching in the dust.

I kept watch from some distance out as the old people got stuck into the Lieutenant and our Sergeant; yet in a little while, it was all smiles and good humour. We had captured a couple of stragglers, completed our search, and were out. Dunphy came over to me.

"They were raided last night, the prisoners are in poor shape and were slow to get out. The old headman reckons the VC stole most of their rice and dried fish. There is nothing we can do about that; he says they went South. Stay on the ball while I make my report."

Eric Sanders wandered over to join the radioman and the Lieutenant, and a minute or so later, the rest of the Platoon were called in for a quick briefing.

"The CO wants us to follow the VC and continue our patrol on to the next hamlet. The country is light forest with low scrub and odd patches of thick stuff. The rest of the company are strung out to the East. I know it's bloody hot, but keep your eyes skinned and watch where you put your feet. Dar, if you will take the lead with your section, we could get going."

I felt better away from the base; this was something to take my mind off her, and worse, my physical longing for her was greater than I could remember. The Platoon was well into its routine of searching hamlets to show the flag and keep the VC off balance, and I was proud to be part of it. We saw ourselves as experienced campaigners who did everything quickly and silently. I remembered thinking at the time that there had been something not quite right about that hamlet, but whether my awareness was clouded by a preoccupation with Jill, I don't know. We were not the first Australian patrol they had seen, and ours had been a copybook search.

We strung out through the bush with the captive VC in the middle. We kept well away from the tracks. It was pretty obvious that one of the prisoners was trying to slow us down; but other than that, the Platoon did a solid day's bash. When we came to a slight rise in the timber, where there was good cover, the Dunphy called a halt for the day. The mines were set, the pickets placed, and we ate our rations as the light fled. In the grey of dawn we did an hour's bash until we found a good place to brew up and have breakfast. The boys felt safe with our routine of moving out of our overnight position. We reached the next hamlet early in the morning. The same routine, and the same sounds and smells, as smokers coughed up their phlegm, mothers scolded their children, pigs squealed, and babies cried.

We left just as quietly as we had arrived. Plenty of smiles all round, and the elusive VC had been and gone. The country had changed, and we came to a small valley with a dry, eroded watercourse at the bottom. I balked at having to cross the open ground in daylight. The options were to follow the edge of the timber down until we found a place to cross. We had a break while I conferred with Myles and Eric, and it was decided I should lead my Section across, establish a position and call them over. I found a good place to cross and signalled my men to follow. As the first of them came through, I noticed where the earth had been disturbed. I yelled a warning as the first mine went off, seriously injuring Bill Pepper. My memory of it was of the shock of the explosion and the scream of men. Their AK-47s opened up and I felt a searing pain in the guts and ran to where Toots was directing his fire. I caught a glimpse of them and ran until I shot one in the face and two as they went to stand up. Silence, and then I found Toots with the side of his head blown away. Chunky was lying nearby and manning our friend's M60. I took it from him and went over and shot our two prisoners in the back of the head.

Dunphy had set up in the trees and was trying to establish our position. Our Sergeant lay quietly in the grass, nursing a nasty leg wound. The wounded were being brought in when Barrel grabbed me by my belt and dragged me into the trees. "Come on mate, you have copped one; we have to get you out of here." My boots squelched with blood but I don't remember feeling any pain. The roaring came in gentle waves, up and down, up and down. I was floating in silence, Nan was holding my hand when my great-grandfather appeared, "So glad to have met you at last; Nan has told me so much about you; she tells me that you are a lot like me. You and I are silly buggers—all my fault I am sure; I should have left a message for you never to join the army."

Great-grandfather smiled a lot. He was young like me, with a shock of ginger hair and just as Nan had said, he had freckles on his nose and cheeks. He was obviously very pleased to see me, and we sat on a log and had a beer. "Cheers, great-grandfather, this is great." They had rolled me over and I could smell the metho; then there was what felt like cold steel on my back. Voices, "you work on that side nurse, this boy is very hot," and they bathed me. The Mighty Hunter lifted me up so I was behind him, "hang on to my belt," and away we went racing through the trees, and I waved to my mother and sister as we wheeled the mob.

There was the roaring and I was floating up and down.

"This is my wife Sandra," Toots said, spreading the photos out on the blanket. "Sandy for short, everybody calls her that. We got hitched when we were seventeen. I got to tell you mate, we had to; she was three months gone. I am an old married man, and there she is, our little girl Linda, cute little thing, don't you reckon?"

"You are a lucky man," I said, picking the photo up and looking closely at the little girl with her long hair and toothy grin, sitting on her mother's knee. "I hope I have a family like yours one day."

"No sweat, you will be able to provide for a family in no time, though mind you, I do not know that I would rush it. Shit, did we have a struggle, serve us bloody right for being so randy."

"Your little girl looks like a hockey player to me; you can tell by the determined look they get," I said, just to get him going.

"No Dar, her mum plays netball so I reckon she will be good at that."

"Toots, I am sure she will."

"Dar, I know what we will do. Sandy has a friend she went to school with. I reckon you and Sally would get on a real treat; hang on, I might have a photo of her here; she was Sandy's bridesmaid. Here mate, there she is, that's us on the big day; she's a bloody good-looking lady. When we get back, you come and stay with us and you can meet her. I have a spare set of clubs and the girls play golf, so it will be great. For a moment, I was standing there with Sally; she had looked lovely. She has her own hair-dressing salon, so you would never have to pay for a haircut again."

There was the roaring and I was floating. I woke to find myself staring at a high ceiling; it startled me to watch my chest rise and fall. Then the thought that I was obviously still alive, there was the foot of the bed, and in the next bed there was a bloke with a tent over his legs.

"Are you awake?" I raised a hand.

"Welcome to the world. You have been out to it ever since you came in last night." "Where are we?"

"Concord Repatriation Hospital in Sydney." Then I remembered, seeing Toots, and I could not stop my tears.

"Mate, you're okay, I've lost both my bloody feet." That was some return to the land of the living.

Wounded or not, I knew I was in big trouble, and some weeks later, and quite unexpectedly, WO Story and Major Holt turned up at my bedside. They were in civvies. Their tour had ended without further incident, and they told me that Eric Sanders was recovering from his wounds in Brisbane. It was not until their visit that the reality of my situation started to hit home. As much as I had thought it through, I was resigned to accept whatever punishment the army dished out. The reality was that I had no regret that I had shot those VC, for in my mind they had been part of the ambush.

"There may be a certain amount of comfort," Holt said, "in knowing that you will face all this bravely, and I wonder if there is anything you would like me to do on your behalf?" What could I say or do? I could only lie there and smile, as Holt continued, "There is not a lot more that life can throw at you Corporal, is there? As soon as you are well enough, you will be formally charged with the unlawful killing of unarmed prisoners of war and have to face a court martial. I expect that when I see you again, it will be as a witness, so it is not appropriate that I make any comment on the case. I believe that you will be subject to the discipline of the Provost Marshal. Charlie Company suffered a grievous loss that day, and on behalf all those in it, I extend to you our best wishes for a full and speedy recovery."

I found Holt's approach overly formal and a little awkward. But I was much comforted by Mick Story's comments. "Corporal, the men hold you in high regard, and that includes myself. I can only say that it has been a privilege to serve with you, and I am sure that you will face the future with fortitude and dignity." I dozed a lot, and would wake to find my sister or one of the boys, who may have been passing through, sitting by my bed. My thoughts of what had gone wrong at Hamlet 267 were by then crystal clear. All that anguish over the VC taking their food was part of it; there had been chooks and pigs wandering about all over the place. I blamed myself; the Mighty Hunter would have seen it in one, and so should have I.

Eventually the army acted; I was charged, flown up to Townsville, where I continued my convalescence. They were in no hurry to deal with me. The papers and television were full of contempt for the war, and in an inexplicable, if spiteful way, that contempt had been spread to include former combatants like myself. The boys wandered in to visit, and oddly enough, the Lieutenant and Chunky came in together. Chunks had yet to report to his new posting down at Puckapunyal. I worried that Myles's career might have suffered; I doubted that any of us would ever be the same again. Reputedly, the army was unforgiving of young officers. We sat on a park bench while Chunky handed out beers and I caught up with the news.

"We were all so down," Chunky said. "I honestly think it was a mass grieving. Battalion sent us over to Vung Tau for a spell; you have never seen anything like it; we all went out and got monumentally pissed. All we talked about was how you and Toots had saved us that day." Myles had been subdued. "It was incredible," he added, "there were many tears shed, which I am certain did us the world of good."

"Myles," I said, "I am sorry about your career, I am pretty sure I would have stuffed that up for you. I can imagine how uncompromising they are."

"Frankly Dar, I would be happier if you didn't feel like that. I was in command and whether I am ever charged or not, we will just have to wait and see. My wife and I have thought about it, and if it happens, I will get out. Dar, the boys are anxious about you. Is there anything you need, or would like us to do, and how is the recovery coming along?"

110

"They reckon I will be as good as new. A close call, fantastic things those choppers, still if I had gone, it might have saved everyone a lot of trouble."

"For Christ's sake, don't talk like that," Chunks said angrily. "I am told a lawyer has been appointed to defend me." Myles nodded, "Good, because I propose to give you such a rap they will think you are a bloody angel. I think the shock of us losing Toots, and your own severe wounds and loss of blood had a great deal to do with it. In our eyes, you are a hero, and regardless of the outcome, nothing is ever going to change our view. I think we should best leave it like that. I can't stay and chat, as I have to catch a plane. The next time we meet will probably be at the hearing. Strange, how they have not set a date. The boys all want to testify, so keep your pecker up. It was a hell of a thing to have our tour end like that." I found Myles very reassuring, and he embraced me like a brother before he left.

"Nice of him," Chunky commented, "he doesn't say much, but I know he is bloody concerned. And mate, the last time I saw you, was not so good, I thought we were going to lose you. Talking of which, Eric has been medically discharged; they may have saved his leg, but he says it will never be right." We sat in companionable silence remembering. "Dar, while I'm here, we all want to know if we can do anything, just say the word. They all want to be witnesses; we want the Court to know that you and Toots got us out of that; can you understand, because it is important to us that you do?

"Chunks, I do."

"Dar, it is great to be back, and all this has made me keen to get out; we cannot wait. And how do they treat you here? I heard MP's can be real bastards."

"I am all right, but I get the feeling things are going to change once the court deals with me, so that might be a good time to check me out." The very thought of that had been nagging at me, and I was glad for the opportunity to say so.

"Chunks, I think it is bloody nice of you to come, but do me a favour and explain to the blokes that I just did what I had to do. We all know you can't go around shooting prisoners, and I do not want them feeling as if I have been unfairly treated. Tell them, I will wear whatever the court dishes out. What I did was bloody stupid, but I wish I could have done something for poor old Toots. I cannot help thinking how his little girl and wife must be so sad. And how about you? I bet your old lady is pleased to have you home. I think this war is buggered anyway, and everyone reckons we ought to get out."

Hardly a day went by without a visit and for a while it seemed the army had forgotten about me. Judging from what the papers were saying, I could not help thinking that Jill would feel more vindicated than ever.

≈ 11 ≈

At last the army moved. My counsel was a barrister in civilian life, and a Major in the Army Reserve. It was his view that the army was taking its time because it did not want the publicity, and that even the politicians were distancing themselves from the war. He thought that the longer it took, the better, and made no comment of the right or wrong of the case, and carefully took me through my life prior to my call up, and my service in Vietnam, in minute detail.

"I am anxious that you fully understand what you are being charged with, the army's case, and our defence." Jeremy took a lofty, if almost humorous view of it, and had opened a briefcase to extract four bulging folders.

"Read these; they comprise The Army Law Manual 1964, The Defence Act 1903-64, The Army Act of 1881 of Great Britain, and lastly, the Australian Military Regulations and Orders. Don't worry if it gets a bit tedious; but if you get the general thrust of it, that will be a big plus. It is important for you to understand what is going on as the case develops. We have more character references than we could possibly need, which will make it abundantly clear just how highly you are regarded. I also have plenty of witnesses who will testify on our behalf. However, this cuts both ways; they can be cross examined, have their stories probed, slanted and contradicted, and of course you must not react no matter what you hear. There are bound to be things that you dispute, but please make sure you tell me and not the Court. I think that you just want to get on with it, and take whatever they dish out on the chin. Have I got that right?" I reassured my counsel that he had it perfectly.

"That is as I thought. I want you to have no such feeling. I want you to fight. I want the court to see the sort of man you are; if we do not get the verdict we want, I want them to at least see you as a heroic soldier who was prepared to fight until your last breath. That is what they will expect, and it will influence the way they think. We are not disputing what happened; what is important for us is to demonstrate the underlying reason. From what I have learned, that is very much your style anyway. I will lead you down paths that will strike you as blindingly obvious. Questions like 'Corporal, when your sister read your call up notice to you over the phone, could you tell us where you were, and how you reacted?' Answer, 'I was driving with my cousin to another shearing shed and I took the opportunity to phone my sister in Sydney to see how she was. There are no phones available to us at the sheds unless the owner will give their permission and allow us to use theirs at the homestead. After being told of my call up, I think I probably swore under my breath, reported for my medical and got my affairs in order, ready to do my National Service.'

You see, what we are telling the court is this, 'I did not shirk and I willingly reported in to do my duty.' Take your time in answering, but do answer the questions fully; we have all the time in the world. This could be a lengthy process. I think you will be your own best witness. I want you to keep a military bearing at all times and present yourself as the crack soldier you are. We do not want to make it easy for them; we want to squash any prejudices and any hang-ups they may bring to court. Do you have any questions?" The more I got to know Jeremy, the more impressed I became as his reasoning sounded fine to me.

"I intend to address the court," he said, "about the international legal view of that war, and in doing so, I run the risk of sounding a bit of a lefty, a 'pinkie' if you like, and a professional whinger. But I will be making a point. The fact is, apart from the growing anti-war sentiment here and in America, there is now a substantial and growing body of legal opinion that holds that the American, and by imputation, our own involvement in the war, is illegal."

"But that is unbelievable," I said in exasperation. I had been quite literally been blown away by the idea.

"Exactly, I want to sow the seed of doubt, and make them feel they are being made party to an even greater wrong. Our approach is based on the view that we and the Americans have illegally intervened in what is essentially a civil war. There has been no Declaration of War, nor can it be justified by any assumed right of collective self-defence. I hope you can follow the reasoning; it is what I would call an international jurist's view. They will no doubt grasp it with both hands, turn it inside out and upside down, and use it against us." I could see it. "No, you go for it, Jeremy, you let it rip."

"Good man, I think we are getting there."

Three weeks later and after a fitful sleep, I was raring to go. "This is your day in court. How do you feel?" asked my counsel.

"Bloody nervous, but apart from that, I'm glad it's on."

"Good, you must listen carefully to the questions, speak slowly and clearly, which will give you time to think." Brasso had encouraged us to breathe deeply during the stress of battle, and I intended to do so again.

"How do you plead?"

"Not guilty." The prosecution stated their case, the bulk of which I could only agree with. Then Jeremy began my defence. "We intend to show the court that in the heat and stress of an enemy ambush unleashed upon the soldiers of this patrol, and the subsequent battle being fought for their survival, that the accused was not responsible for his actions when the alleged incident is said to have taken place. We will show that this soldier was gravely wounded, suffering from a catastrophic loss of blood, was in a deep state of shock, which had the effect of impairing his judgment, separating him from the reality of the events happening around him, and that he was in a state of rapidly approaching fatal trauma. Expert medical evidence will be called to show the near fatal extent of this man's wounds."

The first day closed halfway through the argument about the illegality of the war. I spent a lonely night, churning the whole mess over and over. It was bit late for Brasso, Toots, and all the others, to be told that Regina, the Queen of England, was not at war with North Vietnam, but that apparently as the Queen of Australia she was, although it had never been declared. That was contrary to everything we had been told. My counsel held that it was legally untenable under any reasonable interpretation of international law. My head was spinning in outrage at all the army's nonsense.

"The Crown calls Colonel Evelyn Vernon James."

"Colonel James, were you the Battalion Commander at the time of the alleged incident?"

"I was."

"Would you please take the court through the sequence of events leading to the alleged incident, the alleged incident itself, and what happened immediately after?"

"I planned and mounted Operation Rolling Thunder, a series of sweeping patrols carried out by our companies. This called for a loose extended formation designed to cover maximum ground in the search area. The operational map was divided into grids in which the villages and hamlets were numbered and there are brief notes as to the topography, including known special features and vegetable cover. Each company was given their own area to sweep. All Company, Platoon, and Section Commanders would have known their objective and area of responsibility at all times.

Our intelligence reports indicated that light enemy contact might be made. These aggressive patrols were part of our continual plan to deny the enemy space and time in which to consolidate their influence in the province. During this operation, Companies A, B, and C were deployed while the other three were held in reserve, having just completed their own sweeps. Rolling Thunder was mounted on the second of May and was designed to run until the search area had been covered.

At 1200 hours, I should mention that these signals are logged. I was in the Signals bunker at Battalion HQ where I listened to a report from the Commander, Second Platoon, Lieutenant Myles Dunphy, that he had searched Hamlet 267, and that the elderly headman had told of a raid by up to ten Viet Cong, who had taken all their rice and dried fish and threatened to kill him if he resisted. The patrol had captured two Viet Cong stragglers. I remember feeling particularly pleased at that, as I had wanted the intelligence from an up-to-date interrogation.

Also, I thought news of their capture would spread respect for our force among the villagers, I subsequently learned the prisoners were in poor shape and were being a hindrance. The Viet Cong were reported as having taken the path leading to Hamlet 271, in the adjoining grid. I heard Major Holt, Commanding Officer, Charlie Company, give the Platoon Commander the task of following and engaging them. I did not intervene because I approved, knowing the Platoon was very capable, the reports for the remainder of the day were normal.

At about 0550 hours on the morning of the eighth, I heard the Lieutenant report that he had searched Hamlet 271.

At 1320 hours, the Lieutenant called for assistance; he was under attack and taking casualties, and I marked his position. I heard Major Holt say he was on his way and estimating he would be there by 1500 hours.

At 1327 hours, Lieutenant Dunphy reported the action had been broken off, and that his losses were one killed and five wounded.

At 1343 hours, the wounded were evacuated.

At 1410 hours, I heard the body of our deceased casualty had been recovered.

At 1420 hours, the position of an enemy minefield was given, and the Second Platoon was noted as being on the way to meet with Mr. Holt's force.

At 1450 hours, Major Holt reported that he was with the Second Platoon, I acknowledged.

At 1515 hours, Major Holt reported that two Viet Cong prisoners had allegedly been shot dead by the accused. He reported that it appeared to be a heat of the moment reprisal for the death of Private Peter Morgan, their Section machine gunner and a close friend of the accused. The remains of the Viet Cong were buried. The accused had been severely wounded and evacuated. I recommended they withdraw a few kilometres back along Major Holt's route before harbouring for the night, he concurred.

At 1830 hours, Major Holt reported the situation as normal."

"Call Lieutenant Myles Dunphy." Myles appeared pale and stressed. "Lieutenant, in your own words, would you take us through the action of that day? Just tell the court what happened."

"We had stepped up the pace of our patrol in order to pursue a party of Viet Cong. The country was light forest with scrub underneath and with areas where there was little cover. The Sections were in extended formation, and in sight of the next man. The accused was in the lead.

The prisoners were in the middle. Our route was well away from, but roughly parallel to the main path leading to the next hamlet, I would say we kept four to five hundred meters in from it. The path appeared to be well-used and we were wary of it. The prisoners held us up, which in hindsight, I now realize was a deliberate ploy to gain time to set up their ambush.

We had halted at the edge of the timber, where the country fell away in a wide and shallow hollow, going down to what looked like an eroded water course we would have to cross. It was very hot and the prisoners had just been given a drink, and I remember telling their guard to make them move along and to keep them quiet. The Corporal wanted to find a place to cross where there was more cover, we discussed it, but I decided we should carefully cross in single file, a Section at a time.

That decision was entirely mine. In hindsight, if we had gone further up toward the track, as I wanted, it would have brought us into direct contact. They had taken cover on a rise of low scrub overlooking the slope. I should explain that in Vietnam it had been generally accepted that the accused was our eyes and ears, and the men had faith in him. He was raised out in the Australian bush and has much greater powers of observation than any of us. His ability in that regard was outstanding, he could see things the rest of us missed; his skills have been recorded in the reports of previous actions.

The Corporal began to cross and when he was well down, I saw him look back and signal his Section to follow. He kept watch as they drew level and passed him, when he suddenly turned, made the sign, and screamed 'mines!' But one had already been triggered and simultaneously enemy fire began from our right and men started going down. Fire was quickly returned; our Sergeant had been hit; and those in the open scrambled back." Myles and I were back there. There was silence as the Lieutenant sipped a glass of water and composed his thoughts.

"The action began when the Private William Pepper triggered a mine and the firing began. We reported our position and that we were under attack. Our first major response was from Private Morgan, who sent bursts from his M60 into their position. The accused was running back and yelling for his men to get off that slope; he then charged the enemy position, killing all three. During the brief fire fight, Private Morgan had received a fatal wound to the head and Sergeant Sanders had been shot in the leg. As soon as the firing stopped, we attended to our casualties. We called in a dust off; I spoke briefly with Major Holt and went to check on our wounded. I heard two shots, but was not immediately aware of their significance. After checking my men, I went to have a look at the enemy position, where I found three bodies.

The Corporal had been severely wounded; it was clear to us that we probably owed our lives to him, and the late Private Morgan. When I saw him, he was sitting with his back to a tree; his lower abdomen and legs were covered in blood, as was his shirt; and he seemed unaware that he was badly wounded. My impression was that he was in a very bad way, although he was just sitting there quietly. I remember saying something like, 'Hang in there and we will get you to Vung Tau as quick as we can.' While I was with him, he kept saying, 'The bastards got Toots; the bastards got Toots!' He was referring to the late Private Peter Morgan, and there were tears streaming down his face and I realized he was in shock.

Several of our men were trying to stem his bleeding. The men behaved very well; they collected our dead, and set up a perimeter, so the wounded could be lifted out. It was not until the dust off had occurred that I realized that the bodies under a poncho were those of our prisoners. I asked what had happened, and was told that the accused had shot them with the late Private Morgan's M-60. We buried them before we left for our rendezvous with Major Holt's party."

"Thank you Lieutenant, you may step down."

"Call Major Barrington Holt."

"Mr. Holt, how would you describe the state of morale of the men in Charlie Company at the time of this patrol?"

"Proud, confident, professional, but also they were tired and stressed."

"Could you tell us why?"

"They had melded as a unit; they knew their strengths and weaknesses, had been bloodied in battle, and were confident they could defeat the enemy. The Company had suffered heavy losses, and had won high praise for their participation in an earlier operation known as 'Dingo Drive'. This was mounted to remove the enemy out of the Long Hai Mountains, for which the Company earned unit citations, and individual decorations from the United States and our Task Force Commands.

However, our units are given a heavy workload and there is not really the opportunity given for our men to shed the stress that builds up through losses and continual patrolling. There is a particular doctrine in circulation, a theory of command that holds that stressed and keyed up soldiers are less likely to sustain casualties, I lean toward this doctrine. The unit had suffered losses which the men had to accept. They had a little over three weeks to serve before their return to Australia. The morale of Charlie Company was about the same as the other companies in the Battalion, and was about what I would have expected, given what they had achieved."

"Major Holt, could you tell the court what you know of the state of the accused's morale at that time?"

"I believe it would have been good; he was promoted after 'Dingo Drive', which was to replace the late Corporal John Braithwaite who had been mortally wounded during that operation. They were close friends. I think he would also have been feeling proud of his own achievements, which were considerable, and still be grieving the losses of his Platoon. I would also say that they were a particularly close knit unit.

After talking with Mr. Dunphy, his new Platoon Commander, I instructed our Company Sergeant Major to do what he could to ease the new Corporal into his responsibilities. He said he would run some informal sessions for him and other junior NCO's in order to boost their confidence. WO Story is a Warrant Officer of outstanding ability and with great experience in the training of men. He and I also thought it would be a good plan to ensure the Corporal was kept as busy as possible. At Company and Battalion level, the view had been formed that he was particularly suited to the military life; he was demonstrably fearless in action and had a natural aptitude for leadership. He was popular, held in high regard by his peers, and I and his immediate superiors were very satisfied with his performance.

It is on record that I put in a recommendation for recognition of this soldier's conduct under sustained enemy action during 'Dingo Drive'. I would think it is also highly relevant that Mr. Dunphy, his present Platoon Commander, also made a report highly commending his conduct at the time of this alleged incident. Mr. Dunphy described to me how the Section Commander had rallied his men and had charged the enemy position, wiping out all three enemy. I was also made aware how severely wounded the Corporal was at the time of the alleged incident, and that only a moment before, he had discovered his closest friend had been mortally wounded. I think he would have been overwhelmed.

"Thank you Mr. Holt, you may step down."

"That went well for us," my counsel said, "no harm at all. I think they will want to throw it out. We have clearly established your condition at the time; the army doesn't want this; so keep your pecker up." But always in the back of my mind was the thought that we may have been kidding ourselves. After all, who knew what went on in the minds of such men? Gilbert Soames, the civilian Judge, was from Sydney and no doubt hoped the hearing would be dealt with quickly, so there was time for renewing old friendships with a leisurely lunch or two, and some golf. Phillip Kerry was a Regular Army Colonel, who would have seen that whatever the outcome, reputations would be ruined, and he would have preferred not to be a part of it. In his view, this trial was all about dealing with the great unknown consequences of war, and trying to rationalize them after the battle, and this was nothing more than a layman's way of dealing with the terribleness of armed conflict. The hearing was also to be the last assignment for Brigadier Richard Johnson, who would soon retire as Deputy Director of Military Planning, and who appeared peeved to be ending his career in a display of the Army's dirty washing.

The waiting got to me, and I thought they might be still arguing whether we have been fighting and dying in someone else's civil war. I realized I was starting to think like Jeremy. In truth, all the high-minded talk about the legality or otherwise of the war had washed over me, as deep down I knew they were not about to let me or anyone else kill defenceless prisoners and get away with it.

When the sitting was recalled, the verdict came as no surprise and I was relieved it was over. The finding seemed to go on forever and I was so wound up by that stage that only snatches of it stuck.

"... and there are no circumstances under which the responsibility for the well-being and safe conduct of prisoners of war can be avoided... the sentence shall include the time the prisoner has already been held, including his hospitalization and convalescence, and upon its completion, he shall be dishonourably discharged from Her Majesty's Australian Military Forces."

When the gist of it sunk in, all I could think about was that I only had a few months of incarceration to serve. The way I saw it, this was a much better outcome than had been dished up to those we had left behind.

"On the command 'Move!' convicted prisoner number N X 4739621 will cut the lawn edges. Now Move! Move! Come on, we have not got all day, you low grade bastard." The small pair of nail scissors had rubbed my fingers raw and after snipping away at the thick grass for hour after hour, I was nowhere near finished.

"On the command 'Move!' convicted prisoner number N X 4739621 will clean the toilet block until he can see his ugly face in the urinals and toilet bowls before returning the tooth brush to the issuing officer. Now Move! you useless bag of shit!"

I counted the days.

⚡ 12 ⚡

On the day my younger brother was released, I was up in Townsville to collect him; he had wasted away to nothing, and I was shocked. I gave him a hug and for some time, I was unable to speak.

"What have they done to you?" I asked, which he dismissed with a shrug. "You are coming down to stay with me while I build you up, and you get your life back together."

"Sis, thanks for coming up. I can't tell you how good this is."

"Have they hurt you Dar?"

How could he smile, but he was. "No way sis, but it is bloody good to be alive and out of that place. I guess people gravitate to their own level, being a prison guard would have to be one of the most miserable occupations there is. That is the last time I am going to talk about what has been a bloody awful experience. Tell me about your life in Sydney; is there a man in it yet?"

That was Dar, and I had to admire how he had already put it behind him.

"There is, but it is a bit complicated."

"By that I assume he is married."

"Dar, I am so busy with our catering business since Hanna and I took the plunge that I really do not have time for romance. The current one just happened; you will meet him. Gerard has been through a very unhappy marriage breakup, and perhaps I was lonelier than I knew. Please don't ask me how I feel, because I don't know myself."

I stopped at a pub so that he could relax in the sun and enjoy a beer.

"Dar, the move to Sydney was the smartest thing I have ever done; the business has taken off, and all the connections we made in Adelaide have been marvellous for us. On the commercial side, we are running two staff canteens and catering for boardroom lunches and corporate functions, that's product launches and so on. Hanna and I did very well out of selling the Adelaide business, and for that we have to thank Henri. Those two really adore Sydney and have been very generous to me. They were deeply shocked at what happened."

But really, the strangest thing for me was realizing I was a success, and wanting to share it with my brother. "The boys send their love, and have been wonderful to me. They now bring in stuff from all over the world. Keep your eye on those two, because once they get themselves organized, their business will really take off. And please do not forget to thank Henri; he invested your money and it has grown substantially."

"Sis, it is really thanks to you, but I will; that is fantastic."

"Dar, now that I know what it is like to be in love, sometimes I feel like a beached whale, neither one thing nor the other." My brother laughed. "My first boyfriend," I continued, "made me very conscious of our differences. Hanna and Henri saw through him straight away, and wanted me to end it. Funny, but when I did, it really upset me. Do you think Jill was a bit like that, a little prejudiced underneath her veneer of Christian respectability?"

"I don't know, and who cares; maybe she was, and it is all a bit academic now." I was so relieved to hear him talk like that.

"I was telling you about Gerard," my brother seemed keen to listen, if subdued, "perhaps I am the rebound from his broken marriage. I would not mention him to my friends, certainly not to Hanna and Henri, as they do not approve. Meanwhile it just drifts along." "That's fine," he said, "as long as you are okay. Jill was my dream; up there you needed someone to cling to. It was my thoughts of her and our future life together that kept me on my toes—where we would live; how I would earn a living; and what sort of a husband and father I would be? And at least it got me through it. My mate Toots had this thing about her. 'Dar, old son,' he would say, 'I don't care how bloody beautiful she is; if she's into religion, and disapproves of you having a few beers with the boys, your language and your stream of off-colour jokes, it is not going to work and your life is going to be hell. Mate, she actually thinks you have seen the light, but I happen to know that that is bullshit.' When I thought about it afterwards, I realized he was probably right."

I also thought that Toots had had it right.

"Girls keep track of these things," I commented, "and Coreen wrote to say that she and Ern want another child; they sound very happy, except that he is away all the time, and she says Jill has met someone in the church." We were silent for a while.

"Good for her. Sis, tell me about your friend Heather. She sounds nice."

"You will meet her. She is a very switched on lady. I would leave things as they are so she continues to act for you. Her husband Tom is the Fairburn of Fairburn and Carne, the stockbrokers. Oh, and I never told you, I flew up to see mum and dad. I could not bear the thought of anyone else explaining your case to them. And I did not want them getting it third hand. They were very calm and understood; their love for you is just the same. They know I was coming to get you. Aunty Viv told me they both hit the grog pretty hard when we were taken. To give them their due, the mission did a lot to get them off it, but it has taken its toll, on dad more than her; he is not as strong as he was.

Arrawatta has been sold again, and to another English crowd, and dad says they are letting the place slip. And they are certainly not doing much for our people. I got them the best kerosene refrigerator I could buy and I send them a little extra money, not that it is much use to them up there. They are managing well, no television yet, and they listen to the radio. I think it is wonderful to be able to fly in and out on the mail plane. Mum was insistent that I pass on her love, and to remind you to sing to Nan. Mum told me how she goaded the old men into putting on a fertility dance for the young people. She choreographed it with dad. I can see Nan's influence there; she was worried they would forget how to do it. Isn't that amazing?"

He smiled and said I sounded like our mother.

"Dar, as much as I love mum, of all the influences in my life, I owe my success to Nan; she was such a marvellous woman. All those hours I spent in her kitchen, learning to cook, or pretending I was the lovely Lady Sarah hosting a tea party. That dear old thing, she was such a wonderful teacher and so encouraging; they are wonderful memories. She had a knack of coming down to my age; I often think of it. To think that all those years ago she taught herself from any old cookbook, she could get her hands on. Theirs was a great love story. I am sure it is the prettiest one I have ever heard. I always thought it was lovely being named after her; it was as if she knew what I would do; I think it is really something. There is not a day goes past when I don't sing to her and tell her what I am doing; when I look up and I see her and Fritz, I feel happy."

"Sis, I would not mind betting they feel pretty satisfied as well."

⚡ 13 ⚡

I knew nothing of Sydney's restaurant scene, and when we were seated, I met Gerard for the first time and he was not the sort of person I expected. I was aware he was of Greek extraction, although there was no trace of an accent; he was pudgy, rather than being overweight. Add a pasty face, slicked down hair, gold rings and a watch, and one very sloppy handshake, and that was my sister's boyfriend.

"The likeness between you and Alkina is amazing," Gerard said.

Heather was something else; she had a shock of red hair, a vivacious smile, and an easy yet confident manner. My sister had been so full of Heather's doings on the drive down that when we met, I would never have guessed at her profession. She was a few years older, and may have been a former top model. Alkina had said she had a young family, and as I was soon to discover, she was one very smart lawyer. My sister clearly thought she was as good as Christmas, and some of it must have rubbed off as she had grown in confidence, and had become something of a fashion plate herself.

Heather had a charming manner; she leant across as if what she was about to say was confidential, "Dar, your sister is my favourite client, and your greatest fan. I practically get a daily update. I do seriously, but never mind; she is a very talented and hardworking lady." There was obviously a good deal of mutual admiration and my sister pushed it along, "Dar, they do tend to put it on in Sydney, but if you want to get organized, stay close to Heather." Alkina had a lot of Nan's disarming charm, and told a very funny story about a corporate function where the chief executive's mistress was given an award for outstanding achievement. Gerard ordered drinks and seemed to be there to fetch and carry. The conversation darted from the state of Heather's children, to payroll tax, to a new recipe my sister proposed to serve at a function. There was James and Patrick's business, mutual friends, or something they had seen at the theatre. Gerard seemed to have little to offer other than to sip at his gin and tonic and sit around and look bored.

Heather liked an audience, although most of it was for Alkina's benefit. She had a fund of legal stories and the ladies were in sparkling form, and lunching with them was very different from anything I had known. My sister was talking to Gerard when Heather turned to me. "And Dar, now you are in Sydney. What are you going to do?"

"Have a break before I go back to shearing. Heather, you people are way too fast for me." Looking back, our chat had obviously been preplanned.

"Oh, I wouldn't say that," she said almost disapprovingly. "Your sister told me what happened, and perhaps now it is time to move on. Why not give Sydney a go? It could do you a lot of good; just look at her, she handles it like a trooper. You've have had a pretty rough trot, and sometimes these things can work out better than you think. I don't suppose you know that James and Patrick are looking for someone to organize their warehouse. It is a job that will grow, but right now, they need someone to assemble the orders and do the deliveries. Their business is doing very nicely, thank you." Alkina was making a great show of talking with Gerard.

"Take my card," she said, "give it some thought and give me a call." We chatted about the war, until she leaned forward and lowered her voice, "Your sister would love you to stay, and you never know, you might even meet a nice lady. Perhaps I should not say, but she needs someone she can call on in a hurry, so you can earn a bit of extra cash on the side. She wants to build you up and see you get back on your feet."

My decision was not that hard. I could always go back to shearing; but my decision certainly changed my life. About the smartest thing I could find about "Patrick, James and Co Pty Ltd, Importers and Purveyors of Fine Foods" was the spectacular sign slung across the front. Their dilapidated warehouse had peeling paint, and cracked windows and the state of the rear of the premises, particularly the loading dock, was worse, and the main roller shutter hung by a thread. I had been up for hours for my first day on my new job, and was sitting on the front step as the street slowly came to life. Across the road a woman parked and walked my way.

"Good morning, I am Darain," I announced brightly.

"Good for you," she said, letting herself in, and shutting the door behind her. She was followed by a middle-aged lady who aggressively parked her black Rover, forcing its passenger side front wheel carelessly up on the pavement. She slammed the door and marched up to me. "Would you be a part of this organization?"

"Not yet, but I am about to be; I will be doing the warehousing and deliveries."

"Oh, you will, will you?" I could readily see that she had already puffed herself up and was ready to fly right off the handle. "Then you may not be aware that these people have had my order for over a month; and I am trying to run a business. I simply cannot imagine how they have the audacity to advertise." The front doors were suddenly flung open, and the first lady reappeared, as if finding irate people arguing on her doorstep first thing in the morning was nothing unusual.

"Madam, if you have a complaint you had better direct it at me," and to me, she said, "and excuse me, but who are you?"

"I am here to do the deliveries."

"The brother back from Vietnam? Well thank God for that."

I stood back to let her attend to her customer. When they were done, she came around the counter to me.

"I am Margaret," she announced, "but around here it's Peggy, as you will see the place is a complete shambles. I will show you around, and you had better get used to the complaints, these people are fed up." She found me the keys to the truck and said it was a little way down the road, and disappeared to answer the phone. A quick reconnoitre, and I found the old Bedford where it had been abandoned half way down the street. I nursed it to a garage, had a battery and tires fitted, a grease and oil change, and gave it a quick clean-up. By the end of the first day, I had delivered two loads, and before I left that night, I had loaded the truck so I could make an early start.

Peggy had not exaggerated; those who came in and demanded their orders, provided they carted it themselves, were helped; the rest just waited. Despite this, the phones rang and further orders were placed. James was interstate and Patrick appeared to spend his life on the phone, or being balled out over the counter by irate customers. Those first days nearly put me off having anything to do with the business. I rationalized that I had only taken it on to please my sister. I drove with a map of Sydney spread out on the seat beside me. After a few weeks of finding my way around, things began to settle down.

It would have been an early Friday night some six or so weeks later; Peg was still there, and she seemed at ease with the world; she said the irate calls had ceased, and that the business had picked up. I had wondered about her; she was a good-looking lady, with a ready smile and something nice to say. We had devised the paperwork between us, but she was the only one who knew who was who. Normally she was gone before I got back. "Chaos no longer reigns," she commented, and watched as I backed the truck in and began locking up.

"Peg, that sounds great." Perhaps I was a bit slow, for suddenly it occurred to me that she may have been waiting.

"Dar, the last guy just took the truck and we never saw him again. When it was found a couple of weeks later, the cops said he had probably used it to do some contract carting for himself." She shook her head at the thought and laughed.

"Okay," I said, "that's me for the week." Then I took the plunge, "Peg, why don't you and I go out for a drink?"

"Dar, that sounds like a nice idea." I had supposed she was spoken for.

The local pub was one of those sprawling, much modified, pre-war places that all look the same, down to the same aluminium tables and chairs. The trees were hung with fairy lights. I ushered her to a table and went for our drinks. Taking a sip of beer, I took one look at her, and the scene, and I must have looked pleased with myself.

"You look happy, so do let me in on the secret," she had smiled at me as she said this.

"Peg, it is just that I have not done this for a long, long while."

"You sound like you may have been doing time."

I smiled at the comment, but she was serious. "Yeah,' I replied, "you could say that; my number came out of a barrel and I got a ticket to Vietnam. Peg, believe me, this is a whole lot better." Her frown was still there, but now she was embarrassed.

"Dar, I am sorry. I knew you had been; I was just being a smarty pants." She raised her glass. "Welcome home. It is not a very popular war, is it? I think the public are tired of all the bullshit attached to it. I don't think we ever did understand it." I laughed; it was a comment I had heard before. "I would not worry, because neither did we."

I had to watch myself with Jill, but I doubted I would need to with her. As we spoke of Vietnam, I did not sanitize it; her eyes were glued to mine as she listened. That country could have been in another galaxy. Peg's smile crept out from her eyes; the rest of her expression followed. But it did not seem like the time or the place to trawl over it again, and I changed the subject. "That's enough of me, what about yourself?"

She never held back. "Dar, my life has been rather mundane by comparison. I was the second of four kids, and left school to go to secretarial college. I did bookkeeping and learned how to bash a typewriter. I was a sixteen-year-old kid, who drank too much, got in with the wrong crowd, and married too young. I must have been impossible, and of course it was to the wrong bloke. I can't imagine what I put my parents through. The usual story, I would not listen. But, as these things turn out, my awakening was not long in coming. My dear husband did time for attempting to supplement his income with an armed robbery. At nineteen, he knew it all; mind you, I honestly thought he did. I was all of twenty-one and already a battle-weary wife when he got out. I had waited, and what a joke that was, as he went right back to his former routine of broads, booze, and being a wise guy, and I woke up to myself in a hurry."

She saw herself clearly.

"Dar, may I tell you something? This is the best job I have ever had, and I think those two are the nicest blokes you could ever work for. I mean you and I know they are too soft, effete, and impractical, and they would be the first to admit it. They expect the business to run itself, but of course, it does not and never will. If it wasn't for their great agencies and products, and people like Heather Fairburn and your sister, they would not have survived. Dar, you're good for them; I can see it already;

you know what has to be done and just get on with it. The boys know everyone in the food industry, and I think we have the basis of a very good business. I think what I am trying to say is that you should stick with them."

Up until then I had seen this job as just a chance to have a long break in Sydney, see how the other half lived, and repay a few favours to my sister.

"They don't worry you?" she asked.

"Not at all, but I have often had a laugh, wondering what my mates would think." "Oh Dar, I can imagine, at least there is no mystery about it." People were drifting home or on to somewhere else for a meal. I was still in my work clothes, and would have liked to have had a shower and a change. Although she seemed perfectly content, there was not much in the way of food, other than the usual pub fare of steak sandwiches or hamburgers.

"Heather and your sister are the brains behind the business, and of course your sister knows the industry backwards; they are two very smart ladies."

"Peg, could you handle a steak sandwich with chips?" She must have been feeling the same way. "Thanks, I will have you over to my place another night. This is pleasant. I have not done this for a while; it is nice to be able to relax over a couple of drinks and good company." That had been said with a broad smile. The evening simply slipped away as we talked. When we got up to leave, our hands just slipped into one another's as if they needed to be held. Which was how our romance began, and having become aware of it, Alkina did what she could to help it along.

"Dar, if Peggy wants to pitch in again, she would be more than welcome." The comment would have been made a week or so before one of her weddings. "But do let me know early. I want everyone there by two, the reception starts at six, and there are three hundred guests. Dar, I want you in your dicky-suite as the chief pooh-bah. Please keep our people on their toes, and make sure they offer the guests a drink as soon as they arrive."

I had grown into the routine. Alkina was organized and unflappable, which would have been Hannah's influence, as her functions were staged like a well-planned military exercise.

"Dar, the mission is to ensure our guests have a lovely night. Incidentally, you two have been seeing a lot of each other, so I gather you are smitten. I hope so, because I think Peggy is very nice, and the way she looks at you is something to behold." My sister's mind raced from one thing to another, and certainly she missed very little. Some months had gone by and her comment had been more appropriate than she knew, and I thought I should explain where we were at.

"Peg and I have decided to move in together and see how we get on."

"You may as well, as you practically have anyway. If I may say, I think you two get on very well. Dar, have you read that book I gave you on wedding protocols for different beliefs and customs?" My sister never lost her focus, and I was not going to say that I had not, because I knew that Peggy would have, and coach me when we had the time. Nor was I going to tell her that Peg was developing a suspiciously keen interest in the subject herself.

My sister liked to coach me. "Dar," she might say, "sometimes, the groom or the best man can be overwhelmed by the occasion, the effects of liquor, or both. I expect you to step in and gently get the proceedings back on track. Not that it is going to happen at this one. Sir John Bignam is one of my best clients. He and Lady Bignam are lovely. This is Penelope's day. I will have two warming ovens hidden by a floral display just behind the bride's table; just be sure they whip the meals away during the speeches and keep them hot. Oh, and don't forget to compliment the women. I think a wedding is that sort of occasion." She need not have worried as Peg had already briefed me. I liked to reassure her, "Sis, we enjoy doing them; we understand their success is in the detail."

Those were exciting days. Hanna and Alkina's business was flourishing, and Peg and I were a part of it. But it had not escaped us that Gerard was clearly sponging on my sister, and we were keen for her to ditch him. Peg had embarrassingly caught him stealing cash. It was a very touchy subject. However, the occasion just presented itself when my sister had been applying a little pressure of her own.

"Being able to call on you and Peggy is just fantastic," she had being saying, "and I must tell you that James and Pat are delighted with the effort you put in, and they tell me their business has never been so good. Which brings me to another thing; I would like to see you commit to staying in Sydney. I do not see how you could possibly contemplate dragging Peggy away to the bush."

But there had been no pressure from Peg. But my sister can be pretty insistent.

"Dar, you are earning good money with me, and I know that when things sort themselves out, the boys will come good; they are naturally generous anyway, and they think the world of you. Besides any of that, it is nice having you around, and I think you have picked up a lot more than you realize. Did I tell you I saw Mrs. Vane at the hairdressers the other day? She told me just how charming you had been to everyone at their anniversary party; very nice to hear, and Dar, it is just terrific for business."

"That's nice, look sis, this may not be the time to bring it up, but Peggy and I have been watching Gerard, and that relationship worries us. I have watched you peel off a wad of fifties for him, and I have seen him go to your handbag and help himself. As Peggy says, 'with him it is one-way traffic,' and she has caught him helping himself from the cash box. That is stealing, and it has to stop." I suddenly wished I had kept my mouth shut, for the mask had fallen off, and she was sobbing.

"Don't think that I don't know. I do, and it is tearing me apart." I had triggered a meltdown and tears were streaming down her cheeks.

"No, sis, no, you do not have to put up with that sort of shit, not from Gerard, not from anyone, no you don't!"

"I am trying," she managed between sobs, "and Heather doesn't like him either. I am making a real goose of myself. I know he steals from me."

"Heh sis, that is not Nan's favourite girl talking, not the great grand-daughter of Alkina, who won her Fritzhugh, who loved her till he died, not the daughter of the Mighty Hunter, not the big sister who has always told me to be proud of who I am. Do it for Nan, she wanted you to be proud and strong like her. You don't have to buy any man." I poured her a brandy. "Sip this," I said, "you are far too good for someone like him. It's easy, all you have to do is run your own love life as well as you run mine."

That produced a wan smile, but the matter did not stop there, for not long after there was a message to call Heather at her office. The pretext was my old Army Will, and I have to say that Heather had grown on me.

"Alkina tells me you are heavily into romance these days." The view through the window behind her was nothing flash, just the smoky glass of another office building across Pitt Street. At least her office was handy, a flights of stairs and there was a nice little pub just around the corner. The office was bigger than I had imagined; phones rang, couriers arrived, clients waited, and people scurried about with beribboned files.

"That's true," I agreed, "and probably largely due to you and my sister."

We laughed. "Good, it sounds promising. Now Dar, this old Army Will of yours is not relevant for today. You need one that reflects the current situation. And let's hope I never have to pull it out of the safe for many a year to come." That had been said with well-practiced levity. "I suggest, everything goes to Alkina, provided she survives you by six months, and we only say that in case you both go in an air crash or something as equally bothersome. Should she not, then it goes to mum and dad. I have already discussed that with her. I intend to set up a trust for them so they do not have to worry about money, and administer it from here. A pessimistic outlook, mind you, but you never know when the grim reaper may strike, ha, ha. Then when you get married, your estate can go to your wife, but not straight away, and let me tell you why."

How extraordinary to be sitting there, planning my future, and having that conversation. I could not help thinking of Brasso and Toots and the others. How much I would have liked to have seen them again, to have a beer and share a joke, and to have them meet Peggy. I found it incredible their young lives had been snatched away.

"You and Alkina seem to have my life all stitched up," I commented lightly. "Heather, I am grateful, for all your input, and get a great kick out of watching my sister succeed."

"Your sister is a very talented lady."

"Now Dar, the problem arises this way; if you die, it would all go to your wifey, and there would be nothing left for dear old mum and dad. I think sixty percent to her while they are alive and she takes the rest when they peg out. But do not fuss my boy; we will have to throw the whole lot out if Alkina gets married, which I hope and pray she will one day before I am much older. One cannot anticipate every event in one's life, and it would be boring if we could; so if she gets married and starts a family, we will have to start all over again."

"Please do whatever you think is best," I added.

"Dar, that sounds good! Please be here at the same time next week to execute it." She shuffled some papers about, and brought it up as if it had been purely coincidental.

"And while we are at it, I believe you spoke to your sister about her relationship with Gerard."

"Yes, I had to. She was very upset over it, but I am glad I did; he takes her for every cent he can."

Heather lent forward and wore a very earnest expression. "I must say I find him quite obnoxious," she said. "You can only go so far with these things, and she is a very dear friend of mine. However, I think brothers are different. Please feel free to talk to me anytime about it. I find that relationship a real worry."

She shook her head, as if to make her point, "And while we are on that subject, I have been doing a little checking up myself. I find Gerard has an unsavoury reputation; he says he owns his own business, which I doubt. And I hear he owes money all around the town. There are things I could do, but she would have to agree, and it is an incredible thing to have to say, but I am not even sure she would. Then she sat back. "That's women for you; we are very strange creatures." I was glad we had talked.

One thing followed another, and my steady progression at work had begun. I was having major repairs and an upgrade to the warehouse done, had leased some badly needed extra space down the road, had put on two extra hands, and leased a couple of bigger trucks.

≉ 14 ≉

Just as Heather and I had hoped, my brother had slotted in and got the place moving. I had found that when dealing with the boys, the only way to get anything done was to deal with Peggy, who at least knew what was going on, and made up for Patrick's mad panics, and his and James's complete inability to take managerial control of what could be a very good business. My brother's and Peggy's romance had come as a bonus.

Besides our catering business, my life revolved around organizing functions, and reducing my debt to the bank. They had funded a bigger, fully equipped professional kitchen that gave us the sort of generous working area we needed. But my emotional life was a shambles, as it seemed that everyone close to me had taken a deep dislike to Gerard, indeed Heather was quite exasperated by the relationship. Gerard had me on an emotional string, and knew it.

When he started to help himself to my money, it began with small amounts, which I chose to ignore. Then he began asking me for larger sums to get him through a temporary cash flow or some other crisis. Some of these he paid back, but as our relationship went on, he expected me to agree to whatever he asked. I would feel very let down and call our relationship off, and then he would return and beg me to take him back. I can understand that I was naïve, emotionally dependant, and there is no doubt I was vulnerable. So naïve was I that I even compared my own feelings with those of Nan's for Fritzhugh, until I came crashing back to earth when I found out about his other women.

That emotional shambles aside, those years were a very rewarding time for me, I was very fond of Peggy, and when she called to tell me that she and Dar were getting married, I was thrilled. There was certainly no doubt those two were very much in love. Almost as soon as I got off the phone, I had scribbled out a menu for their engagement party, and sung the good news to Nan.

"I now have two great ladies running my life," my brother had quipped. I offered to put on the wedding, although Peggy had seemed quite overwhelmed by that. Hanna and Henri had filled my apartment with flowers for their engagement party.

"Now we will really have to seriously expand the business to take in all their children," Pat joked.

"I am buying Dar a boat," Peggy told me confidentially when we were clearing up.

"Dar would never expect such an extravagant gift," I told her.

"No, it is not what you think; he puts in a huge week and he's been out a few times and caught the fishing bug. We are looking at one of those old wooden ones he can restore. I am so looking forward to my life with him."

⚡ 15 ⚡

The old timber boat lay propped up on a couple of old timber railway sleepers. I had purchased her through the elderly owner of a boatshed who said she had been sitting unused on one of his moorings for years. Sam had offered me the sleepers and props so I could get her off the sand and scrap her hull while the tide was out. Her barely discernible name was carved on a weathered timber plate screwed to the transom. *Night Winds* had seen better days. As I scrapped, a pile of green and red seaweed, white crusty barnacles and loose clumps of mussels built up on the sand. The seagulls had left layers of encrusted dung on her topsides. Sam said he had forgotten when he had last seen the owner move her from her mooring. There came the steady beat of diesels as fishing and charter boats headed out to sea. As I worked, I took in the sight, smell, and sounds of the sea.

"How's the hull?" Sam asked on one of his many trips down to check on progress.

"Sam, I reckon she looks worse than she is. I only hope there is no wood rot."

"Dar, I always did like her shape; she is typical of the thirties, and these clinker built boats are renowned for handling well in a sea."

"Sam, that sounds good. I will let her dry out while I repack the stern gland and give her four or five days out of the water; then I can slap the antifouling on."

"Shame to let her go like that, when you are ready with the engine! Give me a whistle, but I would think she will be right; these twin cylinder jobs last forever." Sam was a very obliging old bloke. He would wander down to cast an expert eye over progress, often with a couple of mugs of tea.

"I was only thinking, I reckon you would enjoy running a boatshed. There is no money in it, but it pays the bills and keeps a bloke out of the pub." The old chap would pick up a block and do some sanding.

"Sam, for me, this makes a great change to the daily grind."

"I can see. I like it Dar; it is just me the water, wind and the seagulls, and mate, where did you learn about engines?"

"I did a short course before I went out to work in the shearing sheds, and out there, I have helped strip a few down."

"Son, better fix those navigation lights; we don't want the Water Police to nab you."

"Sam, the eyes of the law are right on to me?"

"Ha, ha, they could be, but they would be better off if they kept an eye on a few of them plastic boat owners."

Sam had done a stint in the last war, and given a lead; he might launch into that. "The blokes in the Second AIF put up with whatever the army dished out, and did it with good humour; as a matter of fact, that is what I mostly remember about it. No matter how crook it was, we would always manage to make a joke of it."

"Sam, it is my solemn duty to tell you that not much has changed."

"Ha, ha, well, I have to say that the Second World War was a cock-up right from the start; we had no fighters, very few ships and bugger all of anything else. I mean what a letdown after all the sacrifices our young men made at Gallipoli and on the Western Front. Just think of the politicians' talk and the dedication of war memorials in every town across the country. And still we were caught with our collective pants down; I mean the way we were caught unprepared in 1939 nearly cost us the whole bloody country." My friend still carried the burden of it.

While I worked on *Night Winds*, Peggy spent her time helping my sister and planning our wedding. Every now and again she would turn up to see my progress.

"Darling, *Night Winds* is going to look wonderful, really, if I did not know, I would not have recognized her." That was her, always positive and encouraging. We might have a picnic lunch on the sand, and it felt wonderful to have her care for me like that. "Darling," she said, running her hand over the timber, "she gets prettier every day, and Sam gets a huge kick out of seeing her come back to life." I must admit that I was feeling very pleased with progress myself. It would be hot down on the beach and I would have stunk to high heaven.

"Peg, and all the time her beauty was hidden under a mountain of seagull dung and marine growth."

She had sounded Sam out about coming to the wedding.

"Son," he said, "I really like your missus. I think she's a real nice lady. I would not want to offend her, but we are too old for that sort of caper; that's a day for you and all your young friends."

But later, he had wanted a blow by blow description, so he could tell his wife anyway, so Peg brought the photos down, so he could take them home and show her. Sam had carved and gilded a new name plate and fixed it to the transom as our wedding present.

≠ 16 ≠

Those years of our marriage passed sweetly, and it seemed everything we touched turned to gold. We had a home we had remodelled and loved with a pool and all the trimmings, and we got a great kick out of entertaining our friends. I was the General Manager of a financially robust and expanding company, which I had worked hard to build up from small beginnings. I was paid handsomely, owned shares in the business, and drove the top of the range BMW. Heather was Chair of the Board, and my sister was a director, with a special responsibility for product development and quality control. To get away from the pressure of business, Peg and I would slip away on *Night Winds* and anchor in a quiet cove somewhere. My memories of the war and its aftermath had receded to wherever those things rest, and we were very happy. So the timing seemed ideal to start a family.

I recall that we were driving home after a movie and a couple of drinks in a nice little pub on what had been a cold and wet winter's afternoon. The starting of our family had often been discussed, so there was nothing particularly special about our decision.

"Darling, I am going to stop taking the pill, as I think it is high time you and I made a baby."

"Sounds great to me; let's go home and get to work on it." At that moment in our lives, we would never have dreamed we would have any trouble on that score.

Perhaps, if there was anything on our minds, it would have been our wish that Alkina would meet someone she truly loved. She had so much going for her, she was a raging success, and we were thrilled to be a part of it. Her articles were commented upon, and her books were instant sellers; she was always in the media, yet she remained the same unassuming person she had always been, and she was also embarrassingly generous. My sister dated a succession of charming and successful men; yet, as far as we knew, there was no one great love in her life. Peggy was her greatest fan, and I remembered flippantly suggesting to her that Alkina might frighten them off.

"Dar, don't you dare say that; your sister deserves the very best. Just you sit back and watch; I know it will happen, it cannot be easy to find someone who is even in the same street, let alone as gorgeous." It was great to see how well those two got on. But to return, that was a time when my wife and I were rather pleased with our lives.

"My dear," Peggy said casually, "you did not know I can knit. I am making some baby things."

"Peg, you are right out of my league."

"My being pregnant will be perfect," she replied. She had revelled in the prospect of motherhood. Her thing was to spend a day on the water, throwing a line over the side, while reading and listening to the radio. Perhaps we might just lie back and enjoy the water lapping against the hull, and when the mood took us, we would enthusiastically make love.

Each ANZAC day, I was reminded of how good my life was, when the former members of our unit chipped in to help the families of those who had not come home. But the business of making babies turned out not to be so easy; the weeks became months, which passed into winter and spring. In the meantime, she knitted, shopped for baby things, and we made love.

"I do not understand. It is just ridiculous that a randy couple like us have not been able to do the trick, so I have booked us in to have a check-up," she announced. My doctor made me cough, inspected my equipment, and asked about our love making.

"Well I am damned if I know," he announced. "We had better get another opinion. You seem in great shape to me. It may be something simple like stress, in which case there may be some minor lifestyle adjustment needed. Your wife's gynaecologist says she is as good as gold. You can never tell; some couples only have to look at each other and it happens." My doctor gave me a note to a specialist.

The lobby of the Macquarie Street building was opulently clad in marble and the Tenant Index was replete with specialists, with lots of letters after their names. My man had a thin face, not much hair, and big ears, and he seemed distinctly pleased to have been presented with the problem. The doctor made his inspection, before announcing, "Good man, now go into the room over there and ejaculate into this." I had been handed a small plastic jar with a screw-top lid. My task was further complicated by him carrying on a phone conversation with someone about a disappearing testicle.

"Good show!" he said, having a look and tapping the lid approvingly. "Take a seat while I ask a few questions." We went through my life in great detail. "There," he said. "I think that just about covers it, except we will have to take a few blood samples so they can have a good look at those." He found the vein and filled his vials. "Nothing to it, see you at the same time, next week."

We had thought there could be few lovers like us, and were glad that we were doing something about our problem. We made light of it as we waited for the result. But in the back of my mind was the thought that the son of the Mighty Hunter might be infertile. The evening before, I had gone for a walk and had sung to Fritzhugh and my father's ancestors, and that night I hardly slept.

The medico's opinion was very matter of fact: "Your sperm are not surviving, this coupled with the fact that your count is low, means that fertilization does not have much chance of taking place."

"Christ!" I said aloud.

"Now, about your blood test, there is some evidence emerging, and you are not alone in this, that there may be a link with the defoliant sprays used in Vietnam." Not that war again! I could almost hear the drone, as the planes had flown in line abreast, leaving a fine mist that hung in the air and settled over everything. But there had been plenty of children conceived, and Barrel had only recently called to say he and Kath had just produced twin girls, so I mentioned that.

"I know son, different people, different effects; these things can be quite inexplicable. And in your case, there may be some relationship with your previous occupation as a shearer, and the pesticides used on sheep. We will just have to watch, and see if you come good."

I called her. "Darling, it's me." I was devastated, and headed for the boat, where Sam was hosing down the topsides of a cruiser. We exchanged a greeting but I avoided the usual banter. A light nor'easter was piping in, and I was soon steering into a low swell. I headed for our favourite fishing spot. The boat drifted in the lee of the headland, and I sat in the stern and drank Scotch and water, and tried to come to terms with it. There would be no little boy like Brasso's Timmy—I could still see the big smile of his first teeth—nor little girls like Chris's Annabelle; yet I had to concede that unlike their dads, I was back home unscathed.

She would have been a beautiful mother, but other than getting drunk, there was not much I could do about it. *Night Winds* joggled as the seagulls looked on sceptically as if they knew. I leaned over the gunwale and saw my watery reflection, and it came to me that Brasso and Toots were probably looking down and having a good laugh, "Ha, ha, ha, Dar, the bloody army got you in the end, just like it got us; only this time mate, they got you by the balls, ha, ha, ha…" And in that moment I saw it their way and joined in. When I got home, the place was as silent as a mausoleum.

"Darling, tell me what he said." She pretended it did not matter. "I knew where you had gone, my darling; please don't blame yourself." But life went on, and no one knew but us.

Another day another dollar. "Good morning Pat, morning James, this won't take long."

"Always nice to see you Dar. What is on your mind?" They had never quite accepted their success; it was as if they were expecting me to announce a major disaster, a product recall, or that the bank had suddenly called in our loans.

"Well, we do have some competition out there, and if you can spare a moment, we ought to talk about that. I want us to protect our position and expand our market share in Perth, Darwin, Alice Springs, Townsville, and Cairns." James had pushed his files aside and had placed a clean sheet of paper and a pencil in front of him.

"They are not places we are particularly fond of, and I personally cannot handle Alice Springs or Darwin," Pat observed flippantly, "but never mind; you can't help that." Kid they might, but they knew the value of hanging on to a major customer, the signs of a weakening loyalty and of our loosening hold. None of that had gone unnoticed. The opposition constantly whittled away, till finally we lost them altogether. "My view is we need to consolidate; we don't want to sit around until we are knocked off. I have lined up a deal to use air-freight, so we can trial a daily delivery door to door." That had their attention.

"The times they are a changin', volumes are up, and we have to deliver our perishables fresh, undamaged, and as far as we can, guaranteed on time. That ought to shut out the competition for a while. There will be a small squeeze on margins, but we have the market share and volume to do it, and this ought to give us a boost. I project that with the novelty of it, there will be a significant lift in the first few months. But we would be sitting ducks if someone came in and did it first." James was nodding and doodling away on his paper.

"Sounds good to me," Pat said.

"Yeah, and it makes a lot of sense to me," James added. "Why don't you run it past Heather so we are all on the same wavelength?"

I had come armed with a ream of projections, and would have been happy to go through it on a whiteboard with them. Instead, James suddenly changed tack.

"Then Dar," he said, "we would like you to take Peggy up to Noosa for ten days on us; stay in the best place and live it up; do you both a world of good." There were few secrets; she must have mentioned our problem to my sister, but I had been taken by surprise.

"That's very generous, but first I will have to do a quick whip around, and make sure this scheme actually works. We can get away after that."

But still nothing happened, and we consoled ourselves with the specialist's view: "These problems often right themselves over time." That winter we flew up to see my parents. They had aged, and it was obvious that a grandchild would have delighted them, and there was vague talk of us giving it one or two years before adopting a child.

My life has a habit of serving up surprises, and I can still remember this as clearly as if it was yesterday. A Sunday morning, I had intended to get out on the water early, throw a line over the side, and read the weekend papers. On the way home, I would have my usual couple of beers with Sam. But she had come in at some ungodly hour after running one of my sister's major functions. So I decided to stay home and fix her a late brunch. I wandered down to the shops to get the papers and settled down in the garden to read them. She emerged sometime after noon, and I made her black coffee with scrambled eggs and bacon. She complained of a dull ache in her left breast and we spoke about what she may have lifted, and I got her some mild painkillers. It would have been five weeks later when she phoned me at the office on a Friday afternoon. "Darling, I will catch a cab in, say six-ish, and we can go out for a drink."

"Our pub", as we called it, had not changed much over the years. They could have been the same tables under the same tree, except they now ran to a bistro. It was nice to be there. We chatted about nothing in particular. I was enjoying my beer, and then realized that she was reminiscing about our early days, and becoming quite sentimental.

"Thank you darling, for our lovely life together." she said quietly. "I often think of our first date; we were so unsure of ourselves, and tried so hard to make it work, and it did. Two young people who had been hurt, needing someone to love, and we found each other. The way it happened was so lovely, and I remember it was such a wonderful feeling. I can still recall that first night and thinking what a nice man you were. Darling, I still adore you, and the passing years have not diminished my love for you one little bit." She was going to tell me she was pregnant. Then her eyes filled with tears. "Darling one, I have to tell you that I have just found out that I have advanced breast cancer."

You hear about other couples, and never think it could happen to you. I did what I did best, and comforted her while she bravely got it out. "Darling one, it has spread. I am so sorry, I have been dreading this moment."

"Shall I take you home?"

"No, I want to be here with you, have a few drinks, and if they still make steak sandwiches, have one of those, just like we did on our first date." She had been so courageous; her eyes shone, there was the beginning of a smile, and she looked lovelier than ever. I can recall it exactly, and in that moment, I put a cocoon around my own feelings. Alkina was devastated, and the boys went into an emotional meltdown.

Her oncologist spoke of the efficacy of chemotherapy, but Peg had already made up her mind to have none of it. Not all that many years ago, she had held the hand of a close friend while she had succumbed. She made me promise, "Darling, promise me, never let me go through that; I thought her dying was monstrous." I did everything I could to support her.

"Let me enjoy each day with you. I do not want to end up helpless in a hospital bed, and nor do I want to drag you in day after day. None of that; I don't want a drawn-out dying, and I want to be at home with you for as long as I can, then go quickly, without all the other. And Darling, if you would help me when the time comes, it is the only thing I want."

"Of course," which I promised without a second thought.

"Thank you darling one. I am glad we settled that. I want you to know I love you, and to me that is all that matters."

I had to handle things the best way I could, which hopefully helps explain how I found myself outside the Blue Flame Strip Club in the heart of Kings Cross. It had obviously been a long night for the bouncer, who was happy to chat. It was that time before dawn, when the drunks had collapsed in an alleyway with a bottle of port in a brown paper bag beside them. The pushers had done their trades for the night and squared with their wholesalers, and the customers had returned to their suburbs, having shot up in a doorway around the corner. The last show had finished. Couples, including two women, were drunkenly moving on the floor to a trio who looked eager to pack up for the night. I sat at the bar and ordered a Scotch and water. A girl at the other end flashed me a smile and joined me on the next stool.

"Would you like a girl?" she asked.

"Yeah, I could do. My name's Dan. What's yours?"

"Yasmin."

"Nice name."

"I am a nice girl."

"I can see."

"You are not a cop, are you?"

"No, and how has business been?"

"Slow," she stifled a yawn, "there are a few skinflints around who want to get it away for nothing."

"That's no good; what's the going rate?" I asked, trying to project a sympathetic smile.

"What do you want, to play around or just get screwed? Either way I can work something out for you."

"Like a drink?"

"That's friendly, a Scotch on ice, thanks." She spoke to the bartender, who smiled all-knowingly, and appeared to be contemplating the transaction with some interest. I presumed he took a cut of whatever changed hands, and I slipped Yasmin a handful of fifties under the bar.

"That's for your time."

"Thanks Dan, I got plenty of that."

"I like to talk."

"That's fine, so do I. You keep paying and we can talk the rest of the night. What's the matter? You can't get it up? You can tell me. I don't mind?"

"Yeah," I said, "it is complicated."

"I am the original therapist, unless you prefer men, and if you do, I can arrange that as well."

"You have nice teeth."

"Thanks, it's good for business."

"Yasmin, I have a little problem, tell your friend to go round again, and more ice for me, and we can talk about it. Is that okay with you?"

"Fire away Dan, I thought you might never make it."

"Do you use?"

"Are you sure you are not a cop?"

I made a face at her. "I know all those on the take; if you are, could we get on with it?"

"No, but I need to arrange a regular supply of the best grade."

"Dan, I'm selling pussy, not dreams; you would have just walked past a million dealers, so what is the problem?"

"This is special, here. I owe you," and I slipped her another handful of fifties.

"Dan, you are a man who means to get what he wants."

"You never told me, if you do."

"I do a little recreational; a girl can get down doing this."

"I can understand."

"Dan, I think you are telling me you don't, but you say you need some; so what is happening? You don't look that way."

"I have a friend who is very sick; they need to escape from the reality of it every once in a while. But I do not want to purchase what some doped-up kid has cut down with whatever they fancy."

"Sensible, but that is going to cost you. I won't buy from just anyone myself."

"You have a decent source?"

"Yes."

"Good, Yasmin, how about this—you get me the good stuff and I will pay for the same amount for your own use, so it won't cost you a dollar? Plus I will pay you a handling fee of five hundred."

She nodded to the barman. "Let's go round to my place and get started." We went along Victoria Street and paused outside a former mansion with a "Flat to let" sign in a front window.

"Come on up, this is home."

"Nice."

"It does me and my kid."

"Boy or a girl?"

"Little girl; she keeps me on my toes. Gets a little hectic when I come in a wreck and she wants to play. Are you being square with me Dan? I would never bring a john home."

I produced another wad and peeled a few off to build up her confidence. "What do you need?" she asked.

"I am not sure I know, say three or four a day until the end."

"Is this for your wife Dan?"

"Like some eggs and coffee?"

"Thanks Yasmin, you are a good girl."

"I am not a good girl, but I am a nice girl. Can't life be a bitch? When I am not working, my name is Penny?"

"I need a little coaching Penny. Could you throw that in with the breakfast?"

The sun had warmed by the time I got home. She lay with the drip in her arm and one afternoon Beryl, the nurse, took me aside. "Your dear wife has lost control of her functions so we need to put a catheter in to make her more comfortable." I did not want my wife to be in pain and I gave her the first shot when I woke to find her in distress. There was now a continual procession of friends through the house. A supply of specially prepared meals was delivered daily, as if it was actually possible for her to eat her way to a full recovery. My sister would spend hour after hour with her. Hanna would arrive with masses of flowers and replenished the many vases around the room. The little boxes of delicacies were her doing.

Everyone was embarrassingly generous. Patrick and James would usher me out of the office, with a solicitous, "Dar, we do not expect you to come in; everything's fine; you go home and look after Peggy." It was nothing for them to send around a team of professional cleaners who would do the house from top to bottom, or for someone to turn up to replenish our liquor supply. I played it day by day; as one week grew into another, I grasped at every moment of her life. My sister would take me aside to ask confidentially, "If she was able to eat the Mornay, and the orange and brandy fruit salad Hanna made for her?" I could not very well tell her that she had sicked it up before settling down with a fix of high-grade heroin.

Peg was wasting away, but still orchestrating her life to the end, until she finally whispered, "Darling, I have had a lovely life. I do not want to lie here anymore." I did my best to shepherd her through another couple of days, but her deterioration was making her unhappy. The nurse had been in to wash and fuss over her. And Peggy implored me. I called the nurse in to ask if my wife and I could have a few hours of privacy.

"Beryl, I will call you if she needs anything. Feel free to watch TV, have something nice to eat and drink, the fridge is bursting with it. Please let us have some time together."

Peg was strong to the end. "Darling, this will do, she has to rub me down all the time. I barely have the strength to move, and I am frightened that I may not be able to whisper. Please, it is time for me to go, another love, as quick as you can, hold me tight for a little while." She was smiling at me through her tears. "I love you," she whispered. "I will see you in the stars, now darling, please." I held her close until there was a gentle knocking on the door.

"Thank you, I didn't call you; my wife just wanted to slip away while we were together." The rest of it seems like a dream. I called her mother and my sister. Her doctor consulted the nurse and later joined me for a drink in the garden. The house was full of our friends and neighbours patting me on the back and giving me a hug and I was just hugely relieved to have set her free without any fuss. There had been a moment of doubt when the doctor remarked that he was pleased her death had come so easily.

There was to be a church service for family and friends. James and Pat were inconsolable, and her nurse must have told me a dozen times what a lovely lady she was. Penny sat up in the back, but as she was not wearing her blond wig, I did not immediately recognize her; she left before I could thank her. The local minister, whom neither of us had met, had not been enthusiastic at being asked to conduct the service. But Peg had thought it would comfort her mother and immediate family.

"Was your wife a Christian?" the minister had inquired.

"Very much so," I replied, "as are all her family, particularly her dear mother."

She would have enjoyed her wake. Alkina did it wonderfully, and it featured her favourite chamber orchestra. I should have been prepared; we had talked it through often enough, and the formalities seemed oddly unrelated. I was alone in our home a day or so after all the medical paraphernalia had been removed, when the shock of losing her suddenly hit me, and I found it inconceivable that she was dead.

There were her spice jars in the kitchen, the basket of knick-knacks at one end of the work bench; she was everywhere. It seemed she might waltz through the front door, expecting to be kissed. My big mistake was not immediately returning to work, and getting back into my routine. There would have been sympathy, nice lunches, a few drinking mates, and a chance to talk. But I did not go in, and they in turn respected my privacy. The hopelessness of my empty life simply enveloped me. I could not read, or even watch TV and found myself prowling around the house with a neat Scotch in my hand and my mind filled only with thoughts of her.

I know now that I had wanted to join her, and in desperation, I took out her syringe and gave myself a hit, which was followed by another and another, until her supply ran out. The inevitable happened, and I found Penny sitting at the bar wearing an outrageous get-up and she came over to join me.

"Hi stranger, how are you doing? Will you join me in a drink?"

"Thanks." This was an improvement on being alone.

"Tell me how you feel? I am a pretty good listener."

"Like a bag of shit."

"Dar, I thought it was a very nice service. She must have been a special lady."

"Thanks Penny, she was."

She was looking at me closely. "And you look like a bag of shit. What on earth are you doing to yourself, trying to drink yourself to death? I have tried that and it doesn't work." I had not shaved for days. Of course she knew this was not right; after all, I was supposed to be running a business.

"Aren't you back at work? I think it would be better if you were; you are obviously still very sad." I just sipped my drink and let her chat. She asked after Alkina and Heather.

"Although I have never met her, I would say you and your sister are very similar." She even reminded me to take up her offer. "Dar, it is supposed to be you doing the talking. I am a great listener. If you need to get it away, I understand; just say so."

I had run out of small talk. "I need some more."

"You what?" She was so shocked that not a lot was said.

"I wondered if you wanted me to buy her sachets back?"

"No, I used them."

"Christ no, you shot up the rest of all those carefully measured fixes I prepared for her?"

"Yes."

She was shaking her head in disbelief. "Go on, get out of here and get your own fucking supplier."

⚡ 17 ⚡

Do not let anyone kid you that an addict or a drunk does not know what is happening. It is all a question of them caring enough to do something about it. As weak and sick as I was, I remember being bashed and rolled up in the Cross, just around the corner from Kellett Street and waking up in the gutter and being disappointed that I was still alive. The crew of a garbage truck ignored me as just another derelict. I staggered along and cleaned myself up at the fountain. I had no idea what I had signed for Heather. I knew she had cancelled my cards, and even in that state, there was a niche in my mind that approved. All I wanted was a bottle of dry sherry in the morning, and not to think of my loss.

⚡ 18 ⚡

As his sister, I think I know what had happened to him during his drug and alcohol binge better than he does. As Heather explained, most solicitors experience one of their long standing clients phoning in the middle of the night to tell them their eldest daughter had just killed a pedestrian, been caught with a cache of drugs, or maybe one of their sons had been arrested after a drunken brawl. You take it on, accepting it as part of the great human experience.

My brother had really sunk to the bottom of the barrel, and I had co-opted her help as soon as I became aware. He was never at home, or if he was, he never answered the phone. I heard reports that he was seen looking like a dead beat and hopelessly drunk, either up in Kings Cross or down in Woolloomooloo, and it had been months since I had spoken to him. It was alright for him to walk out on his life, but it had ramifications; he sat at the apex of a business and a lot of people looked to him for their livelihood.

I could see that Heather had had enough, and felt the business should now appoint someone else in his place, and for the company to move on. And so it was that on this day I was aware that he was the main item on the agenda for what was to prove to be a highly emotional board meeting. At least Darain had seen to it that we had a well-trained staff, and there was already someone he had groomed to step into his shoes. The boys and I were having coffee when Heather arrived; James and Patrick were still carrying on as if Peggy's death had only just happened. We all accepted that a great deal of our success was due to my brother's hard work, and of course, he was my brother.

Heather opened the meeting and got to the point. "As our General Manager has not returned to work, I think that it is now appropriate that we appoint someone to fill that role. Could we have some discussion on that, then I shall put it to the meeting?"

James spoke in a subdued tone, "I think he needs help."

"What do you propose?" Heather asked.

"I am not sure. We have lost our dear Peggy and Dar is not coping at all. I am told he is drinking very heavily."

"Alkina and I understand it is much worse; he is avoiding anyone he knows and is believed to be using heroin."

Having it spelt out jolted us all. I was crying while the boys consoled me.

"James and I prefer not to act hastily," Pat announced.

"Then we must cease paying him," Heather said. "We have already been more than generous."

"No, no, that is not an issue for us," James replied.

"I honestly thought my brother wanted his own space."

"It appears we all did," Heather commented.

"He is inconsolable," Pat added.

"They were so close," I said, "but I hate what he's doing, and I know what she would think."

Clearly Heather saw her role as getting him off the payroll, and for the company to get on with its business. Yet, I should never have doubted my dear friend's capacity to rise to the occasion, which of course she did.

"I suggest," Heather said, "that we instruct a private inquiry agent to find out exactly what is going on. There is not only their home, those two accumulated considerable assets, and it may be that I have to quarantine them so they are not just frittered away."

Then a couple of weeks later, Heather and I met for lunch in Martin Place, which was just around the corner from her office. Pigeons shook their wings and strutted around the tables to peck at crumbs that had fallen from the stiff tablecloths. Matrons checked their makeup in their mirrors when they thought no one was looking. Pretty office girls made sure their escorts got a grandstand view of their pale cleavage, as they fluttered their eyelashes and sipped their wine. A nicely dressed matron smiled in recognition, which I politely returned.

"They know his routine," Heather said. "Every couple of days, they tell me where they last saw him; they reckon they all gravitate to the Cross sooner or later. It is better to call a spade a spade, and they say he can no longer afford the going rate, and now wanders around in an alcoholic daze. I was surprised at how much he had already gone through; at least I have been able to put a stop to that."

I grimaced. "Come on, we can handle this," Heather encouraged. "At least now we know, and my dear, the good news is, I think I have found a religious order who will take him in. It's a retreat not far out of Tamworth that takes in men with a chronic alcohol dependency. Some sort of farm, and I have to say it sounds promising, the only stipulation they make is they need to be convinced he wants to beat it," she smiled, "now that might be a tall order."

"You are the most wonderful friend; just tell me where and when and I will deliver him."

"That sounds good, his friends have copped a string of abuse when they have tried to bring him in, and if they do, he just wanders off again. Your brother can be very tiresome; I won't tell you what he said to me."

"Oh blow my brother! Can we enjoy our lunch? And I think we need a drink."

"I quite agree, a glass of wine or two might help restore my self-esteem. As soon as I have their response, I will get cracking. My dear, you are being very brave, these things happen; he has been through enough, and Peggy's death was just too much."

≈ 19 ≈

I am sure I am not the first to have to do this, but my brother had learned to live in the street, I watched him share a bottle with a man with grey whiskers while empty bottles of port and dry sherry lay in the gutter around them. He had no idea I was there. After searching frantically for two nights, finally I had found him. The sight of him in that appalling state upset me; he was lying in a dingy lane like a dirty pile of old rags. Quietly, I crept away, to race for my car before he could move on again. He was light and he stank, and I bundled him into the back. I had chosen the coast road in the hope it would gain me a few days to straighten him out. He needed to understand what was happening. There had been no recognition, and it surprised me that he could have reduced himself to this.

I found a motel on the coast with parking bays in front of the rooms, a few snips with my dressmaking shears and the stinking clothes came away. I wished he was with our father out in the bush. I placed a plastic chair under the shower and turned it on. His eyes were shut against the light; the face was thin; his chest caved as if he may have been starving to death. He had been hastened into old age. I soaped his head, and discovered the revolting sores and scabs. The water had turned a revolting grey. Now there was some resemblance. I trimmed his finger nails and brushed his hair. He was very thirsty, and his breath and teeth were disgusting; and he coughed up most of his omelette.

He was too weak to protest, and on the third day, we managed a walk down to the beach; and when he was tired, I put him to bed. The following day was much better, as he understood what was happening. The air was full of the sea as we walked along the shore, letting the waves wash over our feet. The trunks of the coastal brush had been bent and gnarled by the wind. I sang to Nan, telling her he was going to recover. Things were going well until he suddenly pleaded for a drink. I found that just too much.

"How dare you! You do this for Peggy; do it in memory of her. Pull yourself together. I don't want to hear another word about drink, heroin, or any more of your pathetic self-indulgent nonsense."

I would drive for half a day, find a motel on the beach, endeavour to get him to eat, then we would walk along the shore and then he would sleep. Slowly we made our way north, until it was our last day on the coast before I had to swing west along the banks of the Bellinger River before driving up the cutting into the hills of New England. The deserted beach stretched as far as I could see and the sand was a golden ribbon against the sea. The retreating waves filled our tracks.

"Dar, I am taking you to a place where there is no drink, and no drugs, and you are going to find yourself. When you are recovered, I will come and get you. Until then you are to do as you are told. Look at me. Peggy married a fine man, not a pathetic bum who would be a bloody nuisance to all those who love him." As I spoke, the retreating water made little rivulets in the sand. "Remember her with a clear head, and tell me you will do as they say."

"Okay sis, I will."

"Dar, your head has been full of Marmoo—the evil spirit. I want us to enjoy our last day at this pretty beach, because tomorrow we will be there."

Dar could have been in a trance. Normally we would have chatted about what we saw along the way, and I thought he seemed bewildered. We drove through that lush country without comment, and on through the lovely rolling hills further on from Dorrigo. "You will enjoy living in the country; it relaxes me just seeing it again. I wonder what Nan would have made of all this? Look, the apple gums are in bloom, isn't it lovely?" My brother said nothing. "Nan would have missed us so much; she once told me that you reminded her of Fritz. Please do not forget to sing to her and tell her what you are doing; you will be able to see the stars much better up here. Heather reckons the head of this place is charming. She went to a great deal of trouble on our behalf. Look, the highway is gradually falling away through the hills. This is more interesting than the flat country; you will like this place. I believe it is in the foothills, so you might have a little of each."

At a junction a sign directed me to the Dungowan Valley. There were pretty paddocks of Lucerne along each side of the gravel road. The hills were a hazy blue and an old red tractor cut a fresh brown swathe along the slope. The valley filled me with pleasure; here and there, mobs of fat white sheep ate their way across the paddocks, as I swung through the gate and parked under a tree in front of the Dunraven Priory. It was a very pretty setting and a row of magnificent pepper trees shed a carpet of pink seed around a lovely old sandstone building that reminded me of parts of Hunters Hill. The Abbot must have heard us as his beaming presence emerged and offered us a cheery greeting. He was the character monk straight out of a novel, complete with habit, balding dome, and bulging middle.

"Welcome to our Priory," he boomed. "I am Father David, and this fine gentleman must be your younger brother."

The moment was extraordinary and the rough brown habit appeared such an impractical garment for such a warm day. There were splotches of animal dung and earth down the front, and as I later discovered, it was made of coarse woven wool. Grubby toes protruded from stout-looking sandals. A wide leather belt held the girth in place. He was nut brown, and I thought that what hair remained may have once been sandy. This bear of a man was going to embrace me, and when he did, the smell was of assorted animals, and sweat. His hands were like hard leather; there would be no trouble keeping my brother in line. The Abbot was quite overwhelming.

"Darain, you and I are going to become the best of friends." With this, he had grasped my brother's hands with both of his, as if this first meeting was special for them. But it was wasted on Dar. The Abbot's voice had a timber that could have been an opera singer's; and when it was lowered, the resonance was as smooth as syrup. His delivery brought back memories of evangelists, who had been so certain of everything; the Abbot would be a very persuasive man. "Just a moment my dear lady, while I get your brother organized."

He had led us through the arched front door and across a flagged and vaulted hall. His study was Spartan, my heels clip-clopping seemed inappropriate in such a place. There were two worn leather armchairs in one corner, but nothing that said anything about a former life—no family shot with elderly parents, no children—only posed black and white photos of monks adorned the walls.

"Now say goodbye to your sister," and with that, Father David propelled my brother through the door, spoke to someone, and returned. "Take my word, he will do well here. Our loving God has been very good to deliver your brother." I was not going to argue. His movements were surprisingly nimble as he slipped behind his desk. "Believe me, you got him here just in time."

"Father David, I am sorry he is in such a dreadful state." I was having serious doubts, and feared that any fire and brimstone preaching might break him. I had not felt this apprehensive since I was put in a different home. As these thoughts tumbled around my head, Father David smiled benevolently.

"Alkina, he and I are brothers in drink, and may I assure you, we do understand. You are a wonderful caring sister, so he is much blessed. I was like him years ago so please have no doubt; he will be a different man. Shortly we will have a cup of tea. I am sure you could do with one. The thing is, my dear lady, they never seem to realize how much they intrude upon the lives of their family and friends. They live in complete self-absorption."

"I have noticed," I remarked, "when his wife was alive, I would never have believed this could possibly happen. Do you know the story?" One of the cherubic-faced monks appeared, smiled pleasantly at me, and disappeared.

"Alkina, I had a long chat with Heather, and what a wonderful friend she is, and she told me you are very special yourself. I mean we need to know what we were dealing with. His recovery will take time, but it is very satisfying when they do."

The monk returned with a tea tray. "Thank you, Simon. Do try some of our bread and butter." Brother Simon continued standing to one side. "Our dear Simon used to be a successful pastry cook until he took to demon drink and lost his way." Simon smiled like a scolded child. "Single-handed our Simon declared war on the dear young men and women of the New South Wales Police Force. Fortunately for everyone, he lost. He bakes every day and we have the best bread on this side of the Victorian border. I beg your pardon Simon, this dear lady is the elder sister of the man who has just this moment joined us. Peter is looking after him."

That comment must have been for their own information, as they smiled like a pair of conspirators. The bread was awful, but I nibbled at it to be polite. "No doubt, right about now, they will be having a nice chat." The Abbot's comment caused them to laugh. "Perhaps Simon, you could get our guest some samples of our produce so she may rediscover just how good fresh food can taste." The clear-eyed Simon wished me a safe trip and disappeared. The Abbot may have sensed my puzzlement.

"My dear, dear lady, that was very rude of me; we sometimes forget our visitors do not understand our humour. It was just that we knew your brother was rapidly being made aware that there are other things to worry about other than himself. Almost without exception, that long-forgotten fact comes to many as a rude shock. Incidentally, thank you very much for your generous check." Heather had very smartly discovered what might be required to get things moving.

"Your brother is to have no visitors for a while. When he is ready, he will contact you himself; at that time, I hope he will be something like the brother you remember. Have you time for a quick tour, then we can collect your hamper?"

He was both very gracious and proud. "This is our lovely chapel, where we thank our Almighty God for all the wondrous gifts he bestows upon us." I must admit that it really was quite beautiful.

"Father," I said, "thank you for showing me a lovely sanctuary in which to find peace and quiet, and to collect one's thoughts."

"Exactly, it is where we can collect ourselves and find a connection with our maker. Have you taken the Lord Jesus into your own heart Alkina?" My answer surprised even me; Nan and my mother would have been amused. "Yes Father, I have."

Suddenly I had to leave. "Thank you so much, it's a long drive and I should be starting back."

"Of course, we shall go via the kitchen." I stowed the hamper in the back. Simon had been over generous. "May God go with you; now be of good cheer; your brother is in good hands." I held my breath for the hug.

"Thank you Father David, I shall enjoy the hamper." The balmy air in the valley hummed with insects and a soft breeze gently rocked the trees. I waved as I drove through the gate.

≉ 20 ≉

Brother Peter was an unusually friendly fellow, and when the monk clapped a hand on my shoulder, I nearly collapsed. We had strolled through the building, the monk chatting away like a proud boarding-house keeper, pointing out this and that, until we emerged out onto a sandstone terrace. The range made a hazy backdrop; the afternoon had warmed, and the sun hung like an incandescent ball. A distant diesel toiled away and the spray from the irrigation lines hung in the air.

"Follow me Darain," he said, and the Brother led me to a large corrugated iron shed. "We still have time to load tomorrow morning's first delivery. What a lovely day it has been for you, I am quite sure you will come to love it here, now all you and I need to do is to stack these masonry blocks neatly onto the tray of this truck." A large bay of sand was piled against one wall, and to one side was a hopper for dispensing bulk cement. There were grey metal moulds on the floor and the masonry blocks gave out the unmistakable smell of wet cement. The monk had positioned me next to a pile of dry blocks. Brother Peter picked up a block in each hand and slammed them down in the middle of the tray. "You do it just like that."

In my weakened state, I had no chance. "Never mind, we will do it together; now both hands on your end, good, now lifting together, one, two, three." I almost fainted from the effort. "Good man, we will have this done in no time." I do not remember how we finished loading, other than my hands were bleeding and I ached all over.

"That was good; now drink plenty of water," the monk advised, and seemingly mildly amused. Already I had told myself what a miserable sight I must be by comparison to this robust and energetic man.

"Now we can visit the pigs," he said. This could have been uttered by a well-meaning school master. "And still have time to shower before prayers. I am fond of our pigs, and I used to run the program before I took on the masonry factory."

We entered a long shed with a concrete floor and rows of pens full of noisy pigs. Men shovelled feed into their troughs from a mobile bin. The monk scooped up a squealing piglet and put into my hands, where it soiled my front. "Lovely animals, they put on over a kilo for every kilo we feed them." The sun had disappeared behind the green hills, and I was desperate for a drink. "Scrub your hands; here, this way, we make our own soap; it is very good for healing cuts; jump under the shower, your change of clothes and towel are on the bench." The shirt and pants were former army issue.

"Hurry along, that's a good fellow, or we will be late for prayers." I dozed during prayers. "Time for dinner, come this way." We sat at a long table and Peter introduced me as if I was a visiting guest speaker. "Darain works with me in the masonry factory." They were unfailingly enthusiastic.

"I still remember my first meal here," he told me. "I had been drinking for years, mind you; nobody was really sure how long. We had corned beef, carrots, mashed potato, and cauliflower. It was the first meal in a long time that I had any idea of, and it tasted so good. You will probably be the same. Bangers and mash with fresh beans, all grown on the place; we have the best snorkers for miles around; eat up and put some meat on your ribs. And drink your milk."

The Abbot had intoned his prayer before we ate, during which the monk supervised me. "Chew your food and give your teeth and jaws a decent work out; I bet they have not had one of those for a while, small mouthfuls, and sip your milk." Had she seen it, my sister would have been beside herself with happiness. My expression may have mirrored my thoughts. "Darain, you can see the humour of it; we should take that as a very good sign."

I was asleep as soon as I lay down, and did not hear the bolt being driven home.

"Wake up, hurry along; it is time to start a new day." I was being shaken; the yellow light dazzled me; I had no idea where I was.

"Time to wash before chapel," Peter told me. It was all right for the monk, every part of me ached and I could not stoop to put my shoes on. Peter did it for me. It was freezing and my mouth and throat were parched. The monks made a low murmur as we knelt in prayer. I felt that perhaps this was a very bad dream. The first mug of tea helped. The monk was bursting with vitality and urged me to eat a hearty breakfast. I managed a few mouthfuls of porridge.

"Couldn't you handle a couple of eggs?"

"No thank you."

"Show me your hands; never mind, they will soon heal; we will borrow some working gloves." In the gray of dawn, a mist lay in the hollows across the valley, and I was so stiff, I could barely move, much less bend down to pick up my end of a masonry block. The monk seemed highly amused. "Ha, ha, you will soon get into the swing of it." That first load was the pinnacle of human endeavour. "Come on," the monk encouraged, "drink plenty of water and you can rest while we drive across the city. I really think you are the ideal recruit for the masonry business, and it will strengthen our resolve as we drive past all those sinful pubs, ha, ha, ha, and my friend, there is no way we will be stopping." The city surrendered to the warming morning sun as we slowly made our way through it on the way to an industrial site.

"We had to compete to get this job," Peter explained, "so we do make a good product; just keep watch as I reverse in. This job should keep you and me out of mischief for some time. After we are through here, we will have a brew of tea and some lamb sandwiches. I do not know of a nicer lunch." The monk knew I was done and left me alone while he made another batch of blocks. Each day was a repeat of the last, a couple of loads before lunch and the same after, which was only varied to make another batch. As I recovered, the monk kept lifting our targets. Perhaps, when you climb out of an abyss, you soon forget what it was like at the bottom. Peter had announced yet another load, and I distinctly remembered being unable to restrain myself from stating the obvious.

"We could quadruple our output, using a forklift and pallets."

"Thank you Dar, you make an interesting observation. I knew you would make a fist of this job."

"Well," I replied, "I only mention it, as I could probably get us a pretty good deal on the gear." A couple of days later the monk said, "I was thinking about your idea, but there is a problem with it."

"Yeah," I said, "and I think you will find that it is pretty well-standard practice? Okay, we would need more level flooring for storing pallets and for the forklift to run around on."

"Ha, ha, and if we had done that, we would not have a job for you," Peter replied. The monk had a point. Brother Peter was a good motivator, and as I got to know him, I found him to be a very pleasant and well-meaning man. They were long hard days which began and finished while the stars were out.

"The way you work Peter, you should have been a shearer; you would have made a great deal of money," I added.

"Is that right? Tell me about the life. I have seen it being done here, but I have never had a go at it myself."

"Peter, it is a pretty tough life, and the work is very repetitive, a bit like this; and of course it is definitely no good if you have a drinking problem. I have seen men earn huge checks, and then go on a bender and blow the lot. I hardly touched the stuff in those days, so we did all right out of it." The monk smiled his approval, and took the opportunity to discuss my progress.

"You are sounding good and making a fine recovery and it is good that you have retained your sense of humour. Sadly, for some, they have lost too many brain cells. Do you think it was losing your wife that started you drinking?"

"I am sure it was," I replied.

"Think about her, and all the time you had together, and be thankful for her life."

156

"Thank you Peter," I said, feeling comforted by his comment. "And what about yourself?" His response absolutely floored me.

"Do not collapse, but I was a cop until my life disintegrated around me. We were all on the take, simple stuff, like turning a blind eye to illegal brothels. I have to say it was a wonderful little earner, which came with parties and free sex. We also took a cut from the illegal casinos; they were a booming industry in those days. As a young cop, I had more cash than I could handle.

Once you go down that slope, the opportunities multiply. Meanwhile, the crims who ran those rackets did as they wished. We also turned a blind eye to SP bookies, and sneaky little businesses receiving stolen goods. You name it, we did it; we were the problem, not the solution, and what we got up to still shocks me. There were no excuses; once I joined the older hands in corruption, it just got bigger. If there is a lesson there, it must be about keeping a moral compass and having the discipline to say 'no'. That life makes you arrogant and greedy. Restaurants and bars never cost me a cent. I was drinking so much I did not stop to think. The thought of how obnoxious I must have been still horrifies me. When the axe fell, it cost me everything I had. When I got out of jail, I drank to destroy myself. I was lucky a chaplain got me in here. Then through Father David, I came to love God, and I asked his forgiveness, and now I am trying to put something back, and this is now my home.

We should try to get your life back together. The trick is never to forget where you were, and never let your guard down for a second; I really mean that, not for a second."

"Peter, I let a lot of people down; although when I think about it, I believe I really wanted to die." Peter had the knack of carefully choosing his words, "Time will heal; it sounds trite, but it does. Get your body and mind working, especially your mind; for us, it seems to be the weak link. You need to regain your self-discipline. When you have done that, you will have recovered." I had a high regard for the man, but Peter wanted me to make way for someone else, and I found myself sitting in the Abbot's study.

"Brother Peter tells me you are a new man. I do not think your sister will recognize you. How do you feel?"

"Father, I have not felt so fit in years." The Abbot smiled. I tried to explain myself, "There were times when I thought I would not make it. Brother Peter has remarkable motivational skills. I am sure I tested him."

"Then God was on your side. Peter's program was ideal for you. We find they either drop out or they go on to make a remarkable recovery. I would like you to look after the priory's flock of sheep, which ought to be right up your alley."

I chuckled at the suggestion. "Father, they do need a decent tidy up, I was going to offer."

"Good, now join me in prayer as we thank our loving God." What do you do in my circumstance? And of course I complied. "Yes Father," I said softly.

"Close your eyes," he directed, "and think upon the words."

"Dearly beloved Father," and the Abbot's superbly modulated voice flowed like honey.

"Please make yourself comfortable, while I will read you my favourite chapter from God's word." The richly timbered voice and phrasing were a theatrical experience all on their own. "Perhaps Darain, you might tell me about your early life as a boy on the mission. I am extremely interested, and I wondered if you were ever initiated?" Telling the Abbot of my childhood helped, and after that, I never felt so isolated. He seemed captivated by it.

"Dar, what a childhood! Perhaps you could take me through it when we have these little talks together."

Once I started shearing the priory's very indifferent flock, I would often look up to find I had an audience. We were a closed community and had I wished to hide away, the priory was the ideal place. Apart from the Abbot, and a few visitors coming and going, there was little outside contact. Maybe it was this—the lack of any stress, or the need for any decision on my part—that enabled me to settle into the rigorous routine of my new life.

The Abbot was a busy man. Our counselling sessions had developed into far wide ranging discussions. Should they be about my people? I found it amazing what I could recall, or we might discuss a difficulty facing the priory. I suppose I saw my joining in their religious life as being an expected part of the deal. The Abbot seemed an extraordinary, caring person, for during one of our conversations, he said, "We might pause for a moment and give thanks for Peggy's life and ask our God to clasp her to him." And I found myself kneeling in front of the prayer rail, listening to the father's incantations with tears streaming down my face.

The wool clip had sold well and the Abbot was most effusive. "A wonderful result Darain, and you made such a first class job of it, thank you for all you have done. And while we are on the subject, I wondered what you thought of our sheep?" I was glad to have been asked.

"Without being too critical, they could be a whole lot better, as grazing on these magnificent pastures, they ought to be absolutely first class. And pardon my saying but the rams look very nondescript to me; and I would get rid of them and buy some from an established stud. You will see the difference straightaway."

The Abbot seemed very pleased with my comment. "I am not surprised," he chuckled, "why don't you look after that and buy in what we need?"

I was happy to be given the task, as the district was renowned for its fat lambs, and we were surrounded by suitable studs. But I was curious as to how the place was run, as it seemed to me that the priory must have a huge income, as the labour costs would have been next to nothing. I knew what the masonry factory turned out, and that would have been a healthy income stream on its own. One day, during one of our discussions, I asked the Abbot where it all went; he appeared a little taken aback, but took time out to explain good-naturedly. "Dar, it goes to charity, and it is distributed only after a lot of thought and prayer. Unfortunately, such is the need there is never enough. I must tell you how it all began, as it is a very inspiring story."

I admit to being genuinely curious as he began. "I came here many years ago when I was still a young man and became a chauffeur and general handyman for an elderly doctor, who had recently been widowed." There was a wry amusement in the Abbot's voice, as if the telling of it rekindled pleasant memories. "As you would have heard me say, God moves in interesting ways, because I found my new employer was a chronic alcoholic. Each morning he was drunk by eleven, but he was so adept at disguising it that nobody knew. But as I disposed of the gin bottles, I knew very well, and quite frankly I still do not know how he got away with it. But at least he had the good sense not to drive. You see he had not long lost his wife, and I believe he would have still been grieving.

That is his photo in my study. Doctor McKell was equally charming drunk or sober. Although, in his declining years, he could be forgetful, which, as he told me, was probably the result of his years of chronic alcoholism. He and I got on very well, and before long, he was in the habit of inviting me to join him for a drink, which I should never have accepted. The problem was he was always so charming if insistent about it. You see I was supposed to be the sober chauffeur, yet I would also be well into a bottle of gin before lunch. So it was not long before the inevitable happened, and I hit another car. The doctor was badly bruised and shaken, but I was seriously injured, and lay there rigged up with wire pulleys and all the other paraphernalia orthopaedic surgeons were so enamoured with in those days. After months in that contraption, I had time to reflect, and I honestly thought my life was ended. But after a few visits by the hospital Chaplain, I felt renewed hope and began to pray. Mind you, there was no flash of lightning, nor did I instantly get up and walk.

But I felt a profound peace, a belief in God, and a new faith in the doctors and nurses. You see, I felt I had been heard, and was strengthened, and I resolved to give my life to God. I could hardly wait to share this with Dr. McKell, who was making a very slow recovery because of his age. When he was well enough to visit, he came to see me. That was the measure of the man; he never attached any blame, not at all; and he was very concerned about my recovery. But I found that apart from his initial affability, the poor old fellow was very down. I told him how I had found God, and I asked him to pray with me. That day we asked to be delivered from the grip of alcohol, we were heard, and neither of us ever touched a drop again."

Christ! I had turned back the clock—this was the mission and Jill all over again; but I realized I had brought it upon myself.

"A simple story," he continued, "but that is how it began, and as is widely known, once we had recovered sufficiently, we began the program. He was in no way a martinet, but the doctor clearly saw hard physical work as a way of restoring the body, and in his view, provided it was not too badly damaged, the mind would follow. Most rewarding of all, we found that when they were back on their feet, our patients became our most enthusiastic supporters. We saved many a life, and the most wonderful thing was he arranged his affairs so that after his death, our work could continue. He was a compassionate man, and through his generosity, many men have come to serve the Lord."

There was no doubting the Abbot's sincerity, but for a moment, I imagined I saw Peggy shaking her head in disapproval. I was careful not to offend the Abbot or Brother Peter, and I have to say that Peter had made a huge impression on me; he had not only turned his own life around, he was contrite, worked enormously hard, and radiated compassion. For my own part, I was reluctant to interfere with how they ran their business, but the Abbot increasingly asked for my opinion. There appeared to be no overriding business plan, nor were there any basic systems in place. Their problem was the insatiable call on funds to meet the priory's many charitable commitments. I had long planted the seed, and was not surprised when I was asked to streamline their masonry factory.

After the success of that, I was drawn into the day-to-day management of the priory's many enterprises. I had only recently discovered that Father David was involved with my people; I had no idea. The pretence had been dispensed with. "I would like you to take a keen interest in all that we do," the Father suggested, "we need your valued input. I see it as a valuable contribution to our wider ministry."

My own recovery had been good, and I found it satisfying to see the improvement in the quality of our fat lambs, to watch the wheat ripen, and to feel satisfaction in a newly sown paddock of Lucerne. In the mornings, the air had a special crispness, the dew sparkled on the grass, and the pale sheep made their tracks across the paddocks.

On one occasion, I had started back after a long day of drenching sheep. The Abbot was doing his rounds and had just left a party working on one of his projects. I watched as he gathered his cassock, climbed through a fence, and continued in my direction. An irrigation pump held a rainbow in its spray, and the dairy cattle stood stationary in the late afternoon sun. We called a greeting to each other as he drew near; the Abbot was flushed from his exertions. Usually these seemingly casual exchanges were the Father's way of having a private word with me.

"Dar," he said, "you seem settled. Peter and I are very pleased at how you have knuckled down to the many tasks you have been given, I need hardly ask if you are happy here?" I was wary, and would have preferred they did not delve into my feelings, and their drawing me out made me feel uncomfortable. Jill had used the same ploy.

"I am a tribute to Peter's perseverance," I laughed. "I am sorry if I was a nuisance."

"No more than anyone else," the Abbot said kindly, "and now you make a useful contribution. We think you are a natural farmer, but what I came over to talk about was about you visiting your sister and seeing if you can stay sober."

The suggestion came as a shock, but I was curious to discover how I might have left things. "We believe you are ready," he said lightly, "and we know she is a very caring lady, and that a visit would bring her a great deal of joy. We understand the hazards, and if it does not work, we will come down and get you. Please do not take that as an invitation to resume your old ways. Now, I have to go down to Sydney anyway, so we could travel down together, and if you wish, I could help you tidy up your affairs while I am there. You have been out of circulation for some time?" I was struck by the man's thoroughness.

"Thank you, but my sister writes that she and Heather have that all under control. I imagine they have made a better fist of it than I could have myself."

"You are blessed!" he exclaimed. "They are lovely women. We find a week or so is usually enough the first time around. There is nothing forced about it; you just see how you feel. When you are ready, just call the priory and let us know what train you are returning on. Take a tip from an old hand, and do not put any pressure on her or yourself by making a big deal out of it. Just do it, and feel proud that you are there; it will have been quite an achievement. Remember, if you do not make it, you will not be the first, but you do have to try. Sleep on it, and we can book your ticket and allocate someone to do your work."

Peter was exuberant as we drove past the pubs on the way to the station.

"Sherry and port on special, ha, ha. I used to think there was terrific value in a flagon of either."

"Peter, please, I would rather you did not," the Abbot complained; he was obviously well-versed in the Brother's routine. But when the train arrived, Peter shook my hand warmly and clapped me on the shoulder. "God speed my friend, I am sure you will be fine."

The air conditioning was oppressive after the sweet air of the valley as the train ran down the gentle slope and wound through the rolling hills of Willow Tree and Murrurundi. The Abbot had put the morning paper he was reading to one side.

"Dar, you were telling me about a great walk you once did when you were a boy. I found it so interesting, and was hoping we could continue our discussion. Our ignorance of your people is monumental, and I find the lore your parents taught you absolutely intriguing."

He was an easy man to converse with, and I spoke of my father's prowess with a spear, and of our fishing on the coast, my many memories of that idyllic time, and the sort of things a small boy never forgets. It was surprising how much of it I had retained. The Abbot told of an unnamed legal luminary, who had been on such a long bender he had actually forgotten who he was; but as he recovered, he would stir the priory up by debating both sides of a complicated legal argument over dinner. In what seemed like no time, we arrived at Central Station and parted on the concourse.

Once I was on a bus, there was no compelling urge to rush into the first pub I saw and drink myself into oblivion. I got off a couple of stops early so as to stretch my legs and check my appearance in a shop window. The night was still, and as I approached, I was very surprised to hear her raised voice, and there was fear in it.

I had not specified a time, and hesitated that I may be about to intrude upon one of those private moments couples need. A neighbour's window slammed down in protest. She was pleading; there was what sounded like a slap, and some muffled sounds which made me very apprehensive. All I could do was wait. Her chatty letters had not mentioned her having a new boyfriend and another round of the argument floated down. "Gerard, leave me alone, please go." God Almighty, what was that parasite doing back with Alkina? There was a cry of pain as though she had been punched. Then a plaintive, "No, no, stop it! I will have to give you a check; we banked the takings; I can only spare you three thousand."

"I said seven and I meant seven! Do it before I give you a hiding."

I remembered my conversation with my sister: "No, Dar, it's over, it really is, I do not see Gerard anymore." How relieved I had been to hear that. Now the bastard was back, extorting money from her. Her sobs broke the silence. Then a minute or so later, her door opened and Gerard came down the stairs. I had been standing out of sight in the shadows, and came from behind, intending to simply put him on the ground, and handle the situation from there. But the best laid plans, and using not much force, I had screwed Gerard's head up and around, until suddenly he was limp in my arms. Jesus no! I had not meant to snap his neck, but I instinctively knew that I must have.

From that moment on, I acted purely on self-preservation. Wallet, I only had a few dollars the Abbot had given me. Car keys, leave him there and find the car. A Ford, look for a tricked up Ford; thank Christ, it was close by; and I put him in the boot. I must be mad and my troubles were just beginning. Hopefully I had not been seen. The things the mind can conjure up, and I saw the bright side of a very grim situation and that this was one problem I had solved for my sister for all time. There were no vital signs, and I found myself driving along in her former lover's car, with his body in the trunk. I opened my window and to let the night air wash over me. Hell, that was the second police car I had seen in a few minutes, and all around were ordinary, sane people, perhaps on the way to the theatre. I can remember willing myself to concentrate and breathe deeply.

Without thinking, I was heading for the boatshed, and from then on, things began to fall into shape. The bay was a mirror, and out in the farthest line of moored boats, *Night Winds* rode peacefully in the water. The boatshed dingy was precisely where Sam kept it. I laid the body across the floor and sculled through the silent boats and came alongside. Father David was right; my friends did love me; Sam had kept her pristine; the fuel and oil were full. I lay the remains on the cabin floor and threw a blanket over it, then sat in the stern for a moment, trying to gather my wits and apply some logic to my situation.

Then I motored into the wharf and quickly ran the car around to a quiet street, where, with any luck, it would not be noticed. I grabbed some old chain from a pile of rusting iron to sink the remains, and borrowed a spare can of fuel. The engine sounded sweet as she headed out to sea. A trawler gave a friendly toot and left us in its wake. I passed the headlands, made my way through the anchored container ships and bulk carriers, until well off the shore, where the distant city lights were just a haze.

Everything was in its place and like a dog sniffing for a long buried bone, I rummaged under the floorboards for a spare bottle. As my fingers closed around the cold glass, it was like a prayer being answered. On deck I drank half a tumbler of Scotch. I lifted my second to Peggy, as if she was sitting in her usual place in the lee of the cabin. Wispy clouds drifted across a half moon and the drink calmed me. *Night Winds* lifted with the swell and I welcomed the soft sea breeze and the spray on my face.

I set to work on the wallet, found her check, tore it up and scattered it to the wind. The plastic cards, the wallet and everything in it were cut up with a filleting knife and went over the side. I took a drink and throttled right back. I reduced each garment to shreds before it went over the side, until there was nothing but the body lying across the stern tray. A couple of half hitches of chain around it, and I ran the filleting knife down from below the ribcage to ensure the sneaky little bastard did not blow up and rise to the surface again, and over the side he went.

The faintest zephyr was coming in from the nor'-east and smelled wonderfully of the sea. I threw a couple of buckets of sea water over where he had lain and opened up the throttle and headed back to shore. I watched the breaking dawn of a new day, and sipped a Scotch as *Night Winds* rode the swell in gentle flights. Peg and I often went offshore after snapper, and I could almost hear her say how she loved the low white clouds on the horizon in the early morning. The sun came up as the wind rippled in from the ocean.

Sam and I hugged like father and son.

"Dar, you look good; you do, you look very good; phew, Jesus son, you have been on the Scotch? Son, don't do that; your sister said you were off the sauce; I was so pleased to hear it. She is a wonderful lady; she had me keep your boat ready for you; did she go all right?"

"Sam, she never missed a beat. It was so good to be out again. I found a bottle Peggy and I had stashed away for emergency. Sam, in a way it was, but I'm okay; I am off the sauce for good."

"Well, you don't smell all right, and quite frankly, you don't look all that bloody good either. For goodness sake, don't go and see her like that; stay here while I put the kettle on." The old fellow fussed about with the tea things, obviously trying to figure me out. "No more booze Dar, don't do that; you have come too far." The tea was welcome; perhaps it had been the sea air, but I did not feel too bad.

"Dar, I found Peggy's ashes on board, that was as far as you ever got with them, and I have them at home. Why don't you and I take them out and you can lay her to rest; it's time it was done." I could not remember ever having them. Peter's and the Abbot's words about how blessed I was came to me.

"I am very sorry. Didn't I even do that?" Peter had warned that I would discover things about which I would have no idea. As usual, he had been right.

"Yes Sam, but not today; you and I will do it first thing in the morning."

"And where are you spending the night?"

"On board."

Sam scratched at his stubble, "Would you like to come home?" I still had to dispose of Gerard's car, and besides that, I was not going to impose myself on anyone.

"No thanks Sam, I will be fine."

"This farm, or whatever it is, has pulled off a miracle; we will have our little ceremony for Peggy in the morning, then you go and see your sister. You hitting the grog like that seemed so out of character. I enjoyed our few beers together, and when I told the wife, we were very down. She and I were very fond of Peggy, but life must go on, and son, we have real faith in you." I was deeply touched.

"Thanks," I said, feeling that I had let the side down. "They have done a wonderful job." As I collected Gerard's car, I hoped the locals were glued to their televisions, and five minutes later, I had pulled into a quiet street and carefully wiped any surfaces I may have touched. I found the address on the license and parked it a couple of streets away, then I gave the inside a final wipe and left it unlocked. I am not sure why; perhaps it was in the hope that someone would steal it; that was the best scenario I could come up with. The stress of the previous night began to fall away once I had boarded a bus. I removed each key from the ring and got rid of them randomly as we travelled along. By this time it was getting late, and I decided to find a café and have something to eat.

I was so glad to still have the boat. I was tired and once on-board, I fell quickly asleep. In the early morning, it was the gentle sound of water lapping against the hull that must have awakened me to a beautiful day. I motored in to shower and shave, and made tea while I waited for Sam to arrive. Typical of his and his wife's thoughtfulness, he came with armfuls of native brush and flowers. Peggy's ashes were in a plain cardboard box.

"Dulce, picked these for her this morning," he explained. The emotion I was feeling threatened to overwhelm me.

"Sam, that's very kind of her, and my very good friend, I want to apologize for yesterday."

"That's okay," he said, shaking his head. "Sis will never know, so there's no harm done."

We puttered slowly out through the boats and headed for her favourite fishing spot. The morning was just as she would have ordered. I shut the engine down and let her joggle in the swell while a zephyr came in from the ocean. She was watching, and the seagulls gathered for her farewell.

"Lovely day for it," Sam commented. "You okay? Don't mind me. I think it was part of the problem, as I never saw you cry. I am on the verge myself."

"Thank you Sam. A morning like this was just how she liked it, a mild nor'easter to keep it cool and keep the flies away. She did not care if the fish did not bite; she said that either way it was just an excuse to be out on the water." We were thinking of her as we kept our silence and let the boat drift in the morning zephyrs. Then I stood up on the fishing tray and slowly scattered her ashes and watched as they silently drifted away.

"Goodbye," I called, "goodbye my darling girl; goodbye my love; this is your place forever."

"Jesus, Sam, I feel sad, but she would appreciate that. There she goes, back to the sea and the wind." I felt sure she would have understood, as Peg was that sort of girl. Sam passed me the branches and flowers, and after a while, I got down.

"Sam, it would be nice if you did that," I suggested. "She was very fond of you and Dulce."

"Dar, thanks, it would be my privilege." I was very moved as Sam threw them gently over the side. "Goodbye my dear girl; with much love from Dulce, your loving husband, and me. Pretty, aren't they? Nice of mum to do that for us, a fitting farewell to a lovely lady; let us just sit for a while." We watched as the floral tribute slowly drifted away. "That was nice Dar, Peggy will rest easy now, start her up, it is time for you to see your sister, and for me to open up."

As I stood on my sister's doorstep, I found it unbelievable I was there, and to find her as bubbly as ever.

"Dar, you look wonderful. I am so thrilled to see you. What a change! They have worked a miracle." She was the reincarnation of her namesake, and strangely, I could discover no sign of Gerrard's assault.

"Thanks, sis, you look pretty good yourself. Now tell me all your news." "Heather would love to see you; in fact you should, particularly, as she was instrumental in getting you in. You can come into work with me and make yourself useful, and then we can meet up with her." At least on the surface, she appeared happy, serene, and as usual, highly organized. Yet listening to her, the contrast between my former life and the depths to which I had reduced myself, seemed unimaginable.

"Sis, I am sorry to have let Pat and James down. How are they getting along?"

"I do not know about that; at least you were smart enough to recruit and train some very good people. They are still expanding; the whole thing has been quiet extraordinary really. You know I often think of James's mother; that frightful woman would have been one of the great motivations that drove him on. I find that ironic, James might make a joke of it, but I think it's true. We were all shocked at your reaction, but no one ever talks disparagingly, because Dar, you were a huge part of their success. James lost his father, which was so sad, as you know James could not stand her; and as it turned out, the dear man was large enough to accept the situation, and they remained close. James organized a lovely wake, and had his father's favourite jazz band play him out.

166

His mother had not changed. I still get the shudders when I think of what may have happened to me if James had not stepped in. Hanna and Henry have slowed down. I will ask them over. While I think of it Dar, Father David phoned on Monday night to see if you had arrived safely, he was surprised I had not seen you, I would call him."

It seemed to me that Peggy had intervened on my behalf, and when I told her, Alkina very much approved of what Sam and I had done. "Oh Dar, I am sorry, that would have been so sad for you and dear old Sam. Father David must think you are cured. I cannot imagine how they do it, but whatever it is, please do not stop."

"Well," I said, "they will not have to come and get me after all, they offered to; they certainly know the pitfalls."

"Dar, I had no idea, and of course the place is full of the stuff. I do like my friends to call in; do say so if it should be locked away."

"No sis, the more I overcome it, the better I get, or so they say." I was in good shape and a week later, I had not touched a drop. But the business with Gerard had left me questioning my own sanity, and made my battle with alcohol seem secondary. I rationalized it by telling myself the man was so flabby and unfit, and that his neck must have been his weakness. Fortunately, my sister never once mentioned him. Ernie and Coreen invited me to stay, and said their eldest was at University, completing second year dentistry. A few days later and I had advised the priory that I was leaving the following morning on the 7:45 am Tableland Express.

It had rained and the country looked in great heart. Father David greeted me enthusiastically. "You made it. We shall offer thanks to God in our prayers. We regard that as a milestone, but my friend, there is still a long and difficult journey ahead."

"Goodness me, you came back to us," Peter said, feigning great surprise and slapping my back. "Do not forget to thank God in your prayers. I certainly will."

My days passed uneventfully, and given my deeply felt guilt, it seemed fitting that I should live like a penitent. It was many months later, and I was moving a line of irrigation pipes for an overnight soak; it was very hot work and I was sweating freely; those pipes were almost too hot to move. I saw the Abbot crossing the paddock to join me. The hem of his cassock was coated in dust, seed, and clover burr. Father David gave me a hand until the line was finished, and then we stopped to cool off and to have a drink of water. "Dar, one cannot help noticing that the way you throw yourself into your work, and it seems to Peter and me that you are a changed man."

I could not really say that disposing of your sister's former lover tends to have that effect, or that working my butt off was the only thing that enabled me to sleep at night.

"Father," I said, "I am not so sure about that."

"Peter and I were only talking about it, as we think the spirit of our dear Lord Jesus has entered your heart." Seemingly, I had dug a hole for myself; why on earth didn't I set the man straight by saying something sensible? I could have said, "Look here Father David, I am perfectly happy to set up your systems and develop the long-term business plans for the priory, but I would much prefer it if you would lay off the evangelizing." But, of course I did not, and the opportunity was lost, and also I regarded Peter and the Abbot as friends; and it seemed to me that Father David had a genuine interest in my people.

"Witnessing the change in you has been a most rewarding experience for me," the Abbot continued. "Personally I see it as a re-birthing, almost like you're dreaming places and reconnecting to the land. I am beginning to understand the timelessness of your people. Dar, you have been given some unique gifts; I mean your feeling for the weather; and in that regard, your predictions are usually more reliable than the forecast. Everything you touch flourishes; perhaps your management role here is your true vocation."

What on earth would Peggy have thought of me hibernating at the priory? I could imagine it and I did not like what I saw, for in no way did it fit the way she and I imagined our lives. While I harboured these thoughts, Father David and I connected another spray line. Time just disappeared; our masonry works had become the biggest in the North West, employing over fifty men. The various divisions I had created now spoke in terms of deadlines, contractual obligations, output and variations to budget. The priory hummed with activity, and in doing so had taken a giant leap in its income, and therefore a corresponding leap in its charitable responsibilities.

It was during that time that I was torn between staying and getting out. Meanwhile, Father David and Peter interpreted what they saw as being the result of my profound spiritual conversion. I think I must be living proof that one can adapt to almost anything. One morning, the Abbot and I were leaning over a stockyard fence, watching a load of young steers being loaded on to a truck.

"Dar," he began, "who would have thought we would have prospered so? It seems to me that the time has come to ask for your total commitment, as for some time now, I have had the feeling that God is calling you to his great ministry."

I was suddenly gripped by panic, for at that time, I was not even sure that returning to my former life was such a smart thing to do. Then I began to rationalize—that staying where I was would not really change my life that much; I was practically one of them anyway. As it was, I spent most of my life planning, looking at figures, or running meetings. We would not have gone ten steps, before the Abbot turned to face me.

"Let us pause a moment and bow our heads and give thanks to Almighty God, and ask for his help and guidance."

≈ 21 ≈

I was delighted at my brother's progress, but rather miffed that he so rarely came down to visit. He appeared to have settled down to the Spartan ways of the priory. I was not sure that I approved, yet I had to admire his attitude toward helping other alcoholics. And when I thought about it, I could hardly refute that his current life was a quantum improvement on his living in the gutter. As Heather said, "One eventually gets used to the idea," which was fine until I received his outrageous letter, which had left me reeling. Somehow I managed to hold my indignation in check until I met up with Heather for our usual Friday lunch.

"My dear, this is really a very nice venue," Heather remarked. My editor said we got wonderful feedback from my gossipy stories, and that it had become a matter of intense speculation as to what Heather might wear. On that score, she had never left me short of copy. The maître d' fussed over us. I usually told her what my editor was looking for from our lunches.

"My dear," I told her, "this piece is supposed to be about a change of ownership and a new chef, and I have to say that I know zilch about either. But I will say that I like the décor; now let's see what else they have. I would prefer to choose the restaurant I review, but I had no choice with this one, which is all to do with who you know, and having one's back scratched; so if it is no good, you can blame my editor."

Heather laughed. "I have never seen you pan one yet, which does tend to let them off the hook."

"I suppose it does, but I don't think my readers would want to be a part of a general rubbishing. They want to be uplifted and to live the experience through you and me; they want to know who was there, what we ordered, and most importantly of all, what you are wearing. They also want our view of the restaurant, the lunch, and how we see the world in general."

"Well as your solicitor, I don't think it would be wise to mention that the Premier's mistress will also be in London, when he is supposed to be over there to confer on matters of mutual interest. Not with her," she quipped, "but with important government officials in the UK."

Heather knew how to get my journalistic juices flowing. I laughed. "Smart timing for Wimbledon, and I am sure I read she was almost good enough to have made it on the circuit herself."

"So I heard. Mind you Alkina, if you ever met the Premier's wife, you could hardly blame him."

"Ha ha, don't worry, I have; she's frightful. I did a reception to welcome a delegation of manufacturers from Japan, and she sought me out to tell me the finger food was cold. 'Mrs. Manville,' I said, 'it is intended to be; your husband approved the menu.'"

"Oh, that's her," Heather agreed. "Lovely wine, cheers. I do look forward to Friday."

"And not bad for the price," I added. "I have to say their wine list has been well chosen." Heather was such a nice luncheon companion and friend.

"Oh, and mum said to tell you how much she looks forward to reading your column; she's a huge fan, and everyone in the office devours it."

"Heather, you flatter me, but it is still nice to hear; and how are Phyllis and Harold? I haven't seen them for ages?"

"Oh they're fine, and today mum and dad are out chasing that little white ball." I sipped my wine and nodded approvingly.

"I can just imagine the pandemonium in the kitchen," Heather commented. I shrugged.

"Well, they knew we were coming."

"Then it should be perfect. It has been that sort of week for me; 'tis the season for litigation; it is no wonder I was looking forward to Friday." Underneath the chatter, I battled to suppress my anguish over my brother's letter. Having another sip of my wine, I decided the moment was as good as any.

"I received a letter from Dar," I explained, and passed it across. "Heather, take a decent swig; I think you will need it." Always unflappable on these occasions, Heather had put her glasses on and had begun to read. "I am sorry," I added, "my brother's mad; believe me, it's a real shocker." Heather would also have wondered about the state of my brother's mind, and while she read, I returned smiles, and had polite little chats with complete strangers. I leaned across and said, "I cannot imagine what is going through my brother's brain. I have never read such sheer unadulterated crap in all my life."

Heather had put his letter to one side. "I am glad you showed it to me. I would have been very offended if you had not." My dear friend must have decided she may have missed something, as she gave her glasses a quick polish, and began to read it through again. That letter was really something else and I felt sure that my own brother had been brainwashed.

My dear Alkina,

How is my wonderful sister? I pray as happy and effervescent as always. Our work here is increasing every day; perhaps it is the pressure of our society that men revert to alcohol and drugs as a refuge. Each day is full of challenges for us, and I feel that whatever skill I can bring to this task helps me to repay some of the debt I owe you, this order, and our Lord for my own deliverance. It gives me immense satisfaction to do whatever I can to help repair broken lives.

I do understand you may find this decision quite strange, but I have decided to devote my life to the glory of Almighty God. I shall work to ensure that his offer of salvation and everlasting life through his son Jesus Christ is told to all who may listen. My decision has been made after much study, prayer and meditation, and I clearly hear the call to do his work.

Father David will ordain me into the blessed order on Sunday, the 6th of July, in our chapel, at 11am. The service will be followed by a celebratory lunch, and of course I would like you to attend. I am immensely satisfied and grateful that God has called me to his service, and I shall enter a week of solitary meditation and prayer to ready myself for this holy event.

I send you all my love, and thank you for all you have done for me over the years, especially your great generosity and affection. I shall now answer the call to spend my life doing what I can for others. Please understand that I do not forsake the ancient stories and spirits of our people; they shall always have a fond and private place in my heart.

With much love,
Dar

Heather put his letter down, and looked across with her eyes raised sceptically.

"Dear me, about all that comes to my mind is 'shit!'."

"Exactly, Heather that was about all I could manage. I think it sums it up nicely."

"Well, we cannot say he was not sober," Heather said, with her delicious, dry humour. "I am sorry, but this time your brother has really floored me. I wonder what we can do, not a great deal I suspect. You and I recognize it as a highly emotional letter, could he have been brainwashed, be under undue influence, being kept against his will, although that may be stretching things a little."

"No, Heather, I think he is bullshitting himself." It is in my makeup to feel responsible, and I continued, "Heather, what I object to is that he might be doing the same thing to the very sincere and well-meaning Abbot, who hardly needs to be led up the garden path. He's a gem; he grows on you; just look what he has done; he is an incredible human being. I know they saved his life. Sorry about this; it is just that in the very best light I can put on it. I think it stinks! One thing I am not going to do is tell mum and dad; they have had enough; it would be the final insult to everything they believe in."

"Perhaps," Heather offered, "the thing to do is to keep your distance. It may help to see it clearer, rather than to attend a service and luncheon for something you really do not believe in."

"That's the point. I honestly don't believe for a moment that he does either. I have not decided if I could go; I need to let it sink in for a while. Somehow this whole thing just does not gel with me."

Heather would have received that message loud and clear. "Well, my dear," she said, "if you really are convinced that something is amiss, we could seek a restraining order to slow the process down. No great rush, but it is worth a thought."

"I wonder if my brother has become a bit strange; I mean his life has not exactly been a breeze. Along the way, he has had his great highs and his great lows. He was too young to cope with being taken from our parents, and I would not be surprised if that was part of it. Although, I really thought that with his marriage to Peggy, he had left all that baggage behind. He could not cope at all after her death, so I wonder how much better he really is. Perhaps he has substituted religion for drink; now there is a thought for you."

My friend was tasting her food and nodding her head as if to say she agreed, and I took it as a cue to let my brother and his problems rest.

"Mm, nice vegetables," she commented, working around her plate. And I joined her, "my dear, top quality to begin with, they do look nice, cooked just enough. Yum, homemade mustard with a hint of lemon in the sauce, oh dear, too thin and runny, what a shame." Should the chef come out, I would find something to praise, and only then would I offer a comment. Heather said I went over my plate like a brain surgeon. It must have worked, because in no time at all I would have enough for my column.

"Hmm, why is everyone so obsessed with potato, which I think is far too heavy for a summer luncheon menu? And Heather, how is yours?"

"You know me. Anything I don't have to cook myself tastes divine. But seriously, the sauce is lovely; but don't ask me what's in it, a generous serving and the meat is delicious and moist, so no complaints at all."

"If chef picked up on the detail," I said, almost thinking aloud, "and they tidied up their act at the front, this place could be a real goer." We chatted about this and that, but a glass of wine or two later; and the conversation had returned to my brother.

"Heather, whatever will I do? I would have thought we had enough religion crammed down our necks when we were kids, to put him off it forever. My impression was we had learned to handle it; evidently I was wrong." Heather looked on sympathetically, but made no comment other than nodding her head in agreement.

⚡ 22 ⚡

The stranger had the weathered look of a farmer, and there was something of a former soldier about him—plain, yet casual clothes, neatly groomed with a relaxed and uncomplicated face, as those in the bar of the Townsville pub noticed. He knew exactly where the Regular Army drank; they were creatures of habit, and the new generation of young soldiers was the same. You could tell who was who just by quietly sitting in a corner and watching; he sidled up to a fellow whom he thought was probably a Warrant Officer.

"G'day," he said, "how's the army treating you these days?"

"Good, thanks mate," the local replied affably. "You're ex-army?"

"Yeah, a few years ago now; just checking the old place out, same you know, just the same."

"Vietnam?"

"Yeah."

"Let me buy you a beer."

"Thanks, a Four X for me."

"When were you over there?"

"Sixty-nine—seventy."

"Any problems?"

"Not a scratch, could not have been luckier. Thought while I am here, I would try to find an old friend of mine; you lose track when you return to Civvy Street."

"I can understand. There are still a few of the old coves around; they retire, but they still cannot leave it alone. What's his name?

"Skune, Ronnie Skune, he was just an MP in those days. He was a *bonzer* bloke; it would be nice to meet up with him and his family."

"Don't know him myself, but hang on and I will ask Stan; he's former Provost. Hey Stan, I am having a beer with a Vietnam vet. He is inquiring about an old mate of his, Skune, Ronnie Skune." Stan was obviously a figure of some standing, as he had a circle around him.

"Skune," he said, "now that's going back a few years. You know I got an idea he bought a caravan park down on the beach at Bowen. That's right, he did, and last I heard he was offering a special deal to serving and former personnel; it sounded like a nice place, and if I remember, it was a pretty good deal."

"Thanks mate", called the visitor, "nice to hear; I will look him up."

The stranger had disappeared as suddenly as he had arrived, but had left enough on the bar for another round. It would have been a few weeks later that those in the caravan park heard the telephone ring in the office. The night was balmy, and they would have listened as the water lapped against the shore. The resort lay in the lee of the north arm of the bay. The lifestyle was slow and casual; the only reason to wear a shirt at night was the mosquitoes. The lights shone softly in the caravans as radios and televisions played. Others sat outside under an awning to sip on a drink, to talk and enjoy another peaceful night.

"Good evening, would that be Ronnie Skune?" the voice inquired.

"Yes, Skune here, how can I help you?"

"Mate, it's Don Perrin here from your former unit; we booked a couple of vans for a fishing party of four."

"Yes Mr. Perrin, they are ready for you."

"Good, but we have a slight problem; we have had a breakdown about six miles out on the Mount View Road, and nobody can do anything till morning. If we make it worth your while, could you come and get us? It is just that we are all pretty bushed."

The former military policeman weighed it up; things had been quiet and he needed the money, but thank God, they were not going to cancel. Four guests, two vans with annexes, seven days, boat hire, food, booze, bait, and all the rest of it. And all ex-army, some pleasant male company for a change, the sort of booking that could spread the word around and make the sleepy place really work.

"Certainly Mr. Perrin, I will be right out, leaving straightaway." The black road twisted through the bush, only a very occasional car came through at this time of night. They would have driven from the inland. Wouldn't it be nice to just take off with some mates for a week's fishing? Oh, to break the deadly routine of being up before the dawn to clean the toilets and the shower blocks; then spend the rest of the day picking up all their crap, which they left on the pristine lawns and everywhere else, exactly where it dropped, and having to pretend that it was no trouble at all, and that his life, as the always affable owner was the epitome of how to live in a tropical paradise. That life would be so kind? They all made the same comment: "Ron, lovely caravan park you have here; what we look for in all the places we stay is cleanliness."

Ha, ha, definitely army, and with a few drinks on board, if he was not mistaken, one was dancing around with a torch, and just as he was pulling off the road he got it full blast in the face, and was momentarily blinded. Bloody idiot!

"Is that you Mr. Perrin?"

"Yes."

"Here we are." He got out fuming, "fair go mate, not in my eyes." Then there was nothing but the impenetrable night as an iron arm clamped around his neck, and he felt the cold steel blade against his throat. "Kneel with your hands behind your back." He did not recognize the voice and his hands were bound tightly. "What is this fellas? A prank? If it is, I think it's gone far enough!"

A noose was slung around his neck. Christ! What if they were tripping on drugs? A hundred such thoughts came to him, as he was bundled forward. "Stop this right now." No response; where were the others? The noose yanked his head up, forcing him to the balls of his feet; he was helpless. His car was driven up until it was pressing against the back of his legs. "Get up and stand on the bonnet." He was hoisted up. "You are about to meet your maker."

"No, I have a family; you can have my money."

"I do not want your money. I want to send your soul to where it belongs. We will let the devil take you—simple justice for all the pain you caused while you were here."

"It wasn't me."

"Oh, but it was; there was a witness."

"You are mistaking me for someone else!"

"You may confess before I reverse your car."

"Do not do this!"

"Say after me: Dear loving and merciful God, hear my confession. While I was a guard at the Townsville stockade..."

"Oh Christ, which one are you?"

"...I abused Military Law, and my obligation to the prisoners entrusted to my care. I am a cruel man and got sadistic pleasure from inflicting pain on helpless men. I tormented and tortured convicted prisoner number NX 3961729. I saw this prisoner as an inferior being. I am deeply sorry."

"In the name of the Father, the Son and the Holy Ghost, forgive me!" The car was reversed.

The following day, a monk was seen boarding the overnight bus for Brisbane, and the passengers were struck by his lovely, friendly, open manner. They remembered him telling the children pretty stories. Later that year, a small article appeared on page three of *The Coral Coast Gazette*:

> The Coroner found that Mr. Ronald Skune, caravan park operator of Bowen, had in all probability died by his own hand. His suicide was in the Court's opinion, caused by an amalgam of depression and financial anxiety. There were no suspicious circumstances.

≉ 23 ≉

I called Heather's private line. "I have a letter from Dar, signed Brother Aden, and I am just so mad I can barely speak."

"Oh dear, stay calm and we can talk about it over a drink. Can it wait until about 6:45 at the usual? Is there anything else?" I had sipped at a Perrier and had not the foggiest notion of how to placate myself. I nodded to the barman and got up to plant a peck on Heather's cheek. "Brother Aden, my foot! I would do anything for my brother, but this is ridiculous." Heather took a sip of her wine as she waited for me to get it out.

"I could not bring myself to go. How on earth could he expect me to sit through something like that? Now I receive this loving, and I think, very self-serving letter. Christ Heather, I could strangle him!"

"Don't worry Alkina, I can see."

"The very idea of it has made me feel so uncomfortable that I have worked myself up into a nice old state. I know it is all crap, and I am trying to resist my overwhelming urge to jump on a plane and try to bring him to his senses." Heather was a good listener, and sat there, nodding slowly as if she was weighing it all up, and every now and then she took a sip of her wine.

"If it is any consolation, my dear," she finally said, "I think you were very smart to keep out of it. If anyone should know what makes him tick, it is you. I would think that in the years to come, you may look back at this, and feel entirely vindicated. The thought occurred to me that although he may look as though he has recovered, perhaps he has not. Your brother might carry a few demons around that we do not know about."

She had that wonderful ability to maintain her calm and stand back and look at a problem with great clarity. Yet neither of us had any idea of the great storm that was already brewing as I struggled to unburden myself.

⚝ 24 ⚝

Unknown to my brother and me, an unprecedented homicide investigation was being run in Sydney, which was headed up by Chief Superintendent Raymond Brannagan. As you can imagine, my source was Heather. "I am told," she said, "they are investigating one of the most horrific cases they have ever seen" which, probably unwisely, I just happened to mention to my editor.

Not long after, I was co-opted by a sister magazine to produce a piece on it. There is no connection between my catering business and this whatsoever, other than that it had given me a great entre to the Premier's office. Through them I made the call and got an interview with the chief investigating officer, who turned out to be a very helpful and charming man.

"What struck me," Brannagan explained, "about these slayings was not so much the gruesomeness, and that we now knew we were dealing with someone who had a taste for it. Nor was it the fact that the victims were husband and wife; no, for me, it was the incredible contrast with normality. For I recall driving into the office on a beautiful Sydney morning. I had been up all night, and I can remember glancing at the Opera House and thinking how pretty and pristine it and the harbor were. We do not expect such things in Sydney.

With murders I never wish the victims to become just another meaningless statistic. In death, they are given a whole new persona. They are photographed, measured, and weighed, and there is an explosion of fact—what they had ingested, where and who with, more detail than even they could have imagined. Ah yes, and as tired as I was, it occurred to me that there was still time for a few brief details of their passing to be included in the weekly return to the Commissioner, Lawrence D. Cavanagh AO. Then we hoard all our discoveries, no matter how seemingly insignificant, and do everything in our power to find their killer.

Alkina, a night such as that weighs you down in a way that nothing else can. But you have to get through it, and as a behavioural psychologist, I recognized that I was already in a state of mild shock. I think I operate on what you might call "auto pilot". I like to control things so I do not tell my superiors too much, just enough to make them feel privy to our investigation. It was not until I had returned to my office from what had been a harrowing night, that I realized we were confronting one of the most difficult homicide cases of my career." He smiled at me and said, "Alkina, that is it for now. I really cannot release anymore. You and I could talk when this investigation is further along."

"Thank you," I said, "I can appreciate the situation."

Brannagan was known as being absolutely forthright, and it was that short interview that made me aware of the case, and, when it was finally cracked, has enabled me to gather my material and write about it. This took place several years after our initial meeting.

"As I may have told you," he said, "I was exhausted, suffering from mild shock and needed to talk. In my profession, it helps to have a confidant in these situations, who has seen it all. So once I was in my office, I brought the number for the FBI up on the screen and called. At the other end, my identification would have come up on the operator's screen.

"May I speak to Professor Martin Knowles?" They put me straight through. "I have just come from another one, so I may be in a little shock."

"How long is it since your last?"

"This is the twenty-seventh day, same ritual, down to roughly the same time of death. They were a married couple, late thirties early forties. It was a slaughterhouse."

"Ray, have you ever had a cannibal?"

"No." How smart he was to pull me up, and place it in some sort of perspective.

"Well, you are a very lucky man, remind me to tell you all about it."

"Thanks, but seriously Martin, I believe he is developing a liking for it. No semen again, or none that we have found. I think it would help if there was; it does help to explain."

"Are you sure it's him?"

"Our man leaves his signature; it's a peculiar motif he draws in blood." I don't know that I was fishing for anything; it was more just the relief of being able to share it with another professional of his calibre and I felt confident that whatever my friend had to offer would soon be on its way. "Raymond, I can listen, but right now, I cannot think of anything useful I can add. Son, it is early days, just slip into your routine and hopefully your people might find something. I know you cannot take it home, but don't leave it too long before you knock yourself out. You feel alright?"

"Yes, I'm okay."

Even that short conversation helped, but I was shaken. My wife had been asleep and I had gone for a walk until sunrise. With someone like her, this was not a subject for the morning coffee. Moleander put her head in the door to let me know she understood. "You can call the photos up on your screen," she said, "not pretty; spending a night on something like that, you poor man." Moleander was a handy cushion.

"Ray, he certainly throws himself into his work."

"He appears to like it."

"Mol, last night changed things; we cannot fall back on a jilted lover."

"Ray, some way to treat a former lover; what did the Professor think?"

"He didn't, but I know he will look for a comparable." I was not in the mood to discuss Martin's latest triumph, a medical student who had cooked and eaten portions of his fellow students. I left Moleander to it, "Chief, the media have gone berserk, and Laurence D wants you to go up and fill him in. I gave them the usual preliminaries to shut them up; that you are personally heading the investigation and all the usual guff." I would have been running on adrenaline. Lawrence D's office stank of brilliantine, and despite the ban, his evil smelling pipe tobacco. I spread the photos.

"Ray, what have we here?"

"Last month's psychopath has gone off again, there's no doubt that it's him. Same mutilation pattern; they were bled, and their kidneys removed. The medics say there is no sign of any particular expertise. Again, no semen, he made the same awful mess by wallowing in their blood and kidney fat. What we find strange is that once again, he presumably left there covered in it; there was no sign of towels being used, or of any prints or residues around the taps." Commissioner Laurence D. Cavanagh had come up through traffic, planning, and industrial relations. He had a reputation as an able administrator and someone who did not rock the boat. This was not his thing at all.

"He must stink to high heaven," I explained, "what does he do? He could not very well get on a bus like that. The neighbours never saw or heard a thing; it appears he just walked away. If there is a connection, it might be that the victims were roughly the same age. I want a complete blackout on the detail."

"Ray, of course."

"I have spoken to the FBI's Chief behaviourist." Lawrence D nodded, but I could tell that he had heard enough and that deference had been paid. It still makes me smile, for at that level, the force is like a collection of gossiping aunts. Laurence D was one of the worst; you only told him what you did not mind being spread around. He was where the rumours and the leaks began. He would tell Milton Strong, the Minister, who was a politician of mediocre talent and desperate for publicity.

"Ray, how was the great man?" Moleander asked.

"Lawrence D looks crook most of the time." Mol laughed. I did not tell her that I did not feel so hot myself. Why leave a symbol? The killer had an unusual fixation. I took a clean sheet of paper and drew it while it was fresh in my mind, religious, perhaps a pattern from a church window? Moleander was already running with it.

"Ray, we are rechecking all recent releases, but it will take a few days to account for them all. The media have set up a camp outside; we have worked out a joint strategy, and I have directed that their calls go to Media Relations. You must have pressed the right switch, as there is now a stream of stuff coming in from the FBI."

"Put out a descriptive bulletin, and see it is shared with Homicide Commanders in every State." The twist in this case was that their killer was obviously known to them. They had let him in, and there had been no desperate struggle to survive. Upon my homecoming after the carnage of the previous night, I had slipped into my usual routine, shoes in garage, everything else in wash, suit in plastic bag ready for dry cleaner, a long hot shower, and two neat brandies. Queenie and I have both moved on, and I don't think she would mind me saying that at the time we were no longer physically close. But we got on sociably, and she kept my life on an even keel. It is also fair to say that her temperament had never been compatible with my work.

"Chief, you look absolutely stuffed. Please go home; this place will still be here tomorrow." I could rely on Moleander to call a spade a spade, and that was how this case began, with the team grinding away day after relentless day, and often it was the small reactions that made it tolerable. Mol had been insistent; she was not going to let me get away with running a sloppy interview. "Mol, I have not got all day, and as for that cranky old fart stuffing us about, fancy, his niece had been missing for days, and he did bugger all about it."

She of the lovely eyes would have none of it. "I would not say that I think you are being a bit tough. He was devastated by her death, and feels some responsibility. Chief, I would not mind betting he is older than he looks, and of course there has been the shock. Give him a few more days and I will get him in again. Funny how she had come on; at first shy and demure, a diligent and creative researcher, and now she made a big contribution. "Please Ray, softly, softly this time, an eccentric Englishman if you ask me, and my guess, considerably deafer than he lets on."

"Mol, you win."

She was an IT specialist, brought in to organize our systems. Everything going back to Adam was now just a mouse click away. These days, we took a lofty view of it, and we looked forward to our exchanges. I had been reviewing the response from our targeting of mental health professionals, and the medical profession generally. "How would it be to be treating a patient, and you suddenly had a thought that it might be him?" I asked. "I cannot imagine. I would have left already," she replied.

The trick was to get her to stand back and use her very smart brain, and the thing was she cared. She would nag me for not carrying a gun, which I felt was a reflex response from watching too many rubbishy cop movies, in which they blast the crap out of anything that moves—which, at least to me, says the writer had simply run out of ideas. But I did have to concede that at the time, the tally was five dead.

"Mol, we are not even close; this fellow is just a leaf tumbling about in the wind. The ritual of it is very important to him. Just think, he is someone's son, husband, or brother." Jim Willard, our Chief Forensic Scientist, could be a bit finicky and had to be handled with kid gloves. My technique was to have a quick browse to check on the doings of our cricketers. I was not a huge fan myself, but it was a harmless enough obsession.

I would have led in with something like, "A wonderful innings over in Perth, Waugh's captaincy was inspiring," knowing such a comment would trigger an avalanche. The compensation came when he told me he had managed to separate out some interesting residues from the crime scenes, and here I am referring to blood and fat.

"Major Lavenby is as deaf as a brick," Mol said. "He will be here around ten in the morning." To her, work was work, and as she promised, the irritating old bugger was punctual.

"Chief, you remember Major Lavenby," Mol could easily be heard half a block away, "he is happy to be interviewed again." Her style of super diplomacy, "The Chief Superintendent would like you to call him Ray," she screamed. I was buggered if I would, and was amazed to realize that I was booming myself. "Good to see you Major. We will have a cup of tea and a biscuit; always do at this time of the day."

The old chap reminded me of a recently laid-out cadaver. This one came closely shaved and complete with highly polished shoes, sharp creases, regimental tie, and Harris Tweed sports coat.

"Major, you are aware there have been other homicides similar to the one that claimed your niece?" The old fellow nodded resignedly. Mol was hanging about like an over-anxious netball referee.

"There we are Major, help yourself to milk and sugar; do have a biscuit; your loss was very sad," I bellowed.

The Major made slurping noises, and looked like a friendly parrot as he nibbled. So far so good, Mol should have been a school teacher; but suddenly the old boy was talking.

"Susan was such a lovely girl, but it is no good looking back, and I do not think I am handling it very well. I have to say her death has flattened me. She was so like her mother, always helping people less fortunate than herself." I nodded, aware that his niece's murder had been more terrible than he would ever know. Mol had tired of her vigil. My gaze rarely left the Major's and I nodded and smiled encouragingly.

"She was the gentlest soul, yet she was also a headstrong girl. Loved horses, had her own hack in the UK, good at dressage you know, loved Australia, stayed in the country with some friends of mine. Lovely place down in the Riverina, they wrote me the warmest letter, loved having her, met some of our Koori people and wanted to do something to assist them. She was very keen on the idea. Mind you, I thought it might be a passing fancy. But no, she thoroughly researched them and became quite an authority on the subject. She convinced me that they had been treated very poorly since the white man arrived. I should mention that I had arranged for her to meet a grandson of an old golfing colleague of mine. I thought it might help get her going; at her age, you do not want to be stuck with a silly old bugger like me. They got on well, but I do not think there was anything serious."

Once the flow had started, nothing could have shaken my attention, I was willing the old man on. "One day, some months ago, after she had left for the day, I was just fussing around, folding the newspapers most likely, when I saw a letter she had left open on the kitchen sideboard. Normally I would not dream of it, but it was there and I read it, and looking back, I believe I was meant to. It was from a religious order, and was in response to her inquiry about the possibility of her sponsoring an Aboriginal child. I regret that when she asked for my view, I swamped her with all the negative attitudes of an old man, for which I am now rather ashamed. Perhaps it was a misguided paternal responsibility. My own children have done very well, and are now middle aged." Then came the most surprising admission: "I have done it anyway, in memory of her; I am providing for a little girl."

He had put down his cup and was fossicking about in his inside jacket pocket, "Here is a photo of her," and there she was—floral dress, big smile, and a mop of curly hair. "Ray, she goes to school every day." Right then my Adam's apple was stuck in my throat, and I had a hundred questions.

"Major, I wonder if you remember the name of the church?"

"Here old man, I have their letter with me." You never know which way these interviews are headed, and I had to constrain myself. I had a glance before I put it to one side as if it was nothing. "And could you tell me about the young man she met through your friend?" It flowed like wine, and as we chatted, I worked through my checklist.

At something to 5 a.m., the incoming passengers at Sydney's International Terminal were being expelled through grey nondescript doors, as if from a giant letter-sorting machine. While those waiting for them drank coffee out of styrene cups, and spluttered through the first cigarettes of the day, I watched as my friend emerged, having flown across the vastness of America and the Pacific, knowing that he would feel like the walking dead.

"Morning Prof, sorry to drag you halfway around the planet," it was not the hour to be effusive. "God, I hate planes. I have been looking forward to a swim and some warm Sydney sunshine. Coming from where I have, I find it hard to associate the pleasure of seeing you and Queenie with someone as bad as this guy." Having filled in the gaps on the drive home, my visitor greeted Queenie with a boisterous hug; those two really got on very well and would talk for hours. Martin floated around the pool while I flicked through the morning papers.

"You made page two: 'Crack FBI. Investigator Arrives. Professor of Forensic Psychiatry Doctor Martin Knowles, the FBI's celebrated behavioural scientist is making a brief visit to Sydney and blah, blah, blah'."

"Ray, this is delicious; it was minus four when I left Washington." The Prof rested with his elbows over the pool edge. "You were asking about my cannibal; in hindsight, the signs were there. The students and staff were shocked, but I later discovered that one of his lecturers had thought he was spending too much time in the dissecting room. His girlfriend was a pleasant young lady, and we will probably never know if she was at risk. His childhood seemed normal, the mother a caring type, although she had a black-and-white view of the world, as religious people can do. He was their only child.

The father was the one; he was a horror. My assessment was that he not only knew, but had encouraged him. During an interview, he would adopt an aloof academic manner; the man was an engineer with the Federal Standards Laboratory." The Prof had hauled himself out and was enjoying the sun. "But he shot himself in the foot when I changed tack and told him his son was a very clever young man. It made him smile broadly, which was the first decent reaction I had had, and at last he began to talk, and he became the proud father, living a fantasy life through his son. We discussed his son's early interest in dissecting small animals. And in no time at all, this guy was describing his boy dissecting his own pet rabbit and was smiling as if reliving a private joke.

"The animal had been anaesthetized," I threw in, and he giggled like an adolescent. There it was, and I knew that he had corrupted his own child. At least I had the satisfaction of letting him know I understood."

After that conversation, a few holes of golf seemed like a reasonable diversion. Twenty bucks on the first nine. When you know your golfing partner's game like we did, it is quite difficult to take a dive, and I was relieved when Martin won. Queenie enjoyed having him stay, and was happily doing her thing in the kitchen when we returned. "Lovely day for it boys, and who won the money?"

"I did, but I suspect your ever-loving husband may have taken a dive." That raised a laugh and made me blush.

The following morning we started on the crime scenes. At the first, the lone young female Constable appeared very relieved that someone had actually bothered to turn up. One becomes used to the gruesomeness of our profession, and we could thumb through the crime scene photos without comment. I never mentioned it, but I could not help noticing that the faint smell of death was still there. And to this day, I still don't know whether it was real or imagined.

"Ray, a nice job, a long way better than we generally get served up and it amazes me how they ever get solved." I laughed. "It used to be pretty slipshod; everyone and his dog would wander in and out."

"Ray, they died quickly; it's the aftermath that becomes gruesome." I was glad to have him there.

"Prof, what do you think was the point of this whole drawn-out sequence, or is it a ritual? Did he need to kill, or was it done specifically to remove their kidneys and to bleed them?"

"Well, to me, I think this whole thing, his motif included, says he wants to be caught, but the significance of what we have here is beyond me."

"Prof, for me, it is the motif. There was something about this couple, yet I could not put my finger on it. Their background seemed so average, and there was nothing in their home that said they had been one thing or another. The Chaplain did not read anything into it." My visitor looked puzzled.

"Ray, he certainly does not care what the rest of the world thinks. If we assume that it is a ritual, rather than a compulsion, then to me, it's like an animal marking out its territory." I had been back a few times on my own to try to understand what it was all about.

"Okay Prof, we have a fine collection of prints and pubic hair; dogs mark their territory with pee, but somehow I do not think that's the point of the fat and the blood."

The American was lost in thought. "She was an attractive woman, and yet nothing suggests there was any sexual motive. I think the secret may be in discovering why he chose them."

"Yeah, they let him in, so it is fair to assume they knew who he was. No residues around the taps, the paper towels may not have been touched; you try it, you need the other hand to steady it as you tear it off. He must have been covered in the stuff, and outside there was nothing on the garden taps."

My guest shrugged. "I have all I want from this one, Ray. Shall we move on?"

We were stuck halfway up the same cliff face, and depressingly, I knew the other crime scenes were going to be a repeat of this one.

⚡ 26 ⚡

During my term as Premier, I had very little involvement with it until the killings continued; and it became a hot political issue for my government. Let me commend the author for researching and writing about this case. It is timely, as it removes much of the journalistic speculation, and sets the record straight. However, I confess that as a Premier has to do, I piled on the pressure until it was solved. But let me return to the beginning, as before becoming State Premier, I had risen through the ranks of the Labour Party. I had been prominent in the liquor industry and had bought and sold a few rundown suburban pubs. I would go in hard to get rid of the sleazebags who give a pub a bad name; the drill was to give each pub a theme and then to renovate and decorate them so they could prosper again. In those years, I was still young enough to be full of energy, as you have to be in that industry.

I like to think that when I became a politician, I purposely set out to create an aura. I admit that I enjoyed power, and hopefully, was adept at using it. Thus, it is on the record that at the time of these happenings, I had a staffer summon the Police Minister. Despite the party affiliation and a long-time friendship, Milton Strong, the Police Minister, would not have been used to urgent summonses from my office. In a general sense, visitors were meant to be impressed by the selection of oils by great artists such as Albert Tucker, Elioth Gruner, and Arthur Streeton whose works were on loan from the State Gallery. You have to do this sort of thing to add prestige to the office, and just to let people know who is in charge and to keep them motivated.

"Thanks for coming up, take a seat. Milt, I am beginning to form the view that you are an incompetent. Strong would have had an urge to get up and walk out. "Do you understand why? It's because the Police Force you run, or more correctly, do not run, is not worth all the money my Government throws at it."

"Harley, what could have brought this on?"

"For months now, we have had some deranged bastard out there on a killing spree." "Surely not that again, Harley. Mate, after all the years of hard grind for the party, we ought to be able to sit down and talk about this calmly over a drink."

"No Milt, you, listen to me, the Commissioner's report says some of them were murdered in broad daylight!" With that I picked up Commissioner Cavanagh's report and threw it at my closed door. Milton would have been outraged. "He's knocking off my constituents. I know that because Cavanagh quotes Brannagan as saying the victims were high achievers."

"Are you being funny?" I ignored the question.

"Milt, I suggest you tell the Commissioner to get that prima donna Brannagan off his fat backside, before I do what this morning's papers suggest, and get rid of the three of you."

≈ 27 ≈

I think Queenie was impressed that I hobnobbed with the great and powerful, but she also feared that the Premier might suddenly turn on me. The television and papers were full of it, and as you would expect, they played up the horror aspect of it. At least Martin had been in great form; he was our cushion, and entertained us with stories of his life in Washington. He was a great friend to have and the most flattering of guests. He went out of his way to spoil her with charming little gifts he found while fossicking about in little-known antique and curio shops.

"I think the Premier overreacts," I explained. "He pressures the Minister, who downloads it on to the Commissioner, who dumps it on me. I did not agree with his going public and appealing for information, as all it says to me is that there is panic at the top." Queenie disappeared into the kitchen so Martin and I could talk.

"Ray, where has the follow-up on the victim's letter taken you?"

"Martin, we interviewed the Abbot of a priory which is just out of the city of Tamworth, that's about a five hour drive north of Sydney. I am told he was most co-operative; our local DI is an experienced hand, who also writes a very descriptive report. Among other things, they take in chronic alcoholics and rehabilitate them. He ran a detailed interview, which unfortunately proved to be another dead end." "Listening to your Premier just now, you might have to watch your back. Media scrutiny can make a man like him look ineffectual; he might lash out, and Ray, this screwball could still be around in a year's time."

Some months had passed since the Prof's return to Washington, when he suddenly called first thing in the morning, or what would have been the cocktail hour over there. He had just come in three under to win the money and sounded pretty pleased with himself. "And while I am here, what's happening with your investigation?"

"We have a breakthrough on the residues. They have been able to separate out and identify the source of the ochre he uses to decorate himself."

"Ray, fantastic, that is a major step forward."

"The deposit is in a remote part of Western Australia, and they think the black wool may have been curtain material. The only problem with that is there were traces of soil, pollen, and pig shit through it. So right now we are looking for a black, interior decorator, who gardens and keeps pigs." Martin exploded on the other end, which does much to explain how people like us get our kicks.

I drove home, conscious that there was a psychopath out there, who could go off again. But you never know; perhaps he was back taking his medication and going to work every day. I wondered if he had a wife, brother, a mother, who might have an idea. As unbelievable as it might seem, it appeared that we had an Aboriginal male, presumably living in Sydney, who applies his ochre, gets himself admitted to the victims' home, and that's it. After removing their kidneys, he smears himself with their fat and cavorts in their blood; but I always came back to that symbol. I poured her a drink and told her that Martin had called.

≈ **28** ≈

Ray largely left me to run my own race, and sometimes I found it difficult to wait for the wheels of the department to move and so I wrote my letter at the end of the day. I will freely admit that there had been a time when I had wanted to transfer out of Homicide, but he was so enthusiastic. I do not think that Raymond ever saw it in terms of rotting cadavers and ghastly people with warped minds. It must have been catchy, because I had caught the bug, and now saw each case as an intellectual exercise, and besides any of that, I loved him. Perhaps it had been a toe in the water for him, and I suppose, for myself, and either way, we made no great decisions. The idea had been nagging me for weeks; I would use my maiden name, but writing to an Abbot did seem strange.

The Abbot
Dunraven Priory
Dungowan NSW 2340.

My dear Father David,
I have to thank you for your guidance as to what I might do to assist or hopefully adopt a Koori or part Koori child..."

There followed three pages of compelling reasons why they should accept me. Attached were glowing testimonials from the Mayor of Lane Cove, the Minister of my Church, (obtained under false pretences) and from a Queen's Counsel. That I had an Arts Degree, with a Masters in Communications and Information Technology, seemed quite beside the point. Carefully reading it several times for exactly the right nuance, I sealed it in a plain envelope and posted it on the way home.

I was aware that Jim Willard suggested the man they wanted may turn out to be an artistic person like a potter, someone who might spin and weave their own cloth, and that what he needed was the cloth his strands of black wool had come from.

⚡ 29 ⚡

Anyone who has ever visited a sprawling Queensland city knows that everyone knows everyone else. That feeling of belonging was what knitted the communities together, and so it was with the retired Police Inspector, and of course everyone knew of Owen Nash, who was a much-respected figure. Nash knew how the system worked, and now that cotton was grown in the district, there was plenty of money in circulation. The pulse of life was slow, and the monsoons threw a wet blanket over the city. His comfortable retirement was long settled, which had all been a question of doing the ground work, certainly no rushing around putting the heavies on people; that sort of thing was strictly for amateurs.

He was not the first policeman to ever have been on the take, and if over a long career he had a guiding principle, it was never to get too greedy. These days it was mere tokenism, unlike when he was a young up-and-comer on the force. He would have long rationalized that the punters did not really mind all that much, and after all, if it was outside the tax system, paying for police protection was expected, and they always paid. He had had fingers in so many pies; whoring was huge, turning a blind eye to the sale of stolen grog and cigarettes; and in the early days, the big spinner had been illegal gambling. Now he was harvesting the rewards of a long and distinguished career.

There were Lions, Rotary, a seat on the High School Council, and a Directorship of the Rugby League Club, and only the other day, he had been asked to lend his patronage to the formation of yet another team. He was replete with satisfaction; after checking his watch, he drove down to the sporting fields. Someone was opening up and he parked alongside a nondescript truck.

"Is that you Mr. Nash?"

"Yes, hello," which was the last thing he remembered. He regained consciousness in the most excruciating pain, was unable to move, or understand what had happened. The pain and shock made him slip in and out of consciousness. The gag had filled his mouth with a mixture of foul-tasting whisky and vomit. He had to swallow it carefully or choke; he had wet himself; and it was difficult to breath. There had been a car accident and he was trapped, but as he went numb, he began to realize his predicament. There was the motion of the truck; he was somehow encased and he may be dying.

The monk sang quietly, like the Mighty Hunter after a hunt. He would adhere to the lore and dance and sing his triumph to his ancestors; it was enough to feel the blood and kidney fat on his skin, and have it glisten in the light of his own fire. There was the peace of the bush as he drove without headlights, picking his way through the trees in the moonlight. He went through two more gates until he was in the wild country beyond the dingo fence. What shock his captive would be in, to be trussed up like a fowl; had he ever wondered about the bashings, false accusations, and imprisonments he had perpetrated?

They were in the thick timber where the trees had never been felled since time began. He parked and went back to erase his tracks. He hid the truck and slung the bundle over his shoulder. The smell of burning eucalypt gladdened his heart and as the fire crackled, he stripped off his clothes and began to chant and dance. When the embers had died down to a red glow, he knelt down over the prisoner. The eyes bulged and he saw they understood what had been said; and in a while, there was only the vacant stare of the dead.

≈ 30 ≈

I was in the habit of parking well down the road and arriving at my sister's place at around five thirty in the evening. My day would have begun well before dawn, with my usual round of our enterprises. The drive down to Sydney gave me time to think, and the opportunity to see what conditions were like up and down the Hunter Valley.

Her own business was now so well-established that she was forced to stand back and manage it, and with Heather's guidance, she did very well. I told her I was extremely proud of what she had achieved, and that I hoped my cloistered life would not come between us. It was after 5.35 p.m. when she would have heard me coming up the steps. She made me a cup of tea. I said that I had a good trip down; she apologized that she had a function and had to go. She looked well and seemed in good form.

I would call up a day or two in advance to say I was coming and stay for the day or so it took to attend to the priory's business. She seemed no longer concerned about seeing me in my habit, and nor did she ever mention my haircut, and I will readily admit that my life did take some getting used to. On the few occasions she had sounded off, I would just have to put up with it. I was in no doubt that she viewed the way I lived with a great deal of scepticism.

"Dar," she would say, "it is always lovely to see you. I would have thought you might want to marry again, your life seems so cloistered. I mean, I don't think that, assuming there is a God, he is so uptight that he expects us to spend every hour of every day in a state of perpetual funk about the death of his son, and you know my views on that."

I would never take offence. "Sis, please try and understand that there is a huge need for our work. There are many men out there who are just like I was, and for there to be any hope for them, it has to be done. The priory raises a great deal of money for the needy, and does a great deal of good in the world." I was aware that I was no doubt being unfair and unanswerable, and that I at least had to let her try to get through.

"Dar, I think it is time you came back to Sydney and resumed your life. Patrick and James would have you back tomorrow! You have a privileged standing there, for goodness sake; why not use it?"

I would smile my angelic smile. "You could say I am a victim of our extraordinary success; there is never a spare moment and, as I told you, I am to follow Father David when he steps down."

"Dar, that's all very well, but they will hardly be rewarding you in the way James and Patrick would."

"That well may be," I replied, "but I have taken over the responsibility for our adoptions and foster care. Many are our people, so you can imagine how I view that. I am currently training a Brother to run it."

"Father David is making good use of you."

"I suppose he does, and Peter sent you a couple of his hams. I dropped them off at the cold store; you might scribble him a note with your impressions."

"Dar, that's nice. I have to run. There's a casserole in the fridge. Enjoy, and hopefully I will see you tomorrow."

⚡ **31** ⚡

Susan Wallington-Syms loved her uncle, but living with the dear old fellow did have its difficulties. For one thing, Major Danver Lavenby, hearing aid or not, got agitated every time she tried to adjust it for him; so for much of the time, conversation was difficult. Yet, for an unknown niece from London, he had been very hospitable, and had made her coming to Sydney easy. Her mother had warned that she had not seen her brother for years, and that he might be over-organized, in that over fussy way older people can be. None of that now mattered, as she was simply enchanted by Sydney.

This was her first trip abroad, and she had not told anyone there was a man in her life. The weather was perfect, and for the very first time in her life, she had a decent tan, and in every way, her new life was so much nicer than she had expected. Her lover was a merchant banker, and she had just signed a lease on a tiny new flat that even had a glimpse of the harbor. But, she was not going to make the mistake of burning all her bridges by moving in with Benjamin as she wanted him to propose and for them to marry. There was so much to do and see, and she wondered if her uncle had guessed she had a lover. She had made little attempt to hide it, and having made the move from her uncle's home, the best thing was the freedom.

It was a Sunday night. Ben was due in Melbourne first thing in the morning, and had left to organize his week. She had just settled in front of the TV when there was a sharp knock on the door. Her immediate thought was he must have left something behind.

"Hello, I am from the Dunraven Priory," said the melodious voice. Surely there must be a mistake, but she certainly had written. It was almost comical, as through the wire screen her caller could have been Friar Tuck. "You are Susan Wallington-Syms; you wrote to us, and may God bless you for your generous spirit. I understand you wish to foster or adopt a Koori child?"

She could not help herself. "Good God! I did, but not at this hour!"

"Ha, ha, no you would not." That good-humoured rubbishing did it.

"Oh, I am sorry; I do not mean to be rude."

"Not at all, it is just we at the priory find time is such a precious thing."

"You must be Brother Aden."

"Yes, a random call is the only way to make a realistic assessment. When people expect us, they go to inordinate lengths to dress things up." She invited him in.

"We are just looking for some reassurance that people are who they say they are." With a shock, it occurred to her that her own manner had been most unwelcoming.

"Oh, do pardon me Brother Aden. Please sit down and let me make you a cup of tea."

She died without a sound.

Her warm blood and fat gave him her strength and transported him, and he was a hunter once more. His inner fires were satiated once more beneath the rough brown cassock of the Order.

≈ 32 ≈

Having written to the priory, I was in a panic at the remote possibility I might be successful, and had thrown myself into research. Nor had I yet confided in Ray, who would have been horrified, and so would my mother and sister. What if during their inquiries they contacted them? When I popped in to mum's for a quick drink on the way home, which was an open invitation, as usual the dear lady wanted the latest news on the serial killings. It was not the sort of stuff you tell elderly ladies, and so I spun it out and removed the gory bits to make it palatable. I felt so incredibly silly telling her about my letter.

"Mother, the situation has arisen where I have had to inquire about adopting or fostering an Aboriginal child. I had to, as it was obvious that no one else was going to. Despite all the resources we have thrown at it, this case is going nowhere, and I nominated you and Annette as immediate family and enthusiastic backers."

She had been unflappable as always. "And what are you going to do if they agree?"

"That simply will not happen."

"Your sister has enough to worry about with her own family. Moleander, I think this could be seen as mischievous interference; I assume the department has no idea."

"Mum, we are desperate, and so far I have not heard a thing. I promise you I will call Annette tonight."

"And what if you are right, my dear? I will be in a dreadful state if you do not answer your phone." I had not thought of that, which of course I did not tell her.

The hard grind of our investigation went on week after week. Ray had the entire team in for a review of the case, and had already filled three whiteboards when I arrived. He is an excellent communicator. "The idea behind today's program is to provide a forum where we can pool our thoughts. Feel free to comment at any time. You are about to learn things that have previously been withheld. Please do not put it down on paper, and do not discuss any of it with your colleagues, and that includes your senior officers."

Ray has a commanding presence. "We have been able to put together a profile of the man we are looking for. Ladies and gentlemen, this assessment is based part on fact, circumstantial evidence, and educated guesses. We think he is an indigenous Australian, and we make that presumption because of the recovery of traces of ochre, which, quite remarkably, have been matched with an ancient deposit in a remote area of Western Australia. And we believe he applies this to his body before he smears himself with their blood and kidney fat. The point I would make is this, he knows what he is doing, and this ritual seems to an important part of his behaviour. The problem we have is that for the rest of the time, he is just like you and me, and to his family and friends, he appears quite rational." He wrote it up: "LIVES A RATIONAL LIFE."

"But what of the victims, and here there has been some interesting work done? There is the link of age, twenty-eight to forty-three, the link of earning power—they were relatively high achievers, in a range $60k to $160k. Now here it comes, the one great thing they had in common, these couples were all infertile." That got a reaction. Up it went with a flourish, "INFERTILE". That sparked a vigorous discussion, and when it died down, we broke for lunch, and over a sandwich, I spoke with Detective Inspector Frank Macintyre from Tamworth. One look at Frank said he was travelling well. He had that country stamp of clear eyes and rosy cheeks, and he was filling out around the middle. Probably golf Wednesdays and Saturdays, with a few beers after. Frank was cruising through his last years before retirement.

"Frank, may I ask you about your interview with the Abbot?"

"Moleander, as I said in my report, I found him a very cooperative man."

"Well Frank, I was wondering how he reacted to the Wallington-Sym's letter."

"Oh," he said, "I did not know you were aware of her letter; her inquiry was specifically about in some way being able to assist or foster a Koori child. Father David explained to me that they try to place them with their own people. It's quite wonderful really, as under their sponsorship program, the public may sponsor a child by making a monthly contribution toward their upkeep and education, which was what he suggested she do. Moleander, there was not the slightest hint of evasiveness. I was given full access to their files and he immediately declared those monks and others in their care who had a record. We accounted for everyone, and I do mean everyone—even those who had dropped out; he and I backtracked five years. The Abbot struck me as being a pretty shrewd judge of character. I came away with the feeling that he would have known if they had harboured him. I have been through his list a dozen times, and I cannot come up with a suspect."

"Thanks for that Frank. I find the whole thing gets to me; it is a very intriguing puzzle."

"Moleander, it is, and I wish you could have seen it. 'Dunraven' is well over a hundred and seventy years old, and the sandstone used in the lovely buildings was quarried on the site. The homestead looks over some of the most picturesque land in the district. The Abbot's a real character, and mind you, they are a wonderful success story. Their income goes to charity; the work they do restores one's faith in human nature." Frank had obviously been impressed.

"Frank, may I get you another cup of tea?"

In order to stimulate the discussion during the afternoon session, Ray split us into small groups. There was one overriding message, "That we were well on the way, and that he had every confidence we would crack it." He posed the question, "It appears he has accessed their personal detail. Is he associated with the medical profession? Could he be a public servant? Our targets will be the fertility clinics and adoption agencies, church, and state. Does his wife or lover unwittingly reveal their secret?" Despite all this, I had come away surer than ever. I knew no more than anyone else, other than having a strong urge to follow my instincts, and I could clearly see that we had hit a brick wall.

Lawrence D pontificated to the media, prompting speculative articles to appear in the press, and for good measure, the radio shock jocks gave it a good stir. Harley Manville declared his government would provide the investigation with every possible resource. The media by then had labelled our elusive killer "Kidney Man".

≈ **33** ≈

Quite frankly, I was intoxicated by my lover, and hoped with all my heart that he felt the same way about me. I snuggled up to his naked warmth and listened dreamily to his breathing and shook in involuntary delight as I remembered our lovemaking. At last I had found my mate, and I imagined my great-grandmother's joy when I had sung to her. The dear old thing had said I would know, and with that thought, I fell blissfully back to sleep.

It was Friday again, and I could look forward to another delightful working lunch with Heather. I collected her at the intersection of Pitt and Hunter Streets, and as it was a nice day, I drove with the hood down. I was happier than I could recall, and to that extent, it must have showed. Heather noticed it immediately. "Is it my imagination, or are you looking particularly radiant today?" I unsuccessfully stifled a giggle. "Okay, come clean, do I detect romance in the air?"

"I will admit there could be the first blossoming of it," I replied, trying very hard not to reveal just how elated I felt. "Good, Alkina, it could not happen to anyone nicer." Tony said my dimples showed when I was happy. "Heather, it is a magical day, and I adore your outfit; I really do, it's very nice."

"Well, thank you," she replied. "In my business, it is not hard to do what with all the power dressing and nonsense my legal sisters carry on with, but this little number is straight off the rack." Heather was not in the slightest self-conscious or vain; there was no need for her to be; she was one of those women who added a ton of style to anything she wore, and she looked great in anything. Today it was orange and brown, with dark green and yellow accessories, all cleverly put together, which, with her mop of red hair, turned heads wherever she went. Yet, we regarded our ritual of getting all glammed up and meeting for lunch, as one of life's great pleasures, which if it had done nothing else, had done a great deal to promote our professional lives.

"Care to tell me where you have chosen for lunch?" she asked, as we threaded our way through the city. "One of my chefs has given me a rave recommendation of a new place over in Glebe. I thought we should get in before everyone else discovers it, as it is so much easier writing about places I have never been to before. But you watch, I bet it is full of advertising and legal types; they sniff these places out before anyone else." Heather laughed, and as happens, the maitre d' knew who we were as soon as we walked in the door, and promptly ushered us through to the winter garden.

"Half the Sydney Bar is here," Heather commented, nodding and smiling in recognition. Our lunch was going to be something. The wine had been chosen, and ceremoniously opened. Judge Tom Levine, an enthusiastic trencherman himself, toddled over for a chat. He was about to step down and we talked about that.

"Okay, who is he?" my dear friend demanded once we were alone. I tried to protest, but knew that was not going to work.

"Heather, he is in the wine business over in Adelaide, but I would rather not say much more, other than to tell you that I am very much in love." I felt so self-conscientious over it.

"My dear Alkina, I am thrilled for you, and it is simply a beautiful thing to see you look so happy. Here is to you my dear; that is the nicest news I have heard in a long while."

"Thank you, I do not want to make a big deal of it; we will just have to see how it works out." Every now and then either the maitre d' or a waiter fluttered around. Heather said her terrine was delicious, while I was concentrating on my own, and what I might say about it. My companion may not have been aware, but she also had taken to going over her plate, testing the texture and having a little taste here and there, and pausing to concentrate as she did so.

Heather told me about a case of a supposed fraud, which, as her counsel had dissected the Crown's evidence, the Judge had thrown out. A couple of middle-aged housewives had left their table on a leisurely stroll, supposedly to the powder room, but really to have a good gawk. We pretended not to notice. I told Heather I had just returned from a trip to Perth and Adelaide, and had flown from Alice Springs across to Arrawatta to see my parents.

"How were they?"

"I suppose age is catching up, but it was lovely to see them. Dad still goes out on the camps; mum helps out in the homestead, and in fact she and the manager's wife live in each other's pocket." Our conversation had reminded me, "Heather, may I share a concern I have?"

"My dear, I shall be most offended if you don't."

"I am not sure this will make a lot of sense; it is just that when I go back, I am struck by the air of impermanence that hangs over the place. What annoys me is that my mother was born on Arrawatta, and she and dad have lived there all their married lives. It seems to me that there is always talk of the station being sold, staff being sacked, or they are cutting back for one reason or another. I can see they feel threatened, there is talk of less work, and all the carry on over the station's cost cutting. To me, the implication is that it would be a better outcome for the owners if our people were not there at all." Heather nodded her head as she took it all in.

"I certainly agree," she said, "in an isolated community like that, and at their age, it would be an awful situation."

I felt guilty asking for Heather's help during what was supposed to be a relaxing Friday luncheon. "Our people," I continued, "have dreaming places all through that country that go back to the beginning of time. I hoped you might fire off a letter on my behalf, perhaps to the station owners, the government, and maybe the church, to clarify the position. Surely their rights should be spelt out. Perhaps they could declare a reserve, even if it was only for the next fifty years; at least that would give them peace of mind."

The plates had been whipped away, the iced table water replenished, and our wine topped up, all so surreptitiously it was barely noticeable.

"Alkina, my dear, it will be my pleasure to look into it, I will get our conveyancer on to it; presumably there must be some sort of ongoing leasehold."

"What gets to me," I commented, "is their disingenuous benevolence. My parents are perfectly capable of living on their own resources out in the bush. The problem is that the succession of owners have overstocked the land until it is nearly exhausted. The cattle have diminished our bush tucker, which, when I was a little girl, used to be everywhere. My father often talks about the pressure they put on the land. He says it is why the country takes so much longer to recover from a drought."

"Do you know who the current owners are?"

"Heather, I have no idea, but it has changed hands several times in my lifetime."

The restaurant was packed, and the air crackled with conversations. Every now and then, and no doubt fortified by a few drinks, someone would approach our table to say "hello". The main course was served with suitable ceremony, and I had to refocus on our lunch. The maitre d', as busy as he was, anxiously kept an eye on our progress from a discreet distance. The food tasted as good as it looked, and we thought the chef had made a pretty good effort, and we carried on with our conversation. Heather said she been at it since seven that morning, and that she was hungry.

"This tastes absolutely divine, and have you heard from your brother?"

"Dar is avoiding me as I have not seen him for ages. No doubt he is wrapped in the arms of the Lord; who knows what he is up to? Heather, I don't buy all this conversion business." I leant forward so that my voice would not carry, "I think it is bullshit; I really do. I miss not having him and Peggy around; they were wonderful times. But, if he is up there helping other men get their lives back together, I suppose I will have to be content with that. But between you and me, I know something is not right, I cannot put my finger on it, but I will let you know when I do."

She had this disarming way of cocking an eyebrow and tossing her red hair. "My dear," she said, "that does not sound much better than my week. We lost an appeal, and I recruited a couple of gawky graduates; it is all the running around we have to do, and Sydney is a big city." Just as Heather was about to continue, we were approached by an overdressed matron.

"Oh," she said, "do pardon me, but I am just so thrilled to see you. I simply had to come over and say how much I adore your column. And you just have to be her legal friend?" We were used to it, and sent her on her way with a smile and a "what a nice thing to say". The head chef made a brief appearance, and we chatted for a minute or two.

"That was very nice, thank you chef; you conjured up a subtle combination of flavours." When he was gone, I turned to Heather, "And what did you think?"

"I was so hungry I would have eaten a horse," she laughed. "No, seriously I loved it, and I thought the menu was one of the better ones we have had. The ambience and the service were good, and I could stay here sipping and chatting for the rest of the afternoon, but unfortunately, I have a meeting to get to."

≈ 34 ≈

The weather could have been made to order as the Abbot and I stood ankle deep in pasture, feeling well-satisfied with what we saw. I had just turned over four thousand first cross ewes into a new paddock, and they were heavy in lamb. It had been a season that would have made any farmer happy. I was quite unaware of how it had happened, but I found myself talking about my childhood on Arrawatta.

"Aden, the stories you have told me about those days are quite enthralling. I so admire your wonderful connection with the land. I wish we had it. I think that is one of the white community's problems, a lack of belonging and of continuity." I found it extraordinary that Father David should draw a parallel between my recollections of my childhood and our cloistered life.

"There are so many lessons that we can learn from it," the Abbot said, "but it is comforting to know that our own family is united in our love and service of our dear Lord and creator. I think that gives us strength and hardens our resolve to overcome all the challenges we may face. I must say that in the early days; our founder and I never realized the importance of making that connection with the land. Now, of course, we know how important it is in giving people back their lives. We just never recognized its wonderful healing powers. We help lost men like you, Peter and myself, to blossom again. We have been given another chance by the wonderful grace of our loving and most forgiving God. I thank him every day, and I thank him for sending you to take over the heavy burden of managing it all. I pray that he will grant you guidance as you ready yourself to assume my roll. Be assured your Brothers all love you, and will follow you into whatever pastures you may lead them.

The priory is now a thriving business, and with that we have assumed a very heavy responsibility within the community. We have so many people who depend on us, and I worry what would happen should we ever falter. How much skill and hard work you must have brought to James's and Patrick's business. Should our loving God call me to his heaven, I know the priory and all its enterprises could not be in better hands. It has been a privilege to watch you strive so mightily. The District Agronomist tells me that we are the most productive agricultural enterprise he has ever seen; neither our founder nor I would ever have envisaged anything like this all those years ago."

"Well Father, perhaps you only showed him our more successful projects."

"Ha, ha, Aden, not at all; he enjoys coming out to see what we are doing, which is quite an accolade. However I must go; I have a counselling session to prepare, and I want to have a quick word with Peter."

The exchange left me drained; it was almost as if the Father had access to my emotions. I watched the receding figure and tried to rationalize my thoughts. "Jesus," I prayed aloud, "you know what I have done. I had to end Peggy's life; what else was I to do? Thank you for allowing her to slip away so peacefully." I rarely cried, but in that moment, my tears were flowing freely. "As for Gerard, you know I have little remorse over him. In fact, I rarely think of him at all. Perhaps, you and I should call it quits? But if you want to know, what really haunts me is the sound of my shots thudding home as those young men ran toward me. They were probably just like us; they would have enjoyed a beer and a laugh; and why did it have to be my friends; were their deaths and those of all the others for nothing? And you know, that for me, what stands between you and me is my knowing that if I had to do it all again, I am not sure I would treat those two VC prisoners any differently?"

⚡ 35 ⚡

I drove my truck down the New England Freeway. I had developed almost an antagonistic feeling for the young woman I now knew by sight as Moleander Courtenay. She had not been forthright, and I would not welcome her visit. The priory was a place of quiet redemption, where the lost could recover themselves, and those who answered the call to serve Almighty God could spend the rest of their days in gainful work while readying themselves for the glory of his heavenly kingdom. There had been no need for subterfuge; the priory was an open book, and would welcome the police and their inquiries.

Why had she not declared her connection at the outset, and what was her role in the investigation? That young lady had a brazen sexuality, which she would no doubt use to gain what she wanted. A simple mistake; we should never have banked her check; it had given her an excuse to regard a visit as her right. But these were small matters, and as an agent of the Lord, I had to stand aloof from such mundane concerns. As I drove down the valley, I enjoyed the cool night air; it was after ten, and I still had three hours of driving before I reached the city outskirts. The highway dipped up and down through the hills and valleys as it fell toward the sea. When the moon came out from behind the clouds, it bathed the stock in its pale light.

The Lord had revealed her to me, for when her letter was received, I had set out to discover who she was. The impression she conveyed did not do her justice; she was a most striking young woman. I had followed her on her bus, and had sat in the back near the rear entrance and watched as she settled down to chat with the lady next to her. She appeared to be early for someone employed by the government, or was I being unnecessarily cynical? What was it that kept her so motivated at that early hour of the morning?

The traffic on the Harbour Bridge moved slowly, no doubt a large part of why she left so early. Her fellow commuters appeared more affluent than most. We must have been nearing her destination, the passengers had thinned, and she had moved towards the door. I got out at the same stop. The city was vibrant with energy; she purchased fruit and the barrowman gave her an effusive greeting. The pleasant exchange was between two people expecting to see each other for their morning ritual. Everyone was intent on hurrying to work; she was easy to follow. We went through an arcade where she momentarily lingered by a shop window. The gathering tempo of the awakening city was catchy.

I kept walking as she unexpectedly bounced through the front entrance of Police Headquarters. My breath came in shallow rushes and I paused for a while to make sense of it. Then I set off to attend to my other business.

⋙ 36 ⋙

It was a tough time to be the Chief of Homicide; the shock jocks filled the airwaves with dire predictions and they called for the Minister's and my resignations. They put across such a ragtag of ridiculous theories; they suggested it could be the mild-mannered man next door, and one followed another. As the man leading the investigation, I had to make myself impervious to all this, as from where I sat, I could only lead and reassure the public and spread our net as wide as possible. This was a relentless task of painstaking checking and rechecking. Moleander wore a linen suit for the occasion. She was great backup to have on the day I was to put my job on the line. What if they called my bluff, but knowing those involved, there was simply no other way for me to go? She had turned up just as I was packing my briefcase.

"Ray, you look smart, and I am sure you and the Prof have it under control. Just let me run a brush across the back; these uniforms show the fluff. We know you put in two hundred percent; these people are just a bunch of opportunistic politicians blowing hot air, and trying to save their own hides. I will be wondering how you got on."

"Thanks, I think it is a case of like it or lump it. Distance has helped Martin see my situation very clearly, and I agree that I must confront it head on and deal with it."

I felt surprisingly at ease as I was being driven down Macquarie Street, it occurred to me that this might be the last time I made the trip, and I found it a very sobering thought. One look around the table said that the Premier meant business, for the whole of the inner cabinet was there. This was all about our Premier, covering his backside, and to do that, someone had to be made the scapegoat; and that someone was going to be me. He was going to ensure that whatever was decided was seen as being well-considered and not just him overreacting.

To look at the Premier, it was not hard to believe his reputation as a ladies' man. There was no doubt that he was slick, although in my view, it would be stretching things to say he was handsome. No, I think a pleasant face, perhaps he benefited from the female urge to mate with someone with power. And as for Milton Strong, my Minister looked like a country parson about to deliver a homily. Fortunately, my immediate boss, Lawrence D, was in London, being kept on side with a nice little junket accompanied by his wife, supposedly to liaise with the Metropolitan Police. It occurred to me that if I was going to announce an arrest, Strong and Lawrence D would be flanking me on either side.

The Premier was smiling like a company chairman about to announce a bumper profit, a hike in dividend, and a bonus issue. And then without further ado, we were away.

"Nice to see you all," he announced, "we have a few matters to cover today, which mostly deal with questions of law and order. In relation to that, may I say we are all aware of the outcry from the media over the recent spate of home invasions and attacks on the elderly? I would like us to cover these activities, which I am sure that like me, you find particularly abhorrent. They make us appear as though we are not doing enough, a misconception which my government is very keen to rectify."

A practical opener, and nothing to do with one serial killer, who, as yet, I had not managed to bring in. The deal was to control me so tightly that I would not be able to break wind without Cabinet approval. The strange thing was, having told Queenie what could be in the offing, she had been quite unfazed by it. She said she rather fancied us spending more time at our getaway in the mountains, and having the time to get the garden in shape, and then taking a leisurely trip up through Vietnam, which we were keen to visit. That was her, solid and dependable, and so what if we were in danger of boring each other into premature old age?

Manville invited Police Minister Milton Strong to lead the discussion. Here was a man who could explain the unexplainable away, and never mind the big house in the most expensive part of Killara with a pool and tennis court. One could even harbor the perception that he may have been on the take. I thought it highly likely that perception might be right, and that under another government with a vigorous broom, and he could easily end up on the inside. The veins on his nose said he was hitting the bottle, and if his past was gnawing away at his insides, that seemed likely.

"I have instructed the Commissioner," he announced, as if it was another illustration of his genius, "to review the operations of our suburban command structures to see if we can streamline the flow of paper work, and release more officers for general policing." Now there was a brilliant idea that was at least ten years overdue. "The initial estimate is that we should be able to free upwards of eight hundred to twelve hundred officers state-wide. I will also be seeking Cabinet approval to recruit another eight hundred full-time clerical staff so as to enable the Commissioner to get these men and women back on the street."

Manville looked attentive; his brilliantine held his hair rigidly in place—it was thinning on top and there was not a gray hair in sight; aha, the dear man had to be dying it.

"My department treads a fine line between our government's desire to protect the civil liberties of our citizens and the giving of more powers to our officers. My own view is well-known. I would like my officers to have a general power to apprehend and search on suspicion, including the right to search cars and a suspect's place of residence."

That led to some discussion, which quickly fizzled out. The Premier was making his last-minute checks before he struck; one hand had unconscientiously felt his chin, to reassure himself that he had shaved close enough, the other checked his immaculate collar and tie. Meanwhile the Minister droned on and on, while his audience looked decidedly unimpressed. "I am also having a series of meetings with my colleague, the Minister for Public Transport..." and on and on it went.

It occurred to me that none of it would have been necessary if those two had done their jobs in the first place. This stuff could have been attended to on any day of the week. I could see the headlines now: "Premier Chops Top Cop!" the papers would scream. Milton was waffling on about the newly installed radio command network. Manville was shuffling his papers; the Minister finished speaking, and the Premier took over and positively beamed as he spoke, "This is an opportunity to announce a new initiative my government proposes to take in order to ease the workload of Chief Superintendent Brannagan." The man was actually smiling at me.

"Whilst we appreciate his enormous workload in the hunt to catch the worst serial killer in our state's history, I believe the time has come to lessen the burden. Therefore, I intend to set up a high-powered committee to direct all operations until this criminal is caught, and to give it unprecedented powers and funding." This was just as Martin had predicted. "This committee shall have the instant ability to deploy all the resources of the state, and will enable us to monitor the hour-by-hour progress of this investigation." My heart was pounding. "Under this initiative I will ask Chief Superintendent Brannagan to report directly to this Committee, until such time as this offender has been arrested and convicted. It will be known as 'The Premier's Committee on Serial Crime'. I shall chair it, and it shall comprise The Attorney General, The Police Minister, and The Solicitor General." But where was Lawrence D in all this? No wonder he and his wife had been sent on a junket.

But the Premier had the equation wrong, and I recalled Martin's advice: "Do not have a bar of it; they will ride you until either you have a massive heart attack, a cerebral haemorrhage, or both. They will bring no expertise to your case, or enhance your ability to resolve it one iota. But you had better have a decent exit strategy that is polite, and does not rub their noses in it." I felt surprisingly calm, apart from one pounding heart, as Manville smiled benignly and perhaps assumed it had been done. When I finally caught the Premier's eye, it was a relief to be given the nod to speak.

"Mr. Premier, Ministers, ladies, and gentlemen, I need to apologize that we have not made an arrest; and I would like to state again that I accept the responsibility entrusted to me to do so. May I also assure you that I will not rest until this investigation has been resolved? I also acknowledge the unstinting support and encouragement I and my department have received from this government, and I thank you for it. However, there are certain crimes that are difficult to solve as they lack motive and connection to the victim. When these killings began, they were thought to be random slayings. Yet, there were clear identifying marks left at the crime scenes, and there was no attempt to conceal finger or footprints. Unfortunately, this person has no criminal record; but when an arrest is made, they will ensure he is convicted.

We are getting closer, which may be the reason the killings appear to have stopped. We now know they were not random, and that the victims belong to a clearly identifiable group. I believe it is wise that much of what we know remains suppressed, and I would like it to stay that way. We have now traced where the offender may have lived and travelled within Australia. I understand there are political ramifications, but I see the setting up of this overriding committee as an expression of no confidence in myself and my investigating team. Therefore, if it goes ahead, you may have my resignation first thing on Friday morning."

It was if a vast weight had just been lifted from my shoulders, and there was one of those awkward silences. The Premier was looking at Milton Strong, as if to say, thank you for your lousy advice, and his Minister was blushing. I had had a few offers and I had seen lesser men leave the force and do very well. Manville had not got to where he was by making capricious moves, and it came out without him missing a beat.

"This meeting has been particularly useful; it is always good to hear a wide range of views. I should make it clear that this Government has every confidence in Chief Superintendent Brannagan, and will continue to see that he is given every resource. Perhaps there has been a misunderstanding of what was intended." After a brief diversion into matters of less importance, we were invited into the inner sanctum for drinks. When the opportunity arose, the Premier took me aside. "Ray, I do not see any cause for you to even think of resigning, because as far as I am concerned, your future is assured."

All was cosy and light again, and I wished my American friend had been there to witness it. When I was being driven home, the day caught up with me and I told the driver to take me to Lane Cove. I had a blistering headache and a drink with Moleander would help.

⚡ **37** ⚡

My mother and I have a habit of verbally bouncing off each other, which has been there as far back as I can remember.

"They have offered you twins," she suggested as soon as I arrived, "and my dear girl, the press are giving you people no letup over this wretched man; the media are obsessed with it." And that very much included her. I took a sip of my wine, fossicked in my handbag, and gave her Brother Aden's letter to read.

> My dear Moleander,
>
> Receiving a loving and generous letter such as yours is always proof, I believe, that Almighty God does listen to our prayers. You sound such a nice lady, that I do hope your own prayers are answered in a way that adds richness and real meaning to your life. The plight of little children orphaned, abandoned, or mistreated in any way is one of the great concerns of this Order.
>
> We are very involved with the health and welfare of our indigenous children. Where cases are referred to us, we do our utmost to place them with family members, or at least in one of their own communities, which goes a long way toward maintaining a social and cultural consistency. Having found a home which offers loving care, we offer continued practical assistance to these families.
>
> I have enclosed a circular that shows how you may help our children by making a cash donation, or in a more permanent way, by sponsoring a child. Doing either is of great practical assistance, as it goes toward providing books, clothing, and all the myriad of things they need while they are growing up.
>
> Thank you for your inquiry and may our Heavenly Father bestow his blessings upon you.
>
> Yours in his name,
Brother Aden

"Mum, I found it quite charming."

"Dear, I quite agree, and they sound so very practical."

"I thought it was worth a shot, and I have to say, I do not recall ever seeing Ray so frustrated. Everyone from the Premier down is leaning on him." We chatted over dinner and as my mother is a very good cook, having the evening meal with her is always a pleasure. I helped with the cleanup before leaving.

We think he must have stood in the shadow across the road, from where I was briefly framed by the vestibule light, as I came out and down the steps and on to the pavement. Then the monk must have followed me home. I had worried that Ray would have had a difficult afternoon, and was not surprised when I heard the car door, and him having a few final words with the driver before he came up. I was glad that he had made the effort.

"There was nothing on the news, so I assumed you came through unscathed."

"Manville did the quickest about turn you ever saw; and we are all mates again. Making small talk with those guys over a drink is about as relaxing as a session with the Commissioner."

"Darling, it is over now. I will produce something light then I guess it is a hot shower and bed." His reconstructing of that evening illustrates what our relationship was all about.

"I remembered feeling stiff across my neck and shoulders and falling asleep with her in my arms. Something must have disturbed me, because I lay there half-asleep, and contemplated getting up and calling a cab. Somewhere a diesel motor ground its way up a distant hill. Was I hearing things or was that someone at the front door? Who in the hell could it be at that hour? I could hardly ignore it; probably a drunk on the wrong floor. The diesel had faded into the general hum of the city. She also stirred.

"Mol, there is someone at the door. Do I have a rival?"

"Ray, do be a darling and see who it is; it has to be a mistake; your gown is on the back of the bathroom door." I switched the entrance hall light on and opened her front door.

"Yes," I said. Into the general gloom, the lobby light must have just tripped. "Is there anyone there?" I was certain of what I had heard. "Whoever is there, it is very bloody late!" But on the edge of the light, I began to make out a shape standing in the gloom, who may not have realized their eyes were being reflected. Her caller was obviously confused, about the same height, some sort of cloak falling to the floor, and it was then that I realized how ridiculous the whole scene was.

"You must have the wrong apartment," and I closed the door. Jesus Christ! It was going on three; no wonder they were confused. Then my brain began to function, and with a start, I realized her late night caller had been a monk!

"Mol, wake up, we have to talk." She was having difficulty rousing herself. "Come on, wake up, Mol, this is serious; I am getting under the shower, make some coffee while I get dressed." The hot water helped, the monk had come to kill her. She could not stay there alone. I must get her over to her mother's and under protection. I felt a surge of adrenaline; we had been closing in. What had she done? She had come very close to being spread all around her own living room. Mol smiled sweetly as she sipped her coffee.

"Has there been another killing?"

"Not yet, nice coffee, but we need to talk."

"If that was one of ours, how did they know you were here?" I ignored the question and refilled my cup.

"Mol, that was probably our killer. You are in great danger, but he must have got a surprise when I answered the door." She was startled.

"Ray, I am so sorry! I wrote to the Abbot; it was the Major's niece and that letter he handed in. What have I done?"

"Mol, at least we now know where he is. I want you to stay with your mother; I am putting you under protection. Promise me you will do as I direct; we cannot afford any slip ups on this."

I smiled to make it easy on her. "Mol, we are on our way. Did it not occur to you that you may be offering yourself as a victim? Bugger me dead; he is a bloody monk!" Her eyes and expression told me it had sunk in.

"Dear me, he came to kill me," her voice was faint, "I put our lives in danger." She had gone a deathly pale, and was staring at me. "I have stuffed up; it was that file and that English girl's gruesome death. I could not get that letter out of my mind. I read Frank Macintyre's report again, and while he was down, I went over it with him. I have to say he was very decent about it. He had written so descriptively about what seemed such an extraordinary place, and we were all so busy. Ray, I just felt I should. The Major's niece was so well-meaning, and despite Frank going back over it with me, and he was convinced. But I could not shake off my doubt, and I wrote inquiring about adopting a black child, in much the same way as she had done, and I received the most fantastic reply. I will get you the file."

I was surprised by its thickness, but I did not want to interrupt her explanation.

"Yes, and you were saying."

"My mother and I made a donation. I noted the phone calls, time, date, everything that was said; it is all there. Of course, I never told them where I worked."

"Okay Mol, let's see if I can get on an early flight, and I will endeavour to discover how in the hell we missed him."

"Ray, I imagine if he had killed me," she said as if she was thinking it through, "he would have taken my file." Perhaps she saw a vision of her own mutilated cadaver.

"Ray..." she said, and I caught her as she fainted.

≈ 38 ≈

When I arrived at the restaurant, Marco the maitre d' was all welcoming suaveness. We had met before and he was very good at his job, but our last meeting had been at a different restaurant. "Is so nice to see madam, again.

"Thank you, this is a pretty setting."

"You are too kind." I appreciated the welcome and the restaurant's ambiance; but there is no point in having the best food in town, if the rest of it is second-rate. Waiters scurried about, and the diners were a mix of wealthy matrons, businessmen, and the usual advertising types with their seemingly limitless expense accounts. He intended to display us unobtrusively and had a good memory for detail as my favourite bottled water materialized. Then he disappeared, presumably to inform the kitchen.

When the familiar mop of red hair appeared, Marco swept her up; she had gone for pale cream, and when she walked in, the effect was electric.

"Hi, don't you just love Friday?" she said, with her usual exuberance. "I am so relieved to get out of the office. My girl, you do look swish." Which was one of the things that was so nice about her; she was the star of the show, yet she always made a point of complimenting me.

"Well I do try to keep up, although with your dress sense, I doubt if anyone could. Heather, your outfit is just fantastic."

"Thanks, we had a substantial settlement late this morning; it is always nice to get a result your client can live with, because it lets everyone off the hook. Now tell me about your glamorous life. I am sure you will not want to hear about mine."

"Don't be silly, of course I do."

"You couldn't, a practice where my clients want everything done yesterday—a demanding husband who thinks the household runs of its own accord, the most over mollycoddled and spoiled kids you could imagine, and a mortgage you could not jump over. The whole mess would put a huge strain on any woman. I would much prefer to hear about lovely food that someone else has had to cook. So my girl, what are we doing here?"

The maitre d' had done his thing and a waiter removed the flowers and poured Heather some iced water. "Oh, I heard some very nice reports. It changed hands about six months ago, and they appear to be

216

doing nicely. Three hands-on partners, which I think is an ideal way to go. I have met Marco before; I believe he's one, and he makes an excellent frontman. Manfred Mueller, the head chef, is another; he has a big reputation for running a kitchen and being innovative, which ought to give me something to write about. The remaining partner is also a chef and owns the premises. Now that can hardly be a bad combination."

"Alkina, that sounds good as I have arrived with a head full of clients and their torts, so a glass or two and some lovely food ought to help. What I enjoy so much about our lunches, as well as the company, is that the results are almost guaranteed to be excellent. Which reminds me, our conveyancer said he was having an interesting time with your mum and dad's tenure up there, and he is hopeful of doing something positive. We are corresponding with some London solicitors who handled the estates of your long-departed English relatives. It is all about tracing the title back and trying to ascertain who is entitled to what. I will let you know when he has sorted it out. And while I think of it, we rolled over your deposits; the share market is a bit iffy at the moment, so we should leave them where they are for the time being. I instructed Tom to take up your rights to the new issue of Conway Masters, so you have done very nicely out of them. That is about it; now tell me all about the new man in your life."

"Let's say I am ready to say yes, whenever he asks; and if he does not, I might have to do the asking myself."

"That sounds positive."

"Heather, Tony is the most wonderful man I have ever met, and I am very happy as long as I know he loves me, and really, what else matters? I am not going to be the easiest person to live with; I am over-bossy, over-fussy, and over-everything else, probably in all the ways men find threatening. So you could say I am very much in love. He says he loves me, so it is a very precious part of my life. Oh, and do forgive me, I have been very selfish, and I am busting to introduce him to you. It is just that I am taking it slowly, as I do not want him to feel I am setting him up for marriage. I do hope you understand. I am trying to be ultra-cool."

"That's great, you deserve someone special."

I had already scanned the menu and would go through it in more detail with Marco.

"Heather, love life aside, it has been a hectic week; we did a major function at the Town Hall for a visiting delegation, one of those showcases where the city Councillors strut their stuff. The usual round of lunches, and we put on a major shebang at the Art Gallery for one of the oil companies, which was very smart; they do like to be seen sponsoring the arts."

"I read about it," Heather remarked. Our luncheon was a delight, if you discount those interruptions from complete strangers, and the waiters being over-attentive. The chatter was lively; we both would have been guilty of spicing it up. Heather told of a juicy defamation case and all the *argy-bargy* and carrying on before it was settled.

"We lawyers are great ones for rumours and tasty gossip," she said, "and the other day, I heard the most incredible leak from the Premier's Office. It came through a journalist friend of mine. Mind you, many of the so-called leaks are quite deliberate. This one was about those serial murders that have everyone scared out of their wits. I was told the reason they were hushed up was because they think he is an indigenous Australian." We were again interrupted by a waiter fussing around and topping up our glasses. When the waiter had gone, and for whatever reason, I overreacted.

"Well, I hope that turns out to be crap; we do not need nasty stories like that," I said sharply. I regretted it immediately; poor Heather had gone crimson.

"My fault entirely; I never gave it a moment's thought," Heather said. I can only say I was mortified.

"Heather, please do not apologize; my mother would never forgive me. She would say, if I cannot conduct a civil conversation with my best friend, then I have a serious problem. Heather, I am terribly sorry, please go on."

Heather qualified it. "Well it is only uncorroborated scuttlebutt." But in for a penny and I pressed her, "Heather, do tell me."

"They think it may be a ritual, as each time, the corpses were bled and the kidneys removed; apparently the killer smears himself with the victim's blood and kidney fat, and cavorts about leaving a disgusting mess." My dear friend had just described the basics of the kangaroo ceremony, and it was as if my whole world had collapsed; I wanted to scream. I hoped Heather had not noticed, and I made a superhuman effort to remain calm and to keep smiling. I desperately needed to survive the shock. Could my brother be the serial killer? It just seemed unbelievable. I had to see our mother and father and hope that they would know what to do. I struggled for control, I was not going to let Dar destroy my life. Recalling it later, I have no idea how I got through our lunch.

⚹ 39 ⚹

My decision to get away had been brewing for some time, and despite our close working relationship, I always knocked before I entered the Abbot's study.

"Good to see Aden," the Abbot beamed, "how was Sydney, and did you manage to get through everything?" The Abbot's Bible was open and that morning's newspaper had fallen on the floor. "I did not realize you were back. Have you time for us to pray together? I would like us to thank our dear Lord for today, and to ask for his guidance for tomorrow. There is so much to pray about. You only have to read the papers; there is just so much trouble in the world. I imagine God must be very disappointed when he sees the way we treat each other."

"I am sure he must, but Father, could we talk for a moment, as I have something on my mind?"

"Of course Aden, I like to see you settled and setting a cheerful mood for the others; that is our duty to God. Now tell me what is on your mind?"

"My parents are getting old, and I feel very remiss that I have not been able to see them."

"Aden, you must go and visit them," Father David enthused.

"Father, it will be good to see them and my land again, and to walk some of the dreaming places of my childhood. This may seem strange, but I need to feel the hot wind on my skin once more."

"Aden, you must never forget your past. God has made you big enough to allow them to co-exist in harmony. When will you leave?"

"It will take me a couple of days to tidy up and instruct Brother Damon on what has to be done."

"Aden, forgive me, I have taken your enormous workload for granted, and it was wrong of me."

"Not at all, and if you do not mind, I would like to slip away without any fuss. I shall come and say goodbye."

"Please draw a check to cover your expenses and take a vehicle."

"Thanks, but it is not necessary. I shall wear street clothes and travel light. I can hitch a ride when I need; I do not see any difficulties. I shall take my time and enjoy the journey."

"Aden, I should have suggested it before; now let us kneel and ask our almighty God for his divine guidance as you set out on your journey."

⚡ 40 ⚡

I recall feeling very pleased with myself as I boarded my flight to Tamworth, for now we had a resolution in sight. I stowed my bag in the locker and nodded a greeting to the elderly gent in the next seat, a well-groomed country type with woollen tie and smart-looking tweed sports coat.

"Personally," my neighbour said, "I think they should bring the drinks around before we take off, as it is only a two-Scotch flight to Tamworth anyway. Timothy Caruthers," he said, offering his hand. "Care to join me when they turn up with the trolley? I do hate drinking alone."

"Sounds like a good idea, Ray Brannagan," and we shook hands, "and I prefer not to smell of it at the other end. It's been a very long night."

"Trouble sleeping old boy?" I had to laugh. "You could say, so what should I have?"

"It seems we need not worry; we will be there before they get around to it, ha, ha. Brannagan, I know the name?"

"I am a policeman, but there is no need for us to advertise the fact."

"Certainly not, what we need is a couple of gin and tonics with lemon and ice, a good drink for this time of day that will do us both the world of good, and no one will be any the wiser. I knew a policeman once in the army, decent sort of cove; he would have retired like me many years ago, and well before your time. What do you do in the police force?"

"Homicide investigations, although I doubt if you would have ever come across such a thing."

"Ray, I suppose not."

"And Timothy, what do you do in your retirement?"

"Not much, we have a few acres out on the Manilla Road—sheep, wheat, Lucerne, a few cows—my son runs it now; my job is to putter in the garden and pour the drinks, ha, ha."

"Sounds ideal, would you like an assistant?"

"Ha ha, I have to say you do not match my perception of a policeman. Ah, here come the nice young ladies with the drinks."

Having done a 'bottoms up' and conducted a light banter with Carruthers, I tried some probing myself. "I understand there is a religious order, not far out of Tamworth, who run a recovery program for chronic alcoholics. I wonder if you know of it?"

"Yes, but I hope, touch wood, that I never have to be admitted. Poor buggers; it is sad to think that a man cannot have a drink without wishing to drown himself in the damn stuff. I must say it is part of the nightly routine at our place. I always thought it a good thing; it marks the end of the working day and sets one up for dinner. As a matter of fact, they are very successful exhibitors in the Tamworth show. I believe they run a highly productive farm; of course it is always a help if no one draws a wage, ha, ha, ha. You are not going up to take the cure yourself?" Caruthers rather enjoyed his own humour, and the conversation meandered along; but I knew no more than he did. We chatted, and had a second drink, and once we touched down, we said our goodbyes when my companion was met by his family.

The western clouds were giant swirls of pink and purple, as Detective Inspector Frank Macintyre drove us out to the priory.

"This is no reflection on you Frank, none whatsoever; no one would have suspected one of the monks. We will have to tread very carefully, and it would appear the Abbot had no idea. What we need are a decent set of prints and a match for that fibre. Nice-looking country around here; the cattle look as fat as rocking horses." Great trees draped their shade over the priory courtyard and I was very impressed by the old sandstone buildings. "This is the original Dunraven homestead," Frank explained, "wait till you see through it."

"Frank, you write a descriptive report. I feel I have been here before."

The front door was wide open, and after failing to raise anyone, we chose not to go wandering through."

"Chief, follow me; they must be working outside." A distant diesel made a steady throb and down the slope a truck was slowly backing into a shed. We stood on the rear lawn with the valley rising to the hills behind, every now and then, when the wind was in the right quarter; we were practically asphyxiated by an assortment of farm smells.

Frank pointed out a rotund figure in the distance and waved, which the Abbot returned and headed our way. We set out to meet him and as we drew closer, I saw that for a man of his age, he moved surprisingly well. The photos had captured it exactly—impish eyes, extraordinary haircut, although the pate was nut brown, and the monk had one of those angelic faces that had escaped the ravages of time. Frank's report had said middle to late sixties, and that he might well be a good deal older. Close up there were pearl white teeth, an overpowering smile, and a strong body odour. The eyes sparkled with good humour, grubby sandaled toes protruded from beneath the rough habit, which looked exceedingly hot and uncomfortable. The big man gave Frank a brotherly hug.

"Good to see you Frank."

"And you Father David. I would like you to meet my boss, Chief Superintendent Ray Brannagan from Sydney." The handshake was firm and welcoming, as was the greeting, "Nice to have you here, as I said to Frank, you boys are always welcome."

"Thanks," I said, surprised by the man's warmth, "it is worthwhile just to see the magnificent homestead and the views. Frank writes a descriptive report, and I would imagine that if ever a man could find his soul, this surely would have to be the place." The Abbot laughed, "Exactly, that is our aim, and many of them do." I felt reassured that we would be able to get on with it.

"Father David," I said, "you understand why we are here, and I was hoping you would give me a quick tour of the accommodation, and tell me about the people you have here, and that includes all the members of your Order."

"Of course, and that was very good timing Frank. I was about to come in anyway."

"And would you have taken men into the program since Frank was last here?"

"Yes, they come and go all the time; and if we go around to my office, I can give you a copy of the up-to-date list." We followed Father David across the flagstone veranda into the wide hall and finally into a Spartan study. On the walls were what appeared to be the annual group photos of the monks. The shots had been taken outside on the stone terrace.

"We have around one hundred and eighty men in the program at any one time," Father David explained, "how long they stay depends on their progress and the individual."

We followed him into the administration centre next door, and watched as he rummaged through a file, extracted several pages, copied them and gave the copies to Frank.

"We run a tight ship; if they do not cooperate, we do not let them take the place of someone who will. We have had too many successes for that." I could well imagine that under the veneer of affability, there would be a determined streak to the man. We returned to his study and spent a few moments looking at the photos.

"And Frank tells me the Brothers are all reformed alcoholics."

"Indeed, they are."

"Are there any of indigenous descent?"

"There are two, and of course race is not an issue with us."

"No Father David," I replied. "I do not imagine it is, but would you please identify them for me?" The Abbot immediately did.

"And could you give me a copy of their photos?"

"Certainly, we print them ourselves."

We now had photos and identification. Frank was busy jotting down the details.

"We have our group photos taken six weeks before Christmas day, so they can go out with their greetings to family and friends." We did not tell the Abbot that we were almost certain it was one of the indigenous Brothers.

"Thank you for your help. Now if you do not mind Father David, if I could see their rooms."

Frank might have been on a social visit; he and the Abbot chatted like old friends while I followed and concentrated on taking everything in. The Abbot was justifiably proud of their work.

"We grow our own wheat and mill our own flour, which in turn is used in our highly regarded bakery, and a great deal of their output is given away to hospitals and the like. The same goes for much of our other produce, and of course, good wholesome food plays a very large part in their recovery." As Frank had said, the priory was a hive of industry.

"This is Brother James's room." We were shocked by its austerity. Frank had looked at me and shaken his head in disbelief. There was nothing, other than a couple of timber pegs let into the stone wall, a stand with a few personal items, a small chest of drawers, and an iron cot. "The Brothers all work extremely hard," the Abbot explained. "We rise well before dawn and retire late, and we work and worship the Lord together in a true brotherhood. Our Brother James has Japanese, Afghan, and Koori blood; in what proportion, even he does not know." I believed there was madness there. Frank was trying to find something that might hold a decent print; the Abbot did not demur. "James runs our machine shop; he can do anything with metal and is a wonderful worker for God." Fittingly Frank had chosen a machined ornament. I looked on with approval.

"Good," I commented, "now could we inspect Brother Aden's room?"

On the way, we visited the holy of holies; the Abbot was most anxious to show it to us and so he led us on to the prayer room. I am not sure if I felt overawed, or spiritually intimidated, by the beautifully carved figure of the crucified Christ looking agonizingly down. There was enough room for three or four to kneel side by side at the ornately carved prayer rail.

"This is one of our treasures, and was carved for us by a man who was surely lost. Today he is a very talented sculptor and still corresponds, and I like to think we restored him not only to his loved ones, but to his art; just look at the intricate detail."

We trailed the Abbot down a hall.

"This is our Brother Aden's room," our guide announced almost reverently. There was the smell of death in Aden's cell; his habit hung in front of us. I took it down; the feel was coarse and I wondered how anyone could wear it next to their skin.

"Father, are these made from home-spun black wool?"

"Yes."

It was at that moment I was confident we had cracked it.

"Ray, the fleeces come from our small flock, and we never use dyes and it has become another of our industries. It is most surprising how the interest in this has spread; we are asked to send fleeces to enthusiasts all over Australia."

Frank was inspecting the items on a dresser, and had slipped a silver-plated photo frame into an evidence bag.

"Our cassocks," the Abbot continued, "have a lovely earthy texture; we have some very dear friends who spin, weave, and make them for us." We had just kicked a mighty goal and I gave Frank the nod, and folded the habit over my arm.

"We need to take this," I said, "so we can run some routine tests, and I need to interview Brother Aden."

"I am sorry," Father David explained, "for Aden has taken leave to visit his parents; they are now quite elderly, and regrettably it is many years since he has seen them." There had been unmistakable regret in the Abbot's voice. "He left after matins twenty-two day ago, but I am certain he has nothing to hide."

I could not wait to get out of the place, and was much relieved when we were heading back to Tamworth.

"Well done Frank, to your favourite pub; we deserve a drink after all that. And mate, I doubt that it's premature to celebrate. Christ, this habit is putrid; it has to be him. Have we brought a decent evidence bag? If they get a whiff of that, I will be ejected from the plane. Frank, we hold everything back until we have Willard's confirmation." I phoned him as soon as it was clear we had a fit.

"Frank, Brother Aden is our man; we found blood and fat traces in the cassock. And even at this early stage, Jim assures me the fibres are a match. We have enough to put him away. You had better take a couple of the more experienced hands out to the priory and pick up everything you can on this fellow. The Abbot will be shocked, but make sure he tells you of any contact. Frank, I want everything; I just told the Commissioner. What do you think? Talk about kiss my ass. Thanks Frank, I had better let you get on with it."

❖ 41 ❖

I popped my ears as my flight began its slow descent into Alice Springs, where the rows of little planes sat to one side like a neat arrangement of a child's toys. I had stocked up on glossy magazines for my mother, and anything I could find on the cricket and the football for my father. Not that any of that was any compensation for what I was about to tell them. I waited in the air-conditioned departure lounge until the mail plane was ready.

The vast red country slowly passed below as the waves of warm air lifted the little plane gently up. I chatted to the pilot as best I could against the incessant drone. This was the way of my generation, which now took the outside world to the isolated stations. The bush telegraph had worked in its timeless way; the pilot knew all about me and soon it would hum with the awful news of my brother, the horror of which felt overwhelming. How pathetic it was to be bringing this back to my parents, my homecomings normally were ones of personal triumph, when I could regale them with stories of my life, while they had listened with delight. I would arrive laden with gifts. My mother was easy, a keen dressmaker. I kept her supplied with good quality material and whatever else she needed. Their delight was worth the trip on its own; this time I bore only heartache.

My father sensed it, and seemed wary of my sudden arrival. We drank tea and they waited for me to tell my news. Mum could see I was distressed, but did not press me. We talked of inconsequential things, while I readied myself.

"How are Heather and her family?" This avoidance went on until mum took my hand in hers. "Alkina, what's troubling you? Your father and I can see it, and we can only share it if you tell us." I had difficulty getting it out.

"I believe Dar may be the serial killer the Sydney police have been looking for. The details were never made public, but Heather heard them; they were straight from the kangaroo ceremony you taught him. The victims were bled, the killer took their kidney fat, and smeared that and their blood all over himself, and cavorted in it."

It was the worst moment of my life, and I collapsed into her arms. I just felt so sorry for them. After a while, my poor father had recovered sufficiently to have us follow him out into the bush, where he led us to a place I remembered from my childhood. And still they had no idea their son had taken vows and joined an obscure order of monks. I told them now, knowing it would be splashed all over the media, but compared to what they had just learned, it was no longer important. In a while, my father left us to grieve in his own way; and mum and I just sat in the sand and wailed. We kicked it up and threw it all over ourselves, and stamped the ground in our anguish.

When we had calmed, my mother spoke with such tenderness. "Alkina, you have your own life to live; you cannot live Darain's for him. Your brother is a man now. You and I may grieve, but it is his father we must worry about. He was never able to be part of his son's coming to manhood; I am not sure he has ever got over his loss. My dearest daughter, we are very proud of what our children have achieved. Now we must wait while your father decides what we should do." Mum was an emotional sponge and had Nan's way of coping. A day or so later, the poor thing shared her private thoughts with me.

"Alkina, your father and I have each other to comfort, and we worry about you; we want you to sing to dear Nan; she would want to know and to comfort you. We may not walk our country as much as we would like, but old age has given us the wisdom to see things more clearly. We could bear the grief of losing our children once we knew you were safe. He and I are not unhappy growing old, but we would like to see you married and having children. We could teach them much. I often think of all the things we did, as if it was just a few years ago, and they are lovely memories."

"Mum, remember our great walk to father's country? Dar told me so proudly about their time together, the ceremonies they made, they were never far from his thoughts. I am sure they were what sustained him over the years." I stayed with my parents until it was all said.

≈ 42 ≈

Some weeks after my sister had returned to Sydney, and in fantastic, if unintentional timing, I returned to my boyhood home. I arrived just as the pale light of dawn rose over the misty billabong, where I had frolicked as a child. I lit a fire a little distance away from their cottage, and settled beside it to warm myself and to wait. My thoughts were of those days of so many years ago, spent running in and out to play with my cousins and their friends, of being hoisted high on my father's shoulders, the wonder of hunting and gathering with all the women and children, and coming home tired after racing ahead of Nan and my mother.

I must have been napping and awoke to see the beaming face of my father. The old man let out a whoop of joy, and we embraced. The face had hollowed; the back may not have been as upright; the muscles across his shoulders no longer rippled; but the power of that large frame was there. We were elated to be reunited again. There was the awkwardness of my being out of touch for so long. How should I explain? Peggy and I had not flown up very often and I left it to Alkina to see they had everything they needed. My neglect was a feeble excuse, perhaps unexplainable, like some of the other phases of my life. My father brewed tea and we talked.

"Dad, it has been far too long; I am sorry." My words seemed unnecessary. My father shook his head and his fond expression said otherwise. I tried to explain, "As I walked in, I reacquainted myself with all the wonders of our country. They may have been dormant after all these years, but all the things you taught me were still there, and throughout my life, I often wondered what you would have done in my situation. I have never told you how much I got from being your son. I still think of our hunting trips, all the fatherly talks, and the wonderful stories you told me. They soothed and nourished me as a boy. I took them with me out into the shearing sheds. I carried them to war, into my business life; they were with me in my marriage; and I will carry them always."

My father was nodding as if he was also remembering. "Your mother and I think you are a fine son. You made us very proud, but Dar, what made you turn to their God?" The complete clarity of the question shocked me. I had unsuccessfully tried to explain myself to my sister. Had I really just been hiding from reality for all these years?

"Apart from seeing you and mum, it is one of the reasons I came home. I have never accepted their beliefs in the absolute terms they do. On my way here, I have felt the spirits of our dreaming everywhere. I never lost it, and I think the stories you, Nan and mother told me are just as valid, and as spiritually comforting as theirs can be. It is the reason I wanted to come home to find myself."

Whether he approved or not, my father was smiling broadly.

"Your mother and I missed you, and when Alkina told us how sad you were after Peggy's death, we worried about you. Son, when you and I walk and hunt together, there will be much for us to talk about around our campfire; we will sing to Peggy and tell her how you have returned to your land." My mother had appeared on the veranda.

"I thought I must be dreaming when I heard your voice; come and give your mother a hug." She was frailer than I expected; her grey hair tumbled over her floral housecoat; the smile was still there and the years sat comfortably with her. We hugged, and I let her steer me inside.

"My darling boy, it is so good that you have come home. Tell your father and me what you have been doing, while I make breakfast." While we talked, the Mighty Hunter kept looking at me as though I might disappear, and my mother kept coming over to run her hand over my face. I was overwhelmed to be blanketed in such parental love. My father ate well and after a day and night of catching up, the old man made ready to leave.

"My son, it is time we hunted and talked together." He had gathered his spear, *woomera*, and club. My mother hugged and kissed me goodbye. The skinny legs strode out in front, and after a while, the old man began to point to the things he wanted me to see, and it was as if the intervening years had never been. How strange it was to find I remembered those familiar landmarks, the rocky outcrops, stands of trees, and the skyline of red hills. My father would stop to remind me of a place where our spirits dwelt.

After a while, the Mighty Hunter halted at a water hole and we rested under the trees. He said we were going to a place where there had been thunderstorms, and where there would be new grass to bring in the kangaroos. There were so many things that came back to me: how my father used to lope along and rise on the balls of his feet, the great rippling leg and shoulder muscles taut until the moment of release.

"Dad, when I was a child, I wanted to be a mighty hunter just like you."

"My son, you were a fine warrior, who fought for our country, and you made your mother and me very proud. We understand how you suffered, and how losing your friends must have been very sad. Your mother and I understood what you did; after all I would have told you how our ancestors killed their enemies.

A man can lose too much, and how much you have missed your

lovely mate. What happened to you and your sister was because your father was not wary; yet your great-grandfather Fritzhugh warned us. I should have listened carefully, for our ancestors have walked this land before." My parents must have thought and talked about this a great deal, and I was very touched. "No dad, there is no need to blame yourself, just as there is no point in me making excuses; I know that what I did was very wrong."

It was not long before we came to where there had been showers, and already the new green shoots were poking through. At dusk, while the faded pink of early night stole away, the great reds emerged to feed. The moon bathed the land in its soft light, while a million twinkling stars made everything below seem of little consequence. The Mighty Hunter became part of the night as he circled toward his quarry. Their black noses remained unaware, until suddenly they were disturbed and plunged in alarm. A few minutes later, the hunter was back with a fine young animal slung over his shoulder. I took it from him, and followed my father through the bush.

"We will camp at Nan's billabong, do you remember?"

"Yes, I have often thought of it."

"It was our favourite place. When you were taken, we would come out here to imagine the two of you playing in the sand. This is where Nan and Fritz first mated in their great love, and when it was her time, where she came to release her spirit to join him in the sky. This is also where your mother and I first mated, and where you were born, and where we first held you."

I was much comforted by his words. The flickering flames of the fire danced across our faces as the old man carefully prepared the feast. "Tell me how you and Peggy made your life together?"

"We were just like you and mum; we were very close. I still think of her every day; I did even when I was drunk. Peggy was my life; she filled it with love; living with her was like a beautiful dream; and she was sweet enough to say I had the same effect on her." I laughed as I recalled the feeling. "And what was so wonderful was that she and Alkina were closer than sisters. When Alkina was getting established in Sydney, the three of us worked ourselves into the ground. As you know, she and Hanna had done very well in Adelaide, but it was not until she teamed up with Heather in Sydney that her business really took off. The three of us had a ball, and they were beautiful years. When they discovered Peg's cancer, she and I discussed it calmly, and having seen death before, I honestly thought I could handle it.

I was wrong, and I regret very much not doing enough to support Alkina, as I know she would have been devastated. If there was any consolation, it was that she had a closely knit circle of friends. As you probably know, Peg and I led a very comfortable life and were very happy. The boys paid me well, and as we expanded, so did their generosity. Alkina would have told you that Peggy was a very smart lady, and that she had me sorted out right from the start. Peg never made demands, and made sure my life was as pleasant as she could make it. And it remained like that throughout our marriage. There is a lot I could tell you about her, but that covers the basics. I am sorry I have caused you and mum so much pain. Perhaps if there had been children..."

"How does your life work now?" I had arrived expecting the question; but now that it was asked, I was not at all sure I could answer it. There were things in my life I could never explain.

"Dad, the priory does an immense amount of good, and I suppose that once I had dried out, I began to appreciate the peace and quiet. I just got caught up in it, and began to feel I had a purpose again." I sensed that my father expected more.

"Son, there is something troubling you; tell me about it; I want to try to understand."

"Dad, I am sorry I have left it so long, as we walk, I will try to fill in the years."

The Mighty Hunter carved from the outside, and we began to eat, and it was a glorious sensation as the smell and taste of it rekindled my childhood senses. But my father was not going to leave it there.

"It is many years since Peggy died, and son, we have not seen you. Have you something more to tell me, so that it does not just tear away at your innards? We could talk of it, and sing to our ancestors and spirits."

The way it was put had an implication which my father had not explained.

"No, I came home to see you and mother, to see my land again, and to renew my dreaming." He grunted as if he was not satisfied. "It is good that you have come; it has been far too long since I have seen my son. I remember taking you hunting for your first roo."

"Dad, the memory of it has been with me always, and just being here with you makes it seem like yesterday. Just like now, you chose the best portions for me, you made your boy feel like a warrior, and I want you to know that all my life, I have thought of how good it was. I would have liked to have fathered a boy, and taught him all the things that you taught me; perhaps the three of us could have made the long walk so that you and I could have revealed our totem and our lore to him together. It saddens me to think our secrets will never be passed on."

The settling noises of the night came to our fire: frogs, crickets, and squabbling birds, and the gentle trickle of water over rocks. When we had eaten and talked, my father began to dance, waving his spear at the stars, kicking the dust into the air, singing his chant, calling his

230

ancestors, telling them he was with his son who had come home after a long journey, and what great joy he felt. He whirled his woomera around his head and dared his enemies to come and stamped his feet and made thrusts into the night with his spear. All time for me had stopped; I was a boy again; I joined my father and sung that I was home; the dust rose as I pawed and stamped my country. And the Mighty Hunter sung of his satisfaction that this was so.

⚡ 43 ⚡

My mother rarely phoned, like Nan; she was more comfortable expressing her thoughts in a letter. She sounded upset and the line was very poor.

"Dar came home to see us," she told me in between sobs. "I have embraced my son for the last time. Your poor father has taken him out for their final hunt together; he insists he must do it, but I know it will break his heart, but he wants Dar's spirit to stay in his own country. My darling girl, it has been so long, and we were so glad to see him. They would have sung and danced their dreaming, for your father wanted him to talk about what he has done, and to try and understand it." There was a prolonged silence as mother composed herself. "My darling Alkina, please sing to Dar's spirit; you love him, as your father and I do." My poor mother would have been struggling. "Darling, I must go," she said softly.

Even before my mother's call, there had been weeks during which I had terrible visions of my brother smeared with human fat and blood, and after that call, I saw my father spearing, then striking him down with his club. This ghastly vision reduced me to a state of near collapse. Father and son worshipped each other. I sung all this to Nan, and dug deep into my own emotional reserves. This was not something I could share with Heather, or any of my close friends. I was deeply in love, and was determined to let nothing stand in the way. It was the certainty of that love that kept me going, helped me to maintain my grip on my life, and I threw myself into my business.

There was much comfort in telling Nan of my romance. The way it had blossomed had been surprisingly simple. I had flown over to do the food for a prestigious international medical conference in Fremantle and Tony had flown in from Adelaide to do the wines. We had done it well, and our long days would end with a late supper together while we unwound, and when he had finally kissed me goodbye, for me it was more than just a farewell kiss. There had been phone calls, and a sharing of thoughts, until we met again at a wine festival in the Barossa Valley. "I like the way you did that," he told me after a banquet. "I thought your food complemented my wines very well."

We had laughed, and I had known immediately, just as Nan had said I would. Tony was so professional, so easy to get along with, so attentive and charming. It seemed to me that we complemented each other in every way. His kisses had left me reeling, and his touch had awakened a longing that I had never known before; our desire for each other seemed unquenchable. The D'Cruz family were originally from Spain, and were in the olive oil business, and they adored me and I them. But over the following months, Tony was sensitive enough to know something was troubling me, and to fly across whenever he could.

I do not know how I got through it; the media was full of the case, and although I had been interviewed by the police, for some unknown reason, my brother had still not been named as their prime suspect. I had to tread warily; I loved Tony too much to risk his family becoming caught up in it. My mother was struggling with her grief, and there was still no sign of my father. I had put my life on hold, and had to invent reasons to slow things down. Months went by, and my romance and my busy life continued, although thankfully the media had not yet made the connection. There were limitations on keeping my romance from Heather, who might be offended if I held back any longer, and I decided that she and Tony should meet.

⚡ 44 ⚡

The blast of inland heat hit me with a fierceness that shocked my sense of anything I may have expected. I had been warned to wear a straw hat and sunglasses, and to wear a loose shirt over my shorts, and to ensure I drank plenty of water. But this was a furnace. I began to film and that diversion helped, but I knew I was not cut out to be in the centre of Australia in the middle of summer. At Alice Springs, I teamed up with Sergeant Michael Dodds, or "Mick" as he was known, who immediately made me feel like an alien who had landed on the wrong planet. The Sergeant paid no attention to the heat. He was as lean as barbed wire and as brown and craggy as the land itself, and was said to know the country and understand its people better than anyone. The local approved of my camera and filming, although the sincerity of his remarks was lost on me at the time.

We chatted on the way to the charter plane, although the slow country drawl seemed strange, the bushman chose his words carefully. "Ray, it is a pleasure to finally meet up with you; your reputation stretches through the outback, and I should tell you that my boss told me to do everything I can to assist. But mate, I am in the dark; what do we know about this bloke?"

I was embarrassed at the little I had; most of it had come from the Abbot and the suspect's sister, but as we went through it, I was again struck by the wild deviations in the man's life. But once we had covered the childhood background, Mick nodded as if that pretty much explained everything. Far below, deep gorges crisscrossed a wild jumble of barren rock hills and sheer cliffs, and amply illustrated the enormity of our search. Mick struck me as being the quintessential outback Australian with an independent view of the world, who was completely unfazed as to whether we agreed or not.

"Chief, I did warn you, if this bloke has gone bush, that's it; we may as well pack up and go home."

The pilot put us down on the Arrawatta strip where we were met by the station manager. After a brief look around to get my bearings, I began my interviews. The mother was helpful and articulate, she described how one morning her son had just walked in, which, seeing where we were, was nothing less than astonishing, and how neither the son nor her husband had been seen since, which tallied with the sister's story. She did not mind me filming, and seemed as eager to help as was her daughter, which, given why I was there, I would not have expected.

Using a sort of bastardized English, Mick began with the elders, but it was mostly directed at one grizzly old man, who sat under a tree like a Buddha. The locals squatted around him on their haunches; a cloud of persistent bush flies had attached themselves and irritated the hell out of me, but the old men could not have cared less as they crawled around their eyes. Mick turned to me, "Ray, he says, this man is dead; that he got speared and his father smashed his head in." We paused to consider that scenario. "I do not think we can argue with that. The old bloke's story is that they went out into the sandstone range, which is well west of here, and are no longer on Arrawatta. I have been out in that country myself, and it is as rough as guts; and given the time span, there is no way, even with a very skilled tracker, we can follow."

Mick continued the discussion with the others, before he said, "Yeah that tallies, they are all in agreement, and Dick here is the most respected elder, so in my view, if he says our man is dead, then he probably is. The gist of what he says is that the father took his son out into the bush and dispatched him." Even though I had it on film, I wondered how all this would be received in Sydney, and what with the heat, dust, and the flies that left me exasperated? We did not need much; perhaps some bones, hair, or a few teeth, anything else would have been a bonus.

"Mick, I do not know that we can leave it there. We need to talk to the father and at least have him verify all this. I mean, all I have is an uncorroborated testimony and enough film to make a documentary." Mick would not have a bar of it.

"Ray, I am sorry, but that's it; all we can do is hope the wife will let us know when her husband shows up, and if you like, I will fly out and take his statement. If it had not been for her intervention, they would not have talked to us about him at all. I reckon we have done well to get this far, and even if they knew, they would not tell us where the remains are. So there is not much we can do about it until the father shows up."

There seemed a vast gulf between the meticulous investigation that had taken us this far, and this untidy winding up. My companion must have read my thoughts.

"Ray, cheer up, this is not the first time this has happened out here; there would be the few we hear about, and probably a bloody lot more that we do not. When we get back to the Alice, I will do what I can to put it all down, so it at least sounds believable."

"Thanks, but Mick, where I come from, things are not that simple. I have to terminate this case in a way that satisfies reasonable standards of proof. That means producing some tangible evidence of this individual's death. I do not know what you have seen or read, but there is considerable public interest in this case." Mick looked at me as if I was being patronizing.

"Ray, you must have thought I was kidding. I take your investigation and trip up here very seriously. But we are talking over four thousand square kilometres in the immediate search area. Mate, it is all right for you city blokes to want this and want that; believe me, we are talking about a bloody lot of Australia. We have the elder's mark on a statement, and it seems to me that whether those in Sydney like it or not, they are just going to have to accept the fact that this cove is dead. That is all we have; we are told he is out there somewhere; we do not have the father to interview, and have bugger all hope of finding a cadaver. And you can tell them from me, that unless it was buried, and I doubt it would have been, most of it would have been scattered by the birds and animals all around the countryside.

I knew when to withdraw. "Okay Mick, what do you suggest?"

"I will get the pilot to fly over some of the countryside while you film. When I investigate these cases, I find you cannot have too much footage." I was sceptical, and for me it certainly took some getting around to understand that the mother and sister knew what was intended. The following morning we wrote it up, and whether it was the effect of the few convivial beers the night before, or the air-conditioning and a decent sleep. But when I read the report, it made sense, or it did in Alice Springs.

"...then we interviewed one Dick Nirwarra, a tribal elder, who said he believed that according to tribal custom in dealing with such an outcast, who is believed possessed by evil spirits, the suspect would have been speared, then clubbed to death. The whereabouts of exactly where this happened and the location of the remains are unknown. However, they are believed to be in a vast area that lies approximately three hundred and eighty kilometres due southwest from the western boundary of Arrawatta Station. This is in the impenetrable country associated with the Dreaming Time spirits, which are of great significance to these people...." Several more pages wrestled with the mysteries of belief. Mick took an expansive view of it.

"Ray," he said, "their beliefs are just as valid as ours, or they certainly are to them. And another thing, it seems to me that city people never seem to understand how huge this country is; they think we live in each other's pocket like they do." I could understand the sentiments, and there was nothing I could say.

However, back in Sydney, the wiry bushman had been a better judge of human nature than perhaps he knew. The report made interesting reading. Lawrence D sucked his pipe and nodded sagely as I took him through it. "This is a very politically sensitive situation Raymond, and it would be better if you made the same presentation to the Minister; at least you have seen that country at first hand." Any physical evidence of the suspect's demise or not, the killings had stopped, and it seemed I could do no wrong. As one of the dailies told its readers, "Chief Superintendent Raymond Brannagan and his team have done the people of this State proud by painstakingly resolving this complex series of killings."

≈ 45 ≈

Our Friday lunches had grown out of friendship, and they later had taken on a character all of their own, and once we realized their publicity value, we made them a vehicle to promote our careers. Heather was always so unfailingly enthusiastic. She complemented me on my outfit, which was only a simple frock I had sketched and my mother had run up for me. She had worn a pale rust-collared linen skirt, with a blouse of a divine shade of green, which she teamed with a chunky red, yellow, and brown necklace and matching bangles and sandals. The effect was stunning, and assured that I had something to carry on about in my column. Then Tony arrived, and I was able to introduce them, and for the first time in months, I was able to relax.

"Heather is my dearest friend, and has run me and my business for years—my business very successfully, me, I am not so sure." We laughed and were rewarded with an unconscious toss of her gorgeous red hair.

"Oh, I would not say that; you turned out okay. I knew Tony would be divine, but my dear, this is ridiculous." Heather took his proffered hand in hers, and looked him straight in the eye, so there was no mistaking her sentiment. "Tony, at last we meet, and I am truly delighted. Alkina is my dearest friend and a very special lady."

His other hand had closed over hers in a gesture of reassurance. He had worn a casual navy jacket over an open shirt and looked relaxed. We were deeply in love, but I had kept him under wraps for so long, I felt the need to explain. "We kept running into each other professionally. I suppose our romance began in Fremantle, and really blossomed in the Barossa and then later in Adelaide. It has not been easy to squeeze it in between our commitments. I think it is a miracle we ever found the time."

"Not so Heather," he laughed. "I adored her food, and I think she quite liked my wines; perhaps it was more a meeting of taste buds."

I suspect that Heather and Tony were aware there was something worrying me. But since our romance blossomed, I did my utmost to rise above it. Of course it was wonderful to see how those two warmed to each other straightaway. The conversation sparkled, and like many in his industry, Tony had an endless supply of very amusing stories which kept us entertained. A few days passed before she and I spoke on the phone and after a little prodding, I told her I was worried about my brother. I did not elaborate. She was the only one who knew Tony and I were to be married, and we had asked her to keep it under wraps until we were ready.

≈ 46 ≈

Hanging on my office wall were citations, from the grateful people of Sydney, and the State of New South Wales. Months had passed, when quite suddenly my much-publicized, and supposedly resolved case suddenly took a very embarrassing about turn. The circumstances were so extraordinary that I was embarrassed enough, and I will confess, unwise enough, to try and keep it out of the media. I had been feted and honoured by the Premier, the Lord Mayor, and seemingly everyone else, and no one could have been more surprised at this about face than myself. I immediately advised the Commissioner, who would have rushed to tell the Minister, and I could just imagine how the Premier would have reacted.

As a result, I was still in my office trying to piece it all together when Martin's call came in on my private line. The wall clock said it was nearly midnight, and a desk of flashing lights told me I still had a bank of unanswered calls, all of which was very predictable, as the television hierarchy was in an absolute frenzy over it. But at that moment, I was genuinely puzzled as to how the American had found out.

"Ray, I just heard, and as it took me by surprise, I guess I am just curious." I had an overwhelming wish not to have to explain.

"What did you hear?" I asked.

"That you arrested another suspect 'Kidney Man'. Ray, my source is impeccable. I made the comment, that to my knowledge, it had been wrapped up months ago. So, what has happened? Then it hit me that our Premier was in Washington."

"Martin, this has only just happened."

"Oh, I see."

"Prof, it seems we made a mistake."

"Raymond, I do not believe it!" Martin was having his moment in the sun.

"Listen Ray, I heard all the worse screw-ups years ago."

"With due respect Martin, I doubt that not even you could top this one. We put the wood on the wrong man, and I am trying to piece it together. There will be an exhumation tomorrow; we suspect poisoning. I would give you ten to one on the result. This has to be one of the worst cases of betrayal and absolute bastardry anyone could conjure up. But what gets to me is that this bastard nearly put one over me."

"Okay I get the picture. So what happened?"

"You know how the subconscious works. I woke up very early on

Sunday morning with a persistent headache. I knew what it was all about; I was never really satisfied with the resolution of this case, and it was still going around and around in my head. There had been no interrogation to fill in the gaps, and we had no one to charge. Having got up to take something, I thought of one last possibility we should look at, and first thing in the morning I rang Tamworth and asked them to get me a set of the Abbot's prints. You know what's coming; this most cooperative, and in my mind, absolute prince among men, and of course they matched."

"Raymond, that is incredible."

"Our suspect had been systematically and expertly set up; you have no idea. But what is so terrible is that it appears our original suspect may have been slain by his own father in a traditional act of tribal retribution." The American was silent as I continued. "This case really began years ago with the death of an elderly country doctor. There were no surviving relatives, and as a recovered alcoholic himself, he left his estate for the carrying on of a successful detoxification program he had founded. But the rub was he left it under the control of his former driver, cum handyman, who somehow evolved into our Abbot. My friend, he would have really got up your nose. I thought he was the true Samaritan, one of those marvellous people you read about, but rarely meet in a life.

Now listen to this, the retired medical staff remembered the doctor well, which brings me to the situation I still have to work through. So, all these years later, I now discover there were rumours doing the rounds of the hospital after the doctor's death; maybe it was his age, seventy-four, but nothing was ever done about it. I suppose you can put that down to provincialism, and no one daring to rock the boat. When looked at today, the symptoms were clearly indicative of a poisoning, which is why I am having his remains exhumed."

"Ray, you and I understand the dangers of charismatic mind-benders."

"Point taken, but this bloke's followers believed his every word."

"Ray, you brought him in, and you did that because that fine brain of yours would not let up until you were sure."

"Martin, it really gets to me that all the evidence we thought we were so clever in putting together had been carefully planted. This man assumed our former suspect's identity when he killed. The cunning bastard! You had to see the way they lived and the veneration they had for him."

"Ray, I understand how you feel, but you got him; these people can really worm their way into your head."

≈ 47 ≈

I took the opportunity to jump onto a train so I could thumb through a glossy bridalwear magazine on my way into the city. There was nothing that caught my fancy. I had it clearly in my mind that I wanted peach, with Heather and her youngest daughter in dresses that were to be about two shades paler. I also hoped my designs, with a little alteration, might be used again. When I had it right, I was to send my mother my sketches and the material. There was still no word from my father, and if it had not been for Tony, I doubt that I would have got through that dreadful time. As it was, my mother's letters were heartbreaking.

If there was any light at the end of the proverbial tunnel, it came from the joy of planning my wedding. Tony and I wanted an unobtrusive civil ceremony on the harbor foreshore, with the background of the Opera House, the harbor, and botanic gardens. We thought with just immediate family and close friends, and a few appropriate words to be spoken to each other. Heather was having the reception at her home, and Hanna was supervising the catering.

I emerged from the underground into the sunshine of Martin Place, where scurrying office workers jostled past Japanese newly-weds posing for their photos while pigeons wandered unconcerned around their feet. A procession of buses moved slowly along Pitt Street, leaving a cloud of blue smoke hanging in the morning air. The receptionist ushered me into Heather's office, where we had coffee before going through to a conference room. Her conveyancer was a pale-faced young man with long, unruly hair, who had the look of someone who might be happiest with his nose deep in a book. There was no pretence of a collar and tie, which would have looked out of place on him anyway. He straightened his files, and other than a friendly nod and a limp handshake, he did not waste time on the preliminaries.

"Ladies, in this pile are copies of all the leases; there are fifty-seven in all. Arrawatta has changed hands several times over the years, and parts of it have been sold to neighbours, and so on, I imagine, according to the economics of the cattle industry. I have searched and rechecked all the changes in the ownership. On the surface, and without delving into the history of all of those involved, everything would appear to have been kosher." He paused, and suddenly looked up at me and smiled, as if he had something up his sleeve.

"Following each transfer has been an interesting exercise, and as you will later see, we may have also had some unexpected good fortune. And ladies, as this involves a great deal of research and legalese, I will try not to get lost in the detail. But some ninety-three years ago, there was a foreclosure, which resulted in a change of ownership from the Estate of Lord Handsmere Brancliff to one Oswald Cerry, the eighth Earl of Fairley, which sounds like something out of a Shakespeare play." He smiled at his own words and appeared to be enjoying himself.

"I thought it a reasonable thing to try to understand how that happened, as I could not follow the paper trail with what we had. So I went through your great grandmother's papers and got in touch with a firm of London solicitors who had acted for the estate. This was quite an experience on its own, as their pedigree went back over three centuries, and I did not expect them to give me the time of day. Ladies, as you know, a foreclosure is the result of a default under the terms of a mortgage and is the measure of last resort. Now this is where it got interesting; I was dealing with a retired former partner, who had a keen sense of history, and whom I found to be very knowledgeable. As he explained, Lord Brancliff's family was part of the firm's folklore, and he became as intrigued by the relationship between the two aristocrats, and the widow, as I was.

What he found was that most of their documents had been produced as evidence in the trial of one of the partners for fraud, one Bartholomew Craven, which made him wonder why the Earl of Fairly had been called as a character witness, and therefore, what might have been the connection between him and a former convicted partner, who acted for Lord Brancliff's estate. When Lord Brancliff died, his widow was well provided for. So how much had Fairley known about her husband's estate before he married her? When the partner's conviction is taken into account, it does not look good." My thoughts were of Nan and I smiled in understanding.

"Can we return to that foreclosure again? Now with the benefit of hindsight, there is clear evidence of collusion between Fairley and the estate's solicitor. So when had their plundering of the estate begun? Presumably even before the marriage; the correspondence shows the convicted partner and the Earl were the widow's most trusted advisors. At the time of her husband's death, the property in Australia was un-encumbered, which runs contrary to the correspondence received at this end. There had been a limited personal guarantee to an English pastoral house, so they could purchase goods on the station's behalf and ship them out. Even they may have had an unwitting hand in it, as they acted on instructions from the Earl, when they should not have. Once those two guys got their hands on the estate, money was ripped out left, right, and centre.

Ladies, to reduce a complicated story to its essentials, I reckon the current title fails, as over the years, the State has been transferring and renewing leases to parties who were not entitled to them.

Assuming all this stacks up in court, and I cannot see why it would not, this may well be the situation. Lord Brancliff died, leaving his entire estate to his only son, with a life interest to his widow. That is, she could have the income and live in the marital homes until she died or remarried. When she remarried, the estate, including the Australian cattle station, should have passed to the son, but it never did. After the mother's marriage to the Earl of Fairley, there were years of inordinate delays in handling the estate, for obvious reasons. Then her son, whose name was Fritzhugh, was killed on The Western Front. Ah, but our Fritzhugh left a valid will; upon his death, his estate passed to his widow. Her will, a copy of which I have, left her estate to her great granddaughter entirely, provided she survive her, which she has, and who, as far as I know, is you," he said, looking straight at me.

I was overwhelmed by the implications. The dear old lady had known all was not right, and had virtually said so in her journals. I had assumed Nan's estate comprised cash on deposit, a small holding of shares, and just her personal effects.

"That is what your great grandmother directs in her will. Now here is the intriguing part. I believe she long suspected their marriage may have compromised her husband. His mother had never acknowledged her, and all along, it must have been at the back of her mind that something was amiss. You can see it in her papers; she went to meticulous trouble to write down everything she knew, and to send it to her Darwin solicitors, who incidentally have been very helpful, and to also ensure she left a valid will. Marvellous really, she was obviously hoping that one day, someone would try to unscramble it."

I would have loved Nan to have been at that meeting. But a few weeks later, I was snuggled up to Tony's warmth on a chilly winter morning, when the radio came on with the morning news. I was just about to jump out of bed to switch it off when I caught this news item: "In breaking news, detectives yesterday arrested the Abbot of the Dunraven Priory, which is in New South Wales and near the city of Tamworth. He is to be charged in connection with the serial killings which have taken place in Sydney over more than four and a half years. We shall report further developments as they are released."

I ran to the phone and punched in the number I knew by heart. "May I speak to Detective Inspector Frank Macintyre please? Alkina de Cruz, he knows who I am."

"I was about to call you. Your brother is no longer a suspect. I cannot say much at this stage, and I am very sorry for all the anguish you and your family have been through. This inquiry is ongoing, and if there is anything you should know, I will call you myself."

I immediately called my mother.

⚞ 48 ⚞

My father and I had danced and sung our dreaming by the fading glow of our fire, until the grey of early morning stole through the bush and the birds began to stir. I believe the old warrior's heart would have been heavy with sadness, and so much would he have been hurting, that he would have willingly given his own life not to have to do this. For the law of our people stretched back into the dreamtime, I was his seed and there was no one else. My mother and sister knew what had to be done, and now the time had come. This was our place, where my life had begun, and must now be ended.

I imagine that my father's tormented thoughts may have been of the moment of my birth, when he would have felt my warm nakedness, and heard my first cries. Perhaps, he would have remembered his young son's eyes, which had followed him as we had hunted together in the country of his birth. Those thoughts would have filled his mind and he would have been unable to move on from those days of so long ago. I watched as the tip of his spear drooped toward the ground, for he would have again heard the screams of delight and laughter as my sister and I had splashed along the shore. But that was many years ago, before the great sadness.

What was he thinking? What had happened that I had come to treat life so cheaply? What had destroyed my faith in our ancient customs, and the knowledge of life and death, and all the myriad of things that he had taught me? He must finish me here, for it was the rule of life. His arm lifted, and in that moment he would have seen my skin caked with the dust of my land, and my whole being devoted to stamping and singing my dreaming. The great spear was raised ready to strike, and I smiled at him, and suddenly the Mighty Hunter froze. He had been deceived by white men before. The horrendous news that Alkina had brought, the anguish of my mother and sister, if he believed what had been said, his sadness would never end, it could not be true. Never again! I was his son and a warrior. He would not strike me down; we would walk and hunt together; just as he had yearned to do all those years ago, over our country, to sing and dance in the land of our dreaming. The Mighty Hunter buried our fire and collected his few things; the years had not passed; he straightened his back and began to walk. "Follow me my son, we shall walk our land and hunt together."

~ ~ ~

Glossary

Arrawatta County: in New South Wales is one of the 141 Cadastral divisions of NSW. It includes Ashford. The name Arrawatta is thought to be derived from a local aboriginal word for the area that includes Arrawatta County

Argy Bargy: noisy quarrelling or wrangling

Billabong: an oxbow lake cut off by a change in the watercourse. Billabongs are usually formed when the course of a creek or river changes, leaving the former branch with a dead end.

Bora: the name both to an initiation ceremony of Indigenous Australians, and to the site on which the initiation is performed. At such a site, boys achieve the status of men. The initiation ceremony differs from culture to culture, but often involves scarification and may also involve the removal of a tooth or part of a finger.

Bludger: one who lives off or profits by the work of others while making no contribution; lazy.

Boong: rude epithet for Aborigines

Bonzer: first-rate

Chook: chicken

Cockies; small sheep farmers

Crumpet: a girl

Doss: room

Goolies: testicles

Huey: Bell UH-1 Iroquois (unofficially Huey) is a military helicopter powered by a single turboshaft engine, with two-bladed main and tail rotors.

Myalls: Aborigines living in the traditional way

NCO: Non-Commissioned Officer

Jarrajarra: kangaroo

The Koori: (from Awabakal language *gurri*, as spoken in the area of what is today Newcastle, adopted by indigenous people of other areas) are the Indigenous Australians that traditionally occupied modern-day New South Wales and Victoria.

Norks: breasts

Nulla nulla: or hunting stick is an Australian Aboriginal war club.

Ports: portmanteaus (suitcases)

Poofter: pejorative for homosexual

Roos: kangaroos

RPG: Rocket Propelled Grenade (similar to bazookas).

SAS: The Special Air Service (SAS) is a unit of the British Army founded in 1941 as a regiment, and later reconstituted as a corps in 1950.

Sheilas: girls

Shickered: drunk

Skint: broke

Station: a large agricultural land holding

Woomera: an Aboriginal stick used to throw a dart or spear more forcibly.

Also by Geoffrey Hope Gibson:

The Taciturn Man

An immigrant's tale of an untamed country

Alexander Gibson, my father, was a young Englishman who with his brother settled in Australia in the 1920s. The brothers each married one of the Solomon sisters just prior to the Great Depression. The Taciturn Man begins just after the Second World War when Alexander took up a rough bush sheep-grazing block in isolation among the tall trees of New England (New South Wales).

I was born in 1937, and so I was just three years old when my father went to war, and age eight when he returned. Fortunately, by then I was old enough to absorb much of the material for this collection which I hope you will now enjoy.

Praise for The Taciturn Man

"A delightful memoir with all the emotions of life itself—seriousness, humour, joy and sadness and more. The author's observations of people and lively writing style make it a great bedside book to be savoured, rather than hurried through."

—Deborah K. Frontiera, author of *Fighting CPS: Guilty Until Proven Innocent of Child Protective Services Charges*

"*The Taciturn Man* is a trip through Australia's countryside that feels like a nostalgic summer breeze as Gibson's personal narrative reveals its beauty, culture, and history through his own experiences and unique voice."

—Susan Violante, author of
Innocent War: Behind an Immigrant's Past